POWER

MARGARET MCHEYZER

Cover Artist: The Book Cover Boutique

Photographer: Wander Aguier

Model: Rodiney

Email: hit_149@yahoo.com

Info@margaretmcheyzer.com

Power

He's powerful.

Charismatic.

A widower.

The youngest ever elected President of the United States of America.

My boss called and begged me to take a client on a day I don't usually work.

As a single mom, my weekends are solely dedicated to my bookworm ten-year-old daughter, Emily. But, on this particular Friday I reluctantly agreed to the favor.

Bennett Adams has an esteemed reputation which is highly respected around the world. I've worked with high-profile clients in the past, but I've never been in the same room as the president.

Until tonight.

He paid for my time, but all he really wanted was my body. My name is Reece Maxwell, and I'm an escort. This is how I met the Leader of the Free World. More importantly, it's how our secret relationship started.

Serving at the pleasure of the President means my life is about to drastically change...

For Tash.

The romance world has lost a beautiful soul, and you're deeply missed. This one's for you, beautiful girl.

Prologue

My phone rings and I look down at the number, sighing heavily. I know what's about to happen. "Hello, Sofia," I say as I lean against the kitchen counter.

"I need you to work tonight," she says in her normal, no-nonsense tone.

"You know I can't." I look down the hallway, seeing where Emily is.

Sofia breathes heavily into the phone. "I know you can't but consider it a massive favor to me."

"Sofia, I really can't."

"What if I increase your share?" I grind my teeth as I check for Emily. "Reece?"

"I'm still here. What's my cut?"

"I'll add an extra five grand." I sigh as I let my head roll back and stare up at the ceiling in the kitchen. "I really need you tonight."

"Fine," I say already hoping Tash is available to babysit for me.

"A car will come for you at six."

I look to the microwave for the time. "Fine," I grumble again.

"Thank you; you're a lifesaver. By the way, this one is only for three hours."

"At least I'll be back by ten. I need to go."

"Thank you," Sofia says again.

"Yeah, yeah." I hang up, take a breath and call Tash.

"Hey," she says as she answers.

"Hey. Um, can you babysit tonight? Pretty please?"

"Oh, um, yeah, that should be okay. Work?"

"Uh-huh. Sofia called, and she's asked me to do a job."

"Sure, what time?"

"Can you be here by four?"

"Yeah, I can. But, seeing as this is so last minute, Emily and I are going bowling, and then we're having pizza."

I love my best friend, she's so good to both Emily and me. I smile into the phone. "Thank you."

"I have to go, so I'll see you and Emily later."

"Thank you." I hang up, and head down the hallway to see what Emily's up to. Opening her door, she's lying on her bed completely immersed in a book. "What are you reading?"

"Harry Potter." She shows me the book. "Have you read these?"

"Nope, but we've watched the movies." I sit on the side of her bed. "I have some bad news."

"You have to go to work, right? I heard you call Tash." She sits up in bed and places her book on her lap. "It's okay. I get it."

"I'm sorry. But I'm make it up to you tomorrow."

Emily shakes her head at me. "It's okay, Mom. You have to work." God, I love my kid, she's just so understanding. Like an old soul instead of a ten-year-old.

"Tash is taking you out for bowling and pizza."

"Yay!" Emily squeals with happiness. "Tash always lets me win at bowling." She crinkles her brows, and stares at me. "Should I let her win tonight?"

"Hell no. Don't go easy on her." Emily smiles proudly. I feel terrible having to leave her when I only have her for the weekend. "Are you sure you're okay with me going to work?"

"Mom, I know you have to work. Besides, the restaurant you work at must be really desperate if they're calling you." *Restaurant, right.* "So, it's okay."

I lean in and kiss her forehead. "How did I get so lucky to have a kid like you?"

"How did I get so lucky to have a mom like you?"

Guilt tears through me, because once she's old enough to figure out what I do, I doubt she's going to be so proud of me. "I need to start getting ready."

"Okay." Emily picks her book up, lies down again and opens it to the page she was on.

I head down to my room and get into the shower.

"What are you going to wear?" Tash asks from the inside of my closet.

"No idea," I call as I finish drying my hair. I walk out of my bathroom and stand at the entrance of my massive closet. "I was thinking one of my black dresses."

Tash looks over to the black section of the color-coded closet. She walks over and runs through the hangers of all the black dresses. "This one?" She takes one out and shows me.

I screw my mouth up and shake my head. "Nah, I'm not feeling it."

"Short or long?" Tash replaces the dress and keeps looking through them. I shrug my shoulders as I lean against the wall. "How are you going to do your makeup?"

"I think I might go dramatic. Smoky eye, red lips. What do you think?"

Tash turns and casts a wary eye over my body. "Depends, what are you going to do with your hair?"

"What I usually do, soft curls and down. I'll wear those shoes." I look over to the racks of high heels and point to the pair I'll wear.

"Which ones?" Tash turns and steps toward the racks. "These?" She points to the black high heels. "You always look good in these." She takes the shoes and returns to the black dresses. "I think these, and this dress." Tash holds the heels against one of the black dresses. I start laughing. "What's so funny."

"You picked a dress that cost about two hundred dollars, as opposed to one of the others that costs ten or twenty times that amount."

"Well, it's hot."

"Because it's tight?"

"Because it draws attention to your boobs, and you have the best boobs ever. Must have something to do with being twenty-five. My boobs are saggy."

"You're only twenty-seven. You have good boobs too."

Tash shakes her head and huffs. "These shoes, and this dress."

"I guess." I shrug. "Anyway, I'm going to curl my hair, and do my makeup."

"I'm hungry," Emily announces when she enters my room. She looks over at me and smiles. "What time are you going to work, Mom?"

Tash throws my decoy work clothes on the bed. "I'll be leaving at about six."

"How about you and I head into town, and we can go bowling, then after bowling we can hit the pizza place?" Tash hugs Emily, as Emily nestles into Tash's side.

"Yep."

"Alright, go put your shoes on, and we'll leave."

Emily breaks out of the hug, comes over and gives me a kiss on the cheek. "Wake me when you get in."

"Maybe. But tomorrow morning we'll go out for pancakes."

"Yay," Tash announces enthusiastically. Emily giggles as she looks over to Tash. "What? I'm coming too."

I give Emily a kiss. "Have fun with Tash tonight."

"I will." She turns and heads out of my room. "Have fun at work," she calls over her shoulder as she leaves.

Tash's brow arches as she mumbles, "I'm sure your mom will."

"Hey," I scold Tash as I stare at her.

"Well, come on, I'm sure you will." She backs out of the room. "Be safe," she says as she points to me.

"Always am."

"Em and I are out of here."

"Take care of my baby," I say as I blow her a kiss of gratitude. Tash leaves, and I get ready for work.

— ✹ —

Lucky for me, I live in a community where the houses aren't too close to one another, and everyone minds their own business. So, when a limousine arrives to pick me up, it's not something out of the ordinary. The security gatehouse only needs to be informed when cars are about to arrive.

The black town car arrives, a man gets out of the passenger side, and approaches my front door. With my bag hanging over my elbow, I take my keys off the hook, and step toward the door.

There's a knock before I get a chance to open it. "Miss Maxwell," the formal and stoic man says. "This way please."

"Thank you." He takes a step backward giving me enough room to lock the door. Once done, I follow him to the car. He holds the back door open for me, and I carefully slide in, making sure I daintily maneuver so I don't give him an eyeful of what I'm wearing under this tiny dress. "Thank you," I repeat once I'm in.

He closes the door and returns to the front seat. I notice neither he nor the driver are talking, which isn't unusual when it comes to these transactions. They don't want to make it any more awkward than it already is.

I don't usually ask Sofia who the client is, because I actually trust her. Strange, considering the line of work I'm in. But she's a good boss, and she's proven herself time and time again. She assesses and evaluates clients carefully, so I have total faith in her. I just wish I asked her who I was going to see tonight.

"Gift five minutes out," the guy sitting in the passenger seat says into his cuff.

I notice he's wearing an earpiece and I quietly let out a long breath. Great, another senator or chairman. *It pays the bills.*

"Gift three minutes out."

I straighten as I fix my hair and get myself mentally prepared for the next three hours.

Looking out my window, I take several deep breaths trying to calm the tension crackling through me. It doesn't matter how long I've been doing this; it still makes me nervous.

"Gift one minute out."

Closing my eyes, I clear my mind, take a deep breath, and prepare myself. When I open my eyes, I look out the window to find our destination.

My heart rate speeds and my stomach clenches. *What the actual fuck?*

The car pulls up to gates, and we're waved through. The driver slowly makes his way down the long driveway and comes to an underground garage off to the left and behind the building. My mouth becomes parched, and my hand shakes as anxiety tears at my stomach.

The car comes to a stop, and the back door is flung open. "Miss Maxwell," another man announces. He holds his hand out to me as I extend mine, reaching for his. There's a nervous tingling in my feet and hands as I notice how many men are gathering around, looking everywhere but at me. Funny thing is, they don't appear surprised or shocked by my presence.

The original guy is going through my bag while another waves a wand over my body and professionally pats me down. "Gift is on her way." He hands me back my bag. "Ma'am." He indicates a door. "If you'd care to follow me."

My heart is beating so hard I can hear it thumping in my ears. The lead guy is walking with speed and determination. Even though I'm wearing five-inch heels, I manage to keep up with him. He looks back over his shoulder and smirks when he sees I'm right behind him. I'm surrounded by a group of men, all quite intimidating, and none of them talking.

"This way, ma'am," he says as we reach an elevator. The doors to the elevator are already open, waiting for us. Only he and I enter.

I bring my hand up to my stomach, attempting to calm my nerves as the elevator feels like it's moving at the slowest speed. Shit, why did I accept this job tonight? Why did I have to say yes? *Get it together, Reece.*

The doors open, and I panic as I look around. I should tell him I can't do this and ask him to take me home. *I can't do this.* I try to clear the massive lump sitting at the base of my throat, but it won't budge. "Ma'am," the guy says as he guides me down an opulent hallway. Below my shoes, the dark-gray carpet is thick, springy, and lavish. The walls have a textured navy-blue wallpaper adorning them from top to bottom. Bright artwork compliments the wide hallway, breaking up the dark floors and walls. "Ma'am." He opens the door to a room, then steps aside. The click of the door closing after I enter makes me startle.

"Fuck me," I mumble as I look around the bedroom. The room itself isn't anything too special. A huge four-poster bed is up against the wall. Opposite the bed there are two doors. I take it one is the bathroom, and the other the closet. Clasping my hands together, I look around, wondering who's going to walk through the door.

I roam further into the bedroom and place my bag on the bed. The air is stifling with anticipation as I anxiously pace looking at the artwork on the walls. It's so impersonal and unemotional. Though it must be worth a lot, it's still so *meh*.

The door opens, and I whip around to see the original guy standing to attention. "Sir," he says as he stands as tall as he possibly can.

My heart leaps into my throat as I hold my breath to see exactly who's about to walk into the room.

"I don't have time for that at the moment." *He* strolls in holding his phone to his ear in one hand, while the other is shoved in the pocket of his suit pants.

Holy shit.

Fuck.

Fuck.

Double fuck shit fuck.

I stand taller, waiting for him to look at me. "I said I..." He lifts his chin and stops talking. "I'll call you back." With that, he hangs up and slides his phone into his suit jacket pocket. "Who are you?" he asks, his piercing gaze searing into my soul.

Get it together. "My name is Reece Maxwell, Mr. President," I say as I step forward and extend my hand for him to shake.

"Reece?" He folds his arms against his chest and taps his finger against his mouth as he stares at me.

"Yes, sir." I lower my hand and take a step backward.

The president doesn't move. His tall, slim frame stands staring at me. "Where's Mary?"

"I'm sorry, sir, but she was unable to make it tonight."

"Why am I the last one to hear about this?" he snaps at me with a dissatisfied tone.

His harsh attitude kind of throws me. "I don't know why you're the last one to hear about this. Maybe ask whoever's been organizing your meetings." Oh shit, what the fuck did I just say? I clear my throat and avert my gaze for a few seconds. "I apologize, Mr. President. I can leave and let Sofia know you only want Mary."

"Who's Sofia?"

I roll my eyes closed, feeling like a total idiot that I'd expect someone like the president of the United States to know who Sofia is. "My apologies, Mr. President. There seems to have been a miscommunication somehow." I walk over to the bed and pick my bag up. Standing taller, I hold my head up and try to save myself from any further embarrassment.

"What are you doing?" He darts his hand out and grabs my arm. Heat emanates from him. Stopping, I meet his hardened stare before slowly lowering my eyes down to where his hand is gripping my arm. My chest is heaving with mixed emotions of disbelief and excitement. Gently, he unwinds his fingers from my arm. "I should be the one to apologize," he says. "Please, stay." He steps back and offers me a small smile.

"Of course." I walk further into the room and return my bag to the bed.

"Would you care for a drink?"

"No, thank you, Mr. President."

In the corner of the room, there's a sideboard with a range of refreshments, from chilled water to champagne in a fancy ice bucket. He pours himself a scotch and leaves it on the sideboard as he takes his beautifully crafted suit jacket off and loosens his tie. "Tell me about yourself," he says as he picks the scotch glass up and walks over to sit on the edge of the bed.

"What would you like to know?"

"How old are you?" He lifts the glass to his lips and takes a small sip.

"I'm twenty-five, sir." Usually, I know exactly what's going to happen because I have regular clients, but this is a whole new ball game, and Sofia should've given me the heads-up.

"Twenty-five?"

I nod. "Yes, sir."

He throws back the remainder of the scotch, stands and walks over to the sideboard where he pours another drink for himself. "You clearly know who I am."

Where's he going with this? "Of course."

"Have you signed an NDA?"

Internally I roll my eyes, because seriously, does he think he's the only famous person I've done this with. "It's a requirement at the agency, sir."

"You can't discuss this, not with anyone."

"I'm aware."

"What happens here stays here."

"Yes, sir, I know."

"Who else have you been with?"

I cock a brow at his question. "Who have you been with?" I ask feeling a bit cocky, yet also annoyed at this personal question.

"I beg your pardon?" He stands taller, trying to intimidate me.

"I don't discuss clients with other clients."

He blinks several times, obviously not liking my reply. "I'm the president."

"Yes, sir, you are. But don't ask me for any personal information on my clients, because I won't give it to you."

His expression is hard and unreadable. He's giving me nothing, not a single thing. "Who have you been with?" he repeats the question.

I shake my head. "I'm not discussing that with you."

"I can bring the Secret Service in here and have them interrogate you. Or I could bring the whole weight of my office down on your agency and find out every single one of your past clients."

I wet my lips and take a breath. "I have no idea what arrangements you have with Mary. But I don't discuss clients." I smile and continue, "If you want me to tell you about my clients, then be prepared for me to tell those clients about you."

He strides over swiftly and grips my upper arms, his fingers deliciously digging in. "You'll speak to no one of me." He stares down at my lips. His body is so close to mine, I can feel his rock-hard cock straining against my figure-hugging dress.

My chest is heaving with shock and, surprisingly, desire. God, I want him to kiss me. I want his mouth on mine. "I speak to no one of anything," I say while I watch him staring at my lips.

He steps in closer, tightens his hold on my arms and lowers his head. I can feel his warm breath on me. "Who have you been with?" he repeats, even slower.

There's an ache pulsating between my legs. A slow, torturous energy is rising between us. I wet my lips again, knowing he can't take his eyes off my mouth. "None of your business," I say with a resolute strength. "Just because you're the president doesn't give you the right to know about my clients." I try to pull away, but he strengthens his grip on me again. I'm hungry for the pain. I know he's going to leave soft bruising on my arms.

"It gives me every right."

I stand staring at him, refusing to look away from his dark brown eyes. "Perhaps I'm not the woman you need tonight."

He smashes his mouth to mine, claiming me while he walks me backward toward the bed. When the backs of my knees find the bed, he stops kissing me. Stepping back, he looks me up and down. "Take the dress off. Leave the shoes on." I shimmy out of the dress and toss it to the floor. "Fuck," he says as he stares at my body wearing a matching black thong and black bra. "Twirl around." He indicates with his finger before crossing his arms in front of his chest.

I smirk and slowly turn, making sure I stick my butt out as I take my time to perform for him. I look over my shoulder, making sure to elongate my spine and tilt my head back. It's obvious he likes what he sees, because the bulge in his pants is now quite prominent. He watches me carefully, his eyes all over my body. I make a full circle and seductively nibble on my bottom lip. He can't keep his eyes off my mouth. I bring my hand up, and with the tip of my finger, run it over my lower lip before sucking on the tip.

He gulps, though he continues watching like a starving man who's seen his favorite food served in front of him. "What is it you want from me, *Mr. President*?" I sit on the edge of the bed and spread my legs so he can see everything. I slide my hand inside my thong and rub my fingers over my wet pussy. "Do you want to taste me?" I lift my fingers and coat my lips with my own desire. "Or would you like me on my knees?" I slink off the bed to my knees, slightly part my mouth and look up at him. "What do you want?" I pinch my nipples through my bra as I wait for his answer. "Or do you prefer to watch?"

He unzips his pants and steps toward me. He laces his hand through my hair and stabs his hard cock into my mouth. He thrusts hard into me, fucking my mouth with vigor and passion. "That's it, take it all," he says in a rough voice as he relentlessly clamps onto my hair and ravages my mouth with his thick, hard cock. I use my tongue to flick the head, but his fingers strengthen, as he pumps his veiny cock down my throat over and over again. "Such a good girl," he says with a tight voice.

I knead his balls, playing with them as his hips speed up. He's close; he's about to come hard. He pulls out of my mouth, grabs his cock, and tugs on it once. Ribbons of his cum flow out onto the bed. I watch as he closes his eyes and grunts while his cock spurts. A part of me is grateful he did that, because one of Sofia's rules is that bodily fluids are never exchanged, but another part of me wishes I was on the receiving end.

When he finishes, he opens his eyes and sighs. Holding his hand out to me, he helps me up. "Thank you," he says before tucking his cock into his pants and zipping up. "You can leave."

"You want me to leave?" Usually, men pay me to do more than just suck them off.

He turns away and grabs the second drink he poured. "Yes, you can leave." Well, talk about weird. But, okay. He *is* the client, and whatever the client wants, the client gets. Within reason, of course. I pick my dress up and wiggle into it. "Why are you smiling?"

I turn to look at him. "Pardon?"

"You were smiling, why?"

"I was thinking, that's all."

"About?"

"Um. Usually my clients want more," I say choosing my words carefully.

He leans against the wall, smirking as he sips on his scotch. He gives me a small nod as he watches me. "Thank you for your time."

He's paying for it. "Have a good night," I say as I grab my bag and head toward the door.

When I open it, the original guy is standing right there. He looks in, and the president says, "Make sure Miss Maxwell gets home safely."

"Yes, sir." He gives the president a nod and closes the door behind me.

The whole ride home is silent and surreal. Like the interlude with the leader of the free world didn't even happen.

The main guy comes into the house with me, and checks every room before heading to the door. Thankfully, Tash and Emily haven't returned yet, or that would've been one awkward conversation to have with Tash. And that could've scared Emily, having a big, burly guy in a black suit checking the house out. "Good night, ma'am."

"Good night," I reply as I smile.

He walks out, and I close and lock the door behind him. I lean against the cold wood, still unsure about what happened.

I just gave the president of the United States a blow job.

Well, fuck me.

Chapter One

Bennett

S he challenged me. How dare she challenge the president of the United States. Sitting in my office, I can't get her out of my mind. Reece was brazenly insolent last night.

"Morning, Mr. President," Liam, my chief of staff, says as he walks in.

"Morning," I reply and stare at the screen on my laptop. He stands at the end of my desk, waiting for me. "What is it?" Jamie, my personal aide, enters and hands me a stack of legislative reforms I need to read today. He walks out just as quietly as he entered. I look to Liam. "What?"

Liam discreetly turns, making sure the door to the Oval Office is closed. "Are you okay?"

"Of course, I am. Why?" He hesitates and rocks back on his heels. "Why?" I snap with irritation.

"Your tie is loose."

"What?" I lift my hands and straighten my tie.

"Whenever you're stressed about something, you loosen your tie. Are you okay? Has something happened I should know about?"

"No, nothing's happened." I feel the tension in my jaw as I look back to the laptop. Tapping my fingers on the desk, my shoulders slump forward and I let out a long sigh. "There is something."

"What is it, Mr. President?" Crossing my arms in front of my chest, I relax back into my seat. The door opens and Alison strolls in. "Give us a moment, Alison," Liam says. She gives us a small nod and backs out of the office, closing the door behind her.

"The girl, last night."

"Is this something I need to know?"

"I need you to stop being my chief of staff and be my best friend for a moment."

Liam's forehead crinkles as he steps back and leans on the back of an armchair. I stand, round my desk, and lean against it. "What happened, Bennett? Do I need to get the Secret Service involved?"

"No, nothing like that." I shake my head and shove my hands into my pockets. Liam's waiting for me to give him something about the girl. "I want to see her again."

"I can set that up. Friday night?"

"No, tomorrow."

"Tomorrow is Sunday, Bennett."

"I know, but I want to see her again."

Liam's jaw jumps and he mimics my posture. "I can see if your usual girl is available."

"I don't want her, I want the one from last night."

Liam purses his lips together, and he lightly shakes his head. "This isn't a good idea. She's an escort."

"I know what she is, but I want to see her again."

"If the press..."

"They won't."

"Let me get this straight. You've become fond of an escort?" Liam's brows shoot up, and it's clear he's not impressed. "If it's company you require, I'm sure I'll be able to secure Mary for you," Liam pushes.

"Liam, you need to listen. I want to see Reece again."

Liam shakes his head and rolls his eyes. "Look," he grumbles as he runs his hand through his hair. "Let me run some polls, put the feelers out to see how the people would respond if this became known."

I blink while staring at Liam. "You've got to be kidding me. You want to run polls on how the American public would feel if they found out I'm seeing an escort?" I pinch the bridge of my nose. "Yes, because I'm sure ninety percent would be all for it, Liam," I shout as I slam my hand on my desk. "No, we're not doing that."

"You need to be prepared if this becomes more than the Secret Service getting you a regular girl on a Friday night."

"There's nothing to prepare for, Liam. Nothing." He opens his mouth and quickly closes it when I silence him with a look.

He straightens and nods. "Is there anything else, Mr. President?"

I turn to look out the window. "No."

"I'll arrange it for you," he replies curtly.

"Thank you." I stand, adjust my tie and head back to my desk.

Liam walks toward the door leading out to the reception area where my personal aide and secretary work. "Alison." He gestures for her to enter.

"Mr. President, one of the reporters told me he's hearing whispers that the baggage handlers are about to go on strike."

I look to Liam. "On it," Liam says, rushing out of my office.

"When's your briefing?"

"I have twenty-five minutes."

"As soon as we find something out, we'll let you know."

"Thank you, Mr. President."

A good five minutes have passed when Liam returns to my office and picks up the phone. "Secretary of Transportation." He holds the phone out to me.

"Cary," I say. "What's going on with the baggage handlers?"

"They hit us hard about fifteen minutes ago. They're prepared to stage a nation-wide walkout if they don't get a twenty percent increase."

"Twenty percent?" I ask as I lift my brows in surprise.

"Yes, sir." He waits on my reply.

"When?"

"Tomorrow night, for seventy-two hours."

"Beginning of the work week."

"Yes, sir. They know how hard it'll hit."

"Set up a meeting."

"Yes, sir."

I hang up and look to Liam. "How did we not know about this?"

"I'll find that out." He stands back and nods.

"And brief Alison. Thank you." Liam exits, giving me a moment to think about Reece, before Esther barges into my office.

She walks over and places a stack of papers on my desk. "You have an appointment with the vice president at nine, and nine-fifteen there's a briefing with the secretary of defense. At ten, you have a meeting with the attorney general, and at eleven your mother is arriving."

"She is?" I look to Esther who nods. "Um."

"Nope." Esther shakes her head. "Don't even say it, Mr. President."

"You don't know what I'm going to say."

"Yes, I do. You want me to cancel her, but I'm sorry, sir, I'd rather take your wrath than your mother's." She waggles her finger at me.

Liam bursts through again, holding two files. I look to Liam, then to Esther. She's standing her ground, refusing to cancel my mother. "Fine."

"You need to sign that, please." She opens my desk drawer and takes out a pen, handing it to me. I scribble my name on the paperwork and hand it to her. "Thank you." Esther smiles sweetly before walking out of my office.

"I pulled the files for both Reece, and Mary." Liam waves the two files at me after Esther leaves the room and closes the door behind her.

"You did what?" I ask with irritation. "I didn't ask you to do that."

"My job is to protect you, Mr. President. And this is me protecting you. Mary's file." He hands it to me.

"Is there anything in there more damaging than their professions?"

"Reece has a child."

"What?" I shove Mary's file aside and open Reece's file. "She has a daughter who's ten." I look up to Liam. "This isn't something to discuss in the office." I hand him Mary's file and slide Reece's into my briefcase. "That's all."

"Yes, sir." Liam bows out in defeat. I don't want to talk about this anymore, not until I can get my head around it.

✦

Jamie enters the office and begins packing my things. "You need to go home," he says.

"I have too much work to do." I try to wrestle the stack of papers he's attempting to swipe off my desk.

"It's nine o'clock and you need to be back at six in the morning."

I stare at Jamie from above my glasses. "Are you trying to baby me?" A slow smile stretches across my face.

"Yes, Mr. President, that's exactly what I'm doing, because one of my favorite parts of this job is watching you rest for only a few hours."

"Are you sassing me?"

"I thought I was babying you," he returns, matching my energy.

Smart-ass. I take my reading glasses off and rub at my tired eyes. "I probably should leave." Standing, I roll my neck from side to side.

He packs the papers into my briefcase, then closes my laptop and packs that into the briefcase too. He places my briefcase on my desk, then takes my suit jacket from the back of my chair, holding it out for me. "There's been a change in your schedule for tomorrow, sir. Your meeting with secretary of Homeland Security has been moved up to seven, and your eight o'clock has been pushed to eight-thirty. Also, you have a phone call with the prime minister of Australia scheduled for ten."

"Thank you, Jamie." He walks with me out of the office toward the residence. When we get to the entrance, he hands me my briefcase.

"Is there anything else, sir?"

"No, thank you."

The guard standing at the door opens it for me, and Jamie turns back. I walk into the foyer and head over to the elevator, where my Secret Service agent, Mark, presses the button and stands in front of me. The doors open, and Mark stands to the side for me to enter. "Sir."

I step in and lean against the elevator wall. Closing my eyes, a bright and vivid image of Reece on her knees, taking my cock as I fuck her mouth flashes in my mind. I can't help but smile at the recent memory of lacing my fingers through her hair and using her mouth while her small wanton moans vibrate up my hard cock.

The doors open as do my eyes. "Sir," Mark says as he exists before I do and waits for me to exit the elevator into the residence.

"Thank you."

Loosening my tie, I walk toward my bedroom, where Mark takes position outside of my door. "Mark, could you call down and have the chef prepare something for me?"

"Absolutely, sir."

I walk into my room and throw my briefcase up on the small table between the two sofas. Sitting, I take my tie off and open my briefcase. I put my glasses on and begin looking through all the files. One catches my eye, and I slide it out. Placing all the paperwork down, I open it to find a comprehensive report on everything about Reece Maxwell.

"Wow," I say as I look at her latest tax returns. The knock on my door irritates me, because I have to close Reece's file. "Come in."

Liam opens the door and stands at the entrance. "Mr. President."

"Why are you still here?"

"I'll be leaving in a few minutes. Um." He looks at the file in my hand and pulls his shoulders back. "I'm actually here for that reason." He pointedly glances at Reece's file.

"What is it?"

Liam lets out a small chuckle. "The thing is, Mr. President, she said no."

"What?" I sit straighter and tighten my hand around the edge of the file. "What do you mean she said no?" Another knock disrupts us, and Liam stands straighter. "Come in."

The door opens and my food is delivered by one of the waitstaff. "Sir, your meal." He walks in with a silver tray and places it on the table beside my briefcase.

"Thank you," I say. The waiter smiles and walks out, closing the door behind him. "What do you mean she said no?"

"She said she's unable to work tomorrow night."

"She knows I asked for her?"

"Yes, I made it perfectly clear." Liam smiles. "She's adamant, that's for sure." There's a collective moment of disbelief. "What do you want me to do?"

I stand and pace back and forth. "I've never been rejected by a woman, Liam."

"Oh, I know. You could've had any of them in high school, and in college. But you saw Kathryn, and that was it for you. She was the only one you wanted."

I can't help but laugh. "Remember how many times she shot me down?"

"Do I ever!" Liam relaxes and steps backward, leaning against the wall. "She refused to go on a date with you, and after she finally did, you two were inseparable."

Suddenly, the joy of the memory is overtaken by the pain of my loss. I pick Reece's file up and flick through it. "She's quite a thrifty woman."

"Did you see what's in her savings account?"

I shake my head and flick to her financials. I look up to Liam surprised. "Why has she got that much in the bank?"

"She also has several investment properties too. And, look at her donations for last year."

I skim the numbers and shake my head. So many parts of me are confused by Reece Maxwell. "What was her reasoning for not being able to join me tomorrow night?"

"She didn't give me one. She simply said no."

I stop skimming the information and look up at Liam. "She said no?"

Liam slowly nods. "What do you want me to do? I threw the weight of the office at her, and she wasn't fazed by it."

"If she's not coming tomorrow, then set up a meeting for Monday night. Check my schedule with Jamie and Esther, and block out anything from eight p.m."

Liam nods, then mumbles, "Hopefully she won't say no."

"What was that?" I ask, playfully challenging him to speak up.

Liam smirks and shakes his head. "I'll set that up for Monday night. Is there anything else, Mr. President?"

Yeah, thought so. "No, thank you."

"Thank you and have a good night." He backs out of my bedroom and closes the door behind him.

I look at my food, and the file on Reece Maxwell.

As I pick at my dinner, I thoroughly examine the file, which completely impresses me. For someone who's only twenty-five, she's amassed a small fortune. I'm looking forward to Monday night.

Chapter Two

Reece

Bennett Adams is persistent, that's for sure.

I look through my closet so I can put an outfit together for tonight. I thumb through my dresses and find one I haven't worn before. "I don't remember buying you." I look at the price tag and find myself smiling. "Nope, I definitely don't remember spending four thousand on you." I hold the dark blue, floor-length gown up and tilt my head. "Looks like you're it." I turn and look at my shoes. "I'm going to pair you with gold heels. Six-inch heels might make me as tall as Bennett. Doubt it though, but anyway. Right." I hold the heels up to the dress. "Yep, you're going to work. Now, what about a bag?" My handbags and clutches are lined up beside my shoe racks. "You." I grab the gold clutch and walk out to make sure it's fully stocked with everything an escort needs before placing it on my bed and heading for the shower.

* * * ✦ * * *

There's a knock on my door, and I stroll over to it. The original guy is waiting for me. "Miss Maxwell." He steps to the side to wait for me to lock my house.

"Do I get a name?" I ask as he escorts me to the waiting car.

"My name is Mark, ma'am."

Once the car is in motion, I say, "Here you go, Mark." Handing him my clutch. He opens and rifles through it. I keep watching in case he cracks a smile or gives anything away. However, he's completely professional and doesn't react.

"Ma'am," he says with his normal cold and emotionless voice. He hands me my clutch.

"Thank you." I'm less nervous today, because I obviously know where I'm going and what to expect. The car moves through the Washington streets easily, and when we pull up to the gates, we're waved through.

We get to the underground parking, and I exit, waiting for the agent to wave their wand thingy over my body. The check is quick and not intrusive. Before I know it, I'm on the way up in the elevator. This time the doors open, and I'm in a different part of the White House. "This way," Mark says as he walks down a long corridor, decorated in subtler, yet still sophisticated tones. He knocks once on a door, waits for a moment, then proceeds to open it. "Miss Maxwell, Mr. President."

"Thank you," I hear him say from inside.

Mark steps aside and waits for me to enter before closing the doors.

I quickly see there's a sitting area with two facing sofas and a fairly large coffee table between them. There's also a massive bed, even larger than the one in the first room, as well as a small dining area with two chairs, and a candlelit dinner. The room itself is larger than an over-priced hotel room, though still cold and impersonal. There aren't even any photos on the walls. "Reece, nice to see you again," Bennett says as he walks over to me and kisses me on the cheek. "You look beautiful." He stands back to admire my choice of floor-length, yet still sexy dress. "Although I'm not particularly a fan of you being nearly as tall as I am."

"Mr. President." I straighten my shoulders and wait for his instructions, but my mouth doesn't catch up with my brain. "Why is a dinner set out?"

"I'd like for you to join me for dinner tonight."

If my client wants me to have dinner with him, then I will. If they want me to suck their cock, I'll do that too. If they want to have dinner while I suck their cock, I can do that as well. They're paying for my time and the use of my body. "Thank you. That's very kind, Mr. President."

He takes me by the hand and leads me over to the table where he pulls my chair out and waits for me to be seated before he gently pushes my chair in. The food is still steaming, which means it must have arrived only moments before I did. "I'd like to get to know you, Reece."

I sit straighter and cross my legs at the ankle. I've researched the shit out of how to sit when out at those hoity-toity dinners, even which forks to use, which glasses to use, everything. Because in my line of work, there's some important dinner at least once a month that I'm paid to go to as the arm candy for someone important. I take the napkin and place it in my lap, while Bennett pours us water and a glass of wine for each of us. "Thank you."

"Tell me about yourself," he asks when he sits.

"What would you like to know?"

"Tell me about where you went to school."

I have a feeling he already knows everything about me, including everything about Emily too. "I moved to Washington about nine or ten years ago, where I knew no one and had very little."

"Why did you move here?"

"Because I answered an ad," I reply with honesty.

"To do what?" He picks his wine up and sips it before placing the glass down and dividing the food between my plate and his.

I watch him carefully, then shake my head. My mind is telling me to shut up and answer the questions he asks, but for some reason, I feel like he's testing me, and I don't like that. "Mr. President let's be honest. I'm sure you already know everything about me. You probably even know how much money I have in the bank." He looks over to me, sets down the tongs he was using to divide the food with, and sits back in his chair.

"As a matter of fact, I do." I pick my knife and fork up and begin to cut my meal, one tiny piece at a time. "I just don't understand why someone who clearly has a good head on her shoulders, would continue to be in the profession you're in."

I look at him and blurt, "Because I like sex. I'm good at it, and I like the money."

"But you can do so much more with your life," he says, patronizing me.

"I have a ten-year-old daughter."

"I know, Emily. She attends one of the best private boarding schools in Washington, maybe even the country."

"Yes, because I don't want her knowing what I do."

"Then why not get out of it, and do something else?" he questions. "Obviously, you're intelligent, because you earn good money, and you've created a retirement plan for yourself and Emily. You have investments, and savings in the bank. It's blatantly clear that you can do anything if you put your mind to it."

"Did I come here tonight so you can lecture me?" I have no idea why, but he has a talent for getting on my nerves.

"I'm trying to figure out why you don't want more?"

"More?" He nods. "You'd prefer I leave this job, that I enjoy...mostly," I snarl the last word to him. "So, I can go and become a waitress?"

"That's a more noble profession than what you do."

"Wow. It's a more noble profession, yet you're the one paying me to be here so you can fuck me." The moment the words leave my mouth, I instantly regret them. "I'm..." I look down at my plate and let out a slow breath. "I'm sorry, Mr. President, I shouldn't have snapped." *What the fuck is wrong with me?* I take a moment to calm my erratic breathing before I lift my chin to look at him. He's sitting opposite me with a bemused grin on his face. "Why are you smiling?"

"Because you're cute when you get riled up."

"Cute?" *Stop it, Reece. Stop it now.* "Perhaps I should leave before I say something that ends with me being arrested."

I move to stand, but he darts his hand out, stopping me. "Don't go," he whispers.

He's just a job, like anyone else is, and I have to treat him like a client. Not like the president. I regroup and smile. "Of course, sir." I sit again, put my game -face on, and pick up the flatware to continue eating.

"Why couldn't you be here last night?" he asks.

"Mr. Liam Price was quite adamant. However, last night I was helping Emily with a project before I got her back to school. Usually, Sunday nights aren't so hectic, but last night was an exception. And I'm sorry, but my daughter comes first."

"I understand." He nods. "But if I want your time, then I expect you to be available."

"My daughter comes first," I reiterate. "She'll always come first."

"She's ten-years-old?"

"Yes, sir, she is."

"That means you would've been fifteen when you had her."

My mouth wants to say something smart-ass, like wow, look at you, you can do the math. But instead, I choose the safe answer, "Yes, sir, that's exactly right."

"There's no father's name on her birth certificate."

I still my flatware, and peer up at him. "You checked Emily's birth certificate?" He nods. "You have no idea the line you've crossed."

"I beg your pardon. You'll watch your tone when speaking to the president."

"Not when he's being an ass," I say through a clenched jaw. "You had no right to delve into Emily at all. You've crossed a line." I lower my cutlery, push my chair back and throw my napkin on the plate of food. "Please, don't call for me again." I stand and walk over to grab my clutch.

Bennett is on his feet and stopping me from leaving by blocking the exit. "I'm..." he pauses and runs his hand through his hair.

In all the years I've been doing this, I've never felt so trapped and hopeless. The fact is, Bennett Adams is the most powerful man in the world. And, if I scream out, not one of his Secret Service agents is going to come in here. But if he screams, they won't hesitate in breaking the door down and throwing me into handcuffs. Because, let's face it; he's the president, and I'm just a whore.

I take a step back, trying to find a way to defuse the tension. "Look," I start in a softer, less aggressive voice.

"I shouldn't have dug into your daughter's records. Especially when it comes to her birth certificate."

I lift my chin to look into his softened eyes, happy he's apologized. "I guess that's as close to an apology I'm going to get. Right, Mr. President?"

"Bennett. My name is Bennett."

"I know what your name is."

He leans against the door and sighs. "I'd appreciate if you stayed, please." He gestures toward the table. I chew on the inside of my cheek, contemplating my choices. "I'm trying to wrap my head around why someone who's clearly intelligent, would continue to work in her current circumstances when she has financial freedom and can support her daughter with what she has."

"Because you must've seen that I'm on my way to financial independence. I'm not there yet."

Bennett pushes off the door, walks over to me, and leads me back to our dinner. "I'll have the chef prepare something fresh."

"No need. This will do."

"But, you tossed your napkin on your food."

I pick the napkin up and place it next to the plate. "See, I can move it."

"But..."

"That's being wasteful, and I don't like throwing things out for something so trivial." Bennett waits until I'm seated again before he moves to sit across from me. "You're staring at me."

"I'm looking at your mouth and fantasizing about it being wrapped around my cock again."

Men. Such simple creatures. Give them food, sex, and a few "yes sirs," and they're putty in a woman's hands. This is what I'm here for, for him to use for his pleasure, and hopefully my own too. I cock a brow and smirk. I pick up a green bean and run my tongue over the edge of it. Bennett's eyes are glued to my mouth. The red lipstick always works. *Always.*

"I *am* hungry," I say in a seductive tone while I nibble on the end of the bean.

"I want to see you on your knees," he instructs with that demanding voice.

I drop the bean and lean my elbow on the edge of the table. Bennett sits back in his seat, boldly provoking me with his intense glare. I casually, though intentionally, run the tip of my manicured nail across my bottom lip before biting on it. Bennett sits straighter and pulls his shoulders back.

I'm affecting him. And I'm enjoying every second of this. "You want me on my knees?" I ask as I ease my tongue out and run it across my top lip.

He takes a breath and slowly smirks. "In front of me." He darts his eyes to his crotch, then back to me.

"Do you want me to crawl to you, *Mr. President*?" I say with a sultry whisper.

He thinks he's setting the pace of this encounter, but he has no idea that I'm the one controlling the entire scene. "I want you on your knees," he repeats.

I stand from my seat and walk around to push myself between him and the table. I turn and sweep everything off, allowing it to fall the floor. He doesn't bat an eyelid, and nor do I. The dress I'm wearing, although it falls to the floor, has a massive slit that goes to the top of my thigh. I slide up on the table and cross my legs in front of him, making the dress fall open so that my legs are completely exposed. The bulge in Bennett's pants is growing while his eyes are glued to mine. "Are you sure you want me on my knees?" I uncross my legs and lift my feet on either arm of his chair, giving him a perfect view of my pussy.

"I see you've color coordinated," he says in a slightly husky tone while his eyes stay focused on my open legs. To tease him that little bit more, I widen my stance. My thong barely covers anything. "I do enjoy seeing you wet and greedy." He shifts forward, leaning his elbows on his knees.

I lean back, pushing my butt closer to the edge of the table. "There's something about a man with his face wet from my arousal," I say. Bennett's eyes snap up to me. "His mouth glistening with my cum," I dare him to lap at me. He stares at me while moving his right hand to my left ankle. He tightens his grip as he slowly moves his palm up toward my thigh. "I like licking my taste off of his face." His hand moves higher and closer toward my pussy.

"Do you want to see my mouth fucking this pussy?" Bennett pushes his thumb into me, making me gasp with want and desire.

"I want to lick my wetness off of your face." I arch a brow, challenging him to feast on me.

He lowers his head, and I watch as he pulls my thong to the side and licks me while retaining eye contact. God, this is so hot. I push my fingers through his thick, salt-and-pepper hair, scraping my nails against his scalp. Tightening my grip on his hair, I hold him in place. Bennett growls around my pussy sending a vibrating shock through my entire body. My lips part as my breathing increases, and my blood pounds with the need for release. He grips my hips and pulls my ass closer to him as he continues to fuck me with his mouth.

Jesus, this man can eat pussy with the best of them.

My fingers tighten as I pull him closer. He growls again, making me crazy with his unrestrained moans and sounds. He's loving this as much as I am.

I want him to stay buried in my pussy, eating and slurping as if he hasn't had pussy for years. Abruptly, he stands and wipes his mouth with the back of his hand. "You taste like fucking heaven."

I lift my hand, and using only one finger, gesture for him to come over to me. Bennett pushes my legs apart and stands between them. I sit up on the table, grab hold of his shirt and pull him toward me. I lick his face, tasting myself on him. "Hmm, I do taste good." I pull back and smile.

"I want to fuck you," he whispers. "Get off the table." I slide off the table and stand nearly eye to eye with him. "Next time, I don't want you wearing heels this high." He pulls the dress to the side and looks at my shoes. "Though I do like these."

"You don't like me as tall as you?"

"No. Now, turn around." I do what he asks, and he pushes my head down so I'm bent over the table. He pulls my dress to the side and pushes the thong out of the way. "This is a nuisance." I hear a tear and find he's literally ripped my thong off me.

I look over my shoulder and laugh. "Don't like them either?"

He unzips his pants and takes his cock out. Bennett runs his hand up and down his long, thick cock. "No, they were a hindrance." He looks around the room and crinkles his brows.

"In my clutch."

He points to me. "Stay exactly like that."

"Yes, sir," I say with a smirk. He walks over to retrieve my clutch, opens it, and grabs one of the condom packets. He tears the foil and takes the condom out, carefully rolling it on. "You look quite sexy in your suit pants with your cock hanging out while you're rolling a condom on. Maybe we should take this to the Oval Office, and I crawl under the desk and blow you."

He looks up slowly at me and shakes his head. "Have you got any idea how much I want that to happen?"

"You're the commander in chief. You *should* make it happen." I waggle my brows.

Bennett walks over to me, grabs my hips, and jerks me back. I can't help but turn to watch as he props my body the way he wants it and lines himself up with my desperate pussy. He looks me straight in the eye, then impales me hard, causing me to jolt forward. "That's it." He stills for a second, closes his eyes and exhales a deep breath. "I need you to take all of me."

Oh my God, please don't tell me the president has already blown his load? He rolls his head back and lets out a hard sigh. *You've got to be kidding me, already?* He digs his fingers into my hips and pummels into me, again and again. *Yes!* I watch him and how intense he is while thrusting hard. Fuck, no wonder he graces the "sexiest man alive" lists. There's a vein straining in his neck, and Bennett clenches his jaw as he drives his hard cock into me. He opens his eyes to catch me watching him. I glance to where we're joined, forcing him to watch us fuck. He arches himself over me, and snakes his hand around the front so he can flick and play with my clit. The more he does this, the closer I get to my own satisfaction. Bennett coaxes a cry of desire out of me. "Hmmm."

He bites my ear and whispers, "Beg me."

"I need to come," I purr. "Make me come."

Bennett's chest rumbles with a gruff. "Beg me," his voice is heavy with delicious desire. He's on the edge of his own release.

"Please, *Mr. President,* fuck me until I come hard around your cock."

He stops rubbing my clit, pushes his fingers into the base of my head, and tugs on my hair. His grip is strong, though gentle as he massages my scalp with his fingertips. His mouth comes down on mine as he plunges himself into me over and over again. A gasp ripples through him as his hips slow and eventually stop. My mouth is concealing Bennett's moan. He loosens his grip and lays his head on my back for no more than a few seconds before he pulls out of me and tucks himself back into his pants. He really needs to go throw that condom out. "You can use my bathroom to clean up."

Bennett doesn't meet my eyes again. He turns and heads over to a small bar he has in his bedroom.

I know the deal. This is where I go to the bathroom, clean up, come out, smile and say, "Have a good evening." So, that's what I do, because my job is done for tonight. When I leave the bathroom, I see Bennett standing by the window looking out, nursing a drink. He doesn't even acknowledge me. "Have a good night, Mr. President," I say as I pick my clutch up and walk toward the door. I place my hand on the handle, push down and open the door. There's been a shift in the air, something's happened for Bennett to be totally quiet. Although, who am I kidding? He's been my client twice, maybe this is his normal MO. I guess, since he's paying me, he can be any way he wants. Mark's standing opposite the door. He peers inside, then looks to me. "I need to get home, Mark."

"Of course, Miss Maxwell." Mark leads me over to the elevator and presses the down button.

The entire drive home, I can't get his rapid cold change of demeanor out of my mind. Well, at least if this happens again, I know to prepare myself. He goes from demanding to guilt-ridden in a moment. It's not like I haven't dealt with this before.

He's only a job, Reece. A paying client. Nothing more, and nothing less. He's like every other man who pays me for my company.

Chapter Three

Bennett

Sitting in my office, I'm inundated with paperwork.

"Mr. President," Esther announces herself as she walks into my office and places yet another stack of folders on my desk.

"Is today over yet?" I ask as I skim the top file.

"Sure," she replies sarcastically. "And maybe we can hold hands and skip down the corridor."

I look up from the file, staring at her from above my glasses. "Are you sassing me, Esther?"

"Not at all, sir." A small devious smile stretches her lips. "I just thought we were exchanging fantasies."

"Your fantasy is to hold hands with me and skip down the hallway?" I can't help but chuckle. "That's a pretty sad fantasy."

"It's either that, or a date with Johnny Depp. And let's face it, Johnny is way out of my league."

I laugh a little more. "Get out, before I have Mark forcibly remove you." I look over her shoulder and yell out, "Mark!"

"Yes, sir." He appears inside my office and stands rigidly.

"Get rid of Esther. Remove her from the White House," I jokingly say.

Mark looks to me and then to Esther. "I'm sorry, sir, but she scares the crap out of me."

Esther looks proud of herself. "She's five-foot-nothing and weighs a buck twenty soaking wet," I say with a chuckle.

"Not to mention I'm fifty-five years old," Esther adds to the satire.

"Sorry, sir, but she's scary." Mark juts his head to the side.

"That's it, you're both fired."

"Who's fired?" Liam asks as he walks into my office from the door on the left.

"Apparently, I am," Esther replies. "And Mark's throwing me out before he's fired too."

Liam's brows lift as he stares at me. "I'd like to see Mark try." Esther and Mark both leave my office, and Mark closes the door. "There's a problem in California."

"What's the problem?" I ask, all the silliness now gone.

"A fire has broken out at Angeles National Forest."

"A fire?" Liam nods. "What are we talking about? How big is it?"

"It's burned through about fifteen thousand acres so far."

"How long has it been burning, and how fast is it moving?" Liam goes to answer, but I shake my head. "Get the governor on the line." Liam picks my phone up while I continue reading the file I'm working on.

"Lucy's on the phone." He holds the receiver out to me.

"Lucy."

"Mr. President," she says.

"What's happening at Angeles National Forest?"

"We've got first responders down there trying to create a firebreak, but with these winds and the unusually hot weather, it's proving to be more difficult."

"How close to residential areas is it?"

"At the moment, it's hanging back and all hands are on deck, trying to contain it. We've got airtankers hitting it from above as well as personnel on the ground."

"Casualties?"

"At this stage, none. However, Mr. President, there's a pocket in the park where a lot of homeless live. One loose ember, and..."

"I'll get you some help."

"Thank you, Mr. President." I hang up and look to Liam. "Who have we got in Forest Services?"

"Taylor, and he's already organized more airtankers to head out." I nod my head. "Make a call, get them some troops on the ground. If it spreads, it'll be total chaos."

"Yes, sir." Liam leaves my office and heads over to his. I need to stay on top of this or it could easily turn disastrous, with many lives lost. Both human and animal. Not to mention if it hits residential areas, the devastation it would cause.

Jamie opens the door, walks over, and places a cup of coffee on my desk. "Thank you," I say before he quietly exists.

Leaning over, I open my briefcase to grab one of the supporting files and see the one Liam gave me on Reece. I slide it out and sit back in my chair. Opening it, I take some time to read through the comprehensive findings. I pick my phone up and dial her number.

"Hello?" Reece answers in a groggy voice.

"Are you sleeping?"

"Who is this?"

"President Adams," I announce myself.

"What?" Reece clears her throat, then yawns into the phone. "Who is this?"

"It's Bennett," I say slower. "Why are you asleep?"

"Look, I don't have time for this. I'm tired, and I'm going back to bed. Whoever you are, you're a weirdo." She hangs up, and I'm left feeling somewhat confused. I call her number again. "No, I don't need a new internet provider, my car insurance is fine, and if you're a Persian Prince I have no money. Can you leave me alone now?" She hangs up.

I'm getting quite sick of this. I call her again but when she answers, I don't let her get a word in. "If you hang up on me once more, I'll have

Mark drive down there, throw you in the car the way you are, and bring you to me."

"Oh crap," she sighs when she realizes I am, in fact, the president. "Morning, sir," she says.

"Why are you still asleep?"

"Because, I'm normal. And normal people are asleep at this time of the morning."

Reece certainly makes me smile. "I have some questions for you."

"I can't wait," she says flatly. "What are they, Mr. President?"

"You had your daughter at fifteen."

"Nope, this is a no-go zone. You don't need to know about that." She's fiercely protective of Emily, and I must admit, I like that about Reece. "Do you have any other questions, or is that all?"

"I want to see you again, Reece."

"What day would you like?"

"Tonight."

"I'm sorry, I'm not available."

My hand clenches around my cell as I feel my anger escalate. "What do you mean you're not available?"

"I have a prior engagement."

"With whom?" my voice tightens as does my jaw.

"That's not your concern," she says, her own irritation clearly conveyed through the phone.

"It *is* my concern. Who do you have a prior engagement with?"

"We're not going to get anywhere if that's all you're going to ask. Is there anything else I can help you with?"

"Yes, you can come down here and suck my cock."

Reece sucks in a deep breath. "My availability this week is Thursday night."

"What? Thursday night? No, that doesn't work. I need to see you tonight."

"I told you, I have a prior engagement, so no. I'm not able to see you tonight." My own anger is dangerously close to spilling over. I'm on the verge of calling the agency myself and demand they fire her. "Is that all? Can I get back to sleep now?"

"Tomorrow night," I say, countering her ridiculousness of not being able to accommodate me tonight.

"Thursday night," she replies adamantly.

"Reece, are you refusing the president of the United States?"

"No, I'm merely informing him of my availability."

"I'm the damn president, and I don't wait for anyone."

"I'm sure Mary would be available for you tonight," she suggests.

"I don't want Mary."

"Thursday night at nine?" Fuck, I hate how she won't bend to my needs. "Mr. President?"

I could force her to come here tonight, I could have her fired, I could find out whoever her client is and send the Secret Service to have a *chat* with him. The possibilities are endless of what I *could* do. "I'll send Mark at *eight* on Thursday night."

"Yes, sir."

"Dress like a slut," I say, hanging up without hearing her response. I leave my phone on my desk and stare at it, quite pleased with myself.

"Mr. President?" Liam announces himself, snapping me out of my fantasy of Reece and what she's going to wear on Thursday night. I look up to him. "There's an additional five hundred firefighters making their way over to California."

"Good." I nod. Jamie opens the door and brings another cup of coffee for me.

"The president hasn't even had this cup yet," Liam says to Jamie.

"Yes, sir, I know. It's what he does. I bring the president a second cup about half an hour after the first, because he's too busy and generally forgets about the coffee."

Liam looks to me, and I half shrug. "It's true," I say. I turn to Jamie. "What have I got in the book for Thursday night?"

"State dinner for the New Zealand Prime Minister, sir," Jamie says without even checking.

Shit, I really want to see Reece, but I can't *not* attend the state dinner. "Thank you."

"Is there anything else, Mr. President?" Jamie asks.

"No, thank you."

"Thank you, sir." Jamie heads back to his desk.

"Are you okay?" Liam asks.

"I'm fine. Thank you. I need to make a phone call."

Liam nods once and walks back to his office. I pick my cell up and call Reece. "Hello," she grumbles groggily.

"Did you go back to sleep?"

"Yeah, I did. I thought I wouldn't hear from you again until I see you Thursday night."

"There's a small hiccup. I'll have to see you Friday night instead."

"Nope, sorry, I'm permanently unavailable Fridays, Saturdays and Sundays."

"I saw you last Saturday."

"That was an exception. I'm sorry, but no."

"That's not a word I hear often." I wait on her reply. "Reece?"

"I'm not sure what to say to you, sir. Those are the days I'm completely unavailable. Would next Monday be convenient?" I don't want to wait an entire week to see her. "I'll dress like a slut for you," she adds in a cute sultry voice making my cock twitch.

"Mark will pick you up at six."

"Yes, Mr. President." There's a slight pause. "Can I go back to bed now?"

"Did you even leave it?"

"Well..." She snorts. "No, I didn't."

"Sleep well."

"Thank you."

I hang up again and get back to work. Though if I'm being honest, it's fairly difficult to do when all I can think about is Reece, dressed like a slut, on her knees in front of me.

Chapter Four

Reece

I check myself over in the mirror, then look at the time. I fix my coat and straighten my shoulders when I hear the door.

Picking up my bag and keys, I walk over to the door and open it. Mark's waiting for me, and I'm taken aback by his lack of reaction. "Miss Maxwell," he says in his usual stoic, deep voice. He steps aside, waiting for me to lock my house.

"Hi, Mark. How are you?" I ask, a little more casually than I normally would. "I feel like we're old friends now," I say as I chuckle and walk behind him to the car.

"We're not," he responds flatly.

I snort with laughter. He shoots me an emotionless glare veiled with a hint of sarcasm. Wait, does Mark actually have a sense of humor? He opens the door and I slide into the back. He gets into the front and gives the driver a small nod.

The drive to the White House is silent, as usual. "Here you go." I hand him my bag, which Mark rifles through, then gives back to me. We pull up to the underground parking, and I'm greeted with the normal security check.

"This way, Miss Maxwell," Mark instructs and jerks his chin toward the elevator.

The elevator doors slide open, and Mark steps in, waiting for me. "Thank you." He presses the button and stands straighter. Mark has an imposing stature with broad shoulders, a height that's on par with Bennett's and a hard stare that could weaken a person and bring them to their knees.

Once the doors open, he steps out and walks ahead of me to the bedroom where he knocks and waits for Bennett to respond. "Ma'am," he says as he opens the door and stands aside for me.

I walk in to find Bennett almost exactly where I left him—standing by the window nursing what I suspect is a scotch. His normally pristine hair is disheveled, like he's run his hand through it many times. His tie is loose, and he's shrugged out of his suit jacket. He turns to look at me and startles. "Platinum blonde?" He casts a wandering eye from top to bottom. "I wanted you dressed like a slut," he says as he takes in my appearance. Something about tonight feels different, there's overwhelming tension clinging to the air.

Smirking, I untie my coat and drop it to the floor leaving me exposed in my leather bustier, crotchless underwear, a garter belt and suspenders holding up black fishnet stockings. Bennett's eyes widen as he slowly brings the glass to his lips. "Slut enough for you, Mr. President?"

He straightens as he eye fucks me. He looks at my heels and shakes his head. "I said I don't want you taller than me."

"You don't like my heels?" I purposely draw attention to them by bending at the waist and running my hands up my legs. "I thought you'd like these."

"You're very distracting, Reece."

"Am I?" I bite on my lower lip, forcing Bennett to look at different parts of my body.

"Get over here," he demands as he lowers his glass and places it on the window sill. I drop to my hands and knees and seductively crawl over to him. When I reach him, I can already see his cock is straining inside his pants. His chest is rising and falling quickly. I sit back on my heels and arch an eyebrow as I gauge his reaction. He unzips his pants and steps forward. Opening my mouth, I do exactly as he asks. Bennett has made it no secret that he wants me on my knees, and that's what he's paying me to do. He's forceful, yet gentle too. It's clear though, that he intends to use my mouth for his pleasure. He's still taking the time to tenderly rub his thumb across my cheek. Bennett comes undone in record speed, pulling out of my mouth only a few seconds before finishing off and orgasming on the bed. He takes several deep breaths, tucks his cock away and extends his hand to me. "Thank you, I needed that," he says as he helps me up. "I must admit, I'm a fan of this." He eyes my bustier.

"I knew you would be." Bennett takes his suit jacket off the back of the chair, and places it over my shoulders. "Am I distracting?" I tunnel my arms through the sleeves of the jacket. A faint aroma of black currant and apple gently waft from his jacket. I inhale deeply while closing my eyes. "Mmm," I moan when the scent hits again. "What's this smell?" I lift the arm and sniff.

"My aftershave," Bennett replies. "You like it?"

"Hmmm." I smirk as I nod. "It's sexy."

"Sexy?" Bennett's brows lift in surprise.

"Says the man who keeps showing up in the sexiest man alive lists." I head over and sit on the edge of the bed.

Bennett rolls his eyes and chuckles. "Don't remind me." He motions toward his bar, silently asking if I'd like a beverage.

"Water, thank you." He pours me a glass of water and places it on the small table in his suite, wordlessly telling me he wants me to move off the bed. Standing, I walk over and sit at the table. "Thank you." I pick the glass up and take a sip.

Bennett sits beside me and purses his lips together. Something is definitely going on with him. "I've ordered dinner," he says.

"Mr. President..."

"Bennett," he corrects.

"I don't like assuming things, so if you want me to leave, then please let me know."

"I've ordered dinner for us," he repeats his statement.

"Thank you." It's all part of the service. If he wants me to stay and have dinner, then I will.

"I want to ask you a question without you becoming defensive."

"You do know just saying it like that has made me defensive, right?"

He grasps his glass with two hands and lowers his chin as he releases a sigh. "Why does Emily's birth certificate not have the name of her father?"

I cross my legs and position myself, so I'm angled away from Bennett. "I thought I made myself clear that Emily is a line you don't cross."

"I—"

"I don't care if you're the president, she's someone you don't ask about."

Bennett picks his glass up and places it back down again. His brows furrow as he stares at me. "I'm struggling, Reece," he candidly admits.

"What with?"

There's a knock on the door, and Bennett stiffens. He looks to me and tugs his jacket around my chest, making sure I'm completely covered. "Sir," Mark calls through the door. "The chef has brought your dinner."

Bennett stands and moves in front of me. "Come in." He double-checks that I'm not obviously visible. Mark opens the door and brings in a tray with food. "Thank you, Mark." Bennett takes the tray out of his hands while being cautious. The door closes, and Bennett turns and places the tray on the table. He lifts the silver cloches off the plates and places one in front of me and the other where his seat is. "I hope you're hungry."

I look at the delicious food on the plate. "Sure am." I look at the food and place my napkin on my lap. "What are you struggling with, Bennett?"

He flinches when I say his name. "I'm struggling with you."

My fork stills as I slowly turn to look at him. "Me? Why?"

His neck tightens and a vein protrudes. "I find myself struggling with our arrangement."

"How so?" I delicately cut into my meat and pop a small bite into my mouth.

"I find myself thinking about you when I shouldn't be."

Talk about a backhanded compliment. "What would you like to happen moving forward, Mr. President?"

"Bennett," he corrects again. "I want to get to know you, Reece."

This is dangerous territory, and I'm not prepared for this. "In a fantasy world, I'd like that. But, this isn't an alternate universe, this is real life." I still my hands and place the flatware on the plate. "You're the president, and I'm an escort. That's all this is, and all it ever will be."

Bennett's face blanks as he stares ahead and pulls his shoulders back. "It's been a long day," he says, essentially cutting this line of conversation.

This isn't how I wanted this to go. I stand and move beside Bennett. He looks up at me and leans back in his chair. I reach for his napkin and throw it on his dinner plate before climbing on top of him. "What can I do to make it better for you?" I push my fingers through his hair, grab a fistful and tug his head back.

Bennett's eyes close as a soft groan rumbles through him. Softly, I kiss his mouth before peppering light kisses across his defined jaw. He pulls me in closer and snakes his hands under his jacket to my lower back. I can feel his hard-on growing inside his pants. Grinding against him, I keep kissing his mouth while his fingers dig into me. "You're addictive," he whispers.

I move my hips against him, making Bennett groan with desperation. I unzip his pants and slide my hand to grasp his erection. "I think you're enjoying this, *Mr. President.*" I tighten my fingers around his hard cock and gently pull while my thumb circles around the head. A small amount of pre-cum wets his slit. Bennett purses his lips together, concentrating on the feeling. I lean forward and playfully drag my teeth across his bottom lip before kissing him sensually. Bennett drags me even closer, trapping my hand between us as he lifts his right hand and slides it into the hair at the nape of my neck. He holds me in place as we kiss. His mouth tastes and ravages mine as he explores demandingly. Bennett flicks his tongue against my lips and quickly moves in to nibble.

Coyly, I move backward, not allowing him to kiss me anymore.

His eyes focus on my mouth, and he moves forward to kiss me again. But I tilt my head to the side, a small smile stretching my mouth. "It's like that, is it?"

I cock an eyebrow and stare at him. Lifting my hand, I suck on my fingertip. "I have no idea what you're talking about." Bennett intently watches as I drag my finger down my chin, angle my head back, and keep dragging my finger across the edge of my corset.

"Fuck," he grumbles. He leans forward and buries his head in my cleavage. He licks, sucks and lightly bites, scraping his teeth across my sensitive and heated skin. "I want you, Reece."

"Condom." He sticks his hand into the suit jacket I'm now partially wearing, takes out a condom and tears the foil packet. "Let me." I take the condom from him and while rubbing him, I discreetly roll the condom over his cock. I lean back, lift myself up, and sink down on his erection.

"Fuck," he sighs as he stares deeply into my eyes.

I ride him, making sure to take it slow enough for both of us to enjoy ourselves. Bennett firmly pulls me down, his fingers trembling with urgency as he digs them into my heated flesh. "That's it," I whisper as I roll my hips. "That's it."

Bennett lowers his head and laves his tongue down my neck, leaving a wet trail of need and lust. "Fuck." His sexual hunger reaches a new level as he stands, grabs both my wrists and pins me to the table while he raises my left leg over his shoulder and thrusts into me. "I'm in you so deep." He plunges into me, over and over again. I try to reach up to kiss him, but the way he has arranged my body, all I can do is lift my other leg.

Suddenly, he stops, falls to his knees and fucks me with his mouth. His tongue is magic, drawing me closer and closer to my own release.

Knock, knock, knock. "Mr. President," I recognize Mark's heavy voice.

Bennett pulls back, leaving me needing for him to finish. "What?" he yells.

"You're needed," Mark replies.

There's a slight pause from Bennett. "Fuck," he complains. He stands and offers me his hand to help me up. "I have to go."

I shrug out of his suit jacket and hold it out to him. "I'm surprised this is the first time it's happened."

He smirks as he wipes his mouth. "I should wash my face, but if I'm being honest, I like having your taste on my tongue."

"You're a deviant." I smile, sliding off the edge of the table and looking for my coat. Bennett grabs it, walks over and holds it out so I can shrug into it. "Thank you."

Once I fasten my coat, he stands in front of me and gently cups my face. "I'm sorry I didn't have the time to make you come." He kisses my forehead and wraps his arms around me.

"You do have a country to run, and these things happen. The last president I was with was always running off to save his country," I tease.

I feel Bennett's body tighten as he pulls back and stares at me. "I'm not particularly keen on knowing you're with other men." I blink as I stare at him. Is something developing between us? "Tomorrow night," he says.

"I'm sorry, but I'm unavailable until Thursday."

He steps back and runs his hand through his hair. "I have the state dinner for the New Zealand Prime Minister on Thursday." Bennett shakes his head and sighs. "It was supposed to be last week, but there was an emergency and the Prime Minister had to postpone her trip." He taps his finger to his chin. "Come to the dinner with me."

My brows shoot up in surprise. "I don't think that's a good idea."

"Why not?"

"Will there be reporters there?"

"Of course."

"All it'll take is one reporter to start asking questions, and you can pretty much forget about reelection."

He looks down and shoves his hands into his pockets. "Trust me, that thought has crossed my mind." Bennett shakes his head and softly sighs. "Come, but not as my date."

"No," I say forcefully. "I won't do it."

"Don't worry about me, I can handle myself."

"But my daughter can't." I look up to him. "I'm sorry, but no."

"What if you come with your friend. It's Tash, isn't it?"

My shoulders sink forward as I openly stare at him. "You're kidding me, right?"

"What?"

My stomach clenches as I walk toward the door. "You're unbelievable." He opens his mouth, but I hold my hand up to him. "No. This." I gesture between us. "Means you don't get to say anything. Your invasion of my privacy is astounding."

"What do you mean?"

"You know about Tash? Do you also have a profile on her too?" His silence is a clear admission. "I can't believe you, Bennett."

He straightens and lifts his chin. "Mr. President," he says with his authoritarian voice.

Rubbing the back of my neck, I shake my head at Bennett. "Hmmm." I run my tongue over my front teeth and cast a wary eye over his body. Standing straighter, I pull my shoulders back and say, "I'm sorry, Mr. President, my schedule is no longer open." I turn to leave.

"Get back here, Reece!" he commands. His voice is deep and smooth, and damn it I shouldn't like the way he speaks to me. *But I do.*

"Mr. President, I have a prior engagement," I say as I reach for the door handle.

I don't hear him come after me, but I feel his possessive fingers grip my arm as he swings me around. He pushes me up against the door, trapping me against his hard body. "We're not done."

There's another knock on the door. "Mr. President," Mark says with a little more desperation to his voice.

"Fuck," he growls while staring me in the eyes. "I have to go, and I want you to stay until I get back so we can finish this discussion."

I straighten, refusing to back down from him. "We're done," I say.

He pushes his body into mine, leans down and possesses my mouth. Our kiss is fevered, intoxicating and desperate. I find myself lifting my hands to push him away, but my body is betraying me. Bennett grabs my hands, holding them in one of his. "Don't." He thrusts into me, showing me how hard he still is. "You make me wild, Reece."

I force myself to turn my head from him. The scruff of his beard scratches at my face. "You have to go."

Bennett leans his forehead against mine and takes a long breath. I can smell myself all over him. He finally releases my hands and steps back. "Come to the state dinner."

"I'm sorry, I'm unavailable," I say, holding onto my resolve.

Bennett closes his eyes and purses his lips together. He visibly gulps and slowly opens his eyes. Walking over to the door, he opens it and looks to Mark. "Could you please make sure Reece makes it home safely?"

"Of course," Mark says and looks to me.

I walk out and follow Mark to the elevator. A part of me wants to turn around and see if Bennett is standing there, but another part doesn't want to know.

I guess, we're done. For good.

It's for the best. Nothing good could come from this.

Chapter Five

Bennett

Tuesday

Sitting in the Oval Office, I read through the legislation proposed. I keep getting distracted by the memory of Reece sprawled out in front of me with her legs over my shoulders while I was feasting on her pussy.

My phone is sitting face up, taunting me to call her. I tap the screen right as a text message comes through. "Fuck it," I mumble to myself as I search through my phone for her number. Taking my glasses off, I lay them on the desk and sit back as I wait for her to answer.

"Yeah," she croaks in an exhausted tone.

"Reece," I say.

"Who is this?"

I pull the phone away from my ear and glare at it. "It's Bennett."

"Ugh. You mean, Mr. President?" She releases a massive yawn, making me smile. "What can I help you with, Mr. President?"

"It's Bennett," I repeat. "I'd like to see you tonight; we have unfinished business."

"No, we don't. I'm sorry but as I stated last night, I'm permanently unavailable."

My fingers tighten around my phone. "I'm not keen on the word *no*."

"Aww, what a shame. Is there anything else I can help you with?"

"Reece, I'm asking to see you tonight. I'm thirsty and my tongue needs to be inside you."

She audibly clears her throat. "I'm unavailable," she repeats, holding on to her resolve.

Reece is certainly adamant, but so am I. "Mark will pick you up at seven."

"No, he won't, because I won't be here."

"Where will you be?"

"Out."

"Out where?" All my muscles tighten with her obvious determination to avoid me. "I asked you a question, Reece. Where are you going?"

"I'm sorry, Mr. President, but my time is exactly that—*my* time."

There's a pain in my jaw from clenching my teeth. "Mark will be there at seven." I hang up, not giving her the opportunity to argue. "Mark," I call loud enough for him to hear.

He opens the door to my office and steps inside. "Yes, sir."

"Seven tonight, I want you to go and pick up Reece." He nods once and leaves my office. *Play with me little girl, and see what happens.*

I loosen my tie and pour myself a scotch, waiting for Reece. The chef is preparing our meals and awaiting further instruction. My phone rings, and I look at the number. "Yes?"

"She's not home, sir," Mark says.

"What do you mean she's not home?"

"She's not home. We picked the lock to her door, and she's not here."

That little minx. "Okay, thank you." I shake my head at her audacity. That's not going to cut it, not at all.

Wednesday

Before I dress for the day, I call Reece. "Yeah," she murmurs groggily.

"Tonight, seven. I have a tongue fucking to finish."

"What time is it?" She yawns.

"It's a little after four."

"In the morning?"

"Yes, in the morning."

"Don't you sleep like normal people?"

"I'm the commander in chief. I don't have the luxury of sleeping."

"Well, I'm normal and four in the morning is a stupid hour. Besides, I have prior engagements. So no, I'm not available."

"God damn it, Reece," I snap. "Seven tonight, be ready for Mark."

"I'm going back to sleep."

"Seven."

"Whatever." She hangs up without waiting for me to reply.

"Fuck," I grunt as I roll my head from side to side hoping to relieve the stress Reece is causing me.

Standing, I open the door to my suite, where Grayson is already waiting for me. "Good morning, sir," Grayson says as he steps back.

"When Mark arrives, have him see me."

"Yes, sir."

I close the door and finish dressing for the day.

My phone rings, and I shake my head when I see Mark's number. "Don't tell me," I say as I pinch the bridge of my nose.

"She's not home, sir."

"Fuck!" I yell in frustration and slam my hand on my table. "Thank you." Mark hangs up, and I stare at my phone. I dial Reece's number, but it goes to voicemail. I dial it a second time. "Call me." I hang up and dial a third time.

"What do you want?"

"We had an appointment, Miss Maxwell," my voice is tight with tension.

"My vagina is closed for business. And, while I'm at it, I appreciate if you don't instruct your Secret Service agents to break into my home and search for me."

"I—"

"Yes, you did because you have a problem with boundaries. Now, leave me alone because I'm out." She hangs up, leaving me seething with her petulance.

I dial Mark's phone. "Yes, sir?"

"Track her phone and bring her here."

"Yes, sir."

I pace inside my room as I wait for Mark to bring Reece to me. Nursing my scotch, I keep looking at the time waiting for her. My heart is pounding, because I know how feisty Reece is. She's not going to like me doing this, but I don't care. She makes me crazy with her childish behavior.

Thankfully, I don't need to wait for long, because the door opens, and Reece barges in. "What the fuck is wrong with you?" she shouts. I can't help but smile as I cast my gaze over her body. "Is this amusing to you?" She pokes her finger into my chest.

I've always seen Reece dressed impeccably, with beautiful makeup and her hair always done. "This is by far my favorite look of yours." I draw my gaze up and down her body. She looks down at her jeans, oversized sweater, and sneakers. "I prefer for you to be naked though." I take a step back from her and shove my hand in my pocket while lifting the glass to my lips. "Drink?"

"You've completely overstepped every boundary known to man."

"I'm the president of the United States, I don't have boundaries."

Reece snorts and shakes her head. "You're fucking demented. I'm going home." She turns to leave my room.

"I wouldn't do that if I were you."

"Why?" she spits over her shoulder at me.

"Mark won't let you leave."

Reece stops short of the door, her hand stills for a brief second before she slowly pivots and stares at me. "You had your Secret Service agent track me down, throw me over his fucking shoulder and bring me here—for what?"

"He did what?" I ask, suddenly annoyed at Mark for manhandling Reece. I scramble past her to tear the fucking door off the handles and kill Mark.

"What are you doing?" Reece darts her hand out and clamps my arm to restrain me.

"He touched you."

"Yes, he did, because that's what you told him to do, Bennett." She lowers her gaze to look at where her hand is gripping my arm. She takes in a deep breath, straightens and calmly squeezes my forearm. She opens her mouth and pants lightly. Jesus, she's affected by me, just like I am by her. "What's happening?" her voice is dripping with desire.

I swing to face her, lacing my fingers through her hair and lowering my mouth to take Reece's. "I miss the taste of your pussy on my lips," I mumble against her mouth.

Reece pushes me backward until my back finds the door of my room. She thrusts her body into mine. "Is this what you want?" Reece nips at my chin before licking down my neck. "Is this what you want?" Our intensity is stirring a strong response deep in my gut.

"I want you," I admit. "Every part of you."

She breaks our connection and takes a step backward. Reece wipes her mouth with the back of her hand. "Boundaries, Bennett. Learn them." I move toward her, but she holds up her hand. "No."

I despise not being able to touch her when I want. "Reece…"

She silences me with a hardened glare. "Boundaries," she repeats before moving past me and opening the door. "Can you please take me home, Mark?" Mark looks in and meets my gaze where I give him a small nod.

"Of course, Miss Maxwell."

She walks out without a second look.

Fuck!

What the hell is wrong with me?

Thursday

Knock, knock.

"Yeah," I call as I straighten the tuxedo's bowtie as I dress for tonight's state dinner. The door opens, and Liam strolls in. His jaw is tight, and he shoves his hands into his pockets. "What's wrong?"

"Mr. President, there's a small problem."

"What is it?"

"One of the guests has been flagged by the Secret Service."

I shake my head and shrug. "Why are you bringing me this?"

Liam rocks back on his heels as he stares at me. "It's Reece."

"Reece who?"

"Reece Maxwell."

I snap my head to the side while drawing my brows together. "Reece?" Liam nods once. "Did she agree to come tonight?" I rack my brain and try to think if she accepted my invitation. Liam's jaw jumps. "She's here with someone."

"Yes, she is. What do you want me to do?"

"Who is she here with?"

"Senator Arthur Garrett."

My mouth falls open as I nod. "I'm not even surprised. He's pushing fifty, and he's got her on his arm?" I walk over and sit on the edge of the bed.

"I can ask the agents to deny her entry."

"No," I say way too fast. "Tell Mark to clear her."

Liam hangs back for a moment. "Are you sure?" I lift my head and stare at him. "Very well." He nods and quietly exits my bedroom.

"Fuck." Standing, I pace back and forth. I fucking hate having to sit in a room where she's nowhere near me. Worse still, knowing she's here with someone else. "Fuck." *Knock, knock.* "Yeah?"

"Mr. President," Jamie says. "Prime Minister Clarke has arrived."

"Thank you." Jamie stays for a few seconds too long. "What?" I snap with irritation.

"Are you okay, sir?"

"Yes, I'm fine." Jamie softly nods and backs out of the room. My tuxedo jacket is hanging in the closet, and I walk over to grab it. I shrug into my jacket and head out of my room. Mark is standing by my door and gives me a knowing nod. "Did she make it in with limited fuss?"

"Yes, sir."

My Secret Service detail all work seamlessly. Mark, the lead agent, instructing them through the comms. We head to the North Portico entrance, where honor guards are wearing full dress uniform. I'm not waiting long before Ms. Clarke approaches. "Ava, welcome to the White House." I extend my hand to shake hers.

"Thank you, Mr. President," she says as she looks around.

The next fifteen minutes is spent going through the normal, boring rigmarole state dinners are all about. Actually, that's not fair, I do enjoy these on the rare times we've hosted them. I guess I'm preoccupied knowing Reece is here with Arthur-fucking-Garrett. He better not touch her, or I'll tear his fucking arms off his body.

Ava and I head toward the state dining room, where we're greeted by a standing ovation. I see Reece standing beside Arthur clapping while looking straight at me. Ava has her arm linked through mine as I introduce her to the hundred-odd people here.

Reece is wearing a stunning, body-hugging red dress. Her brown hair is softly curled and cascading loosely around her beautiful face. Thankfully, I'm able to continue conversation as if she's not affecting me, but I look over at her every opportunity I can.

"What a beautiful room," Ava says as she looks around once I drag her chair out and wait for her to be seated. "Thank you." She smiles warmly at me.

"You're welcome." Mark stands behind me, Grayson behind Ava, and there are another four Secret Service agents standing against the walls of the room. The first course comes out, and while the people at the table are chatting casually, I keep staring at Reece. She's doing her best not to look at me, but every few moments, she calmly turns to meet my eyes. God, I want her to crawl over here, get on her knees, sneak under the table, and suck me until I come in her mouth. I want to take her, bend her, and claim her in front of every single guest here. I don't care what she does. I just want her. Arthur drapes his hand over the back of her chair and absentmindedly runs his fingers over her exposed arms.

Liam leans over and whispers, "Are you okay?"

"What?" I break my hard stare from Reece to turn to Liam.

He angles his head so no one can hear us. "If you don't calm down, people will start to notice." I snap my gaze away from Arthur-fucking-Garrett and how he's getting handsy with *my* girl. "I'll have them leave."

"No, don't." I sneak one more look at Reece before pulling myself together. Standing, I offer my hand to Ava. "Would you care to dance, Ms. Clarke?"

"Thank you." Ava stands and places her hand in mine. Leading her over to the dance floor, I begin to lead her in a simple waltz across the floor. As I lead, I can't help but notice Reece's eyes boring into me. Just like mine are zoning in on Arthur-fucking-Garrett's hands on Reece. I hate the fact we can't dance together. Or that I have to see her and know *why* she's here and what she's going to do once they leave. "The room is certainly opulent," Ava says as she looks around and admires the décor.

"In 1809 this room became the State Dining Room. Prior to that, it was smaller and rather neglected, not being used for much. President James Madison was the one who refurbished the room, but it wasn't until 1902 when a renovation included expanding this room."

"There was a seventeen-year age difference between President Madison and his wife, Dolley," Ava says, surprising me with her knowledge. "Quite scandalous, don't you think?" She chuckles. "Although, I'd have to be wearing flat shoes to be dancing with him, considering he was five foot four."

"Your knowledge is impressive."

"I'm quite well versed across a lot of areas."

"I have no doubt. A master's in economics, a master's in political science, a minor in business analytics, and another minor in counseling. You're an impressive woman."

"You've done your research, too," she says with a smile.

"I have, because one of the things I'd like to talk to you about is your Arms Act."

"Of course, I've brought all the relevant research."

The song finishes, and I let go of Ava, step back and bow while Ava gives me a small nod. "Thank you." I offer my hand to guide her back to our table.

We make small talk as we head over to our table. I pull her chair out and wait for her to sit before I push her chair in. That's when I see Reece stand and head out of the dining room. I shoot Mark a discreet look and gesture for him to go after her. "Grayson." Mark flicks his gaze to Reece, then back to Grayson. They're so good at being subtle that their stealth moves aren't even noticed by anyone. "Mr. President," Mark leans down and whispers.

"Excuse me." I push back and stand. Mark walks ahead of me as we leave the dining room. "Where is she?"

"Grayson has her in the private library, sir."

I hurriedly walk toward my library and open the door to find Reece pacing back and forth while Grayson stands by the exit, blocking her. "Give me the room," I say to both Mark and Grayson.

"We can't do this," Reece says the moment the door is closed.

"Why are you here with him?"

"Arthur?" I lift my brows and stare at her. "Because I'm working, that's why."

"Fuck," I curse under my breath as I lift my right hand to rub at the back of my neck. "You're not to sleep with him."

"Excuse me?" she replies, her voice an unpleasant shrill.

"You're not to sleep with him," I repeat a bit louder, in case she didn't hear me.

"What I do outside of our time together is none of your business."

I slam my hand on one of the shelves, making Reece jump back with a startle. "God damn it, Reece, you don't flaunt him here under my fucking nose."

"You don't speak to me like that." She points her finger at me just as the door swings open and Mark has his gun drawn. Reece's eyes widen, and she takes a step backward, her hand on her chest.

Mark looks around the room, then turns his attention to me. He and I need to have a conversation about this, but right now, I need him out of the room. I jerk my head toward the door, and Mark backs out of the room, holstering his gun. I turn my attention back to Reece, who's now on the opposite side of the room leaning against the wall her face drained of color. "Are you okay?"

"He was prepared to shoot me." She shakes her head. "I can't do this, Bennett."

"I don't want you to go home with him."

Reece blinks several times as tears well in her eyes. "He was prepared to kill me."

"I know. Mark and I need to have a conversation. But please." I step closer to her, and she backs herself into the corner of the room. "Please don't go home with him."

Reece is looking down at the floor, softly shaking her head in disbelief. She wraps her arms around her body, shielding herself from what she realizes could have happened. Reece lifts her gaze and stares at me. "I can't do this with you anymore."

I try to reach out, but Reece avoids my touch by sliding past me and heading for the door. Without another word spoken between us, Reece walks out of my library. I take a moment to compose myself, then open the door. "Make sure Grayson stays close to her," I instruct Mark, who relays my instructions through their internal comms.

I head back into the State Dining Room and sit beside Ava. There's pleasant small talk going on around the table, which I add to but notice quickly that Arthur and Reece both stand and walk out of the dining room. Mark leans down and whispers, "She's not feeling well." I nod my understanding, and perfunctorily continue with the rest of the evening. But every single thought is of Reece and what she's doing.

And I hate it.

Chapter Six

Reece

"Okay, what's wrong?" Tash brings me a coffee and sits in the armchair opposite me.

I curl up on the seat, tucking my feet under me. "Nothing. Why?" I take the mug and sip the coffee. I look out the front window and watch the cars driving by.

"Hang on, another customer." Tash stands and walks over to the counter of her cozy bookstore. Tash chats with the customer, smiles, and when the customer leaves to browse the shelves, Tash returns. "Carrie's making her a coffee." She sits again but keeps an eye on the counter. "So, you were telling me what's wrong."

"No, I wasn't," I say as I lift the mug to cover my small smirk. "Cheeky." I look at Tash from over my mug.

"You've been off since you arrived an hour ago. What is it? Is Emily, okay?"

I smile proudly. "Yeah, she's awesome, I've got to leave to pick her up around two."

"What's the plan for tonight?"

I shrug. "Wanna come over for pizza and popcorn? Movie marathon?"

"Sure. It's not like I have any hot dates." She snorts with laughter. "My dates are all these books. They're the closest thing to hot action I'm gonna get. I must admit though, I thoroughly enjoy the romance section. I'll tell you what." She fans herself as her cheeks pink. "There are some things in those books that I bet would make even you blush."

"Doubt it. I've had some pretty freaky clients."

Tash leans forward and whispers, "Care to share?" She stares at me with an eager smirk and wide eyes, waiting for me to give her any gossip.

"You know I can't."

"A girl can dream." She sighs and sits back, totally relaxing in her chair. She lifts her coffee and takes a sip. "So, wanna tell me what's going on?"

"What do you mean?"

"Something is off about you. Is it work?" I shake my head. "Everything is safe?" she asks in a more cautious tone.

"Yeah, it's nothing like that."

"Is it a client?"

I turn and stare at a spot on the wooden floorboards. "It's nothing, really. Don't worry."

"You know you can talk to me, right?"

I look over at her and smile. "I know, but you also know I literally can't talk to you. I can't talk to anyone."

"It's gotta be mentally challenging not being able to debrief after you put your mind and body through something so intense."

I run my thumb over my bottom lip as I stare outside. I notice a black car sitting opposite to the bookstore, with a man sitting in the driver's seat. I squint to get a better look and roll my eyes when I see it's the Secret Service agent from last night. "Seriously?" I mumble as I place my mug on the coffee table and push out of my comfortable position.

"What is it?" Tash turns to look out the window.

"Nothing. Stay here." I run out of the bookstore and cross the road. The agent sees me and gets out of the car. "What are you doing here?"

"I've been assigned to you, Miss Maxwell," he says with a stoic, cold delivery.

"What?" I shake my head and run my hand through my hair. "You're kidding me, right?"

"No, ma'am."

"You have to see how ridiculous this is." I wait for his response, but of course, all I get is a blank expression. "When were you told that I'm your assignment?"

"I was instructed last night, ma'am."

"Stop calling me ma'am."

"Yes, ma'am."

He's not going to do a single thing I say. I look over at the bookstore, and Tash is standing at the door with her hands on her hips, watching us. "What are your instructions?"

"I'm to make sure you're safe without intruding on your personal space."

"Are you to follow my instructions?" He looks down, confirming my thoughts. "Will you at least stay in the car?"

"Yes, ma'am."

I hang my head as I take a deep breath, trying to think for a moment. "This is fucked," I murmur to myself. I lift my chin and meet the hard eyes of a Secret Service agent who has to be cursing me as much as I'm cursing the president. "What's your name?"

"Grayson, ma'am."

"This 'ma'am' business is bullshit. It's Reece." I look over toward Tash, who's inched closer and is standing outside her bookstore on the sidewalk. I jog across the street. "Don't ask." I hold my hand up while shaking my head.

"Who's that?" Tash does the exact opposite of what I asked.

I look over to Grayson and scratch my neck. "I don't know what to tell you, but I have to go."

"Well, he's cute. Is he a client? 'Cause if he is, it would be weird that I'm crushing on him."

"He's not a client." I walk into the bookstore, grab my mug and down my coffee, reaching for my bag. "I have to go," I repeat to Tash. "Tonight though, my house. About seven?"

"I close at six, so I'll come over after work. I'll let myself in if you're not there." Tash looks out toward the black car and places her hand on my arm. "Are you sure everything is okay?"

"It will be." I offer her a forced smile, hoping to ease her worry. "See you tonight." I lean over to give her a hug. I walk out and head to my car. Grayson pulls in behind me and follows me home. He pulls up outside my house and parks. I walk in before dialing Bennett's number.

"I was hoping to hear from you," he says.

"Were you now?" I pace back and forth in my family room, keeping a watchful eye on Grayson.

"I wanted to talk to you about last night, and the way things happened."

"Did you not hear anything I said about boundaries, Bennett?"

"Of course, I did. Which is why I didn't call you today."

I find myself rooted to the spot while tapping my foot. My hands begin to tremble while I try to calm the fury bubbling through my body. "Why do I have a Secret Service agent following me?" My voice shakes with anger through my clenched jaw. There's a second of silence. "Bennett!"

"It's to keep you safe. That's all."

"I don't want him, I don't need him, and it's an invasion of my privacy. The American public would be incensed to find out your *escort* has Secret Service detail."

"I wouldn't call it a *detail*. More like one agent."

"Bennett," I snap. "Get rid of him."

"I can't do that," he adamantly responds.

"Do you ever want to see me again?"

"Of course."

"Good. Then get rid of him now. This is not only a total invasion of my privacy, but my clients' privacy, my family's privacy, and my friends' privacy."

"I can't do that, Reece."

"Can't or won't?" He clears his throat. "If you want to have any chance at all of ever seeing me again, I want him gone. And by gone, I don't mean parked down at the bottom of my street. I mean back at the White House, doing the job he's trained for and is paid to do." I cross my arm in front of my chest, waiting for his reply.

"I'm the man who gives the orders, I don't take them."

I run my tongue over my teeth and softy shake my head. I pull the phone away from my ear and simply hang up on him. I'm too angry to speak to him. I walk out the front toward Grayson's car. He opens the door and stands straight when he sees me heading toward him. "I'm going to be leaving to get my daughter in a short while. I don't want her knowing you're here."

"Understood, ma'am."

"Thank you." He's doing the job he's been assigned to do. I can't yell at him for following an order. I head back into the house to get ready for Emily.

Bennett and I need to talk.

The doorbell rings, and Emily shouts, "Pizza! I'm having a whole pizza to myself."

"Seriously, Em? I don't think you can eat two pieces let alone an entire pizza," Tash teases.

"Wanna make a bet?" Emily sassily replies.

I grab my purse and head over to open the door. Grayson is standing there with two pizza boxes. "I told you to make yourself invisible," I hiss.

"Hey, Mom, do you need help?" Emily asks as she comes to the door. I narrow my eyes at Grayson who hands me the boxes. "You don't look like a pizza delivery guy."

I plead with my eyes that Grayson doesn't give away who he is or why he's here, which I'm still trying to figure out. "Uh, the normal guy's car broke down, so he called me to help."

I release a long, silent breath, grateful he came up with that story. "Oh, well, you're dressed really nice," Emily says. "Thanks for the pizza." She takes both boxes and merrily skips back into the family room.

"Thank you, I appreciate what you did."

"You're welcome. Next time, please let me know you've ordered food."

I look to where his car is parked down the street, then back to Grayson. "Why?"

"It makes my job easier," he says cryptically.

"Am I going to be able to order pizza from there again?" His left eye slightly twitches. I have to remember Grayson is only doing his job. "Are you hungry? Do you want a couple of slices?"

"No, ma'am."

"Have a good night." I go to close the door, but his hand darts out stopping me.

"Is Miss Natasha staying the night?"

I shrug. "Maybe. I don't know." I remember I haven't paid for the pizzas. "Here." I open my purse to take out the money.

"No, ma'am, it's been taken care of."

Yep, Bennett and I need to have a talk. I place my purse on the kitchen counter and take my phone out of my back pocket. There's a message from Bennett. *Enjoy your pizza.*

So much for boundaries.

"Mom, what movie do you wanna watch?" Emily asks as she scrolls through one of the streaming services. "I want to watch *The Hunger Games*, but Tash said she wants to watch *Back to the Future*. So, we're leaving it up to you."

My head is swimming with thoughts of Bennett, so truthfully neither. "I want to watch *The Hunger Games*," I say.

Tash pokes her tongue out at me, and Emily snickers. I sit on the sofa next to Tash and open my reply from Bennett. *Dinner, Sunday night.*

I stare at the reply. There are so many things I want to say, but I'm not going to do it in a text message. Tash lightly slaps my arm. "What?" I look over to her to find she's staring at my phone. Her brows raise in question. "It's nothing."

The movie starts, and Tash leans into me to whisper, "Like it's nothing that the delivery driver was dressed in nice clothes and doesn't look like a delivery driver?"

"You heard?"

"No, Emily told me." She glances at my phone, then back to me. "What's going on?"

I run my hand through my hair and subtly flick my head toward Emily. I'm going to have to tell Tash something, but I don't know what. "Please believe me when I say I literally can't tell you."

"Are you in trouble?"

"God, no. Nothing like that."

"Is it a client?"

"Kind of, but please don't ask anything else."

"Do you like this person?"

Her question throws me, because I wasn't really expecting such an intimate query. "Part of me does, but another part is struggling with the dynamic. Besides, it's not like we can be together."

"Why not? Stranger things have happened." God love Tash, she sees the good in everyone and everything.

Her words hit me hard. I lay my phone face down on the sofa and throw my arms around Tash's shoulders. "Thank you, Tash, for taking us in, and for being our family." I kiss her cheek.

"That's you avoiding the question. It's okay. When you can, I'm sure you'll tell me about this mysterious person."

I pick my phone up and stare at Bennett's reply. **Dinner, Sunday night.** I confirm.

I turn my phone off and slide it onto the coffee table between the pizzas. I want to try and forget about him and his stupid over-protective ways.

If only life was that simple.

Problem is, he's all I can think about.

Chapter Seven

Bennett

"Mr. President," Jamie says as he stands inside my office.
"What is it?" I look up from my laptop and stare at him over my glasses.

"You've blocked out a meeting in the residence, sir."

"Of course. Thank you, Jamie." I return my attention to the laptop to finish with what I'm doing before I stand and head out to Esther and Jamie. "Have a good evening," I say to both Jamie and Esther.

"Thank you," they echo in unison. I return to my office to pack my laptop away and shrug into my suit jacket.

I open the door to the covered walkway between my office and the residence. "Sir," Mark says as he walks beside me. "Miss Maxwell is on her way."

"Good." Once upstairs, I walk into my room, loosen my tie and sit by the window, looking out. I'm struggling with whatever it is that Reece and I have. I know this has disaster written all over it and could surely end my career.

The door opens, and I don't even turn to see Reece enter. "Are you okay?" Reece walks over and stands in front of me. "You look like you're thinking about something."

"Truthfully, I thought you'd come in here and yell at me."

"Oh, that's still going to happen, but something is obviously bothering you." I lift my eyes to look at her without even moving my head. She arches a brow as she takes a step forward. Pushing herself between my legs, she scrapes her nails through my hair. I move my head forward, leaning against her stomach. "The weight of the world might be on your shoulders, but it doesn't mean it has to break you."

"I find myself in dangerous territory, Reece." I rest my hands on her hips, holding her exactly here, where I want her.

"What is it?"

I take several deep breaths and pull back, dragging her down to sit on my lap. "You walked in prepared to yell at me, but something stopped you. What was it?" Reece smirks, tilts her head to the side and raises a brow. "I know, it's still coming. But what made you not yell at me straight away?"

"Your tie is loose, and your hair is mussed."

"So?"

"You run your hand through your hair when you're stressed."

"You know that?"

"I pay attention." I slowly nod with the realization that perhaps I mean more to Reece than just a client. "So, what's wrong?"

I wet my lips and look up at her. "I want more from you." She visibly gulps, stands and takes a step back. Looking around the room, Reece takes a moment to wrap her head around this. Have I made a mistake? Have I put her on the spot? "It made me crazy when I saw you with that prick, Garrett. I wanted to tear his hands off you, and shove them down his fucking throat."

She darts her eyes around, trying not to directly look at me. Shaking her head lightly, she backs up and leans against the window. "I don't know what to tell you, Bennett." I love how easy she is around me. "Other than what we've been doing, we can't be together."

"I don't want you seeing anyone else."

"I'm not *seeing* anyone," she replies.

"I mean, I want you to be exclusively mine."

Reece chuckles as she pushes off the window sill and walks over to the table, where she pulls out a chair and sits. "I have to work."

"No, you don't. I can take care of you."

"I don't need you to take care of me, Bennett."

"But I want to."

Reece exhales a slow, long groan. She lifts her hands and places them on top of her head while tilting her head back to look up at the ceiling. It takes her a few moments to finally lower her hands, pull her shoulders back and sit straighter. "Mr. President..."

"It's Bennett."

"No, it's not. This isn't personal; it's business. I'm an escort. My job is to go out for dinner with people who pay me and sometimes have sex with them. It's to listen to their problems, and to give them satisfaction." She stands and lifts her chin. "You're the president, and I'm an escort. You may hire me, but I'm not yours."

"I want you to be," I openly admit, hoping she feels the same way.

"Mr. President, perhaps we should end our arrangement here." Reece creeps toward the door.

"Don't you dare fucking move," I say to her. A small shiver tears through her body as she audibly gasps. There's too much distance between us, and I hate how she's so willing to walk out of my room. *And my life.* Standing, I walk over and stop in front of Reece. Her chin is tucked down with her eyes closed. "Don't you fucking move," I whisper as I reach out to touch her cheek with the back of my hand. Reece licks her lips before pursing her mouth together. Her chest is rising and falling rapidly. "Why are you fighting this?"

Reece's chin stays lowered. "We can't be more. Can't you see that?"

"I want it." I lower my hand to grab hers and place it on my chest. "You want it." Her fingers flex against my unbuttoned shirt.

"Mr. President."

"Bennett," I correct. "I want you."

She softly shakes her head, pulls her hand out from under mine and steps back. Reece opens her mouth several times, itching to say something. It takes her a few seconds, before she starts, "I came here tonight to ask you to remove the Secret Service detail you have on me. It's a waste of taxpayer money."

"I don't care."

"I do, because I'm a taxpayer, and I would be furious to find out the president is spending my hard-earned tax money on Secret Service protection for an escort." She sucks in a breath, though remains still and cold.

"I'm not spending the taxpayers' money."

"No? Who pays the Secret Service then?" I hate how right she is. "You'll never be reelected as president if people find out you're in a relationship with an escort."

I look away from her, hating how she's referring to herself. "Stop talking like that."

"You'll lose every vote, every seat, every person who's supported you or backed your party. The margin you'll lose by will be the biggest in history."

"Are you even registered to vote?" I ask, trying to deflect from the intense situation.

Reece's jaw jumps as she stares at me, ready to argue. "You're kidding right? You've investigated me, have a file with all of my information, and you have no idea if I'm a voter?" Oh, I do love pushing her buttons. I flick my hand dismissively. "Did you just flick your hand at me?"

"I know you're a voter. Who did you vote for?"

"The candidate's name was Nunya."

I stare at her in confusion. "There wasn't anyone by that name."

"None of ya business. Just like my personal life is none of your business. Like my family and friends are none of your business." There she is my fiery girl who's not afraid to stand up to me, or weakens when we're in the same room together.

"You should work for me." I walk over to the small dining table and pull out the chair.

"What? Work for you?"

"You refuse to allow me to look after you, so you should be on my staff."

Reece begins to laugh hysterically. Tears cling to her cheeks as she holds her stomach. "As what? Your on-call escort?"

"I'd find you a suitable position."

She stops laughing and approaches me. "You know, you're so damn cute when you're being unreasonable." She beams happily. "But you've seen my tax returns."

"Well, yes." I lean back into the chair, quite relaxed.

"What did I earn last year?"

"It was a modest salary with your investments."

"You earn four hundred thousand."

"That's public record," I say, not sure where she's going with that.

She holds her finger to her lip. "Shhh, I have a secret. Don't tell the IRS, but what I declared wasn't anywhere near what I earned." The smirk on my face slightly falls. "You can't afford me."

I lift my brows as I relax my arms by the chair. "Hmmm. We have a problem then."

"No, *we* don't. You do." Her smile fades. "I'm not going to work for you, nor is this a good idea anymore." She blinks several times and backs away. "Please, pull the Secret Service."

"No."

Reece's shoulders slump slightly as she exhales a frustrated sigh. "Get rid of them, Bennett."

I wag my finger at her. "You said we can never be, so it's Mr. President," I throw her words back at her. "And seeing as I'm the president, it's my call on where I send the Secret Service. I want them watching you."

"Stop being ridiculous. No."

This is turning quickly. "I want you."

"No!" she adamantly replies. "You can't have me the way you want."

"I can have anything I want, and I want you."

"Great, because I'm for sale," she says with seriousness.

"I want more," I counter.

"Mr. President, all I can offer is my body and time."

I stand and with determination I walk toward her. I grab her arms and pull her into me. "I want more," I repeat and kiss her mouth with vigor. Reece's body instantly reacts to mine. Our bodies are both on fire, each desperate for the other person. She pushes her chest into mine and lifts her leg to wrap around my hip.

"We can't do this." Her mouth says one thing, but her body betrays her. I tug on her other leg, making her jump up and wrap her other leg around my hips. "We shouldn't do this."

I walk us over to the bed and lay her down on it. Reece lifts her arms over her head, while I kiss her chin, down her neck, between her breasts and farther down, lifting her sweater to reveal her taut stomach. "We positively should do this." I unbutton the top of her jeans and lick from one hip bone to the other. She brings her legs up to rest her heels on the edge of the bed. I stand and stare at her while unbuttoning my shirt.

"I have to say," she begins as she props herself up on her elbows. "You deserve to be on all those lists."

"Are we talking about my skills as president or other lists?"

"Other lists," she says with a cute little smile.

"I thought we said we're not discussing those."

"*You* said *you're* not discussing those." She nibbles on her bottom lip as she watches me undress. "I, on the other hand, am really glad you're on those lists."

"The bane of my existence."

"The youngest president to ever hold office, and the sexiest one too." She waggles her brows at me suggestively.

Knock, knock. "Mr. President," Liam calls through the door.

"Fuck!" I grumble. I quickly put my pants on, and loosely pull my shirt on and start buttoning it up. "Just wait there," I instruct Reece.

"Do you want me wet?"

I run my hand over my neck and turn away from her. Smiling, I shake my head. "You're going to be the death of me." I walk over to the door, open it and step into the hall.

Liam's completely professional and doesn't even bat an eye when he sees I've clearly rushed to get dressed. "We need you in the cabinet room."

I finish buttoning my shirt and tuck it into my pants. "What's going on?"

"We've had a sub go silent in the Yellow Sea."

"What? One of ours?" Liam nods. "Why did we have a sub down there?"

"We've been on a recon mission."

I look to Liam and nod. "How long has it been since the sub has been heard from?"

"They're fourteen minutes over their schedule."

"Okay." I fix the cuffs around my wrists. "Give me two minutes, I need to finish something here."

"Of course, Mr. President." Liam stands back, opposite my bedroom door.

I turn to Mark and gesture toward my bedroom. He lifts his hand and calls Grayson. Opening the door, I find Reece standing by the table with her bag in her hand and prepared to go. I sigh as I look down toward the floor. "I know, you have to go."

"I do," I say. I walk over to her and wrap my arms around her.

"Will you assign Grayson to someone else?"

"We'll talk about it tomorrow.'"

"Tomorrow?" She pulls out of my arms and looks up at me.

"I want to see you tomorrow." I kiss her forehead, staying in this spot for a moment. "I really have to go. But, tomorrow?"

"What time?"

"Eight, and I'm going to sit down and actually eat with you."

She blinks several times as a small smile tugs on the corners of her lips. "Fine. But, only because we're going to talk about this whole Grayson situation."

I cross my heart sarcastically. "I promise."

Reece rolls her eyes and nods. "Yeah, sure."

I kiss her once again before opening the door to my bedroom where Grayson is already waiting for her. "Miss Maxwell," Grayson says as he falls into place.

"Hey, Grayson. This is ridiculous, isn't it?" She looks me dead in the eyes, waiting for Grayson to agree with her.

"I take my job seriously, ma'am," he responds.

I smirk when Reece huffs because she doesn't get the answer she wants. She and Grayson disappear down the hallway to the elevator. I love watching Reece's ass as she walks away. It's tight, and delicious, and makes me damn hard.

"Mr. President," Liam encourages.

"Give me a moment." I walk into my room to get my suit jacket. "Okay." I walk out, and we head down to the cabinet room so I can be briefed on what's happening.

Chapter Eight

Reece

I walk behind the counter and jab my fingers into Tash's sides. She squeals and jumps as she turns around. "Jesus, Reece." She lifts her hand and places it to her chest. "You scared the shit out of me."

"I should say sorry, but if I do, I wouldn't mean it."

Tash chuckles. "Coffee?"

I hit my arm to make a vein pop. "Intravenously."

"You're a dork." She heads over to the coffee machine and makes each of us a coffee. "So, what's going on?"

"Not much."

"You're not working?" Tash hands me a coffee and walks around from the counter so we can take up residence in our usual spot by the front window where the perfect amount of sun beams in.

"Not until tonight."

Tash glances at the door, places her cup on the coffee table and stands. Her face hardens with deadly seriousness. "Who are you?" she asks as she walks over to someone.

I turn to see Grayson standing like a statue at the door. "Shit!" I jump to my feet and rush over to Tash before she attempts to serve Grayson his balls on a platter. "Tash."

"I've got this, Reece."

Tash reaches for him, but I stop her before she manages to touch him. "He's with me," I say quickly.

Tash screws her nose at me. "What? Who is he?" I grab her arm and lead her back to our seats. "Do you have a bodyguard now?"

I cringe with the fact I have to stay silent. "Um."

"Are you in trouble?"

"God, no. Nothing like that."

She stares at Grayson before turning her attention back to me. "Who is he?"

"His name is Grayson."

Tash lifts a brow. "He's cute. But, why do you need a bodyguard? What's happening?"

I sit forward and clasp my hands over hers. "Please trust me when I say I'm safe, but I can't say anything. And, I'm fairly sure Grayson's not going to stick around for long."

She scoots forward and looks around. Lowering her voice, she whispers, "Has something happened at work?"

"No." I shake my head but lower my chin. "Please trust me, there's nothing bad. It's just a crazy time for me at the moment."

Tash takes in a sharp breath. "Promise that if it's bad enough that you need a bodyguard, you'll tell me."

"Absolutely," I say, knowing it's a lie. I can't tell Tash anything about my clients. Not a single word. Especially about Bennett. If she knew about him, I'm fairly certain she'd freak out.

She flicks her gaze to Grayson again. "He is cute though. What info have you found out about him?"

I look over my shoulder and can see the appeal. He's always dressed impeccably, and he stands with that authoritarian, intimidating stance. "Nothing, really. What do you want to know?"

"You know. Is he single?"

I snort with laughter and shake my head. "I'm not asking him if he's single."

"I think you should help a sister out." Tash glances at Grayson again. "He's got that dangerous vibe; you know what I mean?"

"Dangerous vibe?"

"Yeah, the *if you look at me, I'm going to pluck your eyes out of your head* vibe." Tash smirks. "Very John Wick. Hmmm, Keanu Reeves, now there's a man I want to do dirty things to. Man, he doesn't even need to participate, he can just lay there and let me do all the work."

I sip on my coffee and shake my head. "How did we go from him?" I point over my shoulder behind me. "To doing nasty things with Keanu?"

"Oh, my God." Tash's eyes widen as she peers around the bookstore. "Have you and Keanu ever..." She links her fingers and smashes her palms together.

"What?"

"Has he ever...you know..." She motions with her eyes.

"No, he hasn't."

"You'd tell me though, right?"

"If it was Keanu, I'd scream it from the rooftops."

Tash links her fingers together in prayer and bats her eyes at me. Oh shit, what's she going to ask now? I'm scared. "Give me one famous person, and I promise I'll never ask about anyone again."

"If I give you even one name, then I can only imagine the questions you'll ask. So... no."

Tash smiles broadly. "You *have* had famous clients."

I shake my head. "No comment."

She smacks my leg. "You're no fun."

"Oh, I'm plenty of fun. Just ask..." I pause and see Tash become super invested in the name she's expecting me to share. "Ha! Not telling." She groans and rolls her eyes. My phone rings, and I dig around my bag to find it. "Hello," I answer.

"Darling."

"Hey, Sofia." I hold a finger up to Tash. Luckily, Tash is considerate when it comes to phone calls and knowing it's Sofia. She stands and walks away giving me a moment of privacy. "What can I do for you?"

"You have a new client."

"New? Who?"

"He's a cardiologist who's here for a conference."

My stomach churns and I screw my mouth. "Um, I'm not really looking for new clients, Sofia. I have my regulars, and I'm quite content with them." Anyone who may overhear this conversation isn't going to think twice about my words.

"I've vetted him, and he's willing to pay big," she throws in, hoping to appeal to my pecuniary side.

"What services is he interested in?"

"He wants company, and straight sex, not even oral sex. He picked you out from the photos, and he wants you dressed in a school uniform."

Ugh, I hate those ones. They creep me out. I get it, everyone has a kink, but school girls aren't mine. I've been asked to mimic everything from elegant to furry pet play to skanky. Some clients want straight sex, some want more, some just want company, and some have even smeared peanut butter on my toes and licked it off. "How long is the booking for?"

"Two hours this afternoon. Four until six."

I sigh and shake my head. "Fine. Send me the address."

"Thank you. I'll text through the details."

I hang up and balance my phone on my thigh. I pick my coffee up and take a sip.

"Everything okay?"

"I have a new client." I roll my eyes and grumble with dissatisfaction.

"Why didn't you say no?"

"It's an easy job," I reply without giving away too much.

"Oh, before I forget, I'm going out for drinks later tonight with a guy I matched with. I forgot my black sweater at your place, can I let myself in after work and grab it?"

"Why are you asking? I gave you a key for a reason, Tash. You don't have to ask to come over, you know that."

She beams happily. "I know, but still, it's the right thing to do." She flicks her gaze over at Grayson. "I can cancel my date if you hook me up with him." Tash juts her head to the side toward Grayson.

"Nope." I lift my hands in surrender. "Not even asking." I finish my coffee and release a puff of air. "I have to go. I need to start getting ready."

"Be safe and take care."

"I'm always safe. I probably won't be home when you get there."

"Okay."

I slide my coffee cup over toward Tash. "Thank you for the coffee."

"Love you."

"Love you too." I approach Grayson and stand beside him. "I'm ready to go." We walk to where his car is parked. "I take it you know what I do."

"Yes, ma'am." He opens the passenger side door for me.

"I have a client at four." He remains stoic, not responding in any way. Not even a facial twitch. *Nothing*. "I need you to not follow me."

"I'm under instructions, Miss Maxwell."

"Can you at least stay in the parking lot?"

"Where's it at?" I give him the hotel name, and he ponders over it on the way home. "I'll check what the protocol is."

"It's all I ask." I guess the Secret Service probably hasn't had to deal with an active escort being part of their detail. But of course, my mind is spinning rapidly thinking about his words. He'll check what the protocol is. Does that mean there *is* a procedure in place for an active escort? Because if there is, it means previous presidents have been in the same situation. I suppose there was that one incredibly public incident with a blue dress, but she wasn't an escort. I start laughing as I think about the second time I met with Bennett. I was wearing a blue floor-length evening gown. I'd best check it for...*stains.* Grayson's eyes quickly shift toward me as he's driving. "Sorry," I say through my laughter.

He doesn't give me an audible response. Instead, he merely nods.

Thankfully, I settle by the time we arrive back home. He pulls up into the driveway and I get out. Grayson catches up to me and holds his hand out. I look at him, not knowing why he's doing that. "Keys."

I roll my eyes and sigh. "It's my home, Grayson, you don't need to check it." He gestures with a hand curl and stares at me. "This is ridiculous. No one knows anything, but people will put it together if you keep hanging around all the time."

"I just look like your boyfriend who spends all his time here."

"In the days you've been with me, this is the most you've spoken. Yes, because my boyfriend would be out in his car most of the time. Makes total sense to me."

Grayson finally cracks a tiny smile. However, he continues doing his job. He unlocks the front door and tells me to wait while he does a quick scan of my house. "You're fine to go in."

"Why thank you," I sarcastically respond. "You can sit in here, if you want." I flick my hand around my dining and kitchen. "Instead of having to go back out there."

"No, thank you, Miss Maxwell."

I shrug as I head into my bedroom, and Grayson returns to his car.

I hate making myself look like a school girl, especially considering Emily is ten years old and at school. I check my two pigtails, grab a lollipop and stick it in my bag. I never take anything that has my address or full name on it when I meet with clients. That's always left in the car. My bag consists of a range of safety items for my protection and the client's. I pull my coat on, slip my feet into heels and pull my socks up to just below my knees.

Walking out to the kitchen, I double-check everything, swipe my keys off the counter and head to the front door. Locking up, I hear someone clear their throat behind me. "I think you should wear a bell to notify me when you sneak up."

"I'll be accompanying you, Miss Maxwell."

I intake a sharp breath. "You can wait outside."

"Yes, ma'am." Grayson opens the passenger door and waits until I'm inside.

The ride to the hotel isn't too long, maybe fifteen minutes. There's a nervous flutter vibrating through me. I have my regular clients, and I'm always a little nervous when I meet someone for the first time. But work is work. I sit in the car for a moment to get my nerves up and focus on what I have to do. I close my eyes and take several deep breaths. "Okay," I say as I work myself up to become the woman the new client needs. I fix my pigtails again, pull my shoulders back and get out of the car. Grayson follows. "Please," I say as I indicate for him to not follow me.

This is hard enough as it is. The fact I'm developing feelings for Bennett almost makes me feel like I'm cheating on him. But the reality is, he knows what I do.

"I understand."

We both enter the hotel and walk over to the elevator. I hit the button and wait until the doors open. I'm getting a few looks from some of the people, judging me by my pigtails, bright red lips, heels and socks. We get to the floor, and both exit the elevator. I just need to find the room. "Stay here," I say pointing to a spot opposite to where I need to be.

Grayson stands against the wall, his hands clasped in front of his body.

Fuck, I really don't want to do this. I should turn around and leave. Instead, I knock on the door. I wait a second, then the door opens. The man, maybe in his late fifties, smirks. He looks me up and down and licks his bottom lip. "Yep," he says as he steps back.

I walk into the room. "Hi," I say as I loosen the tie around my coat and let it fall open.

"God damn it, you're fucking beautiful."

I quickly scan the room and see lines of cocaine on the small table, an array of sex toys on the bed, and a bottle of vodka with the lid off and a portion already missing. Fuck, my gut churns with desperation. I've been in situations like this in the past. My quick thinking has always saved me, so I know I can defuse the situation if need be. "Thank you," I say as I take my coat off. I look at the chair closest to the door and indicate toward it. "May I?" I motion my coat and bag.

"Please." He unfastens the top few buttons of his dress shirt, then rolls his sleeves up as he watches me walk to the chair, place my coat down, and put my bag over it. It's a tactic. If anything happens, swoop up my bag and my coat, and run. "Come sit on my lap." He sits in front of the lines of cocaine and pushes the chair back to accommodate both of us. He taps his thigh and licks his bottom lip again while eye-fucking me. I walk over and sit on his lap. He instantly leans in to kiss me, and the smell of alcohol burns my nostrils. "Hmm. You taste like a little girl."

Balk. I try my hardest not to throw up in my mouth. "Do you like what I'm wearing?" I ask as I soften my voice to make it sound more innocent.

"Sir," he corrects. "You'll call me sir."

"So, you like what I'm wearing, sir?" I play with the collar of my light blue shirt that's tied at the waist into a knot. Slowly, I trail my fingers down to my plaid mini skirt, forcing him to keep an eye on my body.

"Does my dirty little girl like to party?" He looks toward the lines of cocaine. I turn to see the remnants of the lines he's clearly already snorted.

"No, sir, I'm not the partying kind."

"Really? Because with an ass and tits as tight as yours, I think you're lying."

He's getting creepier. But still, this is part of it all. "No, sir, I don't party." I flutter my eyelids at him trying to be the innocent school girl he requested.

He looks over toward the bed and jerks his chin at the toys. "I want to spank you, while you're wearing a butt plug." This isn't what was agreed upon. It was supposed to be straight sex, no extras. He leans over me and snorts two lines with a rolled-up bill. "Here." He offers me the bill.

"No, sir." I shake my head.

He grabs onto my pigtails and thrusts my head down to the drugs. "I said have some. You wouldn't want to upset your teacher, would you?" He pushes my head further.

"I said *no*," I say more firmly. If I don't get the upper hand, this is going to escalate quickly. I've got some moves, and I'll be able to put him on his ass, but when drugs and alcohol are involved, these fuckers seem to have super strength.

He pushes my head further down; my nose is only a mere inch from the drugs. "May I have a drink please, sir?"

He instantly releases my hair and I sit up. Grabbing the bottle of vodka, I stand and walk over to the bed. I take a small sip, making sure to spit most of it back into the bottle without him noticing. I lick my lips and stand as innocently as I can with my knees angled in and my right hip higher than my left. He unzips his pants and shoves his hand in to pull out his cock. I'm sure it's somewhere there in his hand, I just can't see it. "Pick one of those." He eyes the toys on the bed.

"That wasn't agreed to so, no, I won't be doing that. We can have fun without those."

He stands and stalks over toward me. Grabbing my neck, he forcefully throws me on the bed totally exposing my back. "You'll do what the fuck I want, you fucking whore!"

This is escalating too fast. "Stop!" I yell.

He turns me over and slams his fist into my face. A splitting pain echoes through the entire left side of my head. "You're just a two-bit hooker, and you'll do whatever the fuck I want you to."

He manages another punch to my face and as I lift my hands to protect it, he delivers another blow to my stomach, winding me. "Stop!" I scream with everything I have.

"Fucking slut!" He grabs me by the hair and yanks me off the bed.

All the air has been knocked out of my lungs, weakening not only my voice but my strength, too. "Stop!" I scream. "No!"

He jams his damn shoe into my side before lifting his foot to smash down on my head. I close my eyes and bring my hands up to protect my head.

Chapter Nine

Bennett

Wile sitting in my office listening to everyone's debrief for today, I find myself distracted by the fact I know Reece is currently with a client. Liam and Alison are both in discussions while my Communications Director, Elizabeth, and my Deputy Communications Director, Gavin, argue about something completely unrelated. The four of them are vying for attention, and I'm not hearing any of them.

Jamie enters my office and hands me a piece of paper. I open it, and my stomach clenches when I read the words. *Miss Maxwell has been attacked.*

I look up at the four standing in my office and stare at them. "I have to cut this short." My pulse races as I lower my hands under the table and clench them into fists.

"Mr. President?" Liam asks, reading my concern.

"That's all, everyone."

"Thank you," they all say. All but Liam shuffle out of the room.

"Is everything okay?"

Standing, I grab my suit jacket and shrug it on. "Reece," I say to Liam.

"I don't understand."

I make sure the room is secure before saying, "She's been attacked. I need to get to her. Find out where she is."

"That's not a good idea," Liam retorts.

"What?" I close my laptop and pack it away into my briefcase. "Why?"

"Think about it."

"Mark!" I yell. He opens the door to the Oval Office and steps inside. "Where is she?"

"Grayson has taken her home."

"What? Why isn't she at the hospital? What happened?" I ask, completely ignoring Liam's plea.

"You can't go," Liam echoes.

"The hell I can't. I'm the damn president. I can do whatever the fuck I want." The hair on the back of my neck stands at attention as my stomach contracts with anger.

"Bennett," Liam says, changing from my right-hand man, to my best friend. He walks over and places his hand on my shoulder. "Please, calm down." He takes a breath.

I stare at him for a moment. I look around the office and find Mark's left. "Mark!"

The door opens and he stands with rigid control. "Sir?"

"Take me to her."

"You can't go," Liam pleads.

"I'm not doing this with you again."

Liam stands in front of me and pulls his shoulders back. "How do you think her neighbors are going to respond when the motorcade—including Cadillac One—shows up and closes off the entire street? I can guarantee the press will be called, and then you're going to have to explain why the president is at an escort's home."

I grimace at his words, because all of them are true. "I can't leave her all alone."

"Grayson's with her," Liam reiterates.

My jaw jumps as I take a breath trying to figure what the next most logical step is. I turn to Mark and stare at him for a moment. "Mark, bring two unmarked cars. Not Cadillac One."

Mark takes in a breath and flicks his gaze to Liam. "No, that's not a good idea," Mark says. "We don't know what threat there might be at her house."

I look out the door and notice the sun is falling in the sky. "We'll be going under the cover of nightfall. Take two of the plain cars. We'll be completely undetected."

"Bennett," Liam whispers. I look at him and he slowly shakes his head.

I turn my attention to Mark. "Make it happen."

"Yes, sir." Mark leaves, closing the door behind him.

"What are you doing? All this for a whore?" Liam asks. I turn and smash him in the mouth, making him stumble backward to catch his fall. The shock of me hitting Liam stuns both of us. He nods slowly as he rubs at his chin. "I thought so," he says as he walks over to me. "She means a lot to you."

I pinch the bridge of my nose as I shake my head. "I can't believe I did that. I'm so sorry," I apologize to Liam. "I don't know what came over me."

"You care for her." He places his hand on my shoulder again and nods. "There's nothing wrong in feeling something for her. But this is going to become complicated incredibly fast."

"It doesn't have to be. We can sneak in there, and sneak out."

"Sure. Tonight, you can. But what about the next time she's hurt?"

"There won't be a fucking next time." My forehead crinkles as I pull my brows together. "She's not working anymore."

Liam grunts with a half-smile. "Oh, she's not? You've already talked about this with her?"

"She'll do what I tell her."

Liam shakes his head. "You don't like her because she does what you tell her, Bennett. You like her because she doesn't." He steps back and rubs at his jaw again. "It's the reason why you loved Kathryn, too. She challenged you, and you thrive on people standing up to you." I find myself nervously shoving my hands into my pockets. "We've been best friends for years before you even thought of running for president. When it comes to your women, you like them with a backbone. Kathryn...Reece."

"I…" I shake my head and lower my chin to look at my shoes. "I'm going to lose the presidency if it's found out."

Liam chuckles. "Probably, my friend." He pats me on the back and walks over to the scotch, pours two drinks and hands me one. "But, look at the scandals this house has had to endure over the years." He holds up a finger. "Thomas Jefferson, and his advances weren't even wanted, but she had no choice but to fulfill his wishes."

"That's different. They weren't in an era of social media, where with one click of a button, the entire world knows what's happening within moments."

"Don't forget, we've also had a president impeached twice."

"He wasn't reelected, much as he tried to convince the nation otherwise, Liam."

"You never know what the future holds." He shrugs as he throws his scotch back. "I'm just saying, yeah, you may lose the presidency over this, but if it's what your heart wants, then…"

"Mr. President?" Mark announces as he barges into the Oval Office. "We have two cars, sir."

I click my tongue to the roof of my mouth. "Thank you." I throw my drink back and look to Liam, offering him a small appreciative nod. "Right." I take my briefcase as we walk out. I look at Mark and grind my teeth together. "Get me everything you can on the person who did this to her." He gives me a silent, knowing nod. I'm going to destroy the fucker who put his hands on my woman. He's going to wish he was never born.

I walk into Reece's home, surprised by how comfortable and large it is. "She's in the family room, sir," Mark instructs as he leads me past the kitchen to the left and down the hallway. The moment my eyes land on Reece, I suck in a breath. *Jesus.*

She looks up to see who's in her house and gasps. "What are you doing here?" she asks. I walk over and sit beside her where she's huddled under a blanket. "Stop looking at me with pity."

"Your face is bruised, and you look like you've been beaten up."

"That's because I have been," she replies sourly.

I look to my men and flick my gaze at them. "Give me the room." All the Secret Service leave, except for Mark. I jerk my head to the side, indicating he needs to leave, too. He heads out of the family room, but I can see his shoes peeking out from the hallway. I reach across to touch Reece's bruised cheek, and she flinches as I run the back of my hand down her face. "You can't do this anymore."

"What?"

"You can't keep doing this anymore, Reece. Look at what happened to you. If Grayson wasn't there..."

Reece points to her face and tries to smile. But her lip is busted and inflamed. "This isn't the first time, and it won't be the last. It's an occupational hazard."

"The fuck it won't be the last. You're to stop. Right now."

"Yeah? And how do you propose I feed my daughter?" she counters.

"Get a different job. You're smart and talented, and easy to get on with."

"What job do you know that can pay me thousands of dollars each week for only a few hours work?"

Her stubborn resistance is beginning to irritate me. My jaw tenses as my hands grip onto my knees. "Enough." I point to her. "This stops now."

"Yeah? Are you going to provide for me?" Reece lifts a brow as she rolls her eyes. "Thought so." She mistakes my silence for hesitation.

"Yes," I say as she huffs.

"What? Yes, what?"

"I'll provide for you and Emily."

Reece's eyes widen as she slowly turns to look at me. "Who the..."

"Mr. President." Mark walks in and leans down to whisper, "Her friend Tash is here."

I look up at him and give him a nod. "Let her in."

"Let who in?" Reece asks. "You better not be getting me another Secret Service agent."

"What the fuck, Reece?" I hear a woman's high-pitched voice screeching as she walks in with thunderous steps. "Why are all these people in your house?"

I stand and straighten. "Tash, what are you doing here?" Reece asks.

"Holy shit, what happened to your face? Did the..." She looks at me, returns her attention to Reece. then back to me. "Are you the president?"

"Yes, ma'am. Hello, Tash." I hold my hand out to her.

Tash's mouth opens as her brows furrow while she continues to look to me, then Reece. "Yeah, right. You look like him, but whatever." She walks over to Reece and tears the blanket off her, wrapping her arms around her. "What the hell happened?"

"He *is* the president, Tash," Reece whispers.

Tash sits back and runs her hand through her hair. "Did you do this to her?" She stands to approach me, and Mark intervenes, standing between us.

"Mark." I lift my hand slightly telling him to back off.

"Can someone please explain to me what is going on?" Tash steps backward until her knees find the sofa where she plonks down.

"Okay, listen," Reece starts. I sit beside her and place my hand on Reece's thigh.

Tash's eyes go directly to where I'm touching Reece. "Wait. What?"

"Bennett didn't do this." Reece points to her face. "My client did. He was high, and drinking, and it all went to shit pretty quickly."

"Okay, I'm keeping up with that." Tash looks to me. "But why is he here?" She lifts her hand and points to me.

"Because, um..." Reece grumbles, not sure what to say.

"Because we've been seeing each other," I say.

"You are?" Tash asks. "What? Huh?" She opens her mouth several times to say something, but closes it. She runs her hand through her shoulder-length bob several times. "I'm so confused." She lowers her chin and stares at the floor. "So all of those people out there are Secret Service?" She indicates to the front of the house.

"Yeah," Reece says.

"And you two are together?"

"Kind of," Reece replies.

"Yes, we are," I answer. Reece slowly turns to look at me. "We are."

"But." Tash points to me. "You're..." She points to Reece who nods. "And he's..." She points to me, Reece nods again. "And you know what her profession is?" Tash looks like she's about to explode if I shake my head.

"It's how we met," I say.

"What are you doing?" Reece whispers. She turns to Tash and wets her lips while reaching for her hand. "You can't say anything."

"I'd never say a word, but why didn't you tell me?"

This conversation is between the girls. They need to sort out this among themselves. "I couldn't," Reece says. "Besides the fact I've signed an NDA, you know I never talk about my clients." I clear my throat, not particularly appreciating the word *client* when she uses it to refer to me. Both Tash and Reece look to me before returning their attention between themselves. "If it makes you feel any better, I wanted to tell you."

"Oh my God! That explains the cute guy hanging around you."

"Cute guy?" I ask. My voice deceives me.

"She's talking about Grayson."

"Yeah, him. He's Secret Service?" I nod my confirmation. Tash nibbles on her bottom lip as she remains quiet, deep in thought. "That's an abuse of power, Mr. President. You can't order the Secret Service to be your girlfriend's bodyguard, especially considering Reece's line of work. If the public finds out, she's going to be in a world of pain. Not to mention you, and let's not forget Emily, either."

"Reece is quitting her profession," I say.

"No, I'm not," Reece pipes in to reply.

"Yes, you are," I react adamantly. "There's no question about this, Reece. You're not doing this any longer."

Tash's lips purse together before making a popping sound. "Look, are you okay? Do you need to see a doctor? Have you called your doctor?"

"No, I'm fine. The only thing I'm concerned about is how I'm going to explain this when Emily comes home on Friday." Reece points to her face. "And obviously, I won't be able to work until all the bruising and swelling goes down."

"You're not working again," I say with conviction.

Tash's eyes widen as she looks everywhere around the room, attempting to avoid looking at either of us. "Um, are you okay? I'll cancel my date, and stay with you."

"No, don't do that. I'm fine. I'll draw a bath and relax. I just need to get today over with."

"You'll come home with me," I say.

"Can you stop?" Reece says to me.

"Um." Tash shakes her head. "Are you sure? I can stay, we can eat ice cream, you can tell me all about..." She slightly angles her head toward me, giving Reece big eyes. When she peers over at me, she smiles innocently. "Or not." She shrugs. "Look, I don't know what the deal is here. You're you." Tash points to me. "And Reece is my best friend. I'm not sure what the proper thing to do is."

"In this room, I'm Bennett."

"I have to be honest, I got patted down out there, and Grayson looked through my bag, and there's like forty-five million Secret Service agents out there. It's a bit hard to have a conversation with Reece while you're here."

"Forty-five million?" I ask smiling.

"Maybe a slight exaggeration," Tash replies. "Maybe ten agents out there, and that one around the corner." Tash points toward Mark's feet. "We're getting away from the point that Reece is hurt."

"I'm really not *that* hurt. It's superficial. You don't have to worry about me. Go on your date and enjoy yourself. Call me when you get home to tell me how it's not going to work out because one ear is bigger than the other," Reece teases Tash.

"That's not fair." Tash crinkles her forehead, then cracks a smile. "Actually, yeah, it's a fair representation of what'll happen." She stands and looks at me. Wringing her hands together, she finally points over Reece's head. "I'm going to grab my sweater." Tash looks me up and down, then back to Reece. "Take care of her. Don't let her stay here alone tonight."

"It's already decided; she's coming home with me. She's in good hands."

"It's not decided," Reece argues with me. "I'm perfectly fine here."

Tash puffs her cheeks, then slowly blows out the air. "Mr. President, I say this with all sincerity, but, good luck with this one. She's iron-willed, and you're going to need luck on your side."

I chuckle. I like Tash, she's an interesting person. "Have a good night with your date, Tash."

She rolls her eyes and huffs. "It won't work out. I'm too picky. But, hey, if you're bored one day sitting over there in the Oval Office, you could always set me up with Grayson."

"I'm not a matchmaker," I say.

"Tash!" Reece scolds. "Go." She flicks her hand at Tash and shakes her head.

"Love you, and I'll call you later." Tash leans down and gives Reece a kiss on the top of the head. There's an awkward silence when she looks at me. "Bye?"

"Goodbye, Tash." She leaves the room, and I turn to make sure she's out of hearing distance. "She's an interesting one."

"She saved Emily and me when we first moved here. I owe her everything, and if she ever needs me, I'm there in a heartbeat. There are two people I'd give my life for, and she's one of them."

"How did she save you?" I ask as I sit back and make myself more comfortable on Reece's sofa.

"It's a long story, and I'm tired. I think I'm going to go to bed early, Bennett. Do you mind leaving?"

"I'm ready to go when you are."

"I'm not going with you. I'm perfectly fine here in my own home."

"You'll be even better in my home, where I can keep an eye on you."

"Do you have any idea how stalkerish you sound?"

I stand and reach for her hand. "Come on, you need to get ready."

"I'm not going." She drags the blanket up over her torso, snuggling into it while leaning her head on an oversized cushion.

"Get up, now."

"No. I'm tired, and I'm not going anywhere."

I click my tongue. "You have no other option, Reece. You're staying with me." With her eyes closed, she waves me away. I grab the blanket she's snuggling into and pull it off her.

"What are you doing?"

"You're coming with me."

I bend, grab Reece, and toss her over my shoulder in a fireman's carry. "Are you kidding me?" she attempts to argue. "Put me down!" I walk out of the family room. "Put me down."

"Get the car ready," I tell Mark.

"It's in the garage, sir." Mark is a couple of feet ahead of me, leading us to the garage. "This way, sir."

"For God's sake, stop being a caveman," Reece is still trying to argue.

In the garage, the back door to the car is already open. I slide Reece to her feet. "Stop acting like a damn child, and I'll stop treating you like one."

She looks to Mark and shakes her head. Without another word, she slides into the back of the car. The car pulls out, and thankfully, the dark windows give us the gift of privacy. "My face hurts, my neck is sore, I don't have clothes and I want to wallow in my own self-pity."

"Good, you can do that from my suite." I reach across and drag her over to me. Reece's resistance quickly fades as she relaxes into my arms and lays her head on my shoulder. I'm careful when I lean over and kiss the top of her head. A small mewl passes through her as I tenderly draw lazy circles on her arm while she nestles closer to me.

"Bennett?"

"Yeah." *Please don't argue with me, not now.*

"Thank you." Reece lays her hand on my thigh and angles her body closer to mine.

I kiss the top of her head again and tighten my arms around her.

Chapter Ten

Reece

Opening my eyes, I instantly feel like crap. Last night was a cauldron of emotions mixed with hours of broken sleep. I tried to put on the strong and confident persona I always carry with me, but in truth, the beating scared the shit out of me. I'm forever grateful Grayson was there, because I don't think I would've been able to fight him off.

My head is pounding in a constant, dull reminder of the trauma I experienced yesterday. I stretch my arm out to find the bed is empty. Bennett was nothing but a gentleman when we returned to the residence. Though I was robbed of my bath, considering I fell asleep within moments of arriving.

I sit up in bed and blink several times, painfully aware of the throbbing throughout my face and body. I look around the dark room, but I can't gauge what time it is exactly. It's dark and there's no light peeking into the room from the windows. I reach over to the night stand for my phone and have to focus on the screen to see it's nearly eight in the morning. "Whoa," I say to myself as I place my phone back on the nightstand. I close my eyes and roll my head from side to side, trying to stretch out the muscles in my neck. "Ah," I grumble as I rub at the tension in my neck. I take several breaths before standing and walking toward the bathroom.

Finished with the bathroom, I head out and sit on the edge of the bed. I pick my phone up and dial Sofia's number. "Darling," she answers.

"Hi, Sofia. I need you to cancel my clients for the foreseeable future."

"No, darling, that isn't going to work for us. You have your regulars who'll be disappointed if you can't make their scheduled appointments."

"Sofia," I start in a small voice. "Yesterday's client..."

"Oh yes, the cardiologist. How was it?"

"I didn't call you yesterday because I was swept away from home."

"I don't understand," she says, her tone filled with worry. "What happened?"

"He beat me. He was doing drugs and drinking. He had toys he wanted to use, he tried to get me to do the drugs. It was a mess. I barely lasted fifteen minutes in there." There's a long pause from both of us. "Sofia, are you still there?"

"But I vetted him. Ran all the checks thoroughly. I..." She sucks in a breath. "I..." I close my eyes as I lean forward and hang my head. "I'm sorry, Reece. I had no idea. He's a fucking cardiologist!"

"Well..."

"Where is he now?"

"I honestly don't know."

"Did he rape you?"

I shake my head as a gut-wrenching pain twists my stomach. "No, he didn't get that far."

"What happened? Did he stop? Did you hurt him? I hope you did."

I let out a small groan. "Um, Sofia, I need to go."

"What happened?" she repeats.

I slowly shrug. "I honestly don't know yet. But once I find out, I'll let you know."

"What do you mean you don't know? Reece, are you okay? Are you safe?"

"I'm fine."

"Where are you? I'll come to you."

"No, please don't. Look, I'll call you soon and we can talk further about what happened. Just know, I'm safe, and I'm being looked after."

"Where are you?" Sofia is persistent, I'll give her that. "Are you in the hospital?"

"I'm not in the hospital, and I'm not at home. Look, I have to go, but can you please cancel all my clients for now? I'll let you know if I return."

"If?"

Damn, she picked up on my resistance. "I've got to go, Sofia."

"Call me if you need anything."

"I will, thank you." I hang up and toss the phone beside me on the bed. I look around the room and decide I'm going to use that magnificent bath in the bathroom. Standing, I walk into the bathroom and start the water, getting it to the perfect temperature. I need to unwind and relax, and consider what my next steps will be. I can't go to clients with a busted-up face, and based on the way the rest of my body feels, I know I'm not going to be able to work for at least a month, if not longer. I have to consider Emily and how she'll react when she returns home for the weekend. I also need to speak with Bennett and find out what happened with the cardiologist. Do I need to give a statement to the police? Did it even go to the police? Will there be charges against me because I was soliciting?

I don't know. This is all too much for me right now.

My mind needs to rest and relax and not think about what could've happened, or worse still, what's *going* to happen. With the tub full of warm water, I take off my clothes and sink straight into serenity. Closing my eyes, I lean my head back while offloading all my worries into the water. However, there's an ache in the back of my throat as I think about Emily's reaction. She's going to freak out and worry. Of course, I can't tell her the reason *why* my face is bruised. Jesus, maybe now is the time to get out of this business altogether. I don't know. Maybe I'm letting one dreadful encounter dictate my future. Ugh. I hate feeling indecisive.

With my eyes closed, I take several deep breaths, attempting to push those horrible moments out of my mind. I can't let Emily grow up without a mom. Suddenly, the weight of the situation collapses upon me, And my eyes begin to drip with the pain of reality. "He could've killed me," I whisper to myself.

I curl my legs up, hugging my knees while I cry. Man, this is a fucked-up situation. I hate feeling like a victim.

As the water cools, and my tears ease, I take the plug out and let the water drain. Climbing out of the tub, I reach for a towel and wrap it around my body. Jesus, even the towels are luxurious and fluffy. I head out to the bedroom, startled to see Bennett standing by the window. "Shit," I say as I place my hand on my chest. "You need a damn bell." Damn, he certainly looks good in a dark suit with a crisp white shirt and dark green tie. *Really good.*

He casts an eye over my towel-clad body. "I see you got your bath."

"Not a bubble bath, and no wine, but that's okay. And by the way, that's not a bath, that's an indoor lap pool." I point to the massive tub.

"I've laid out some clothes for you." He motions toward the bed.

"I need to go home, Bennett. I can't stay here."

"Why not?" There's a knock on the door and he groans. "I have a meeting in about five minutes, it'll be over in thirty-five minutes. I've then got forty minutes before my next meeting. I'll come up and have breakfast with you."

I stare at him and tilt my head to the side. "So, you've got forty minutes where you'll come have breakfast with me?"

"Today I've got back-to-back meetings, Reece. If I could reschedule any of them, I would."

I lift my hand and wave it. "It's okay. Look, I really do need to go." I glance at the clothes on the bed. "These are your clothes, and I need to get back home. So, don't worry about breakfast, but, I do need a ride."

"No, you'll stay here until we have breakfast together. There are a few things we need to discuss." There's another knock on the door. "I'll be back in exactly forty-one minutes."

"Forty-one is a very specific number, Bennett."

"By the time I walk down there, have the meeting, then return..." He shrugs. "Forty-one minutes."

"Fine, but then I need to go home."

"I'll let my chef know to send breakfast in forty-one minutes." He begins heading to the door but stops. Turning, Bennett walks over to me, then lays a gentle kiss to my temple. As he's about to leave the room, he turns and with a cheeky glint in his eyes, he says, "You look good in a towel. I'd prefer to see it on the floor though." I untuck the towel and drop it to the ground. Bennett is stunned by my brazenness and quickly closes the door, making sure no one sees me naked.

Chuckling at Bennett's hasty exit, I grab the towel and finish drying off before changing into his clothes. A blue dress shirt and boxer briefs that swim on me. It's a good thing the waist is elastic.

I guess I better call Tash and see how it went on her date. I dial her number and she picks up straight away. "I tried calling you last night, but um...*he* said you were asleep."

"Bennett?" I ask.

"Yeah. I don't know what to call him."

"I have no idea," I say. "I guess I can talk to him and ask him, if you want."

"Well, I don't know. Are you two a thing now?"

I look down at his clothes I'm wearing. "Honestly, I don't know what we are. But, how did your date go?"

"Can you spell disaster?" Tash laughs into the phone. "Let me see. I show up at the restaurant looking hot, but I'm totally worried about you and your face."

I smirk. "My face?"

"Yeah, your face. Anyway, the guy shows up, and he's totally catfished me. He's a head shorter, which usually doesn't bother me. But how's this—all he does all night is talk about him and his ex-girlfriend, and how she would let him smell other women's toes. Seriously, smell their *toes*, Reece! Then he asked if we go on another date if I'd have a problem with him smelling other women's toes. He went on and on about this *toe's* thing. Look, whatever floats his boat, but my God, I think he had a toe fetish. Not a foot fetish, but a toe fetish. Anyway, he tried to go in for a kiss at the end of the night, and when I said no, he told me I was a freak because he's so desirable and did I realize how lucky I was because he chose me out of a pool of women."

I'm laughing at her adventure. "Stop making me laugh, my face hurts."

"How is your face? Will it recover or will you be stuck with what you had?" she teases.

"I'm in pain, but I'll recover."

"Alright, so what happened with the guy who did that to you?"

I shrug. "I have no idea. I think that's something Bennett wants to talk to me about. We're going to have breakfast in thirty minutes."

"Wow, sounds so spontaneous," she says with heavy sarcasm.

"You have no idea, but I can't really talk about it."

"Yeah, yeah, I know. Are you home? I'll come over after work. Wouldn't want you walking around with a smashed-up face and frightening all the kids who see you."

"I'm not, but I will be. I'll call you when I return home, okay?"

"Did you stay—"

"Yep," I cut her off before she says the words. My paranoia is in overdrive, and I have no idea if anyone is listening to my calls. "Don't say anything about that, okay."

"Jesus, it all sounds so ominous."

"I have to go, but I'll see you tonight. Hey, any chance you can do me a massive favor and pick up Emily on Friday? I really don't want to show up at her school with my face like this. I'd rather explain it to her in the privacy of our own home."

"What are you going to say to her?" I blow out air through my lips. "Yeah, good luck with that. I have to go; I need to make a coffee. Love your face, even when it's all smashed up."

"Thanks for the sympathy."

"You're welcome," she chirpily replies.

I hang up and chuckle. Tash can always lift my mood, but she's also fiercely loyal and will take my back with no questions asked. Lying on the bed, I let out several yawns before closing my eyes for a short nap.

I can feel something on my cheek, and when I try to swat it away, *it* starts laughing. My eyes flutter open to find Bennett chuckling as he sits on the side of the bed. "Are you watching me?"

"I tried to kiss your cheek, but you hit me."

"Did I?" I yawn and sit up in bed. "What time is it?"

"It's time for breakfast. Are you hungry?"

"Yeah, I'm starving." My stomach growls in response to my words, as if it was waiting for me to wake before it grumbled. "Thanks, stomach."

Bennett laughs again, leans over and kisses my forehead. "You're adorable when you're sleeping."

"You're a weirdo to watch me sleep; that's creepy." He stands and offers me his hand. "Thank you, sir."

"You're welcome, ma'am." I notice the table is gone and I look around wondering when and how it disappeared.

"Where's the table that's normally here?" I point to the void.

"I have a private sitting room through that door over there."

Wow. "You do?"

Bennett laughs again. "Did I not give you a tour of my room?"

"We're usually preoccupied either fighting or having sex."

He shakes his head with a massive smile on his face. "You're quite honest, aren't you?" He pushes on one of the doors and it opens into another room about the same size as his bedroom. "Breakfast is served."

Inside the room there's an extravagant sofa facing a massive TV. The dining table is now located on the far side and has an opulent spread of different foods covering it. "That's a lot of food."

"I didn't know what you'd like for breakfast, so I had the chef make a range of things." He walks us over to the table, pulls my chair out, and waits until I'm seated before he sits. "Help yourself." I look around quite taken back. "What's wrong?" Bennett sits back in the chair and crosses one leg over the other. "Do you not like any of these things? Are you in pain?"

"Every time we start a meal, it's formal. Should I..."

"Do whatever you want, eat however you want." He reaches across the table for a pancake and slides it onto his plate. "I'm really quite a relaxed man."

"Yes, of course you are." I lift my brows and grin. "So relaxed."

"Are you sassing me?"

"Who me?" I place my hand to my chest. "Absolutely." I take a piece of buttered toast and notice the delicious looking fluffy eggs. I spoon a good amount on my toast and lift my flatware to start eating it.

"You know, we need to talk about yesterday."

"What happened to the guy?" I ask.

Bennett stills his fork and clears his throat. "I'm dealing with him."

"That sounds quite menacing, Bennett. What do you mean by 'dealing with him'?" He pulls at his necktie and flicks his eyes away from me. "Bennett?" I push further. "Was he reported to the police?"

"No, he wasn't. If Grayson reported him, it would've exposed not only us, but you too."

My jaw tightens as I shake my head. "So, what happened to him?" There's a long pause from Bennett. He's purposely forming a statement that'll avoid an answer. "Don't you dare go all political on me."

He straightens in his chair and pulls his shoulders back. Here we go, his response will be worthy of his Mr. President status. "I'm having my people look into him, and when there's something to tell you, I will."

I haphazardly toss my flatware onto the plate. "You can't do that, Bennett." He too lowers his flatware and waits for me to continue. "You can't talk to me like you're the American president."

"But I *am* the American president."

"Then you and I know I shouldn't be here because other than certain parts of Nevada, prostitution is illegal everywhere else."

He lowers his leg and leans forward. "I'm struggling with how I feel about you, Reece."

"Why am I here?" I look around the room.

"Because when I was sitting in my meeting, and Jamie informed me what happened to you, all I wanted to do was fucking kill that bastard. And I've only ever felt like that about one woman before. But you..." He points to me, and shakes his head. "You pose a conundrum for me."

I find myself biting on the inside of my cheek, nervously trying to grasp his intensity. "I need to be honest with you, Bennett. I don't know how to reply to you. My biggest worry is Emily."

"I understand that." he acknowledges. "She needs to be protected at all times."

"You have to know she's my number one priority. The reason I send her to board at school from Sunday night until I pick her up on Friday afternoon, is so she's not around what I do. Obviously, I don't bring clients home, but I still need to work."

"You have to stop."

"Oh, I will until my face isn't so messed up."

"No. Reece. You need to stop, period. You can't go back to being an escort."

"And how am I going to provide the tuition Emily needs for that fancy school? Or what if I get sick? I don't have the luxury of having my medical expenses taken care of for the rest of my life. And where would I find a high-paying job? I didn't even finish high school."

"You can work for me."

"You've offered this before. How do you think that'll be received by three-hundred and thirty-three million Americans, Bennett? No need to get your team to run a poll on it, because I can tell you. You're the youngest president in American history, who lost his wife tragically days after inauguration. Now you're sleeping with an escort who got pregnant by turning tricks at fifteen."

Bennett rakes his hand through his hair as his eyes harden. "I'll deal with it if it ever comes to light. We can keep it quiet." He clicks his tongue and returns his eyes to me. "You can work for me. Full medical and all the other benefits."

I tilt my head to the side and smile. "You're persistent."

"Starting salary is forty thousand."

"Seriously?" I snort. "Forty grand a year?"

"With medical and benefits," he says proudly.

"Between my investments and my job, I earn more than that in a month."

He flexes his jaw as he stares at me. "I want you out of that job, Reece. First, it's illegal."

"But *you* pay for escorts."

"Did. I don't anymore."

"That's not going to matter to the American public if it's ever leaked. Not one little bit," I counter.

"Second, it's obviously not safe."

"No, it isn't. But what job is a hundred percent safe?"

"Working for me." I tilt my head to the side and angle my chin down, staring at him with an 'are you kidding' look. "These are all inconsequential. You're not going back to being an escort."

"Bennett..."

He slams his hand on the table making me startle backward. "I don't want you fucking other men."

"But fucking other women is acceptable?"

"No, no. Not at all. I don't want you having sex with anyone but me." I stare down at my fluffy scrambled eggs. I pick my fork up and shove them around a little before lifting some and eating the now-cold eggs. "Reece."

"What's happening here, Bennett?" I motion between us.

"I've been grappling with that very question." I stare at him, waiting for something. "I don't like you having sex with anyone but me." I arch a brow, though remain quiet, letting him state his reasons. "I'm painfully aware that this is your profession, Reece, but I want more."

"More?"

"I want you." His words are raw and direct. "I want to see where this can go."

"Why?" I push.

He stares at his food on the plate and nods his head. "Because I find myself attracted to you."

"I'm a twenty-five-year-old sex worker with a ten-year-old daughter. That in itself will absolutely destroy your presidency. Unless, you decide not to run for reelection."

"I'm going to run," he says without missing a beat.

"You won't win if this becomes anything more."

He releases a cynical chuckle. "That ship sailed the first night I met you. I knew right then that I wanted you, just as much as I do now, sitting across from you at the breakfast table."

Okay then, I wasn't expecting such brutal honesty. "Bennett, I need to protect Emily."

"I understand."

"I'm terrified that once this gets out, my photo along with my name, her name, and probably her school will be splashed across every news outlet in the country. That's too much for Emily to handle."

"Yes, it's a lot, but if it becomes challenging for her, we can have her homeschooled."

"No." I shake my head. "You don't make decisions about my daughter. We're not there yet, Bennett." I pick at my food, suddenly not as hungry as I was when Bennett woke me. He smiles at me broadly. "What?"

"You said *yet*. You said *we're not there yet,* which means you feel like I do." He clicks his tongue to the roof of his mouth. "But I do want to ask you about Emily." I pick my toast up and nibble on the corner waiting for the question I'm sure he's going to ask. "You were fifteen."

"I was fifteen when I became pregnant with her, yes." My body tenses as I wait for more questions.

"Do you want to talk about it?"

"No." I shake my head. "No, I don't, Bennett. It was a horrible and difficult time of my life." I notice his right-hand flex into a closed fist. I lower my gaze to stare at the table filled with food. I wet my lips, ready to tell him my story when there's a knock on the door.

"Fuck," he grumbles as he exhales loudly.

"Mr. President." Some guy walks in and looks to Bennett. "Ma'am," the guy greets me with a crisp tone and a nod.

"Jamie?"

"Sir, Liam needs you."

"Give me a moment."

"Yes, sir." Jamie closes the door behind him, giving us our final moments of privacy before Bennett has to leave.

"I have to go, but I want to continue this conversation."

"I'm going to go home, but obviously, I can't walk out like this." I look to his shirt and boxer briefs.

"I want you to stay until I return later. If you need anything..." He stands and pushes his chair in.

"No, I'm not going to sit around and wait for you. It's unfair to me, and you'll be distracted. I'm going to go home, and we'll see what happens later."

"You'll return," he says with adamant control.

"Maybe." I try to smile, but my face hurts. "I need my own bed."

Bennett looks toward the closed door to his bedroom. "My bed is perfectly comfortable."

"You have a country to run, and I'm going home."

He walks over to me, places his finger under my chin and tips my head. Leaning down, Bennett gently kisses my lips. He pulls back and squats in front of me. "Tomorrow, I'll have Grayson bring you here."

I place my hands on his forearms and grip them, feeling the delicious tension of his muscles. "Sunday night, I'll come over. I need tomorrow to myself so I can process...*everything*."

"Friday Emily returns from school." I nod, confirming that's exactly what happens and why I'm unavailable until Sunday. My hands slide down his arms as he stands, but he manages to link our fingers together. "Okay then." He kisses me on the top of the head and steps backward, breaking our connection. "I have to go."

"I understand." I watch him step backward slowly, not wanting to go.

He smiles at me and looks at all the food. "I'm sorry we haven't been able to eat a meal together yet."

"I told you, I understand."

For a brief second, he pauses, and an unexplainable flicker of something passes between us.

He takes a deep breath and smiles. "I have to go," he repeats. His words hold a certain amount of regret. He opens the door and walks out the room, though it's obvious there's a great deal of hesitation in his steps.

Although I know we're going to have to talk about my past, and Emily, I'm not ready to open up to him about that.

Not yet.

Chapter Eleven

Reece

I hear the front door unlock, and I jump to my feet so I can see my baby girl. "We're home," Tash calls from the front.

Emily's footsteps soon follow. "Mom!"

"I'm here."

"Tash said you're not feeling...whoa, what happened to your face?" Emily's eyes water as she steps backward when she sees me. "Are you okay? What happened? Does it hurt?"

"I was in a little accident."

"A car accident?" She looks toward the garage, then back to me.

"I was in a cab, and it was involved in an accident. My face suffered the most, but I'm okay."

Emily steps forward and lifts her arms to embrace me. "Can I hug you? Are you hurt anywhere else?"

"Of course, you can hug me." I pull her in and wrap her in my arms.

"Was anyone hurt badly? Other than your face."

"Everyone is fine, sweetheart." She tightens her arms around me and snuggles into my chest. "Tell me about school." I lead her over to the sofa, where Tash, Emily and I all sit together. "Anything interesting happen this week?"

"One girl punched another girl."

"What? Who? Why?" Tash sits forward, intently listening to Emily.

Emily flicks her hand at Tash. "No one really interesting. Besides, I didn't want to get involved."

"Don't tell me, you buried your nose in your Harry Potter book?" Tash asks.

"I did," Emily confirms proudly. "They're two older girls from higher grades, and something happened between them. I don't really know, but everyone was talking about how one punched the other. Apparently, someone recorded it on their phone, and uploaded to social media." Emily shrugs. "I don't know. I don't care, either."

"Are you kidding me?" My posture slightly slumps as I look to Tash, then Emily, then back to Tash. "Someone actually filmed it and uploaded it?" Emily nods and reaches for her book, clearly unaffected. Tash and I are both equally surprised. "Emily." She looks over to me. "If anyone sends you that video, I don't want you to open it."

"Why?" she asks so innocently.

"Because if you watch it, you're giving power to the bully and I don't think you want to do that," I reply.

"Especially considering you have no idea why they even fought to begin with," Tash adds, backing me up.

"Okay." Emily shrugs indifferently. "What's for dinner tonight?"

Young minds are so easy to mold and influence. "What do you want?"

"Pizza." Emily smiles.

"Basically, your favorite," Tash teases.

Emily smiles widely. "Yep."

"I'll order it," I say. "Usual?"

"Yep," both Emily and Tash chirp in unison.

I stand and walk into the kitchen to get the phone number of the pizza place we like. I dial and place our order. "Okay, pizza will be here in about an hour."

Emily dramatically rubs at her stomach. "This needs food before it gets angry and starts screaming at everyone."

Tash and I both chuckle. "Well, you have to wait for about an hour. Wanna play a board game?"

"Monopoly!" Emily's eyes sparkle as she jumps to her feet and runs toward the hallway closet to get the game.

"Now we're in for it," Tash grumbles as she sinks to her knees and clears the coffee table in the family room. "She's going to want to play it for hours."

"I'm the car!" Emily announces as she walks in holding the game.

We set up the board while Emily happily chats about her classes and what she's been doing at school. The game starts, and I'm distracted by the course of the last few days. Thankfully, Tash notices my distraction and easily falls into conversation with Emily, taking the pressure off of me.

I sneak a look over at my phone and feel kind of down that Bennett hasn't called or texted. I know he doesn't have time to sit around and talk to me, but a quick message would give me some hope in us. I chuckle to myself and shake my head. Who am I kidding? If we haven't been able to finish a meal together, when is he going to have time to message me?

"Pizza!" Emily cries as the doorbell rings. She leaps to her feet, swipes my purse, and runs to the front door.

"Emily!" I call as I head out after her. Grayson stands at the door, holding the pizzas I ordered.

"Who are you?" Emily asks as she gives me my purse. "Wait, you're the same guy from last time, right?"

"Yeah, I am." Grayson makes quick eye contact with me as he hands her the pizzas.

"Thanks." Emily takes the pizzas and hurriedly makes her way into the family room.

"Here." I pull out money, but Grayson shakes his head, lifts his hand and steps backward. "Do you want to come in for pizza?"

"No, ma'am. I'm nearly finished with my shift for today, and my replacement will be here soon."

"What's it like?" I ask, genuinely curious. Grayson rubs his hand over his chin with confusion. "Being a Secret Service agent?"

"It's Secret Service *special* agent, ma'am."

"What's the difference?"

"About five years of civil duty before being able to apply for the PPD."

"PPD?"

"Presidential Protection Duty."

I nod my head in understanding. "Is it exciting work?"

Grayson chuckles. "Jonathan Wackrow said, *'It is prolonged periods of boredom only broken up by moments of sheer terror.'* That's the best way to describe it."

"Who's this Jonathan guy?"

"He spent fourteen years in the Secret Service, four of which he was on PPD with President Obama."

Those words resonate with me. "You're not paid to protect me, Grayson. You're trained to protect the president and his family."

"Mrs. Adams passed away, ma'am," he says with indifferent coldness. "My team go where they tell me." He stands rigid with his shoulders back as he speaks with me. "Is that all, ma'am?" His team? Wait, there's more of them?

I take in a long breath. "Yeah. Thank you." Grayson nods curtly and walks back to his car.

I half-heartedly toss my purse on the kitchen counter before heading back to the family room, where Tash and Emily have already started in on the pizzas. "Hurry up, Mom." Emily waves me over as she bounces up and down while devouring a slice of pie. "It's your turn." She swipes up the dice and holds them out to me.

I quickly scan the board to see where Tash's and Emily's pieces are. "Thank you." I take the dice and throw them on the board. "Double four." I move my piece and look at what I've landed on. "Yep, I'm buying it."

"Here we go, Emily." Tash lightly smacks Emily's arm. "You know what she's going to do, don't you?"

"Yeah, she's going to buy everything she lands on."

"You and I need to team up to beat her."

"Hey!" I protest. "I'm sitting right here." I look at the pizza boxes. "Pass me a slice of cheese." Suddenly, I hear my garage door opening. I turn to Tash, who's staring at me with the same perplexed, confused, terrified look on her face that I'm wearing. I gesture for her to keep an eye on Emily, who appears oblivious to what's going on. I lay my pizza down and stand to go and see why my garage door is opening.

The door between my kitchen and the mudroom off the garage opens. I look around in panic, searching for the closest thing to use as a weapon. If I yell, Grayson will hear me and come running. I'm just about to scream when Mark enters, followed by Bennett. "What the hell?"

Bennett smiles as he approaches me and wraps his arms around me. "I missed you."

"What are you doing here, and how did you get in my garage?"

He carefully kisses my mouth, being cautious of my swollen lower lip. "I told you. I missed you," he says as he pulls back to stare and gently rub his thumb over my bruised cheek. "A lot."

"You have to leave."

"Why?"

"Do you not listen? Emily is home, and we're eating pizza and playing Monopoly, so..." I step backward and flick my hand at him. "Shoo!"

"Are you embarrassed by me?"

"No, but I have no intention of answering her million questions about us." I gesture between us.

"Mom!" Emily calls from the family room. "It's your turn. What are you doing?"

I look toward the family room, then back at Bennett. "You have to go."

He smiles cheekily. "No, I really don't. My Friday night schedule is completely clear." I place my hand on his torso and try to push him back. But he's built like a tank and won't budge. "I like pizza and Monopoly," he says.

"Mom!"

My jaw jumps as I shake my head. "You did this on purpose."

"Absolutely," Bennett admits. "Because I knew if I didn't do this, then I'd never meet Emily."

"You're an ass." Mark smirks as he tries his best to look around, being all protective and shit. "I don't want Emily feeling intimidated. Can Mark stay out here?"

Bennett takes in a sharp breath before slowly nodding. "Sir," Mark objects.

"Stay in the hallway, I don't want the girl to see you."

"Yes, sir." Mark walks ahead of us and positions himself in the hallway so Emily can't see him. But I know, at some point, Emily's going to want to go to the bathroom or her room, and she's going to freak out when she sees him.

"Hey, Emily," I call as Bennett and I walk into the family room.

Tash's eyes widen, and she scrambles to stand, but Bennett discreetly shakes his head. "Yeah, Mom?" Emily turns and notices Bennett. "Who are you?"

"This is a friend of mine. His name is Bennett."

Emily chews on her pizza while staring at Bennett. "You look familiar."

"Do I?" He walks over and looks at the spare place beside her. "May I?" Emily shrugs. "Are you playing Monopoly?"

"Yeah." She's still staring at him. "Who are you? And where do I know you from? Are you an actor?"

I snort with laughter causing both Bennett and Tash to look at me. "No, I'm not an actor. Do you know who the president of the United States is?"

"Yeah, some guy named Bennett Adams." Emily shoves more pizza in her mouth, but she chews it slower, like she's thinking. "What did you say your name is again?"

"Bennett," he replies.

"Oh. Like the president."

"Emily," I say, not believing the words that are about to come out of my mouth. "This *is* the president..." I pause waiting for it to sink in. "Bennett Adams."

Emily squints and stares at Bennett. "Are you sure?"

It's Tash's turn to laugh out loud. "Yeah, it's him."

Emily appears as confused as a ten-year-old girl can be. "How do you know one another?"

Yeah, I should've prepared for that question, but I had no idea this was going to happen. "I met him at the restaurant where I work," I say the first thing that comes to mind.

"Yes, your mom was the server on duty, and she serviced me."

Dirty bastard. I narrow my eyes at Bennett. Tash is holding in the smirk. They're both dirty bastards. "And we've been friends ever since."

Emily nods slowly, then turns to Bennett. "Should I be calling you Mr. President?"

"I prefer you call me Bennett."

"Huh." She takes another bite and nods. "Okay." Emily is unfazed by him, and I like that about her. "Want pizza?"

"What toppings did you get?"

"Mom likes cheese, so there's a cheese one, and a pepperoni and mushroom pizza."

"Can I have a piece of cheese please?"

"Sure." Emily takes the box and opens the lid offering it to Bennett. "Want to play?" She looks at the game we've already started. "You'll be behind, but it doesn't matter because Mom will beat us all by the end of it anyway."

"I don't always win," I say as I sink to the floor to sit in front of the game board.

"Oh no." Emily shakes her head. "We're in for it now. When Mom does that." She points to me sitting on the floor. "It means she's out for blood."

"Is that right?" Bennett asks. "Well, I've been known to win at Monopoly. Why don't we make this more interesting?"

"What have you got in mind?" I ask. My competitive diva is poking her head out, ready to take on any bet he wants.

"Emily, want to be on my team?" he asks arrogantly.

"Are you good with money?" Emily asks innocently.

Tash and I both lose it, laughing hard. Bennett silences me with a glare, but I can't help but snicker. "The GDP forecast looks to be up by four percent by year's end, and unemployment is shrinking to a modest two-point-five percent."

"What?" Emily questions. "None of that makes sense to me. Are you good with money, or not?"

"I think I'm doing okay."

Emily looks to me and shakes her head. "Can I be your partner, Mom, I don't know what he's talking about."

"Most of us don't," Tash says.

"Okay, you can be my partner, but please don't use words I don't understand. But I have a question for you."

"What is it?"

"Do you believe you're a good president?" Wow, what a hairy question to be asked by a ten-year-old.

"I try my hardest to do right by everyone, and to be the best president I can be."

"Huh." She picks up the remaining starting pieces and holds her hand out to him. "Which one do you want to be?"

Bennett picks the top hat, and Emily puts his piece on the starting square. "What about homeless people?" she casually asks Bennett. "Why do we have so many homeless people in America?"

Bennett pulls his shoulders back and quickly switches into politician mode. I swear, if he tries to school Emily, I'm throwing him out of my house and never seeing him again. "We have a big problem with people who are homeless," he finally responds.

"Maybe you should fix it," Emily says. "You said you're trying your hardest to do right by everyone, so...do right." I'm so proud of my little girl. She has no idea how impactful her words are, because to her it's simply a conversation, but to us as adults, she's going for the jugular without even realizing. "Don't you like the pizza?" she asks with innocence.

"Yeah, I love it." Bennett shoves the remainder of his piece in his mouth and chews.

"I didn't think you'd be allowed to eat pizza," Tash says. Both Bennett and I look over to her. "Don't you have to have your own chef to cook for you, just to make sure your food isn't poisoned?"

"Do you?" Emily asks.

"I'm invested in this now, I need to know more," I say.

"Actually, it's a team of chefs, and they're always being watched to make sure nothing happens with my food. But considering no one even knows I'm here, and you've all eaten from the pizza, the chances of me being poisoned is nonexistent." Bennett reaches for another slice, hesitates and pulls his hand back. "Unless that's just what you want me to believe." He casts a wary eye over us and stops at Emily. "Are you trying to poison me, Emily?"

She shrugs and shakes her head. "I didn't even know who you were until Mom and Tash told me."

Bennett throws his head back as he brings his hand to his stomach. Booming laughter vibrates through him. "This is true, Emily. So, I don't think you'd poison me."

Emily's brows squish together. "I mean…" She looks to me and lifts her shoulders.

"Mr. President," Mark announces as he enters the family room.

Bennett stands and huddles away from us, whispering with Mark. He runs his hands through his hair and nods. I watch as they discuss whatever it is they're talking about. He steps back and walks over to us. The look in his eyes and gloomy heaviness of his tense shoulders screams volumes. "I have to go."

I stand and walk over to him. "I understand. Everything okay?" His jaw tightens making his neck tense.

"Walk with me." He motions with a flick of his head. "Goodbye, Miss Emily. It was a pleasure meeting you." Bennett holds his hand out for her to shake.

"Nice meeting you too." She shakes his hand.

"Bye, Tash."

"See ya." She lifts her hand and casually waves to him.

Bennett wraps his arm around my waist as we walk toward my garage. "Dinner, tomorrow night," he says.

"No." I shake my head.

"What?"

"No. Emily is home tomorrow, and I'm spending time with her."

We stop walking when we get to the door leading between the kitchen and the mudroom-slash-garage. Bennett tightens his arms around me and softly kisses my forehead. "Sunday night, I'm not taking no for answer."

"Well, you're going to have to."

He lifts his hand and gently tips my head back. "I'm not taking no for an answer, Miss Maxwell," he repeats.

"I heard you the first time, and my answer is still no. I'm spending Sunday with myself after I take Emily back to school. So, you're going to have to accept what I say, which is…no."

He runs his tongue over his teeth, before clicking it to the roof of his mouth. "Monday night. No negotiation."

A small smile pulls at my lips. "Monday night." Mark stands imposingly by the garage door. Although his back is turned to us, he can hear everything we're talking about. "Unless something happens."

"Monday night." He kisses me one final time before taking a breath and heading out to the garage.

"Hey." He stops and turns. "We need to talk about this." I point to the garage.

A giant beaming smile graces his handsome face. "Monday night."

I roll my eyes and shake my head. "Good night, *Mr. President*," I say in a husky voice. He stops walking and shakes his head. Yeah, good. I like knowing how much I affect him. I head back to the family room and sit on the sofa. "Emily?"

"Yeah, Mom." Emily sneaks Bennett's money into her pile as she packs his piece away.

"You can't tell anyone Bennett was here."

"Okay. Why?"

"Because a lot of bad things will happen if anyone finds out."

"Like what?"

"Stuff at school, stuff with me, stuff with him, maybe even stuff with Tash."

"Me?" Tash asks as she places her hand to her chest. "Like what?" She nibbles on her lower lip.

"I'm just saying, this stays here, with us. Okay?" I specifically look to Emily. "No one can know."

"I won't say anything." She crosses her heart. "I swear."

"Okay, well, let's get on with the game. I'm poor and need money. But I'm coming after you." I point to Emily.

"Me? Why me?"

"Because you boosted Bennett's money, and kept it for yourself."

"What?" she shrieks with a wide smile. Picking up the dice, she rolls them, and the night continues.

It's definitely not the way I thought tonight was going to go.

Chapter Twelve

Bennett

"I need your signatures on these please, Mr. President," Jamie says as he opens the files for the documents I'm to sign.

I catch Liam walking in from the other entrance. "Where are my glasses?" I search my desk, trying to find where I placed them.

Jamie shuffles some papers and finds them buried. "Here, Mr. President." He holds them out to me.

"What have we got tomorrow morning?"

"Nothing until seven-thirty," Jamie responds.

"Excellent." I sign the documents and hand them to Jamie. "I'm leaving for the day."

Jamie smiles as he packs my desk. "This must be some kind of record for you, sir."

"Why's that?" I ask.

"You're actually leaving before eight." He packs everything into my briefcase and hands it to me. "Have a good night."

"You too." Jamie leaves my office, and I turn to Liam. "What is it?"

"I was going to see if my friend Bennett wanted to grab a couple of drinks."

"Not tonight. Rain check." Liam's features tighten, but he nods and starts walking away. "Liam?"

"Yes, sir?" He pivots and stops just inside the Oval Office.

"What is it?" I know something is bothering him. "Everything okay?"

Liam shoves his hands in his pockets and nods. "Yeah," he says casually.

I stare at him for a moment. "Have a good night," I offer. "And, Liam, unless we go to DEFCON 3, I don't want to be disturbed tonight."

He nods in understanding before adding, "Enjoy your evening, sir." Liam vacates my office, and I grab my briefcase to head up to the residence.

"Miss Maxwell is on her way, sir," Mark informs me.

"Thank you." This gives me enough time to grab a quick shower before dinner.

The door opens, and Reece walks into my bedroom. "Do I see you in something other than a suit?" she asks, noticing my jeans and sweater.

I walk over to her and bring her into my arms. "Aren't you a sight for sore eyes."

"Yes, my bruises could make any man envious," she nervously chuckles. I don't laugh, because I don't find what happened to her amusing. "Oh, come on. That was a little funny."

"Not in the slightest." I lean down and seal my mouth over hers, shutting her up with a kiss. Reece's arms tighten around my waist as she relaxes into my body. "I want nothing more than to stay here and kiss you, but I'm making us dinner."

"What?" Her eyes widen in surprise. "You can cook?"

"Why are you so stunned?" I link our hands together and lead her across the hall to the residence kitchen.

"I had no idea you could cook. Where did you learn?"

"Are you impressed?"

"Not yet. You might give me food that tastes like crap."

"You'll have to smile and bear it," I say.

"Hmmm." We enter the kitchen, and she stares at all the equipment. "Thing is, if it tastes like crap, I'm so going to let you know."

I chuckle as I open the fridge and start moving the ingredients to the counter. "I'm making a real carbonara."

"Real? As opposed to a fake carbonara?" Reece asks as she props herself up on one of the stools and watches me. "What's that?" She points to the meat.

"Guanciale."

"Of course, it is." She furrows her brows. "Which is what exactly?"

"It's the pig jowl. This is the recipe I was taught by an Italian chef."

"An Italian chef? Wow, look at you go. When were you taught to make this?"

"This is something I learned when I was about twenty. The way I was taught is to cut this in chunks. But first, I need to put the water on to boil." I look around and scratch my chin trying to recall where the pots are. "Aha, over here." I open one of the doors and I'm rewarded with what I'm looking for.

"Is it fresh pasta?"

"What?" I look up from the sink where I'm adding water to the pot.

"Is it fresh pasta?" she repeats.

"What do you take me for, a heathen? Of course, it's fresh."

"Oh, because the dried packaged stuff isn't good enough for you. You're a food snob now, are you?" she teases as she watches me turn the gas on and place the pot on it. "Millions of people eat dried pasta, and there's nothing wrong with them."

I swing around and lift my hand, pointing at her. "You're putting words into my mouth."

"You could have your mouth full with something else, if you want." She is not backward about being forward.

I shake my head as I throw a good pinch of salt into the tepid water. "You're in a world of trouble tonight, Miss Maxwell."

"Unless there's another interruption. Which I'm getting used to."

"Nope, no interruptions tonight. I've given clear instructions that unless we're under attack, I'm not to be disturbed."

"That's a welcome change. Though, like I said, it's understandable if you're called away." Reece places her elbow on the island counter and rests her head on her fist, watching me.

"You're watching me," I say, trying to swing the conversation from me always abruptly leaving.

"You're kinda sexy to watch." I smirk at her words as I prepare the space for what I need. I take out a chopping board and place the chunk of guanciale on it. "The chef who taught me this recipe told me that in the Roman times, they'd cut the meat into big chunks."

"Aha." Reece stands and eagerly watches as I slowly chop the meat. She kneels on the stool and wiggles her ass in the air attempting to distract me. "Are you trying really hard not to get *hard* right now?" She waggles her butt again.

I blink several times but hold it together. "I'm not getting hard," I lie through my teeth. Just having her in the room with me makes my cock stir.

"That's a good thing." Reece leans forward making her top gape so I can see she's not wearing a bra. Her nipples are pert and erect, and perfectly ready for my mouth and tongue to lave them with attention.

I clear my throat and look at the chunk of guanciale. "Um...what was I doing?" Jesus, she's so distracting. I take a few seconds to center myself before I pick the sharp knife up and cut the guanciale into smaller chunks. "So, the secret to a good carbonara, is it starts here." I point to the pieces I'm cutting. "Grab a frypan."

"Oh, you brought me here so I can cook for you?"

Reece hops down and heads around the island counter to search for a frypan. She leans over, gifting me with a perfect view of the jeans hugging her taut ass. I stop chopping so I can stare at it and my cock responds by getting harder. I drop the knife and grab her hips, thrusting up into her through our clothes. "The things I want to do to you."

Reece straightens and turns in my arms. "Hey, you said you're going to cook." She glances at the meat, then back to me. "So, cook." She steps back and looks around my kitchen. "Frypan?"

I return my attention to the meat. "Over there somewhere, I think." I flick my head toward the cupboards near the range.

"Found it. Now what do you want me to do with it? If you say something freaky, I'm leaving."

"Freaky?"

"Yeah, freaky. Like have sex with the handle."

"No! What? No." I shake my head. "I'd rather watch you get yourself off with a sex toy, than the handle of a frypan. Hmmm, speaking of which..."

"Who says I don't have a toy in right now?"

I tighten my grip on the handle of the knife and stop cutting the meat up. Good Lord, she's going to be the death of me. I clear my throat again and motion toward the range. "Put it on a high heat." *Get it together, Bennett.*

I hear the burner tick on. "Now what?"

"Nothing, you can go sit down before you cause me to spontaneously combust."

"What? I haven't done anything," Reece says with fluttering eyelashes, all false innocence.

"You're evil."

She walks away and I swat her ass forcing her to hop forward. "Oh, Mr. President, but I do believe you're trying to turn me on."

"You like being spanked?"

Reece arches a brow and seductively runs her tongue over her lower lip. She makes me crazy. "Maybe you'll get to find out." She looks at her nails and lifts her shoulders. "Or maybe you won't."

"I should take you over my knee."

She flicks her hand at me. "Promises, promises."

My cock is straining, and I'm desperate to be buried deep inside her. "Um." I shake my head, struggling to concentrate on the job at hand. "Stop distracting me," I warn. "Now, the meat goes into the frypan with a tad of olive oil." I drizzle the olive oil over the now-hot frypan and throw the meat in. The water has come up to a boil, and I find the fresh pasta the chef has already prepared. I throw it in the rapidly boiling water. "Next step to a good carbonara is two whole eggs, and an extra egg yolk." I crack two eggs into a bowl, and separate the third egg tossing out the part I haven't used. I go to the fridge and find the already shredded fresh parmesan cheese. "Now, usually I'd say we have to salt the eggs, but the guanciale is a cured and incredibly salty cut, so we don't need additional salt."

"You're like an infomercial." Reece laughs. "Or a contestant on a cooking show where they all compete for a grand prize."

"Enough from you over there." I beat the eggs together. "Season with a generous amount of black pepper." I grind some pepper into the eggs. "Now, the tricky part."

"Tricky?" She raises a brow as she stares.

"Yes, Miss Smart-ass, tricky."

Reece snorts with laughter. "You're so bossy."

"Now comes the tricky part," I repeat. "We have to beat the eggs and the cheese together."

"I must admit," Reece starts. "Watching you cook is a turn-on. I could get used to this."

"A turn-on?" My hand stills as I mix the parmesan and eggs. Now that I know, I'll be sure to cook for her more often. I click my tongue and clear my throat, slightly distracted by her statement. "The cooking meat has released quite a lot of its own fat. So, now we need to turn it off."

"You're sexy as fuck."

She's sending me crazy with her silky voice. "Let me check the pasta." Using the tongs, I take a piece out and chew on it. "Yep, it's ready. Perfect actually. Now, we drain the pasta, and throw it straight into the guanciale."

Reece walks around and leans against the kitchen counter, watching me. "Why did you turn the guanciale off?" She crosses her arms in front of her chest, causing her breasts to perk up. I can't tear my eyes off of her. "Bennett?"

"Um." I shake my head trying to dislodge every filthy thought I have of her. "Because we're going to mix in the egg and cheese and we don't want to scramble the eggs." She arches a brow and continues to watch. I catch my breath, refusing to look at her. Otherwise, I'm going to forgo cooking to bend her over the counter and take her hard from behind. "I drain the pasta, and throw it straight into the pan with the cooling guanciale, making sure to coat all the strands of pasta with the fat from the pork." Out of my peripheral vision, I see Reece push off from the counter and walk behind me. Her body presses into mine as hands drag up my thighs to my hips. "We then add the egg and cheese." I tip that into the pasta and quickly mix it around. Reece's hands slide under my t-shirt, and she pushes her fingers into the top of my jeans. "I um…"

"You what?" she whispers before taking the lobe of my ear into her mouth. My hands still and my eyes close as I roll my head to the side. She peppers kisses down the column of my throat. I drop my hands from the pan, and she darts under my arm and pushes me backward as her mouth finds mine.

I grab her hips, digging my fingers into her. "Do you have any idea how crazy you make me?" I murmur against her lips.

"Do you have any idea how much I like watching you cook for me?" She wraps her arms around my neck, kissing me with passion.

It takes every ounce of strength to push Reece off of me. "Then let me feed you."

Reece looks over her shoulder at the nearly finished pasta, releases her arms from my neck and steps back. "Yes, sir. Feed me."

I hate that I had to let her go, because Reece feels right in my arms. "You're a tease," I say.

"I'm not the one teasing you!"

"Come here." I reach for her, but she hops backward.

"Nope, feed me, and then maybe I'll let you kiss me."

"I could make you," I warn as I point at her.

"Feed me," she counters as she smirks with a cheeky leer.

I shake my head as I reach for two big bowls, separating the pasta into two equal parts. "Follow me," I instruct as I walk into the adjacent dining room.

"How do you do it?" Reece enters the room, slowing only to take in her surroundings. "This dining room is bigger than most people's bedrooms. You have so much space."

There's a niggling feeling of regret churning through me. "Honestly, the residence is designed for a family," I say as I place the two bowls on the table next to each other.

Reece draws her lower lip into her mouth and nods. She walks over and sits in the chair I've pulled out for her. "What happened with your wife?" There's a part of me that doesn't want to talk about Kathryn. My hesitation must be concerning to her. "It's none of my business, I shouldn't have asked." Reece picks her fork up and pushes her food around. "I'm sorry."

"No, don't be." I have to talk about it, it's only fair Reece be made aware of what isn't public knowledge. "Um, Kathryn…" I suck in a deep breath, trying to figure out where to start. "I guess, she was the love of my life." I look at Reece, her smile is broad and genuine. "We met when we were in high school, and she was one of two people who wasn't afraid to be herself around me." I twirl a small amount of pasta on my fork and bring it to my mouth. When I finish chewing, I continue. "We got married young, and she wanted to wait for us to have kids because she really wanted to push for me to become president."

"Isn't it more favorable to have a president with a family than not?" Reece asks a poignant question.

"Basically, yes. But she wanted us in the White House."

"You didn't want it?"

"Oh, I did. I mean, I do, absolutely," I pause for a few seconds. "So, we waited to start a family. We decided we'd start trying about midterm, but..." I shake my head. "It was exactly eight days after inauguration when Kathryn woke and said she wasn't feeling well. She was a bit pale and tired, but our life had been so hectic that neither of us really thought much about it. I told her to see the doctor, she said she was exhausted and just needed to sleep."

Reece reaches out and places her hand over mine, gently and reassuringly squeezing. "I honestly shouldn't have asked, I'm sorry," she tries offering another apology.

"She went to sleep and said she didn't want to be disturbed. I had the day from hell, so time just slipped away from me. Before I knew it, I had Esther telling me it was nearly four in the afternoon, I hadn't eaten and I was irritated. I made a mental note to call up to the residence to see how Kathryn was feeling, but again, business interfered, preventing me from calling her." My chest constricts as I'm talking about that horrible day. "It was at four-thirty-two that Esther burst into the office and demanded I go to the residence." I shake my head as my throat closes. "I've never moved so fast in my life. The doctor was there working on Kathryn, but I knew when I saw the gray tinge of her skin, she was gone."

"Bennett." Reece stands, pushes her way in front of me, and straddles my lap. "I'm so sorry."

"Thirty-three and she died from a heart attack. She had a congenital heart condition that none of us knew about. She didn't even know about it." Reece tightens her arms around me, and I close my eyes as I snuggle into her. "The coroner said she died in her sleep."

"She was only thirty-three." Reece gently places her hands on either side of my face and gives me a sweet kiss. "It wasn't your fault, Bennett."

"Of course, it was. If I wasn't distracted, I would've called up here. I would've had time to come and see her. But I put my job before Kathryn."

"It wasn't your fault, Bennett," she repeats slower. "She had a heart condition. This could've happened to anyone."

"I'm the most powerful man in the world, and I was completely helpless to bring her back."

"You're not God," Reece whispers. "You're an intelligent man, and you know you couldn't have done anything." Reece leans her forehead on mine as she wraps her arms around my neck. I'm tightly holding on to all my emotions, refusing to allow them to penetrate through my armor. "You don't always have to be so strong," Reece whispers as if she's sensing my worries.

"Of course, I do. I'm the damn president of the United States."

"You're also a man," she quips without missing a beat. "You can let go, Bennett."

I pull back and gaze into her eyes. Slowly my focus follows the lines of her face and settles on her clavicles. "Is it wrong that you're here?" I whisper as I try to wrestle with the guilt coursing through me.

"Does it feel wrong?"

"No." I shake my head as I lift my chin to meet her beautiful, soulful brown eyes. "I want you here."

"Then it's not wrong." Reece moves her ass closer, nearly sitting on my cock, concealed by my jeans. I can't get close enough to her.

"Do something for me." I kiss her nose, then peck her lips.

"What?"

"Stay the night with me." There's a brief moment of tension crackling between us, a feeling that this is right. *We're* right.

Reece is quiet for a moment as she stares into my eyes. "I'll stay," she says.

A sense of relief falls over me. I don't ever want to let her go.

Fuck, what's happening to me?

Chapter Thirteen

Reece

Opening my eyes, I'm rewarded with a perfect view of Bennett. He's lying on his side, with one arm tucked under his head, facing me. I watch as he sleeps heavily, snoring and mumbling at the same time. Bennett moves his right arm and absentmindedly reaches out for me. He lays his hand on my hip, but that only lasts a few seconds before he rests it on the top of my ass and pulls me closer to him. Funny thing is, he's totally out of it.

I can't help myself. Reaching out I gently trail my fingertips down his nose, around his lips and across to his strong jawline. "If you keep doing that, I might never let you go," his voice is gravelly and thick with sleep.

"I didn't want to wake you." I move my hand away to let him sleep. "I shouldn't have woken you. I doubt you get a lot of sleep."

He opens his eyes and blinks several times. Bennett lifts his head and looks over my shoulder at the digital clock on the bedside table. "Ugh. It's just after three." A guttural sound escapes from his throat. "Why are you even awake?" He kisses my forehead before turning to lie on his back. I can't help but notice the tent under the covers. I swing my leg over his thighs, and Bennett's hand soothingly rests on my leg. I slide over and sit on his thighs. "I could get used to this, Reece."

Reaching across his taut body, I grab a condom from the other bedside table. I tear the packet open and carefully roll the condom on his hard cock.

Sinking down on him, I roll my hips. I close my eyes, arch my back and extend my neck. "Mmmm."

Bennett's strong fingers grip the curve of my ass as I slowly swivel my hips trying to find the right spot to trigger my own release. "What are you doing, Reece?" Bennett whispers.

"I can stop if you want?"

"God no, don't stop." Bennett's breathing changes while his hands dance around my body, gripping, tightening, claiming. Neither of us last long. Both of us needed it more than we thought we did. I collapse on top of him as he hugs me close to his body. "I like waking up like this." Bennett draws lazy patterns on my back as I catch my breath.

This moment feels like so much more. It's as if an unspoken emotion passes between us. I lie on his chest as I watch the moments tick over, one to the next. Neither of us are talking, simply enjoying the now of this quiet time together. Of course, my head gets in the way, overthinking everything and the potential danger I've put both of us in by staying the night. If the press gets a whiff of this, his presidency is over, not to mention what Emily will go through. "I should leave before anyone sees me." I try to push off him, but he tightens his arms around me almost like a vice. "Bennett, what are you doing?"

"I want you to stay."

"This is complicated." I successfully maneuver out of his grasp and sit on the edge of the bed.

"There's nothing complicated about it."

I snort as I shake my head. "Except you're the president. And, I'm a twenty-five-year-old escort with a daughter who's ten." I turn to look at him over my shoulder. Sighing, I stand and head into the bathroom. When I return, Bennett waltzes past me and I search for my clothes that are scattered over the room.

"What are you doing?" Bennett asks as he struts back to the bed, completely naked.

"I'm going to go home."

"Nope, you're not. Come here." He crooks his finger, summoning me back to the bed.

Hesitating, I nibble on my lower lip as I consider everything. "This should end now, before something drastic happens."

"Tell me about Emily." His words throw me off; I'm not prepared for this. I shake my head as I stare at the crumpled bedding. "If we have any chance, you need to tell me about Emily."

"I can't," I say with a shaky voice.

"Why?"

"I can't be here anymore. It's too much of a risk to her...and you."

Bennett lifts his hand and tucks some of the hair falling over the side of my face to behind my ear. "I'm not letting you go, Reece. You need to talk to me, and tell me about Emily."

I stand and resume putting my clothes on. "I can't," I say as I hold onto my tears.

"Why? Will something happen to you if you tell me? I'll protect you."

I gather all my courage and look to Bennett. "We really need to talk about Grayson. He can't keep protecting me, Bennett. You need to let him do his job."

"He is. He's protecting you," Bennett counters.

"No." I lift my hand and wave it to him. "He needs to get back to being here, not sitting in a car outside my house. Bring him back here, let him do what he's trained to do." Bennett drops his gaze as he thinks about my request. "You need to be smart about this."

"About what?"

"Me. Us. Everything."

"Tell me about Emily," he pushes again.

I finish getting dressed and walk over to the opposite side of the room trying to put distance between us. Part of me doesn't want to tell him, but I also know, Bennett isn't the type of man who's going to give up without a fight. "If I tell you about her, I need you to promise me that you'll recall Grayson, and not assign another Secret Service agent to me." His hesitation tells me he's weighing up all his options. "If you can promise you'll do that, I'll tell you about Emily."

Bennett finally nods. "Okay, I'll have the Secret Service withdrawn."

I let out a long sigh and smile. "Thank you." I pick up his boxers and throw them at him. "Get dressed. You're distracting, naked like that."

Bennett stands and pulls up his boxers, then his jeans. "I need a coffee." He opens the door to his bedroom, where we're met by another Secret Service agent standing to the side. "Good morning," Bennett says as we walk out.

"Good morning, sir," the agent replies.

When we both walk across the hallway into the kitchen, the agent stands at the door with his back to us. "How do you take your coffee?" Bennett asks as he fiddles with the fancy coffee machine.

"Like, coffee," I say with a smile. Though on the inside, my stomach is twisting with anticipation of what I'm going to tell him.

"Black? Cream? Caramel? How?"

"Cream no sugar." Bennett prepares two coffees and carries them back to his room and the agent silently resumes his previous position. I close the door and turn to look at Bennett. "How do you do it?"

"Do what?"

"You get no privacy; there's always someone with you."

"I get to close my bedroom door, and switch off even if it's for an hour. It gives me a moment to unwind." He walks toward his private room where the sofa, TV and library are. "Come on." Bennett places the two mugs of coffee on the dining table and drags out a seat.

"I'll stand," I say as I grab my coffee and slowly pace back and forth. "I'm aware you're watching me."

"I am."

My stomach tenses and my heart feels like a hand is closing around it, squeezing the life out of it. "When I was twelve, my mom's then-boyfriend came into my room when he was really drunk, pulled the covers back and slid into bed with me."

"What the fuck?"

I turn to look at Bennett and shake my head. "I just need you to be quiet while I tell you what happened." He presses his lips together and nods slowly. "Nothing happened, but I was terrified. I couldn't tell Mom because she was a horrible woman who would find any reason to beat me, or humiliate me, or degrade me."

"So, you couldn't do anything?"

I shake my head. "He had pinned me under his body, and I couldn't move. When he woke in the morning, he was shocked at what he did and begged me not to say anything to my mother. Which of course, I didn't. I knew if I did, I would've been in so much trouble because she would've made it my fault. So, I said nothing."

"Okay." Bennett breathes heavily, but I notice he brings his mug up to sip on his coffee, covering the angry breaths.

"It was about a week later, he did it again. He and Mom liked to drink a lot, most times to the point of passing out."

"Do you have any siblings?" I shake my head. "Okay, go on."

"The visits to my room became more frequent, and his drinking became less while Mom's increased."

Bennett sighs and rubs his hand across his forehead. "Fuck."

"It didn't take long before he started touching me, which then escalated. I was twelve. I had no one to turn to, so feeling helplessly alone, I felt I had no choice but to let him do what he wanted." I feel sick even talking about this. "Then one morning, Mom burst into my room and found him on top of me."

"When you were twelve." His face is hard.

"Yeah, it was about a week before my thirteenth birthday."

"Tell me she called the police on his sorry ass."

I snort with a dry laugh and shake my head. "No. She grabbed me by the hair, and dragged me through the house, and tossed me out. *Naked*."

Bennett leans an elbow on the table and exhales with pity. "My God," he whispers with pain in his voice.

"The guy opened my bedroom window and threw out some clothes, and my phone and told me to wait for his call because I could go live with him." I let out a humorless chuckle. "He even winked at me." I feel like I'm going to be sick.

"I don't even know what to say or how to react to this. What happened?"

"He kept calling, but I never answered."

"Where did you go?"

"During the day I tried to stay invisible, and at night, I'd sneak back home and sleep under the house." Bennett stares at me. The pain in his eyes is too much to look at. I turn away. "Then one day, about two or three weeks later, Mom called and told me to come home because she found out he was cheating on her with someone else. And I could come home as long as I promised not to try to steal her boyfriend again."

"Steal him? He's a predator who abused you." There's a long silence between us. With shaky hands I lift my coffee mug and sip on my drink, Bennett does the same. "What happened after you returned home, Reece?"

"The next boyfriend was a mean drunk, just like Mom. Actually, he was worse. He'd fill her up on alcohol then beat the shit out of her, then he'd try to force his way into my room. But I learned from the first guy, and when I returned home, I stole a lock from the hardware store, and installed it myself."

"Good for you. That was a smart thing for you to do, Reece."

"It didn't stop the next boyfriend, it merely slowed him down," I say, bursting Bennett's bubble. "He was nasty, rough, and mean. He'd bite me so hard I'd bleed. But thankfully, I have no physical scars from him."

"How the hell did you get out of there?"

"Mom caught him and tossed me out. I had just turned fourteen when she caught him doing things to me. Of course, I was blamed, and she accused me of flirting with him, and leading him on. He didn't even have to convince her, because in her mind I was the one who was at fault to begin with."

"What happened?'

"I was out on the streets again. I was fourteen years old. I had no money. I couldn't go to school. There were no resources available to me, because where does someone that age go? I did the only thing I knew how to do."

"Which was?" his words drag as if he already knows the answer, but he needs it confirmed.

"I figured out that men like sex. So, I stole a packet of condoms, and I sold myself." Bennett closes his eyes and rubs at the center part of his forehead between his brows. "It was either that, or starve. And I chose that. I managed to be able to hire a room at a really nasty motel where I lived for a little over a year."

"How did no one ask questions? How did you do this?"

"Who's going to ask questions, Bennett? My mother? She wouldn't know me if she tripped over me. The police? They didn't even know I was homeless. I was street smart. I blended in and made sure I wasn't seen during school hours because that would've been a red flag."

"Men paid you to have sex with them at the age of fourteen?" His eyes water as he shakes his head. "I'm sorry," he says.

"Most of it was okay, but there were times I was terrified. Overall though, I got really lucky because I had somewhat decent clients. I guess as decent as they could be when they were screwing a child." I shake my head at my own words. "I'm trying to say, I could've ended up a statistic, and I'm glad I didn't. I realize now how it made them feel better that they were paying me for a service, although we both know the type of people they were."

"I'm lost for words."

"I know. This is a lot to take in. Tash knows a considerable amount of this, but not as much as I'm sharing with you."

"Thank you, for trusting me with this."

I place my mug on the table and sit opposite him. "I got a new client," I continue with how I ended up with a baby at the age of fifteen. "He gave me the creeps. He wanted me to wear diapers and crawl around the floor. He was..." I shiver with revulsion. "He was..." I don't even know what to say about him. "The third time I was with him, as he was having his way with me, his hand moved between us. I had no idea until after he climaxed, that he'd torn off the condom and came inside me."

"Shit."

"Yeah. Nine months later, Emily was born."

"What about that fucker? What happened to him?"

"I don't know. He never came back after he did what he did." I take a moment to compose myself. "I got myself tested, kept working, and then found out I was pregnant. I was terrified," I say as I choke back the tears. "How could I bring a baby into this awful world?" My eyes water, and I find myself crying.

"Sweetheart," Bennett says as he stands and moves to console me.

"Please." I wave my hand to stop him. He sits back down and takes in a sharp, long breath. "I'm not ashamed to admit that I considered having an abortion. I was tempted. I thought that I'd be selfish if I kept this baby and then I thought I'd fucking hate looking at her knowing how she was conceived. I thought of killing myself because without me this fetus growing inside me couldn't survive. I really had no one. What was I supposed to do? Here I was, fifteen, a whore, and pregnant."

"The decisions you made were forced on you, you did what you had to do to survive."

I look at him with tears clinging to my cheeks. "Obviously, I made the decision not to abort, or kill myself or put her up for adoption. But I also made the decision that I was going to give her the best life I could. As the pregnancy developed, I made friends with another woman who was a hooker named Peggy. She was a little older than me, maybe late twenties, I don't really know." I shrug as I lift my t-shirt and wipe the tears from my face and eyes. "She was kind, so kind. She pretended to be my mom when I went to the hospital, and when they asked questions, she put on a brave face and lied through her teeth for me. But once I had Emily, I basically took her and left." I smile at the remembered, though painful, memories. "She helped me with Emily. She'd look after her so I could work."

"You had a lot of pressure on you at such a young age."

I nod as I swallow back the tension stuck in my throat. "Tash knows a little of this, but not everything." I look up toward the ceiling, attempting to avoid Bennett's concerned eyes. "Peggy helped when she could, and for a little while it was working. I made sure Emily had everything she needed. She never went without. Then one day Peggy saw an ad somewhere for teenage actresses, in D.C., actually."

"I sense this isn't going to go well."

"Well, I called and a woman said they had a role for someone who was in the eighteen to twenty bracket. I lied and said I was eighteen, and she asked me for a head shot and a body one too. I was skeptical but she said she wanted a photo of me in clothes. That eased my mind and I thought, why not? If I could get some roles where I play a teenager, then what do I have to lose?" I let out a humorless chuckle. "If only it was that easy."

"What happened?"

"I packed all of my and Emily's worldly possessions into one suitcase, which I found on the side of the road. We jumped on a bus and made the eight-hour trip here."

"Okay. That's not a bad thing."

"I had about a thousand dollars to my name, a baby who was under a year old, and I hedged all my bets on becoming an actress." The lump of shame grows in the pit of my stomach. "The actress job ended up being porn. The woman took one look at me, saw I had an infant in my arms and said, '*You'll be perfect because you look like a girl who likes to party. Do you do threesomes and anal?*'"

Bennett runs his hand through his hair. "I don't even know what to say at this stage."

"It was at that moment that I made a decision. Did I really want Emily growing up knowing what I do?" I shake my head. "I decided I was going to protect her from my life."

"Which is why she thinks you work at a high-class restaurant."

"Yep," I say.

"I have to admit, your story makes me feel sick to the core," Bennett admits.

"That's not the end of it."

He pinches the bridge of his nose. "Of course, it's not." Bennett lifts his chin to look at me. "Please, continue."

"Like I said, I had about a thousand dollars to my name. I didn't know anyone here, and I had nowhere to go. Do I return to the hellhole I came from, or do I make a fresh start here? I knew that a thousand dollars would buy me a month, two at most, in a cheap motel somewhere, or I could buy a car and use it to live in. Which is what I did. I found a car for four hundred dollars, and I bought it. I was lucky because I bought it from a mechanic, and I think he felt sorry for me so he even knocked twenty dollars off the price so I could buy gas. He said he did that for all his customers." I chuckle at the thought. "Clearly, I know better. Anyway, I was driving down one of the streets and my eye caught on a help wanted sign in a window of a coffee shop. It was either that or go back to soliciting. Luckily, Emily was asleep, so I parked the car outside the coffee shop, and went in to ask for a job. They asked me how old I was, and I told them seventeen and I didn't go to school anymore so I could work as much as they wanted me to. I'm so grateful to them, because they gave me a job."

"What did you do with Emily while you were working?"

"She'd stay in the car that I parked outside the shop so I could keep an eye on her."

Bennett tenses, his jaw making the veins strain in the side of his neck. "You left her in a car?"

"I had no choice, Bennett. None. I knew no one, I had nothing. What was I supposed to do? Do you have any idea the lack of services and resources for girls like me?" I feel myself firing up as I defend my actions.

"I'm truly sorry, Reece. I'm overwhelmed and frustrated because all of this could've been avoided if you were able to turn to someone for help." A slow, strained smile stretches my lips. "Please, continue."

"I was working for about a week or so, and I had met a few regulars, one of whom was Tash. She was the nicest customer, always so polite and always tipped me. Her coffee was three dollars, and she'd leave me a five-dollar bill. And the worst thing was I really had no idea how to make a coffee because I was still learning everything. Anyway, they had asked me to work until closing, and I could see Emily was going stir-crazy in the car, but I had no options to do anything about it. I needed the money to be able to rent a room for us. Oh man." I clutch at my chest. "That one night, Tash returned. Thing is, just before Tash walked in, I was outside checking on Emily to make sure she was okay."

"Did Tash see this?"

I nod as I click my tongue. "She did, but I didn't know that until later. She came in and ordered her coffee, then we got to talking, and she said she was new in town and didn't have any friends and asked if I wanted to come to her apartment for dinner."

"That was sweet of her."

"Yeah, it is. I knew in my gut she was a good person, but I dreaded telling her I also had a child so I wouldn't be able to. Funny though, when I told Tash, she just shrugged, nodded, and asked me what my child's name was. She wrote down her address on a napkin and told me to come after work."

"I take it you went to her apartment."

"Yep. Emily and I both went. It was a tiny, one-bedroom apartment with one bathroom. She made a home-cooked meal. I'll tell you what, I had never eaten so much in my life. Emily inhaled the pumpkin and potatoes like no one's business. Then, when we were about to leave, Tash asked me why I was checking on Emily outside work."

"What did you tell her?"

"She caught me out on the spot, and I said because we're homeless and living in my car. Tash shook her head and said we were no longer homeless, because Emily's and my new address was her apartment."

"The three of you lived together."

"Yes, we did. For a long while. Tash worked from home doing accounting and bookkeeping, so she'd watch Emily for me so I could work. Tash has always been a gift from the universe." I smile with warmth.

"How did you go from working at a coffee shop, to being an escort?" Bennett asks, still quite vested in my story.

"There was a woman who came in on certain days. Monday through Thursday, and she had to be one of the most beautiful women I'd ever laid eyes on. I noticed the way she'd talk, how she did her makeup and hair. She was out-of-this-world classy and elegant."

Bennett scrunches his forehead trying to see the connection with my description of her and where I ended up. "I'm following," he says slowly as if he's missed the link.

"She was a regular, but quite reserved. I mean, she always spoke eloquently but she never made small talk or anything like that."

"Okay." Bennett lowers his eyes and looks at the mug.

"I began to emulate her. I'd study her walk and the way she carried herself. I looked at her makeup without looking like some kind of freaky crazy stalker person, and tried to replicate it. I even paid attention to the way she styled her hair, and the next day I'd try that style." Bennett lifts his coffee mug and notices it's now empty, so he places it on the table again. "She'd walk in with her shoulders pulled back like she was the most important person in the room, and she'd often get stares because of her magnetic presence. And I wanted that. Not for the attention, but because she honestly appeared to have her entire life together. She was confident without being cocky. She was sensual without being gaudy. She simply was breathtaking in every sense of the word."

"You paint a perfect portrait."

"One day, I think she noticed. And she asked me if I was copying her. I was mortified because here I was, seventeen at this stage, trying to be this woman whom I only knew by her order, which was always the same. I remember being so embarrassed and I apologized and promised I'd never do that again. She asked me why I was trying to copy her, and I told her because it made me feel powerful and beautiful."

"Did it make you feel powerful and beautiful?"

"Absolutely. I felt in control and like I was untouchable."

"How did she respond?" Bennett leans back against the chair and lifts his arm to lean on the back part.

"She asked me how old I was, and that was the first time I actually told the truth. But, that was it. She didn't say much more. She continued coming in, and she started giving me tips. She'd say things like, 'When you're speaking to a person lift your chin and look them in the eye.'"

"Why?"

I snicker. "I'll get to that part. This went on for a few months, then she asked me to have coffee with her one day. I said yes. She told me she'd pick me up after work, and she'd take me for coffee to a place she knew. I thought that was weird, because I worked in a coffee shop, and she always frequented it. But anyway, she met me at the coffee shop, and we walked over to her car. I nearly died. She was driving a Porsche, and it was just as pristine as she was!"

"Did she trick you into this lifestyle by flaunting her wealth at you?"

I shake my head. "She didn't need to trick me into anything. She asked me if I ever had sex before, and I told her how I have a two-year-old daughter. She explained that she was a madam and ran an escort service for clients with money. She told me how I fitted the image she has for her escorts, and asked if I wanted a job. I earned from my first client what I did at the coffee house for two weeks' work."

"How could you go back into that line of work with all the trauma you had from past experiences?"

"Careful Mr. President, your ignorance is showing," I say as I stand and stretch my arms over my head. "I had a daughter I needed to feed, and earning four dollars an hour would keep us way below the poverty line. I had very little education, even fewer career prospects, and a child."

"But..."

"Don't you dare say anything about 'respectable jobs' when you know there's a demand for what I do. Or do you forget how we met, Mr. President?"

"You're right. It is hypocritical of me to judge you for the choices you had to make. I apologize. You did what you had to do in order to make a better life for you and your daughter. But..." His jaw clenches as he stares at nothing. "I saw your tax returns, and you yourself said you earned more than that. You have a property portfolio. Why would you continue to be an escort when you've clearly earned enough to set yourself up for the rest of your life?"

"I love sex," I reply earnestly. "And money."

His eyes widen and he tips his head to the side. "But you've come from so much trauma around sex."

"Yes, I have. Thankfully, I found a wonderful therapist who's been helping me through it all. I've been seeing him for years, and I've come to realize that I'm not a product of my experiences. I'm so much more than that. I could've stayed on the streets, selling myself for next to nothing, but I decided *what* I'm worth. If a man wants my company, he's going to have to pay me well for it."

"You're a breath of fresh air, Reece. It's confusing to me, because I find you wildly attractive, and incredibly determined for being able to turn your life around the way you have. But I have to be honest and tell you how much I despise the fact you used to sell your body."

"Used to?" I ask as I gauge his reaction.

"You can't be serious? You're going to go back to it?" Bennett abruptly stands and paces back and forth. "No, I refuse to allow it."

"I beg your pardon? You *refuse to allow* it? Since when do you own me, Bennett?" I match his elevated tone.

"What the hell is wrong with you, Reece? That guy beat the fuck out of you, and you want to go back to it?" He steps into my space, passionately expressing himself.

"I have no idea if I'll be returning to it. But *you* don't make that decision. *I* do."

Bennett's eyes bulge as he steps back and brings his hand up to fiddle with a tie that he's not wearing. He paces back and forth for a few seconds before he stops, turns and straightens. "I'm sorry, Reece, but I have to forbid it."

"*I'm sorry*, Bennett, but you don't have a say."

"God damn it, yes I do."

"My driving factor is *not* what you want, but what I need to do for my daughter."

"Get a job in a coffee shop again," he says in a higher pitch.

"Yes, because if either she or I get seriously sick, my coffee shop wage will pay for whatever treatment is needed. Do you have any idea that the number one reason for people declaring bankruptcy in this country is because of medical debt? Do you know that?" I push.

"Why is this turning into a debate about medical and bankruptcy? It's about you being an escort, and I'm telling you, it ends now." He points to the ground with finality.

"The reason why this is turning into a debate about medical bills and bankruptcy is because if something happened and I lost everything, Emily and I would go back to living in a fucking car. We don't have a back-up plan, we don't get a pension and paid medical after our time in the White House. We're not entitled to Secret Service agents being with us until the day we die; we don't get any benefits. If I don't work, and something happens, we lose it all. And I'll tell you this right now, hell would have to freeze over before Emily will ever have to turn a fucking trick the way I did just to survive." I step back, my heart beating so fast it feels like it's about to bounce out of my chest. "It ends, when *I* say it ends."

Bennett and I are at an impasse. There are a few seconds of awkward and crackling tension between us. I can feel it coursing through the air, making it hard to take a deep breath. "Reece." He steps forward to hug me, but I counter his movements.

"I think I need some space."

"We really need to discuss what we're going to do moving forward."

"I've offloaded a lot on you today." My mouth is dry, and my stomach is tight with upset tension. I have no idea how this will affect Bennett. "We should never have met," I admit quietly.

"What? Why?"

Tilting my head to the side, I stare at Bennett. "Because this is a surefire way to end your term in office. I'm nearly positive this is cause for impeachment."

"Let me talk to my lawyer."

"Seriously?" I scoff. "You want to talk to your lawyer about us? What about the oath you took to the American people? You owe it to them."

"Being with you is not impeding me in doing my job. Of course, I'm going to serve the American people."

"Then serve them." I'm trying to pick at anything to force him to walk away. "When your term is over, then maybe we can consider being together, but we can't do this now."

I begin walking out of the room, but Bennett leaps forward and grabs my upper arm. "Why are you doing this?"

"Because we're not supposed to be together." I shouldn't have told him what I did. It's too much for anyone to handle which is why I've kept most of this to myself and vowed I'd take it to the grave with me. But now, I've let someone else in. Not just anyone, but the president of the United States. I know what I'm about to do is a dick move, but I'm doing it to protect us all. "I can't do this with you, Bennett."

He appears to be as surprised as I am by my words. "Do what?"

A sharp pain shoots through my chest. "I can't see you anymore."

"What? Why?"

My hands wring together as I open the door leading to his bedroom. A deep burning ache courses through my veins. Because *this will destroy him, Emily, and me if the public finds out.* "When you were elected, you had a wife who wasn't an escort. Whatever we have, has to end."

"No, I'm not letting you go."

I slowly gather my things and start to head toward the door. "I made good on my promise, Mr. President. I told you why I'm an escort, now you have to make good on yours." I look to the door indicating Grayson, then back to Bennett. I place my hand on the handle and turn to him. "Please, don't contact me."

"Reece," he calls as I open the door to his bedroom. His Secret Service detail is standing rigid in the hall. "Reece!" I walk out to find Grayson waiting for me. The door opens as we head to the elevator in silence. "God damn it, Reece!"

I refuse to turn around as I wait for the elevator. Grayson blocks my path so I can't make a quick getaway. "Ma'am." He looks over my shoulder.

Turning, I silently plead with Bennett. With my chin quivering and tears brimming in my eyes, I hold onto my dignity and pride with everything I have. Bennett runs toward me and enshrouds me in his warm hug. "Please," I beg. "This has to end."

"I can't let you go," he whispers as he kisses my cheek.

The elevator door opens, and I step backward, breaking his hold. Grayson moves out of the way. "You have to," I say as I step into the elevator flanked by Grayson. I lower my chin and look down at the floor. The doors close, and I watch as my tears fall to the floor.

He's the president.

And I'm an escort.

I have to do what's right for him, and Emily, and three-hundred and thirty-three million people.

We can't be together.

Chapter Fourteen

Bennett

S itting at my desk, I'm reading over the agendas for a few meetings I have coming up. I promised Reece that I'd pull her Secret Service detail, and I'm a man of my word, so I need to arrange that. While distracted by the agendas and thoughts of Reece, I'm unaware that there's anyone else in the Oval Office, not until Liam clears his throat and I look up. "Liam?"

"Mr. President, there's been a mass shooting."

"Fuck," I grumble as I run my hand through my hair. "Where?" I take my glasses off and place them on the table as I steeple my fingers together and tap them to my lip.

"A music festival." He goes on to tell me the state and the county where this tragedy has taken place.

"What are we talking?"

"One shooter fired into the crowd. Police were on scene and shot him but not before he opened fire and killed at least forty people."

"Do we know anything else about this?"

"It's total chaos." Liam stands and waits for my reply.

"Esther!" I call. The door opens and Esther walks into my office. "Cancel all my appointments for the rest of the day."

"Yes, sir." Esther leaves the office.

"Get Air Force One ready," I instruct Liam.

"Yes, sir." Liam walks out of my office, giving me a few moments to try and clear my head.

"Mark." Mark enters my office and stands rigid with his shoulders pulled back. "I want Reece's detail pulled." I gave her my word, and I intend on keeping it.

"Yes, sir." He exits quietly, leaving me alone.

I sit back against my chair and think about the shooting. At least forty people have lost their lives because a stranger opened fire on them. This is unacceptable. Mass shootings are happening almost daily, and they're happening on my watch.

"Wheels up in three hours," Liam pops his head into my office to inform me.

"Thank you." My mind is churning with so many thoughts. "Liam, come in and close the door."

Liam walks in and leans against the back of the armchair opposite my desk. "What do you need?"

"Do you know anyone who does private security?"

Liam's forehead crinkles and he shakes his head. "We have the Secret Service."

"I know that, but I want someone *other* than the Secret Service."

"For you?" I lift my brows to stare at Liam. "For Reece," he says in understanding. "I do know of someone. His family is friends with my parents."

"Who is it?" I ask trying to think of who he's talking about.

"Brice Lowe. He started Elite Security shortly after he graduated college."

"I've met him."

"Yep, you have. At my parents' wedding anniversary. At the lake house."

I smile at the memory I have. "That's when Kathryn's shoe got caught on the pontoon bridge, she lost her footing, and fell into the lake."

Liam and I have a moment of shared laughter. "When her head popped up from the water, she was so mad that we were all laughing."

"I jumped in after her to make sure she was okay, and we both ended up soaked and laughing so hard we were crying," I say, still remembering how her hair was plastered to her face and her makeup was running down her cheeks. "Your mom was horrified."

"Mom ran into the house to get towels for her. Dad grabbed his camera and started taking photos. Everyone's cheeks were hurting because they were laughing so much."

"It was a calamity of untimely errors," I say, still fond of the memories we made together.

Liam's laughter dies down as fast as mine does. "You like her," he says.

This moment now is not between a president and his chief of staff. "I never expected to find a connection with anyone again after Kathryn. And you know what's the most bizarre part?"

"What?"

"Reece couldn't be any more different if she tried, but I think Kathryn would've liked her."

"Kathryn was always such an accepting and gentle person," Liam says. "But I see Reece makes you happy, Bennett."

I smile as I look down at the laptop keys. "Reece is most certainly unexpected, and I think there's much more to her than she lets on."

Liam's brows lift as he nods slowly. "You won't be reelected if it leaks."

I tighten my hands together as the muscles in my arms strain against my shirt. "Trust me, I know," I admit. "But, I don't think that's going to matter anyway, because Reece has broken it off with me."

"What?" Liam's tone raises. "*She* broke it off with *you*?"

"Yeah."

The door opens and Jamie waltzes in with my second cup of coffee. The first is already cold. He places the hot one down and takes the cold one away. Closing the door, he leaves Liam and me alone again. "What happened?" Liam asks.

I arch a brow as I relive the night and morning with her. "I think Reece is trying to protect everyone around her, including me."

"Protect you?" Liam's eyes widen as he pieces it together. "She's protecting you from scrutiny?"

"I think she's worried for me and for her daughter. Which is understandable, of course."

"And for herself," Liam adds. "She's not used to having her every move analyzed by the press, or by the American public."

"Obviously not, but I honestly don't think she's worried about herself. More about Emily and me."

"Is that why you're removing her protection?"

"We made a deal. She upheld her end, and I'm upholding mine. I told her I'd remove her Secret Service detail." A slow smiles tugs at the corners of my lips.

It doesn't take long for Liam to laugh as he pushes up off the arm of the chair. "You think she's going to respond well to what you're going to do?"

"She won't know," I say with absolutely no conviction. Liam scoffs. "I've convinced myself she's not going to find out."

Liam straightens and clicks his tongue. "Well, I'll prepare the vice president to take office."

"Smart-ass," I call as he's walking out of my office. "I need the number for Brice."

"Of course, Mr. President." And just like that, we're back to our professional dynamic.

"Governor Mallory Shepherd," Jamie whispers as we approach ground zero. Jamie is good about reminding me of names.

"Mallory," I say as I take in the havoc surrounding us. "I'm sorry I'm here under these horror-filled circumstances. What do we know?" I've already been briefed on the plane over, but what more has happened?

"The shooter has been killed."

"Talk to me about the injured and killed." I feel sick to my stomach looking at the mass graveyard in front of me. It's not the first time I've seen body bags, and it never gets easier.

"Fifty-three people have been killed, and thirty-two have been injured. Three are being operated on as we speak."

"I know the shooter is dead, but tell me about him. What could possess a man to open fire at a damn music festival?"

"He had a fully automatic assault weapon. His name was Bill James, and he was thirty-eight years old." Fuck, he's my age. "He lost his job because he's a drug addict, and he got his hands on a weapon." There are so many problems in that one statement.

"It wasn't just a weapon, it's a fully automatic assault rifle."

"Yes, Mr. President." Governor Shepherd says through clenched teeth. She and her party are staunch supporters of easy access to all weapons. "He didn't purchase the rifle here in my state," she says probably aware of what I'm about to say.

"This is a gun-friendly state, yet you have one of the highest gun violence rates in the country. After seeing this do you still believe background checks aren't necessary to purchase weapons?"

"He didn't buy it in my state," she argues stubbornly.

"Tell that to the fifty-three people in these bags and the thirty-two who've been injured. Go to each of their families and tell them the shooter didn't obtain the weapon in your state."

"Mr. President—"

"What's the age range of the people who died?" I ask, completely and coldly cutting her off.

"The youngest was ten, and the oldest was thirty-one."

Ten fucking years old. The same age as Emily. I flash a look to Jamie, who distracts Mallory, allowing me a moment to walk away from her. The deathly scene before me is heart-breaking, soul-destroying. We can't keep seeing devastation like this on a daily basis. This violence is mindless, and *I* need to do something about it.

I notice a woman sitting on the edge of the sidewalk. Her head is down and her hands are up around her head. It's obvious to me she's grieving the loss of a loved one. I walk over to her and sit beside her on the sidewalk. Mark is close by; the other Secret Service agents are fanned out around me. I gesture for them to back away. "How are you doing?" I ask the woman who looks up and startles back when she notices who's talking to her.

"Mr. Pres—"

"It's Bennett," I softly correct her. "Did you lose someone here?"

Her eyes are red, and her cheeks are streaked from the tears falling from them. "Both of my daughters," she says in a whisper. "My *only* two children."

"I'm so sorry for your loss," I say as I reach out to place my arm around her quivering shoulders. Mark clears his throat, telling me in his own way that I shouldn't do that. But protocol be damned. This woman is hurting.

She lifts her head to look at me. "Tahlia's only twelve, and Jessica's seventeen. I bought them the tickets for Christmas." I can't comprehend how harrowing this is for her. "I should've gone first, not them." She points to the mass grave. "This isn't the natural order of death." She breaks down, howling with pain. I pull her toward me and let her cry on my shoulder. In this moment, she could very well be a threat, she could easily pull a knife out and stab me through the heart. It's a risk I'm willing to take to show her a bit of kindness and compassion. She's just lost her daughters, and she's going to be hurting for a long time to come. She finally pulls back and straightens her shoulders. "I'm sorry, I shouldn't have cried on you." She darts her gaze toward my shirt. "Your shirt is ruined."

"Don't worry about my shirt. My heart is breaking for you."

Absentmindedly she reaches her hand out and gently places it on my forearm. "Please don't let their deaths be for no reason." She holds eye contact with me before standing and walking toward someone who's calling her.

My mind is shrouded in a horrible darkness as I try and make sense of the travesty that's occurred. I hate this part of my job, but I know I can make a difference, and this is the very reason I chose to run for president, and why Kathryn supported me. Because we believed we could make a difference. I *can* make a difference.

Standing, I walk back toward Mallory. Jamie is a step behind me, and Mark is to my side though slightly ahead. The rest of the Secret Service agents surround me, watching to make sure nothing happens. "Mr. President," Mallory starts as I walk to her.

I extend my hand to shake hers. "Mr. President, we need to leave," Jamie says as he places his body between Mallory and me once we've briefly shaken hands.

"Mallory." I give her a curt nod and a glare, still fuming at her lack of compassion for the victims. Instead, she wanted me to know that the shooter obtained the rifle from some other state. "I need you to find out where the shooter got the rifle, and I want to know everything about his background," I say to Jamie as we walk toward the armored vehicles waiting to take us back to Air Force One.

Staring at the center of this ruinous scene as we drive away, I can't help but feel an impotent rage. "Mr. President," Jamie's address snaps me out of my growing anger. I look to him and wait for him to repeat what he's already said. "Air Force One is ready for you."

The drive back to the airstrip is filled with tension and my mind is racing to think of what I can do to stop this from happening again. I need to call a meeting when I get back. "I need to see Liam in my office when we return."

Jamie nods, brings his phone to his ear and in a quiet voice, makes the call.

———— ✹ ————

"How bad was it?" Liam's already waiting in my office as I walk in.

"Bad is an understatement."

"What do you need?"

I sit at my desk, firing up my computer as I search for my glasses. "I'm going to lose the election," I start. "It's only a matter of time before the public finds out about Reece, and when that happens, I'll be out."

"You don't know that." I look up at Liam before resuming my search for my damn glasses. "You're probably right though."

"I want to look at gun reform."

Liam groans and rolls his head back to look up at the ornate ceiling. Folding his arms in front of his chest, he sighs. "May I speak freely?"

"Of course, Liam."

"This is career suicide."

"I'm out either way. Let's go out swinging. Gun violence in our country is an epidemic."

"What are you proposing?"

"We need to look at other countries that don't have the gun violence we do."

"Japan, United Kingdom, Australia, Norway and New Zealand have low gun violence. However, they have a combined population of under two hundred million people. They don't compare to us."

"But what's their gun violence rate per one hundred thousand people? If it's lower than ours we need to look at it and try to figure out what we can do to lower ours. I have the reforms from New Zealand, let's start with those and look at what we can do."

"You'll have half the country wanting to overturn your term."

"And I might have the other half wanting to keep me."

"You know this isn't going to be easy, and the likely chance of it happening is..." Liam stops talking as he shakes his head. "But you still want to try?"

I sit back in my chair and loosen my tie. "This shouldn't be the next guy's problem. We can't keep seeing these kids die because we're not doing enough to curb violence."

"What are you talking about? What exactly do you want to do?"

"I don't know, Liam. But, I need ideas on how to try and move in a more peaceful direction."

"People are going to be rioting if they think we're going to take their guns."

My point exactly. "Liam, I don't ever want to see again what I saw today. Children's lives were taken from them simply because they were out enjoying themselves. I spoke with a woman who lost both of her children. She'd bought them tickets to the festival as a Christmas gift."

Liam steps backward and slowly nods. "Let me do some research and present you with some workable options."

"Thank you." I'm interrupted by my cell vibrating in my pocket. I slide my phone out of my pocket and instantly smile when I see Reece's name. "Hey," I say as I lean back against my chair and close my eyes.

"I saw you on the news."

"I had to see the destruction for myself. Show my support for the families."

She sighs into the phone. "You don't need to justify your actions to me. But I just wanted to see if you're okay." I don't answer her immediately, because I'm trying to formulate a reasonable response. "Bennett?"

Opening my eyes, I stare down at my laptop as my shoulders droop forward. "I don't think I'll ever be able to get that image out of my head. It's burned into my memory."

"You're avoiding my question. Are you okay?"

"Yeah, sure I am," I say as I shake my head in contradiction.

"You need to talk to someone about this."

I scoff at her ridiculousness. "No, I'm fine." I rub at the tension across my forehead. "I'm fine," I repeat.

"Why are you lying to me?"

I despise how in tune with me she is. But what I hate more is the fact she's not here with me. I pull my shoulders back and resume my duty as the president. "Reece, you said we can't do this anymore—"

"I was calling to see how you were, Bennett," she interrupts me.

The hardest words leave my mouth. Maybe she's right, maybe we shouldn't do this. I'm the president, and she's an escort. We can't be together. "It's Mr. President," I say.

I hear the sharp intake of air, almost like she's disappointed. "Right. I'll lose your number, Mr. President."

"I think..." She hangs up before I get the chance to finish my sentence.

I toss the phone on my desk and lean back in my chair looking up at the ceiling. What got into me to make me think we could've worked?

I'm the president and my responsibility is to the people. She's an escort and she'll ruin my life.

I'm done thinking with my dick.

Chapter Fifteen

Reece

"Your face is looking so much better, Mom," Emily says as she slides into the car.

"Well, thank you so much for your kind words, kid." I lean over and give her a kiss on the cheek. "How was school?"

Emily shrugs. "It was school," she replies with no passion. "I came first in an English exam, and I came first in a math exam too."

"First?" I pull out onto the road heading toward home. "You came first?"

"Yeah, it was pretty good." I hold my hand out to give her a high five. She quickly smacks my hand, then looks down at her phone. "What are we doing this weekend?"

"I was thinking, maybe we can pack the car and drive."

"Where to?" Emily eagerly asks.

"Anywhere. What do you think?"

"Who's coming? Is Tash coming with us?"

"No, she's working."

"What about Bennett, is he coming?"

I don't want to tell her the truth about us, but I also don't want to lie either. "No, it'll be a girls' weekend. Just you and me." I need to get away from all the pressures of home. Thankfully, Grayson is no longer around, which makes things easier for me because I don't need to explain it all to Emily, although she was chill about Bennett.

Emily turns in her seat to stare at me. "One." She holds a finger up. "When can we go? And two." She holds a second finger up. "Can I bring books to read? Oh, and three." She holds a third finger up. "How far away are we going?"

"As soon as we pack. Yes. Let's just drive and stop when we're tired," I answer her questions in succession.

Emily excitedly claps her hands together. "Yes, this can be a choose-your-own-adventure kind of weekend. This is going to be so much fun!"

"Yep, it is." I look over to Emily and smile before returning my attention to the road.

The sun has fallen, and the night sky is now full of twinkling stars. Emily is struggling to keep her eyes open, and I know I'm an hour or so away from falling asleep behind the wheel myself.

"Mom," Emily says in a small, groggy voice.

"Yeah?"

"No matter where it leads, I think we should take the next exit off the highway."

"Next exit off the highway, you say?"

"Yep." She opens her mouth and releases a massive yawn. "I have a good feeling about it."

The next exit fast approaches and I look over at Emily who's struggling to keep her eyelids open. "I'm taking the exit." She lifts her hand and gives me a thumbs-up. We continue driving for a while and Emily is doing her best to stay awake. If she goes to sleep, it'll only be a matter of time before my eyes close too. "We're coming up to another sign," I say.

Emily blinks several times, yawns, and sits up straighter in the seat. "Does that say Hope River?" She squints to see in the distance.

We quickly approach a weathered sign pointing to the next turn off. "That's exactly what it says."

"Must be a sign." Emily starts laughing. "See, it's a sign, so it must be a sign." She points toward it. "Can we go that way?"

"Sure can. I think you're delirious, though. You need to sleep."

She's still laughing. "I'm so funny. I should be a stand-up comedian."

"Let's not talk about your career as a comedian quite yet," I say as I turn toward Hope River. It doesn't take Emily long before her laughter stops, her head slumps to the side, and she begins to softly snore. I come to a bridge where there's a sign that reads "Welcome to Hope River. Population 1486, 1487, 1489, 1488, 1493, 1509." I snort with a chuckle when I see the numbers crossed out.

I drive toward the town and find it's dead quiet. There are no cars traveling through, no signs of life. It's quite eerie, if I'm being honest. Where on earth have we ended up? The lights of the car catch a sign reading McGrath's Bed and Breakfast. The house looks impeccable and well looked-after. The lawns and garden are clearly maintained, and although this small town looks like a scene out of a horror movie, the bed and breakfast is inviting. But driving for seven hours straight has taken its toll on me and Emily. We both need a place to lay our heads, even if it's only for tonight.

I pull up out the front of the bed and breakfast and nudge Emily. "Emily?"

"Yeah?"

"Come on, I think I've found somewhere for us to stay."

She opens her eyes and with a bewildered gleam she looks around. "Where are we?"

"We're in Hope River, and that over there is a bed and breakfast. I want to check it out and see if they have room for us, we can find something more upscale tomorrow."

"Okay, Momma," she replies in her thick, sleepy voice.

I get out of the driver's side and walk around to the passenger side. Opening the door, I wait for Emily to hop out so we can see if there's room at the bed and breakfast. I try the door, but it's locked. There's a note on it directing guests to call a number. I call the number and it rings only a couple of times. "Hello," a woman answers.

"Hi, um. I'm standing outside the bed and breakfast, and I'm wondering if there are any vacancies for tonight?"

"We do have a room available, and I can be there in the next ten minutes."

"Great, thank you."

"You can wait on the porch swing if you like. I shouldn't be too long."

"It's not too late for you?" I ask, in case I'm putting her out. Although, she doesn't sound like I woke her.

"Oh no, not at all. I won't be long. What's your name?"

"I'm Reece."

"Great. Give me ten."

"Thank you." We both hang up, and I move us over to the porch swing. "Emily, they'll be here soon, so if you can sit there, I'll go grab our bags."

"Okay." With heavy footsteps, she drags herself over to the swing and sits.

By the time I get our two small suitcases from the car, another car approaches. The woman jumps out and rushes up to the bed and breakfast. "Reece?" she asks as she unlocks the door with a swipe card.

"Yes, hi." I smile as I nudge Emily. "And this is my daughter, Emily."

"I'm Yasmin." She pushes on the door and steps in, holding it open for us. She walks behind the front desk, and I can't help but look around.

"This is so cute." I notice a picture on the wall and walk over to it, studying it.

"That picture is this house before Hope got to it."

"Wow, it's amazing. Hope? Who's Hope?"

"She's our local celebrity. It's a bit of a story, but you can ask her about it tomorrow at the festival."

"What festival?" Emily asks. She's awake now that she heard that.

"Hope River holds a festival every six weeks or so down on Main Street. Tomorrow's is the curry festival." I stare at her waiting for the punchline. "I know," Yasmin says. "It was a little quirky for me too when I moved here."

"You're not from here?" I ask.

"Oh no. Hope owns this, and her brother's wife, Tabitha, was friends with me many years ago. Anyway, I screwed Tabitha over, and we fell out. But, couple of years ago we happened to meet up, and our friendship has rebuilt over time. Tabitha is the chef here. She'll be in around five to start on breakfast for the guests. Anyway, I'm boring you, and you're probably tired."

"I am," Emily pipes up.

Yasmin smiles. "We only have one room available, which means you'll need to share the bed. But, rest assured, it's a big bed and it's comfortable. You're upstairs, in May's Room." I look at her with confusion. "The rooms are named after key people of the town."

"Oh, okay. I thought for a moment May was in the room."

She laughs and shakes her head. "No, not at all. Now, breakfast is served from six until nine. But, if you want to have a sleep in, I can ask Tabitha to prepare two plates and keep them in the kitchen for you, if you prefer."

"We'll probably be down at about eight-thirty," I say.

"Sure. I'll be here, so if you have any questions, I'm happy to answer them." She types away on the laptop, and before long Emily and I head upstairs and find May's Room.

When I open the door, Emily heads into the bathroom while I look around the room. "How cute is this place?" I call to Emily.

She comes out of the bathroom, nods, and flops on the bed, still in her clothes. "Too tired to move."

I take her shoes off and Emily crawls into bed. It takes her only a few moments before she's totally out of it. I dim the lights and sit at the cozy sofa beside the windows, looking out into the night sky. Reaching for my bag, I slide my phone out, kick off my shoes and snuggle up on the sofa. There's a part of me that's hoping Bennett will reach out, but I know that's not going to happen. We're done. The way he spoke to me was clear and to the point.

It's for the best.

So why am I tearing up? Why does it feel like my heart has been ripped out of my chest?

I take another look at my phone before sending Tash a message to let her know we're in a sleepy small town called Hope River. Although I'd love for Bennett to message me, I know in my gut that won't happen. I turn my phone off and throw it into my bag. This weekend is about Emily and me, and no one else.

I lean my elbow on the back of the sofa and stare out at the beautiful, clear night sky.

Bennett and I are clearly done. It would have been easy to fall for him, and I'm grateful I didn't let my heart connect with his.

But why does this hurt as much as it does?

"What a weird town," Emily says as we walk along the main street.

"Good afternoon," someone greets as we pass by them.

"Hi!" Emily smiles happily. Once past the person, Emily turns to me and says, "Everyone is so friendly."

"I know. It's bizarre, but refreshingly awesome too," I reply.

Ahead of us, an old lady moves to stand, but drops her cane. Without a thought or encouragement from me, Emily runs ahead and picks up her cane. The old lady and Emily speak only for a moment before I reach them. "This beautiful young girl was just saying you're both staying at the B&B," the old woman says.

"Yeah, we decided to take a road trip for the weekend, and this is where we landed." Emily sidles up beside me, and I wrap my arm around her shoulder.

"Which room are you in?"

"We're staying in May's Room," Emily says.

"Oh, that's my room. I'm May."

"I'm Reece, and this is my daughter Emily."

"Hi!" Emily offers her a small wave.

"Have you had any of the curry yet?" May asks.

"Oh, no. We're not really part of the town."

"Pish posh. Sit your asses down and eat." She points to the two available chairs beside her.

"Oh, um." I look around and see a café behind us. "We can go in the café..."

"I'm going to whack you with my cane if you don't sit down."

"We'd better sit down, Mom," Emily says as she looks up to me with pleading eyes.

"Do you want to try the curry?" I ask. Emily eagerly nods. "We won't be disturbing you?" I double-check with May.

"No, you won't be disturbing me." She pointedly looks at the chairs. "Sit, and enjoy the curries. That one there I made." She points to a rich looking curry. "All the vegetables came from my garden."

"You have a vegetable garden?" Emily asks. "Is it big?"

"It's decent-sized, and I have chickens. They roam around everywhere. They give me eggs too."

"That would be so cool."

"When do you leave?" May asks me.

"Tomorrow at some point. We were thinking about leaving this morning and moving to another town, but Emily really wants to go to the beach."

"Hope River is close, down that way." May points over her shoulder. "It's lined with grass and trees and it's really pretty. Tabitha does a nice picnic basket if you're interested."

"She's the chef at the B&B?" I say.

"And my niece."

"Oh, wow." I crinkle my brows trying to piece together the relationships.

"Yes, I know. Hope River is quite intimate, but once people come here, they don't want to leave."

"Who doesn't want to leave?" another woman boldly asks as she walks over and gives May a kiss on the cheek. She looks at us and smiles. "Hey. I'm Hope." She holds her hand out to shake mine, then Emily's before plonking into a seat beside May.

"Hope? As in the woman who owns the B&B?" I ask.

"The one and only."

"I know you," Emily says. "I've seen you on TV. You have a show, *Restoring Hope*, right?"

"Oh wow, that's you," I say as I instantly recall the few episodes I've watched.

"That's me. Please." She holds her hand up. "No cameras, I'm super shy." May rolls her eyes while Hope is smiling. "What?" Hope asks May when she catches the eye roll.

"Can your ego get any bigger?" May teases with mirth in her voice.

"Do you wanna see?"

"Hey, Hope," a guy says as he walks past. "Gran." Hope and May both wave and smile.

"Oh, sorry, do you want us to move for your grandson." I point to the guy who's already walked by.

"Grandson?" May looks at Hope with confusion.

"Yeah. He called you 'Gran.'" I point to the guy.

Hope chuckles and flicks her hand dismissively. "May becomes Gran once she trusts you. Everyone in Hope River calls her that."

"Not everyone," May says with pursed lips. "Some people are assholes, and I refuse to let them call me Gran. Some have tried, but I ignore them until they call me May."

"It's true," Hope says. She spots the curry Emily is eating. "Oh my God, is that your sweet potato curry?" She turns to May and waits for her affirmation. "Did you make extra for me?"

"You know where I live. You can come over and get the extra I've made."

"Aww, you do love me." Hope reaches over and hugs May, who appears rigid and uncomfortable. "Now." Hope takes the container with the curry, and slides it over in front of her. "I need a fork." She looks around.

"No, you're not eating directly from the container, girly."

Hope's shoulders slump forward. "Fine, I won't." She looks over to me. "So, what brings you to Hope River?"

"Mom picked me up from school yesterday, and asked me if I wanted to do a girls' weekend. Just her and me, not Tash or Bennett." I stiffen when she says Bennett's name, hoping no one picks up on who she's talking about.

"The two of us each packed a bag and drove until we found ourselves here," I say attempting to distract Hope and May.

"Hey, Emily, wanna do something with me?" Hope asks.

I sit straighter, feeling protective of my daughter, but there's something about these people that puts me somewhat at ease, too. "What?" Emily asks.

"There's a bouncy castle down there and I really want to go, but the last time I did, I split my pants and I wasn't wearing underwear. It was totally embarrassing, and I've never been able to go back. Now, I can absolutely use you for my cover. I can say, 'Hey, I'm showing the new kid around.'"

I snort with laughter at Hope's blunt honesty. "You split your pants?" Emily asks slowly.

"Oh yeah. And, once when we were filming an episode of *Restoring Hope*, my pants got caught on wire and they totally ripped open. The producers wanted me to change, but hey, that's me. We kept it in, and it ended up being one of the highest-rated episodes. With the exception of the one we did in New York for the restaurant, Table. Do you remember that?" she turns and asks May.

"Do I remember it? That episode had me in tears."

"Anyway, what I'm trying to say is, I do stuff like that all the time. I can't guarantee I won't completely embarrass myself, but wanna go?" Hope eagerly looks to Emily. "Please?"

"I can agree with Hope," May says. "She does make a fool out of herself. Tell them about the time you broke your nose."

"There are impressionable young ears at the table, Gran. I don't think our new friend Reece would want to subject her daughter to that story."

Emily sits forward and clasps her hands together like she's praying. "If you tell me, I'll go to the castle with you." She quickly turns and looks at me. "Can I?"

"Sure."

"Fine, but don't say I didn't warn you. If you've seen the show, you know I work with my husband, River." Emily and I both nod. We've seen a few of the episodes, but I really like Hope, so when we return home, I'm going to binge all the seasons. "Before we were together, we had history."

"And she was caught in her own head," May adds.

"Listen, old lady, keep your opinions to yourself," Hope says with a massive smile.

"Call me old lady again and this cane is going somewhere the sun don't shine."

Their banter is priceless. "As I was saying. River and I weren't together, and one morning I went down by the ocean to buy a coffee and donuts, because…donuts are life." Emily giggles and I wrap my arm around her to pull her in for a hug and kiss. "Anyway, as I was enjoying my coffee, I spotted this guy swimming in the ocean. Basically, I was appreciating the view until I noticed it was River. Well, before I knew it, he was standing in front of me, I was drooling, and in my haste to get away, I tripped on the step and my face kissed the pavement. My nose was in the way and I ended up breaking it. But!" She holds up a finger. "I was particularly annoyed with myself for dropping the donuts and leaving them behind."

"You were more worried about the donuts than your nose?" Emily asks, still giggling.

"Duh, donuts." Hope stares at her like the obvious thing to have done would be to have picked up the donuts. "They're good donuts. You should go tomorrow morning to get some. Anyway, you owe me a visit to the bouncy castle." Hope points to Emily, then turns to me, waiting for my approval. "The castle is right down there." Hope points to the town center.

"We walked past it and I said to Mom that it looks like fun."

Hope abruptly stands. "Let's go, kid."

Emily turns to me. "Have fun," I say, giving her permission to go with Hope.

"I like your kid," May says.

"Thank you." I smile.

"Where are you and Emily from?" May asks.

"Washington, D.C," I reply.

"What do you do?"

I hesitate for a split second. "I'm a waitress at a high-end restaurant."

May arches a brow and tilts her head to the side. "Waitressing must be a dangerous business."

"No, not especially. Why do you say that?" She points to my yellowing bruises. "Oh, no, I was in an accident." May's eyes penetrate through my soul, unnerving me. "It was nothing."

"How old is Emily?"

"She's ten," I reply and look at the curry I've dished out into one of the disposable bowls. I push the little remaining around, trying not to look directly at May.

"Is that the story you've told Emily to protect her from the truth?"

There's a part of me that feels like May is some kind of snake charmer. "Are you psychic?"

"No, but I'm old. I've been around for nearly seventy-five years, Reece, and I can read people very well. I know a good egg when I see one, and I know you have a heart of gold, regardless of the trauma you've been through."

I swallow the lump in my throat as a chill runs up my spine, causing me to tremble. "How do you know?" I ask in a small voice.

"Sweet girl, you look young enough to be that little girl's sister, not her mother. How old were you? Twelve? Thirteen?"

I clear my throat and look around in case anyone can hear me. "I was fifteen when I had her."

"I'll make a wager that the circumstances were anything but favorable."

"How do you know?" I repeat in a barely audible voice.

"I've seen a lot in my years, and helped many women. But you don't need financial help, do you?"

"It's like you're reading into my soul. Do I have a tattoo across my forehead?"

"I told you, I'm very good at reading people. So, tell me, are you running from someone? Because I'll tell you right now, if you're running from the bastard who did that to your face, no better town than Hope River to protect you."

A sense of ease falls over me. May is protective, without even knowing me. "No, this guy has been dealt with." I crinkle my forehead as I look down at the bowl. "I think."

"What are you running from?"

"A complicated relationship that can never be," I answer earnestly.

"Why can it never be?"

"Because of his job, and because of mine."

She cracks a smile. "Aha, so you're not a waitress."

"No, I'm not. But that's what I tell people, so they don't ask me any more questions about it."

"Why can't you be together? Is he in the mafia?"

I snort and shake my head. "No, not quite. He's a public figure, and if it got out that he was seeing me given what I do, it would absolutely destroy his career. Not to mention the damage it would do to Emily."

"Kids are resilient, and quite smart. You may have been successful in hiding your real career from her, but there's going to come a time when she's going to figure it out."

"I only hope she doesn't figure it out before I have the opportunity to tell her."

"She's ten today, and before you know it, she'll be eighteen and ready to move away from home so she can go to college."

"She already boards at school."

"Huh," May says as she taps her chin and narrows her eyes. "Interesting." She stares at me for a moment. "Are you a drug dealer?"

"God, no! I have no interest in that."

"Ahh, I see. So, you're a prostitute then." I feel the heat rise to my face as I suck in a breath. "Good for you."

"Imma...I'm a... No." My mouth dries as I try to dig myself out of it.

"I'm a vault, nothing will break me. But like I said, good for you. If that's what you need to do to support that sweet girl down there, then I'm all for it. Not like you need my approval." She casts an eye over me. "Judging by how nice your hair is, the length of your nails, and your and Emily's beautiful clothes, I'd say you're a high-class escort, right?"

I clear my throat, still shocked by her accurate analysis of me. "I... How?"

"This man you can't be with, I take it he knows about your occupation?" I nod as I lower my chin and look down at my lap. "He doesn't like you being an escort?"

I lift my head and smile weakly. "It's a complicated situation that would put all of us at risk of scrutiny. I won't put her through that." I point to over my shoulder.

"I take it this man isn't her father, either." I keep shaking my head. "Does she know he's not her father?"

"Of course, she knows he's not her father. All she knows about her father is he wasn't in my life much past him finding out I was pregnant." *Again, not the entire truth.*

"He sounds like a great guy," May says sarcastically, lifting her brows.

"Again, it's complicated and not ideal. But I've made the best of the situation, and I have vowed to be the best mother I can be to Emily."

"You're a good person, Reece, don't let something like your profession stop you from loving the right man."

"My *illegal* profession," I point out.

"Sometimes we can be a backward country. You're an adult and you should be allowed to do with your body what you choose. As long as it's sane, safe, and consensual, then sell it if you want." May shakes her head. "There aren't many things that tip me over with anger, but telling a woman she can't have an abortion is the first thing that irritates me, and telling a man or a woman they can't sell their body is another. If there's demand for the industry, then legalize it and make it safe for the workers."

"I must admit, you're quite a forward thinker for someone who's..." I shut my mouth instantly regretting the words.

"Were you about to say for someone my age?" I cringe in shame as I nod. "My life has been a fortunate one and I'm grateful to be able to see things for what they are. For example, I see a beautiful young woman sitting here doing the best she can in circumstances that I think may have been challenging. Why should I judge you for the decisions you were forced to make?"

I feel like crying. I've kept this part of me so tight and closed off that I'm terrified of telling anyone outside of Tash about what I do. "I have to be honest with you, never in a million years would I have ever imagined that I'd be sitting in this small town, having curry and talking to a woman your age about my occupation."

"Darling." She flicks her hand dismissively at me. "You forget, I was young once and I had my fair share of fun when I was in my twenties, and thirties, and way beyond."

Her entire persona is infectiously beautiful. I feel like hugging her. "I wish I had a parent like you."

"I'm old enough to be your grandparent." She sternly stares at me.

"I never knew my grandparents, or even my father. Mom tossed me out when I was fourteen and I've never been back. I don't even know where she is or if she's still alive."

"She might be looking for you."

I scoff and roll my eyes. "No, that's highly unlikely. She's a... she *was* a horrible drunk who chose her boyfriends over me. There's nothing she could say to me to make feel anything for her. She was never a good parent, and I don't want to find her and relive those horrible years of my life."

"You're entitled to tell her to fuck off if you ever do cross paths with her. You have every right to say whatever you want to her. But I will say this to you, Reece, and take it from an old broad like me."

"What is it?" I feel like May speaks from her heart with every word she says.

"Don't carry hatred inside you, because that's something that'll fuck you up when you're older."

"Trust me when I tell you that one of the first things I did when I started making decent money is find myself a good therapist. It was the best decision I ever made for myself."

"Good for you." She nods. "I have to ask you something though. If I don't ask, I'm going to regret it." The atmosphere has loosened and isn't so tense.

"What is it?"

"First." She looks over her shoulder and leans forward. "Have you had sex with anyone I would know?"

I snort with a chuckle. I lean forward to mimic her posture. "I've signed NDAs, but let's just say..." I smirk and cock a brow.

"Ohhh, if only you could tell me. But, I understand you can't. Second question. How good is the money?"

I laugh a little too loud. "Even though I didn't finish school, I'm smart with my money and have invested a lot of it in property. Last year, my tax returns said I earned around three hundred."

"Thousand?" May shouts a little too loud.

"That's what my tax returns said."

"Girl!" she shrieks. "Holy shit, you got it going on."

"Remember I also have property."

"And you said that's what your tax returns said, which means it's probably significantly higher than that. I'm incredibly impressed by you, Reece. You've taken a situation where life could've chewed you up and spit you out, and you've made it work for you. Well done."

"Even with what I do?"

"Your job doesn't define the person you are. Your heart does, and it's in the right place. Don't ever let anyone try to slut-shame you. You're bringing Emily up and doing it with class and pride."

"Mom!" Emily yells from behind me.

I straighten in my seat and pleadingly look to May not to breathe a word to Emily. "I'm a vault." She smiles, and for some reason, I really do believe that. I've never had an older person take an interest in me the way she has. It's refreshing and heartwarming.

"Hope didn't split her pants," Emily happily says. Her cheeks are pink and she's sweating from her time in the castle.

"That's always a plus," I reply as I turn to see Hope strutting over. "Did you have fun?"

"Did I ever? I love the bouncy castle; it's one of my favorite things to do." She turns to Emily and holds her hand out for a high five. "Thanks, kid. Want ice cream?"

Emily immediately turns to me. "Can I?"

"Sure thing."

"Yay!"

Hope and Emily walk away leaving May and me alone again. "I just wanted to say thank you, May."

"Hi, Gran," someone else says as they walk past.

"Does everyone in the town know you?"

"Absolutely every single person. You could say I'm the town matriarch," she admits proudly. "They all gush over me, and would do anything for me. I pretend it irritates me, but I secretly love it." She instantly lifts her hand and points her skinny finger at me. "That's my secret and you're never allowed to tell anyone."

"I'm a vault," I say, repeating her words.

"That I believe," she replies with sass.

"Mom, Hope bought me a strawberry and lemon swirl ice cream. Want some?" Emily holds it toward me. "It's so good."

"Yep, it's my favorite," Hope adds as she licks hers. "Honestly, I'm so lucky I live here. It's the best small town ever. The festivals are nearly always about food, and I *love* food."

"Because she can't cook," May teases.

"I don't need to cook, River does that. I just need to be fantastic with my building and design skills."

"I've seen some of the episodes of *Restoring Hope*, you're fantastic," Emily says.

"Aww, I really like you. You're now my favorite kid named Emily."

"How many Emily's do you know?" she asks.

"Well, there's you." Hope holds up a finger. She stares off into the distance as she devours her ice cream cone. "Nah, just you."

Emily sassily smiles. "Well, I guess you're my favorite adult named Hope."

"Oh my God, you're so cheeky!" Hope turns to me and smiles. "I love it." Emily is lapping up the attention. "Crap, I have to go. Nice meeting you both. Emily, you and I are soul sisters and the next time you're back in town, someone here will have my number. Call me so we can hang out."

"Okay," Emily eagerly replies. "Thank you for the ice cream cone, and bye."

"Do you need a lift home, Gran?"

"Tabitha will be on her way to pick me up."

"Okay." She turns to Emily. "See ya, kid." Hope jogs away leaving Emily, May, and me.

"I'm afraid it's my turn to leave too. Since the stroke, I find I get tired easily."

"Do you need help?" Emily asks as she speeds up eating her cone so she can help May.

"Not at all."

"Maybe we should head back to the B&B," I say to Emily. "We've had a pretty long day."

"When are you heading back home again?" May asks.

"We'll be leaving fairly early tomorrow. It's a long drive back, so I think we'll head back after breakfast."

"Do you have your phone on you?"

"I do. Hang on, it's in my bag." I rustle through it and find my phone. Turning it on, I find a couple of messages from Tash saying how much she misses us and to hurry home. "It's been nice having this off for most of the time we've been here."

"Take my number," May blurts her number. "I'm always available to talk. And here, enter your number on mine, too. I want to be able to call you anytime I want. And you better answer." She points her skinny finger at me.

"I will." I make a cross over my chest. "Thank you," I say with genuine heart. May is a beautiful old lady who's so far advanced for her era. "Well." Emily and I both stand awkwardly. "This has been refreshing and what my heart and soul needed. Thank you."

"Every six weeks we hold a festival." May lifts her hands in surrender. "I'm just saying..."

"Can we come back?" Emily asks. "Wait, do you know what the next festival will be about?" She looks to May for answers.

"I do believe it'll be the snow cone festival."

"Snow cones?" my voice pitch increases in surprise.

"Any excuse for the town to come together," May replies.

That really is a beautiful thing. "May, thank you for..." I pause to think about what I'm thanking her for. "...being you."

"I'll see you both again, soon."

"Bye." Emily waves as we walk away and head toward the car. "I like it here, Mom."

"Surprisingly, so do I. It's so relaxed."

"See you next time," a woman calls as she walks past us.

"Bye," Emily and I reply in unison to the stranger.

"Mom, even though I really like it here, I can't wait to get home."

I sling my arm over her shoulder and give her a kiss on the side of the head. "Me too."

I've liked being here, but there's a huge part of me that's missing Bennett. In an ideal world, we'd be able to be together.

This is anything but an ideal world.

I have to forget about him, and the short time we shared together. I need to push all of the feelings I was developing for him so far down that they'll never see the light of day again.

After all, he *is* the president.

And I'm the furthest thing from being first lady material.

Chapter Sixteen

Bennett

"I feel lost," Liam says as he struts into my office.

"I have plenty of work for you if you want it," I reply as I take my glasses off and relax back in my chair. "I must admit, it's been unusually quiet. I don't think we've had a day like this since we've taken office."

"It feels almost like the calm before the storm." Liam chuckles and takes a seat on the sofa in my office. His leg bounces as he reclines and places his hands on his head.

There's a tense silence in the office making me uncomfortable. "What is it?"

Liam clicks his tongue to the roof of his mouth. "What's happening with Reece?"

"I told you, it's over. We're done."

"You *do* know you've been a miserable bastard for days now, right?"

"It's the shooting, it…" Liam's brows lift as he nods slowly. "You don't think it was the shooting?"

Liam lowers his arms and slowly raises his shoulders. "If you say it was the shooting, then that's what it is."

Closing my eyes, I pinch the bridge of my nose. "I can't stop thinking about her, Liam."

"If you weren't the president, I'd be telling you to screw what anyone else thinks and to do what's right for the both of you."

"But," I add, waiting for his reply.

"I don't need to tell you, Bennett. If this is leaked, your career is over. The people won't be able to see past it. Regardless of what you do and what happens, you'll forever be known as the president who was with a prostitute." My eyes flick up to Liam, angry at his words. He holds his hands up in surrender and shakes his head. "That's how you're going to be remembered. Not to mention Kathryn was so loved by the American public that anyone you choose to be with after her will mean they'll be closely scrutinized and viciously compared to Kathryn."

I look up to the ceiling and sigh. "I don't know what to do."

"As your chief of staff, I can only recommend you be cautious of who you let into your life. As your best friend, I'd tell you to do what makes you happy. Does Reece make you happy?"

"I like her," I reply.

"But, does she make you happy?"

It takes me a few seconds to reply. "More than I ever thought."

"Then you're stuck. Because if you go for it, you're done in politics forever. But if you don't go for it, you run the risk of losing Reece. I guess the question is, which one can you live without? Politics or Reece?"

"Do you think it hurts me that I'm one of only six presidents who haven't fathered a child?"

"In this case, I think that's what might save you if people find out."

"Save me?" I scoff knowing I'd be torn apart by every single person who had an opinion on my personal life.

"If you and Kathryn had a child, and you brought Reece into the mix, you'd be crucified, as would Reece. At least you don't have a child to draw into the middle of this."

"But Reece has a daughter." That worry has been on my mind from the very moment I knew I was developing feelings for her.

"Unfortunately, Reece and her daughter aren't your responsibility."

My eyes focus in on Liam. My jaw tenses as I clench my hands together, irritated by his words. "Don't," I warn.

"Reece is old enough to look after herself."

"Emily is only ten, Liam. She had no idea who I was when I..."

"Wait. You met the kid?" Liam asks as he shifts forward on the sofa. "Shit, Bennett. When did this happen?"

"Yes, I met her," I reply matching his tone. "Emily is none of your damn business."

He stands from the sofa and paces back and forth in front of my desk. "I hate to tell you, Bennett, but this whole thing is my damn business."

"You'll watch your mouth," I caution.

"Are you kidding me? I'm trying to protect you from yourself."

"What the fuck?" I stand with enough force to tip my chair backward. "Protect me from myself?" I yell as I round the table, ready to confront him.

"Yes, protect you from yourself because you've decided to fall in love with a fucking prostitute, Bennett." He pulls his shoulders back and stands up to me.

"You'll speak about Reece with respect." I lift my finger and point at him.

"Why, what are you going to do?" he pushes in a condescending tone.

I don't know what comes over me, my right-hand balls into a fist and I take a swing at Liam, making contact with his jaw. Liam's head angles to the left as he takes several steps back. The door opens and Mark and several of the other Secret Service agents are in here with their guns drawn. I step back and shake my head at them. "Leave," I instruct Mark and his team.

He quickly flicks his gaze between Liam and me and motions his team out of my office. I walk over to my cabinet and pour both Liam and me a scotch. Handing one to him, I throw mine back in one movement. Liam takes the drink, and silently walks over to sit on the arm of the sofa again. He nurses the drink as he looks down at the floor. He finally lifts the glass and finishes it in one swallow. "We've been friends for as long as I can remember, and if you can't take those words from me, how are you going to react if this gets out?"

I sit opposite Liam. "I'm sorry," I say, truly ashamed of my temper. "I don't know why I did that."

"Because you've fallen for her."

"And I can't have her," I add.

"Maybe you need to consider announcing your resignation once this term has been completed."

"I should be able to have both," I say, although in my heart, I know I have to make the decision. "I was an asshole to her when she reached out after the shooting."

"Bad enough for you not to redeem yourself?"

I chew on the inside of my cheek. "She's dragged her ass out of the worst of situations to make a life for herself and her daughter, and I treated her like..." I pause, hating myself for the words about to tumble out of my mouth. "Like a prostitute."

"What do you want, Bennett? What's more important to you?"

I lower my chin and look down at the carpet beneath my shoes. "I shouldn't have to choose."

"Do you know what? If you were a CEO of a company, it would make maybe page five of the newspaper if it were found out. But you're not CEO of a company. You're the president of the United States, and if it's discovered, it'll be on the front page of every newspaper and every social media site. Every person in the world will have an opinion."

"I know." My throat constricts with worry for Reece and Emily. I pull my shoulders back and lift my chin. "It's over."

"Are you sure?"

"Liam, you've been my best friend since I can remember. You, of all people, should know if I say it's over, it's over. I can't put either of them through the toxic dissection from the public. I'm fine with whatever happens to me, but I won't have them torn apart by relentless reporters."

"The reporters are the least of their problems, and you know it."

I exhale loudly and slowly nod. "I know. They'll never have a moment of peace, which is why it *has to* be over." I hate having to even think about never seeing Reece again. But it's what I have to do to keep her and Emily safe.

Liam stands and moves past me. He stops to the side and places his hand on my shoulder. "I'm sorry you have to make this decision, but it's for the best."

"Yeah, it is."

Liam pats my shoulder twice and heads toward the door. "I'll see you tomorrow, Mr. President." He's switched from best friend to chief of staff.

"Thank you, Liam." He looks at me and nods a silent, *I've got your back.*

No quicker than he closes the door, Jamie opens the one leading out to where he and Esther work. "Mr. President," he announces when he enters my office. I take a second to compose myself before turning my attention to Jamie. "You have that dinner with Vice President Massey."

"Thank you." I stand and walk over to my chair, grab my suit jacket, and shrug into it. Jamie is already packing my laptop and papers into my briefcase. Jamie and I walk out into the foyer where Mark is already waiting for me.

I need to push Reece out of my mind. I signed up to be president, under constant scrutiny from the American public. Reece didn't. And for that very reason, we can't be together.

<hr>

The loud banging wakes me from my sleep. I turn on the bedside lamp and sit up in bed. Looking at the clock, I have to blink several times for my eyes to adjust. It takes me a moment to focus on the time, and when the banging happens again, I know I wasn't dreaming. "Yeah," I call as I sit on the side of the bed and rub my hand over my eyes.

"Mr. President," Liam announces as he opens the door to my room.

"What is it?" A quick scan of his body tells me he's been home and changed because he's wearing a new suit. "What happened?" I'm already on my feet and looking for suitable attire. I can't exactly approach whatever's happened in my boxer briefs.

Liam doesn't speak, he hands me his tablet and taps it to life.

All the air leaves my body as I take a step backward and sit on the edge of the bed.

Fuck.

Reece

"Yeah?" I answer my phone in a groggy voice without even checking who's calling.

"Reece," I instantly recognize Bennett's deep voice and open my eyes.

"Mr. President," I reply, knowing we're well and truly finished.

"Where's Emily?" he asks, his voice dripping with worry.

"Why?" I jump out of bed and start pulling my jeans on. "Why, Bennett? What's happened?" My skin pebbles with sheer terror as every possible worst-case scenario plays over and over in my head. "Bennett! What's going on?" A lump of bile shoots to the back of my throat, and I'm about to lose it if...

"Turn on the news," he says.

I run to the back room, find the remote and turn on the TV, keeping the volume low. I feel the blood draining from my body as I flick through news channel after news channel. All of them have the same breaking story.

The words are blunt and callous with no remorse civility to them at all. *The president and his whore.* A picture of me is splattered across every single station I switch to. I sink to the floor, staring at the disgusting words flashing on the screen. "Oh..." My legs tremble as all the air leaves my lungs, completely winding me. "Emily," I whisper as I hang up and frantically try to call her. No, wait, what am I doing? I shouldn't call her. No, um. I need to go and get her; I can't leave her at school. This is erupting and she's going to be on the receiving end of so many things. She doesn't know what I do. I feel like I'm about to throw up. I run into the bathroom, flip the lid and heave into the toilet. My stomach is tight as I keep dry-retching over and over again. Nothing but bile comes up.

With tears in my eyes, I run to the garage, but someone knocking on the front door startles me. I change direction and open the front door only to have the security guard from the gatehouse at the front of my gated community standing at the door. "Miss Maxwell, there are paparazzi at the gates asking for you."

"Oh my God," I whisper, entirely dumbfounded by how quickly these people found me. "Um."

"Do you need help?"

"I don't know," I earnestly reply, holding my hair back from my forehead.

"I'll wait out here in case you need me." I look behind him and he smiles kindly. "We've got it covered. Don't worry; they won't get up here."

"Thank you," I reply. "Can you stay here for a few minutes."

He nods and warmly says, "This isn't my first rodeo, ma'am. If you need help, I'm here for you."

"Thank you," I whisper. Closing the door, I try to think of what I need to do. I do the only thing I can, I call Tash. Her phone rings out, so I keep going until she finally answers.

"Why on earth are you calling me at stupid o'clock?"

"Tash," I manage to say through my heavy tears and constricted voice.

"Reece, what's wrong? Are you okay? Is Emily okay?" worry drips from her voice. "Is it Emily?"

"They know," I whisper.

"Who knows what? I'm on my way over."

"They know," I repeat in a smaller voice. "Turn on the TV."

"What?" I can hear a rustling of something, then Tash mumbles, "Oh fuck."

"Yeah." I can barely keep it together, there are so many things going on in my head. "The press has found me."

"Shit, what do you need me to do, Reece?" I shake my head, unable to think straight. "Reece?"

"Um." I swallow the lump in my throat and hold in my emotions. "Can you go and get Emily from school? Don't bring her here. Take her to your house. I'll call the school and tell them you're on your way to get her. Please, don't talk to anyone."

"I'm already getting changed."

"Thank you." I sink down the wall, running my free hand through my hair and gripping at the strands. "Don't bring her here."

"I promise you, I won't. Reece, how do they know?"

I shake my head as I lift my shoulders. "I don't know." My eyes sting from the tears threatening to fall. "Please, take care of my girl."

"I will. Hang on, I'm about to go outside, let me check that it's clear," Tash pauses, and I hear her front door creak open. I hold my breath, waiting for her reply. If the press has found her, then Emily won't be safe anywhere. "We're good." I exhale with relief. "Call the school and let them know I'm coming to get her."

I nod and wet my dry lips, still attempting to come to grips with what's happening. "Don't tell her anything until I can talk to her."

"What am I supposed to say, Reece? She's going to ask questions."

"Tell her I'll call her when you get back home. Can you send me a text when you have her, and when you're home?"

"Of course. I'm about to drive, so I'll go."

"Thank you, Tash."

"I'd do anything for you and Emily, you know that. Stay strong." She hangs up and I'm left sitting on the floor, powerless to protect my daughter.

I quickly call the school to inform them that Tash will be picking Emily up as there's been a family emergency. Thankfully, they don't ask any other questions, but I suspect they're going to know rather fast why. Especially when the press camps outside the school to snap pictures of Emily.

My phone is blowing up with phone calls from unknown numbers. In my gut I know it's the press wanting my side of the story. I need to speak with Bennett. I dial his cell. "Reece. Are you okay? Is Emily okay?"

"The security guard from the gatehouse is up here, he told me there's press and paparazzi down there."

"Where's Emily?"

"Tash is on her way to the school. She's picking her up. But, Bennett, what do we do?" There's a long pause. "Bennett?"

"I can't be seen with you at the moment, Reece." My brows lift with his cold words. "I'll send a car to get you and Emily, and I'll have them take you somewhere safe where you won't be harassed. But until I can do some damage control, I can't be seen with you. It's just not a wise move for me."

Shards of ice pierce my skin, causing a small tremor to tear through my body. "You can't be seen with me at the moment?" I ask in a small, eerily controlled voice.

"You have to understand, Reece, this is not good for me."

A humorless laugh rips through my lungs. "Not good for you? Did I hear you right?" Anger is quickly replacing my worry and fear. "Not good for you?" I repeat in an elevated voice.

"I'll have someone come and get you," he offers.

"Fuck you! Not good for you? You're sitting there worried about your job, but not giving a fucking shit about my and Emily's lives. Fuck you!"

"Reece, it's..."

"It's Miss Maxwell to you," I say coldly.

"Reece," he starts again.

"You know the blame and responsibility always falls on the woman. The man is forgiven. The public will feel sorry for you because your wife is dead and men have urges, while I'll be painted as the criminal because I sell my body for sex. You'll be unscathed, while I'll be villainized. Don't worry about me. I'll look after my family, because that's all I've ever done. You just sit there in your tower, surrounded by your Secret Service and loyal staff. Congratulations, Bennett, you've not only lost me, but you've also lost my vote. Fuck you, Mr. President, fuck you." I hang up and throw my phone on the sofa in boiling anger. He's hung me out to dry and doesn't give a damn about me or Emily. I can't deal with him at the moment.

I pace back and forth trying to think of what to do.

I head to the front door and open it. "Ma'am," the older security guard says. "Everything okay?"

"I need to get out of here."

"I can organize that," he says. "It'll take about twenty minutes. Does that work for you?"

Twenty minutes to pack clothes for Emily and me and to get out of here. "Yeah, it does. Thank you so much for your help."

"It's my pleasure, ma'am."

I close the door and run into my walk-in closet where my safe is. Opening it, I take out the emergency cash I have stashed. I pack a suitcase with what I need, then head into Emily's room to pack another suitcase with her clothes. I double-check everything, and when I'm ready, I roll the two suitcases out to the door. Opening it, I see there are now two security guards standing outside. The younger of the two turns and looks at me. "Are you ready?"

I quickly scan the neighborhood, and I'm relieved to find no one peeking out of their windows. Perhaps it's still too early for anyone to know. "I'm ready," I say.

"This is what we're going to do," the older of the two says. "You're going to have to trust me. You're going to get in the trunk of your car, which I'm going to drive out the gates. Ritchie here is going to follow us to a meeting point away from the paparazzi."

I crinkle my brow at him. "And you think this'll work?"

"It's worked in the past," he says and winks. "But time is of the essence here. If we don't get out now, there will be even more reporters at the gate. How many are down there?" he asks the younger one.

"There are two news vans, four reporters, and a few photographers."

"The longer we leave it, the worse it'll get," the older one says to me.

"I'm ready, tell me what to do."

The older one turns to the younger one. "You know where to go. Like last time."

The younger one nods and leaves, while the older one closes the front door. My stomach churns with worry. "Do you know why there's press out there?" I ask, trying to gauge the damage this is going to do in my neighborhood.

"I know," he says.

"Why are you being so nice to me then?"

He holds his hand out for the keys to my car. "Because it's none of my business what you do for a living, Miss Maxwell."

"But, the president—"

"Is the one who should be held accountable. You've lived in this community for years and there has never been a problem with you. You have to do what you have to in order to provide for your little girl. I can't fault a person for that." He pops the trunk open. "Now, at the risk of sounding like a serial killer, get in the trunk." He pointedly looks at the empty space.

"Thank you." I step in and give him a hug before climbing into my trunk. Thankfully, I can bend like a pretzel and the trunk is fairly spacious.

"I'll be putting your luggage on the back seat." He closes the lid, and in this moment I'm forced to come to terms with this horrible situation. My mind won't stop spinning, trying to figure out who would've tipped off the press. Why did they do it? Have I been followed? Could it have been Grayson? The car moves for what feels like hours, but in fact it's probably been five minutes before it stops. I hear footsteps, then the trunk lid opens. "I hope I didn't hurt you," he says as he extends his hand to help me out.

"I can't thank you enough for what you've done."

He smiles proudly. "I'll look after your house while you're gone. But you look after that little girl and yourself. And, I'm sorry for the journey ahead for you." His kind eyes sparkle even under this moonless sky.

"How are you going to get back?" I ask as I look around attempting to get my bearings. "Oh." I point to the security car about fifty yards down the street. "What you've done..."

"I've done it for people I don't like, and I've always liked you."

I hug him before I walk to the driver's side and slide into my car. As I pull away, I look in the mirror to see him walking toward the security car. That man, whose name I don't even know, has shown me more kindness in one hour than my own mother ever showed me in a lifetime.

I need a plan of attack. A phone call snaps me out of my chaotic thoughts. I look at the number on the screen and see it's Emily's school. "Hello?" I answer, surprised, because I only spoke to them less than an hour ago.

"Miss Maxwell, this is Justin Smith, the principal."

I'm confused because I've already cleared with them that Tash will be picking Emily up. "I've already given my permission for Tash to take Emily out of school."

"Yes, that's not what I'm calling for," he says in his snooty, stuck-up voice.

"How can I help you?"

"I'm afraid Emily won't be able to return to the school."

"What? Why?"

He clears his throat. "This is a school that has an elevated standard of prestige and class, and you didn't disclose your...occupation to us when you enrolled Emily. We don't condone or support *people* who are flamboyant."

"Are you saying that Emily has been a problem student?"

"No, Miss Maxwell, this is solely based on you and your lifestyle choices."

"You're right, Emily doesn't belong somewhere with a principal who is so self-righteous. Must be nice to sit on your throne of lies." I smirk at the dig. "I'm sure your wife knows all about your..." I pause for dramatic effect. "*Lifestyle choices*."

"Miss Maxwell," his voice suddenly escalates.

"Thank you." I press the end call button on the screen. "Fucking hypocrite." He must not recall the time he tried to pick me up when I was at a dinner with a client. He slid into the available seat beside me while I was at the bar and tried to give me his number. He looked me dead in the eyes and asked if I'd care to join him and his *male* companion for drinks, *or more*.

I drive in a daze, not sure where I'm going or what else life is about to throw at me. My phone rings, and I groan as I look at the number. "You've got her?" I ask Tash.

"Yeah, she's sleepy, but I have her."

"Mommy, are you okay?" Emily asks.

I smile with relief when I hear Emily's sweet voice, I'm so glad Tash has her. "Yeah, I'm okay. But, in the morning we need to have a conversation."

"Alright."

"Tash," I say.

"Yeah?"

"Do you mind if Emily and I crash at your place for the night."

"Why are you even asking? Of course, that's fine."

"Thank you."

"Love you, Mom."

"Love you too, sweetie." I hang up and rest my head back on the seat as I drive toward Tash's house. Once I arrive, I drive past her house once, then park down the street a safe distance away. I'm too wired to fall asleep, so I keep an eye on any cars that drive down here. I'm grateful when she pulls up to her house. I start the car and drive toward her. Tash motions for me to put my car in the garage, and she parks on the driveway. "Thank you for doing this." Emily is asleep on the front seat, so I quietly open the door, release her seat belt and carry her into Tash's house.

"Put her in the guest room," Tash says.

I carefully lay Emily on the bed, take off her shoes and place the covers over her. When I walk out into the family room, Tash already has the hard liquor out. I slump down into the chair and let out a long breath. "I don't know what I'm going to do, Tash."

"Look, you can stay here for as long as you like."

"No, we can't. The press will eventually figure out where you live, and they'll be here and at the bookstore harassing you."

"Don't worry about me. I can look after myself. Have you got any idea who would've leaked this?" I shake my head slowly, pick up the glass with the liquor and throw it back. "If you're more comfortable, I can move to your house and you can stay here."

"Why would I do that, Tash?"

"You bought this for me." She looks around. "It's the least I can do."

I reach across the table and place my hand over hers. "Do you forget the night you saw me checking on Emily because we were living in our piece of shit car? And you asked me to dinner, and told me your tiny little one-bedroom flat was now my and Emily's home?"

Tash looks down at her empty glass. She shakes her head as tears well in her eyes. "It's what anyone would've done."

"No, it's not. It's because of you I've been able to achieve everything that I have. I'll never ask you to leave here, unless you want to buy a new house, then I'll buy that for you too."

Tash looks over toward the hallway and sighs. "This is a mess, and I don't know how to help you."

"Do me a favor, if the press start sniffing around, tell them you had no idea that I'm an escort."

"What?" Her brows furrow. "Why would I say that?"

"You need to be protected too, Tash."

"Fuck that! I'm proud of you, Reece. You should hold your head up with pride. Don't you dare let them make you feel ashamed, because I'm not. But don't worry; my official statement will be, 'no comment.'"

"I'm not asking you to do this."

It's her turn to reach out and place her hand over my arm, giving me a gentle squeeze. "You don't ever have to ask me to do anything. I'll always straighten your crown and protect your back. Because that's what queens do."

I stifle a sniffle and choke up with how beautiful Tash is. "Thank you." Standing, I bend and give Tash a kiss on the cheek. "I'm going to try and get some sleep because the morning will bring difficult conversations, and some hard decisions."

"Love you, Reece."

I look over my shoulder as I head toward the guest room where Emily is. "Love you, too." I offer Tash a smile before disappearing into the room.

I toe off my shoes and climb into bed beside Emily.

My mind won't stop, but my eyes are stinging from exhaustion. Maybe after a few hours' sleep I'll be able to think straight.

Who am I kidding? This is going to get a lot worse before it gets better.

I curl up behind Emily, close my eyes and try to find a moment of peace.

S itting in my office, the team are all scrambling, trying to spin this positively.

"I think you're going to have to address this, Mr. President," Alisha says.

"The president deeply regrets..." Elizabeth starts as she outwardly pens my speech.

"No, I don't deeply regret being with Reece," I say as I stare at them.

"You have to say something about this," Gavin, my Deputy Communications Director, says.

"If you say nothing, then you're allowing yourself to be a target all around the world," Alisha agrees with Gavin.

"Presidents and sex scandals isn't something new," Liam says.

"Yes, you're correct, but we're talking about *our* president who we fought to get elected into the White House," Alisha argues. "We need to get ahead of this and keep the upper hand on the narrative, and we need the American people, and the world to see it was a temporary lapse of judgement. We can push forward with Medicare and..."

"No," I repeat. "This wasn't a temporary lapse of judgment."

"Mr. President, we can't have you stand up there and tell people you hired an escort and expect them to deal with it," Gavin urges. "This is all about how we spin it. We can make it appear like you're lonely and craved female companionship or the world will tear it apart and make you look like a sleazy predator."

I let out a long breath before turning to Alison. "What do you think, Alison?"

She purses her lips together and shakes her head. "I think whatever you say is going to be torn apart."

"Do you think it's best if we don't comment on this now?" Liam asks. "You're the one who knows the press room, Alison."

"I think if you go out now with a half-hearted apology, you're going to be ripped apart and you'll lose the respect of the people."

I nod as I link my hands together and lower my chin to look at the carpet in my office.

"The president is in deep reflection," Alison says as if she's addressing the press corp.

"No, I'm not," I say as I shake my head. "I'm not in deep reflection, and I don't regret it."

"You can't stand on that podium and tell people you don't regret sleeping with an escort. That won't work for the American people," Alisha argues.

"Alisha," Liam scolds with an undeniable tone of dissatisfaction.

"Liam." I hold my hand up to him. I'm making sure I keep the dynamic in the room as honest as possible. "I need to hear from everyone."

Liam will protect me, I have no doubt, but I can't have the staff too afraid to openly discuss this. "Mr. President, the American people will be demanding to know why you went this route," Alisha says.

"Because he's the president, and going to a bar to meet someone is out of the question," Liam replies.

Mark opens the door and stands in his rigid form. I get up and walk over to him while my advisors all try and figure out the best way forward. "Did you get her out safely?" I ask Mark.

"Mr. President, she was already gone."

"Gone? What do you mean?"

"I sent a team, including Grayson, and she'd already left. He said it appears she packed a bag for herself and her daughter, and has left. Her car is gone too." He stands without saying anything else.

"Can you find her?"

"I can find anyone," he replies confidently.

I take a step back and run my hands through my hair. I said some horrible things to Reece, and I need her to know that was a knee-jerk reaction. "I'll let you know."

Mark quietly leaves my office, and I head back over to sit with my advisors. Liam glances toward the door, then back to me, silently asking if everything is okay. I give him a nod and attempt to focus on what my advisors are throwing around.

Where is Reece? Has she gone to Tash's to hide? What about Emily? Is Emily okay?

"Mr. President?" Alison asks.

"Sorry, what?" I reply trying to listen, but all my mind can think about is Reece and Emily's safety. "Give me a minute." I stand and walk to the door and open it. Mark is standing by the door. "Mark."

"Sir."

"Have you checked her friend Tash's house?"

"No, sir. They were under instructions to report back to me once they reached her house."

The muscles in my neck strain as I run my hand through my hair. Even though I was a total dick to her, I also need to make sure she's safe. She can't fend for herself with this broad scale clusterfuck. She's not prepared. "Check the friend's house, and if she's not there..." I run my tongue over my teeth. "Do whatever you have to in order to find her." With all the power of the world at my fingertips, I'm going to find her and protect her.

"Yes, sir." Mark immediately turns to one of his team and clearly gives them instructions as I return to the office.

"Mr. President," Alison says as I sit.

"Our official policy is to not comment on my damn personal life," I say with determination.

"But—"

"That's it, guys," Liam interrupts Alison.

"Thank you," they all echo, shuffling out of my office.

Liam stays seated, not moving. The door closes, giving us a moment. "She's gone, hasn't she?"

"Yeah."

"What do you want to do?"

"I've instructed Mark to find her." I can feel the tightness in my jaw where I haven't stopped grinding my teeth together. "Are we any closer to the leak?"

"I have a meeting with the reporter who broke the story, but I don't think he's going to be giving anything up."

"Do you think it was someone here?" I stiffen in my seat, as thoughts of suspicion run through my mind. I'd hate to think one of my staff would do this.

"It could've been anyone. There's nothing concrete, but clearly someone was given information and with some digging, they found out."

I look down at the rug with the presidential seal in my office. Specifically, to the eagle's talons holding the olive branch, a marker of peace. This situation has invoked a cacophony of discord and mistrust. "Find out what you can."

"I will."

"Liam," I call. He turns and waits. "Thank you. I know this must be difficult for you."

The right side of his lip slightly tugs into a smirk. "You've got the weight of the world on your shoulders, who you sleep with shouldn't even play part in this." He shakes his head and scoffs. "That's fucked." He turns and leaves the office.

I have to agree with Liam. It *is* fucked, and never in a million years did I think I'd ever find myself here.

But I can handle the political turmoil that's going to come. My concern is Reece. I need to find her, or at the very least, call and speak with her. I rub at my temples, stressed and worried.

• ——————— ✹ ——————— •

Reece

"Mom, your phone." Emily nudges my arm before collapsing back asleep in a nanosecond.

"I'm awake," I say as I sit up and clear my groggy throat. I look at the time and grunt. I've barely had three hours of broken sleep. My phone tells me I've got over a hundred missed calls, along with a ton of emails and messages. I scan through the numbers, and nearly all of them are unknown to me. Bennett has called me a handful of times, but he made his position clear with me.

I can't be seen with you, easily translates to *you're on your own*. My phone rings again, and this time I see May's name pop up. I push the covers off and tiptoe out of the guest room and go into the kitchen. "Hello?" I whisper trying not to wake Emily or Tash.

"Seems you got yourself into a bit of a pickle there, lady."

"Oh no. You've seen?"

"I think most of the population of the world has seen." My stomach churns and flips. "Are you and that kid of yours safe?"

"Define safe." I let out a humorless chuckle. "We're at my best friend's house, but I know it's only a matter of time before the press finds me. It won't take long." I lean against the kitchen counter and run my hand through my hair.

"Get your butts down here. I have a retreat on my farm, and at the moment, no one's using it."

I smile at her beautiful, generous offer. "Thank you, but—"

"Nope, I'm cutting you off right now. This town is built on integrity and loyalty. I can tell you no one here will say a word about you being here. Pack your car, and your kid, and get down here."

"May, I really couldn't impose. If the media finds out..."

"They won't. I'll text you my address, and I expect to see you here by lunchtime."

I pull the phone away from my ear to double-check the time again. "It's five in the morning."

"Yep. Get out of there now, before they find you, because once they do there's no chance of you or Emily escaping them."

I look down at my bare toes on the kitchen tiles. "Yes, you're right."

"Of course, I am. You can stay here for as long as you need. I know a few of the teachers in town and they owe me favors. They can homeschool Emily."

"My own mother tossed me aside like I was nothing. I met you for all of an hour, and now you're treating me like your blood runs through my veins," my voice cracks as I try to hold in my emotions.

"Sometimes, we all need help. I'll see you soon." May hangs up without another word, leaving me speechless at her incredible kindness. I set to making a fresh pot of coffee because I know I'm going to have to wake Tash to ask her opinion of May's offer.

It doesn't take her long to walk out to the kitchen in her pajamas, yawning. "Why are you up so early?"

"My phone has been blowing up."

"I'm sorry." She walks over to me and wraps me in her arms. "This is fucked."

"Yeah, it is." She pulls away and reaches for two coffee mugs as the coffee brews. "May called me."

"May?" She crinkles her brows. "Oh, the old lady from Hope River, right?"

"Yeah, that's her. She called me, and invited Emily and me to hang out down there for a while."

"I think you should go," Tash responds without a doubt. "How long do you think it's going to take before the press finds you and harasses you?"

I pour the coffee and hand Tash hers before wrapping mine in my hands. "Bennett's been calling, but I'm not answering any of his calls."

"What happened with him?" I give her the abridged version of what happened, and when I finish, Tash pulls her shoulders back as she lifts her head. "Next time he calls, I'll deal with him."

I sip on my coffee as I stare at the floor. "I think it's a good idea if Emily and I head to Hope River. We can lay low for a little while, and I can try to figure out what to do."

"You know I love you and Emily, and I'd do anything for you both. But, in this case, I absolutely think it's the right thing to do."

"Okay then." I place my near empty coffee mug on the counter. "I should get Emily up and get her ready. She and I need to have a conversation about everything." There's a heavy, solemn feel to the air.

"Actually." Tash purses her lips together as she stares at me. "I have an idea."

"What?"

"Let me get dressed and go fill my car, and we'll swap cars and phones. That way if anything gets tracked back, the trail ends here. Do you have cash?"

"No, I can't ask you to do that, Tash. You've done so much already."

"Don't be a turd," she says breaking the seriousness of everything.

I can't help but lightly chuckle. "Thank you, Tash."

"Let me get dressed and I'll go out and gas my car up while you get Emily up." She tips the rest of her coffee out and rinses her mug before disappearing into her bedroom.

I take several deep breaths knowing these next few hours are going to be difficult to explain to Emily. I walk into the guest room, and sit on the edge of the bed staring at Emily. I hear the front door open, then close. "Emily," I say as I gently rouse her from her sleep.

"Hmmm?" she grumbles and rolls over.

"You have to wake up."

"Why?"

"Because we're going somewhere."

"Where are we going?" She rolls over again, places her hands under her head and blinks at me several times.

I tuck some of her loose hair behind her ear and smile. "We're leaving here for a little while."

"Why? What's happened?"

"I promise I'll tell you everything in the car, but I need you to get up now and get ready for us to leave."

Emily's eyes redden. "Have I done something bad?"

"No, sweetheart, not at all."

"Have *you* done something bad?"

My throat constricts as I stare at my little girl. "No, I haven't, but again, I need you to get ready because we have to go really soon."

Emily yawns, but nods her head. "Okay, Mom." She pushes the covers back and sits beside me on the bed. Emily lays her head on my shoulder, and I kiss the top of her head. "Love you." She stands with a moan and heads into the bathroom.

I quickly make the bed, then grab our suitcases to get a change of clothes for both of us. When she comes out, I pointedly look at the bed. "Fresh clothes for you. What do you want for breakfast?"

"It's too early to eat."

"Okay." I kiss the top of her head again, take my clothes and head into the bathroom to change. By the time I get out of the bathroom, Emily is dressed and curled up on the bed.

I hear the front door and then hear Tash call, "I'm back."

"That was quick," I say as I walk out to find her in the family room.

"Yeah, I only needed to top it up. Now, just so you know." She looks over my shoulder for Emily.

"She's laying down," I whisper.

"Okay, I need you to know the story is everywhere."

I close my eyes and rub at the tension across my eyebrows. "I feel sick."

"Well, pull it together for Emily. You can do this, Reece." Her warm arms wrap me in a tight embrace. "In the car there's a couple of bottles of water, some snacks, and I bought a burner phone for you too. I thought if we swap phones, someone will be able to track you down. This is the safest way."

I open my eyes and step back. "Are you sure you're not FBI? Who thinks of things like that?"

She taps her nose and smiles. "I got you covered, girl. If you need to stop for gas, try to do it while it's daylight. I'll give you a hat you can wear with your glasses, and hopefully no one will recognize you."

"You're scaring the shit out of me, Tash."

"I own a bookstore, I read a lot of crime and thriller books. And romance," she quickly adds before shaking her hand at me. "I'm glad I like my crime and thriller books now."

"What about romance?"

"Oh, I'm living vicariously through them. Maybe one day, I'll be swept off my feet by my brother's best friend." I screw my nose up at her. "Not that I have a brother." Tash shrugs. "But you have to leave. Like right now."

"Mom," Emily says.

"I'm gonna miss you, squirt." Tash walks over to Emily, envelops her in a hug and plants kisses all over Emily's face.

"Aren't we coming back?" Emily asks. Her brown eyes fill with tears as I see pain coursing through her.

"We will, just not for a little while."

"Mommy, what's going on?" Emily asks from the safety of Tash's arms.

I flick my gaze to Tash before settling a loving look on Emily. "I'll explain in the car."

"Okay, I'll see you both real soon." Tash kisses Emily on the head, before she walks us to the front door and opens it. She checks and gives me the thumbs up.

Handing me the fob to her car, I pick up the bags and walk toward her car. I look over my shoulder at Tash and can feel my own tears threatening to fall. "We're taking Tash's car, Emily."

"Why?"

I unlock the car and place our bags on the back seat. "Come on." Emily sits in the front and buckles in. Once we're away from Tash's house, I try to prepare myself for the conversation we're about to have.

"What about school?"

"You're no longer going to that school."

"Why?"

"The principal called and said you can't attend anymore."

"What?" her little voice breaks my heart. "Did I do something wrong?"

"No!" I reply, still furious over the hypocrisy. "No, you didn't."

"Then why can't I go back? What did I do? Can I be better?"

"Emily, it's because of me."

There's a long pause as she stares out the front window. "You? Did you say something mean?"

"No, not at all."

"I don't understand what's happening, Mom. What did you do to make the principal say I can't go back? Did you do something to him?"

"Not directly to him."

"Mommy," her voice trembles. "I don't understand."

I take a deep breath, trying to find the right words. But, there aren't any right words. "Emily, do you know what a prostitute is?"

"Yeah, it's a lady or man who sells their body for sex."

I take another breath and slowly nod. "In America, there's only one state where being a prostitute is legal, and it's only legal in parts of that state. Everywhere else, it's against the law."

I chance a glance at Emily. She's chewing on her lip as she attempts to figure out what this has to do with us. "So? What does this have to do with you?"

"You know how I told you I work at a restaurant?"

"Yeah?"

"Well, I don't work at a restaurant," I say slowly, really hating that we're discussing this while she's still so young. Emily's brows crinkle together.

"Then where do you work?"

"I'm an escort."

"What's that? Are you a prostitute too?"

"A prostitute sells their body for money, while an escort sells their time for money. Some men pay me for sex, while others pay me to just go to dinner with them, or to sit with them so they can have company."

Emily crinkles her brows and purses her lips together. "I don't understand, are you prostitute or not?"

"Some people will say yes; some people will say no."

"What do you say? Are you, or aren't you?" her question is innocent, yet quite confrontational too.

"I sell my time, and when I have sex with these men, then yes, I'm a prostitute. But, I'm an escort."

There's another drawn out stint of silence. "Why do you do it?"

"Because I enjoy sex, and the money is very good."

Emily slowly nods. "And my school found out you're an escort, and they threw me out because of it?" she naïvely asks.

"Not exactly."

She slowly shrugs and stares at me. "I don't understand."

"One of my clients is Bennett."

"I like him," Emily says.

"Yeah, me too. But, he's the president."

"Why does that matter?"

"The president of the United States paid me for my time, during which we had sex."

"Aha." Emily becomes silent for a moment. "Are you in trouble because he paid you to do something that's not allowed?"

"Yes."

"So, does that mean because he's the one who paid you that he's in more trouble than you?"

"I'm not entirely sure what's going to happen to Bennett."

"What did he say when you talked to him?"

My hands tighten around the wheel as I clench my jaw. "We're not exactly talking."

"Didn't you say you like him though? How many times did you see him? Did you have sex with him all the time?"

"I do like him. *Liked.* Like. I don't know."

"Are you in trouble because you have a job that's not allowed?"

I shake my head. "I'm in trouble because I had sex with the president."

"I really don't understand what's happening, Mom. If you're in trouble, then he should be too because he's the one who paid you. Right?"

"It doesn't always work like that."

"Why? Is it because you're a woman?" I'm speechless and unable to answer her question. "Is it only my school who knows?"

"No, baby. The whole world does. That's why we're driving Tash's car and going to Hope River. We need to lay low for a little while until I can figure out what to do."

"Wait? We're hiding? What'll happen if people find us? Will they hurt us?" Emily starts fidgeting in the seat.

"No one is going to hurt us," I say with assurance. Though in the pit of my stomach, I have no idea what anyone is capable of. "We're going to stay with May for a little while."

"What about my friends?"

"I'm sorry, Emily, but for now, you can't even turn your phone on. We need to be extra careful until I can figure this out."

"Will Bennett hurt us?"

"No, not at all."

"We're in Tash's car because you don't want anyone to find us, right?" My fingers relax around the wheel as I nod. "Why is being a prostitute not allowed?"

"I have no idea why it's illegal, especially in today's day and age. But, I guess it has to do with people and what they think is morally right."

"Morally?" Emily asks. "What does morally mean?"

"Um, best way I can describe it is what society thinks is acceptable. And, they don't think selling your body should be acceptable."

There's another long pause, and I gather that Emily is thinking about our conversation. "Has anyone forced you to do this?"

Loaded question, Emily. "No one has forced me to do this."

"And you said you do it because you like sex, and the money is good."

"Yeah."

"Why can't you get a job that pays the same as what you're getting paid by these men?"

"I make more in one day than most people make in a month."

"What about Bennett?"

"What about Bennett?" I repeat her question back to her.

"He knows what you do?"

"Yeah, because he hired me to..." I take a breath, not really sure how far to go with this with her.

"To have sex with him?"

"Yeah," I let out a sigh.

"Sex is supposed to be private, isn't it?"

"It's whatever the people involved want it to be. For my clients, yes, it's private."

"Then what does it matter if Bennett paid you to have sex? If no one forced you to do it, and Bennett knew that by paying you he'd be buying your company, then what business is it of anyone else's?"

"Because of the position Bennett holds. The entire world knows who he is."

"And now they know who you are too."

A low grumble escapes past my lips. "Yes. This is why we need to get away from it all for a little while."

Emily lifts her hand and rubs it on my arm. "I'm sorry, Mom. If the world knew how awesome you are, maybe they'd leave you alone."

I turn and briefly smile at Emily. "Maybe some people will leave me alone, but most everyone will have an opinion."

"You're not hurting anyone, so I can't see why it's anyone's business."

I place my hand on her thigh and give her a gentle squeeze. "Thank you, Emily, but it's not that simple."

"Well, I support you, Mom. You're doing the best you can. Besides, if it gets me out of school for a while, then I'm okay with that."

This conversation has gone a lot smoother than I thought it would've. I guess the only thing left now, is to wait this out and make a plan to move on with our lives. One thing I know for sure though. Emily is a lot more mature and open-minded than I thought she would've been.

If I'm going to be making decisions for the both of us, she'll have a say in it too.

Chapter Eighteen

Bennett

Reece hasn't answered any of my calls, and I'm going out of my mind crazy not knowing where she is. I hit dial on her phone again, this time she answers. "Where the fuck are you?" I snap without giving her a moment to actually speak.

"I beg your pardon?"

"Wait, this isn't Reece. Who is it?"

"Who's this?" the woman matches my tone.

"Who's this?" I throw right back at her. She doesn't respond, forcing me to speak again. "Hello?"

"You haven't answered my question. Who are you?"

"It's um..." I swallow the lump in my throat. "Where's Reece?"

"If you don't tell me who this is, I'm going to hang up."

"It's the president," I reply with confidence. The woman doesn't respond. "Hello?"

"I'm here," she says with a clipped tone. "Why are you calling?"

Her attitude takes me aback. "Is this Tash?"

"It is. What do you want?"

"I need to speak with Reece."

"Good for you. But, I'm not giving her the phone. You hurt her."

I close my eyes and lean back in my chair. "May I speak with Reece, please?"

"No, you can't." Tash is one headstrong woman.

"I need to speak with her, Tash."

"That sounds like a 'you' problem," she snaps.

"I'll remind you who you're speaking with," I warn.

"A jackass who threw her under the bus."

Both Tash's and my tensions are running at an all-time high. "Tash..."

She cuts me off. "What?" I really like her, she's deeply protective of Reece and Emily.

I pull myself together and get a grip on my frustrations. "Is she with you?"

"No." Tash is giving me nothing.

"Do you know where she is?" Again, there's another uncomfortable and long pause. "Please tell me Reece and Emily are safe? You don't have to tell me where they are, just that they're safe."

"I don't owe you anything. But..." Tash takes a breath. "Yes, they're safe."

I'm not going to push Tash for any other information, because I know Mark will find her. It's unfair for me to compromise Tash and Reece's relationship any further. "Thank you, Tash."

"Hmmm," she grumbles and hangs up.

I lay my phone on the table and try to get to work. Jamie opens the door and walks in, placing a pile of papers in front of me. "Can I have your signature on these please, sir?"

I start signing the papers and stop to look up at him. "Jamie?"

"Yes, sir?"

"What do you think about this situation I find myself in?"

Jamie's brows rise as he slowly lifts his left shoulder. "It's not my business what you do in your personal time, sir."

"But, she's an escort."

"She's making a living the best way she knows how to. I don't know enough of her background to judge her, and even if I did, it's not my business what she does."

"It doesn't bother you that I've paid a woman for..."

"For her company? No, it doesn't bother me. Don't forget, sir, she's an escort, and selling her time is how she makes her money, regardless of whether you've had a sexual relationship with her. Remember, sir, you're not the first president to do this, nor will you be the last. Let's also not forget, you're also a widower, and it would be unreasonable for anyone to believe you'd go all this time without..." he clears his throat as he smirks. "Female attention," Jamie carefully adds.

I tap my pen on the desk as I consider what Jamie has said. He pointedly looks at the documents I need to sign. I return my attention to them, and when I finish, I hand the stack back to him. "Thank you, Jamie."

He quietly walks out of my office, closing the door behind him and leaving me with my thoughts. I really screwed this up with Reece. She reached out to me so I could help her, and I pushed her away. I've broken whatever we were heading toward.

Fuck.

My door opens, and Jamie stands at the door. "Alison?" I gesture for him to let her in. "You can go in, Alison."

She walks in and stands on the opposite side of my desk. "Alison, what do you need?"

She clutches the papers she's holding closer to her chest and looks down, breaking eye contact. Alison takes in a sharp breath and lifts her chin. "One of the press has been approached by a man who says he knew Reece when she was *younger*."

Her implication of the word younger means he's probably one of the mom's boyfriends. "What does he want?"

"He's asked for ten thousand for his interview."

I shake my head and clench my hands into a fist. I want to bring him in here and pummel his fucking face in. "Thank you," I say to Alison as I try to figure out what to do in this situation. As she walks out, Mark walks into my office and closes the door. "Did you find her?"

He stands tall with shoulders pulled back and his arms behind him. "She hasn't used any of her cards, or her phone. Her car is a hybrid, which makes it easier to track. However, she's left her car here with Tash."

"Which means they've swapped cars."

"Yes, sir. Tash's car is older, and we can't track it." *Fuck.* "We're already moving toward checking traffic cameras."

"No." I wave my hand at him. "Cease the search."

"Yes, sir." Mark nods and leaves my office.

"What a mess," I groan as I stare at my computer. She doesn't want me to find her, and I can't use government funds inappropriately. Standing, I walk out of my office straight over to Liam's.

"Mr. President," his personal assistant says as she starts to stand.

I wave her down. "Does Liam have anyone in there?" I head toward his door.

"No, sir."

I knock on his door and open it. "Mr. President," he acknowledges.

"Did you send me Brice's number?"

"I did. But I can get him on the phone now if you like?"

"Yes." I sit opposite him as he dials Brice's number.

"Brice, it's Liam." He smiles. "Yeah, I'm good. How are you?" He listens for a moment before getting straight to the point. "I have the president here with me, and..." He nods and hands me the phone. "Brice, sir."

Liam stands and begins to head out of his own office. "Liam, stay." He sits again, and types away on his laptop. "Brice."

"Mr. President."

"I need you to come to the White House," I say.

"Of course, when?"

"At your earliest convenience, though the faster the better."

"I can be there in an hour."

"Good. I'll hand you back to Liam so he can coordinate with you."

"Of course, sir."

I hand the phone back to Liam. "Thank you."

Liam takes the phone and continues with the conversation as I walk back to my office to get some work done. I slip my glasses on and stare at the laptop, but all I can think about is Reece. I still have a job to do, so I push every thought of her as far out of my mind as I can.

At least, for now.

Chapter Nineteen

Reece

Waking, I stretch and reach for Emily. Panic takes over when I find she's not in the bed. "Emily!" I shout as I jump out of bed and run through the retreat on May's farm. "Emily!" Barefoot, I run to the sliding door and near take it off the railing as I search for Emily.

"She's over here," May calls.

"Hey, Mom." Emily pokes her head up from where she is.

My heartbeat instantly calms when I see she's safe. I head back into the retreat and slide my feet into a pair of flip flops. Wrapping my arms around my torso, I walk out to where May and Emily are. "What are you doing out here?"

"I woke up to go to the bathroom, and I heard May. So, I came to help her. Look at the garden, Mom." Emily eagerly points to the massive vegetable garden. "Over here she has zucchinis, and there's eggplants over there. Look, she's even growing potatoes in this tub here. There's also arugula too." She snaps a few leaves off a plant and eats it.

"Hang on, you can't just eat that," I scold her.

"Yes, I told her she can. Besides, I don't use pesticides on anything, it's all natural and organic." May turns to Emily. "We'll collect some chicken eggs soon, and I'll make you both some breakfast." May leaves Emily to pick some vegetables while she heads over to me. "How are you holding up?"

"Um. I'm not really sure. Do you want to sit and we can collect the eggs?" I ask as I notice her leaning on her cane.

May screws her nose up and stares at me. "No, I don't need to sit, but when I do, I'll let you know."

"Sorry," I murmur.

"Yeah, so you should be," she teases in response. "How did you sleep?"

"I slept like a log. I tell you what, I desperately needed it too. Thank you for hosting Emily and myself."

May shuffles back toward the vegetable garden. She flicks her hand at me. "Pish posh, Reece. No need to thank me." She looks at Emily. "Emily, leave the zucchini and arugula over there, and let's get some eggs."

"Okay." Emily has a bunch of the arugula she's picked from the garden, and a decent sized green zucchini in her other hand. She places both on the edge of the verandah and skips to catch up to May. I hang back, and soon they return with Emily holding four eggs and May holding two. "May's going to make us breakfast." The smile on Emily's face is enough to make my heart spark to life.

"Come on in," May calls over her shoulder toward Emily and me. "Okay, straight through there is the kitchen, and, Emily, down that hallway to the left is the bathroom. You can clean up in there." Emily places the ingredients down, then rushes off toward the bathroom. "Can you cook, or are you as useless in the kitchen as Hope?"

"I'm not a master chef, but I can throw things together."

"Good. Get your ass over here, and start preparing." I walk around the island counter and wash my hands. "I'm tired, so you can make breakfast." I swing around to look at May. "I wasn't tired ten minutes ago."

May brings a smile to my face with her cocky-old-lady ways. "What am I making?"

"Do you know how to make a frittata?"

"Sure. Frypan?" May points toward one of the lower cabinets and I open it to find a neatly arranged cupboard.

"Emily and I had a chat this morning. You explained to her what you do."

"I had to," I admit in a small voice. "It's unfair to keep this from her considering it's affecting her life. The principal of the school called me to tell me Emily is no longer welcome there."

"I bet you were paying a pretty penny for that school too."

"Yeah, I was."

"Judgmental assholes," May says without a quiver to her voice. "I can guarantee those dickwads haven't always been so righteous in their own lives." She huffs and shakes her head.

"Well, you're right, the principal certainly hasn't been. He once tried to pick me up, and wanted me to have fun with him and his *friend*." May gasps and I think I may have overstepped my sharing. Perhaps she's not as advanced in her thinking as I thought she was. I mean, she is a seventy-something-year-old woman. "I'm sorry," I instantly apologize. "I shouldn't have said anything."

"What? Why not? I'm not a prude by any means."

"Do you want me to help?" Emily asks when she returns from the bathroom.

"I've got everything under control," I say as I prepare the ingredients for the frittata.

"May, do you have any of the Harry Potter books?"

"Do I ever! Hell yeah, I do. The bedroom that's right next to the bathroom, if you open the door, you'll see there's a bed in there, and I have all the Harry Potter books, along with all the Divergent books, and Hunger Games and so many others. But you can't read the ones on the top shelf, they're my spicy books."

"Spicy books?" Emily asks innocently.

"Books with sex scenes, Emily," I clarify.

"Oh, eww! Yeah, I don't want to read those."

"That's why I was warning you," May says. But you can lay on the bed, or take any book and sit out on the veranda. Whatever you want."

"Thank you, May." Emily skips down the hallway, happy to know May is a collector of books.

"I like her," May says. "Does she read a lot?"

"Her nose is always in a book, and she likes playing board games." I break the eggs into a container and lightly whisk them. "She's a good kid."

"What about her father?"

"Let's not talk about *him*."

"Okay, let's not talk about him. But, what about you and our fearless leader the president?"

My egg whisking stutters and starts up slower. But I owe an explanation to May. "I wasn't even his regular girl."

"So, how did it all happen?"

"His regular girl wasn't able to make their appointment, and my boss offered me more money to go because it was on a night I don't usually work." I turn to see May is thoroughly invested in this. "Anyway, I went, and we just..." I take a breath, trying to formulate a cohesive sentence. "He was an ass who wanted to know things I refused to tell him."

May snorts a chuckle. "Sounds like most men."

"But I don't know. Something happened between us." I shrug as I shake my head. "I don't know what to tell you, May. My relationship with him went from professional to personal rather fast."

"Am I right to assume this is more than a paid service now?"

"I thought it was. I really enjoyed spending time with him, and the sex was great. He even cooked for me."

"A man who cooks, he's one who's good to keep around. It's also a bonus that he's not a two-thrust wonder." I nearly choke on my own spit. I turn to stare at May, surprised by her blatant honesty. "What? I love sex, and I can tell you, having a man—or woman—who can move their hips...or tongues, is crucial to a healthy relationship."

"I'm not really sure I know how to respond to that."

May crinkles her brows. "I didn't take you for such a square! Pffft." She flicks her hand. "Anyway, so who ran to the press to tell them about you?"

"I have no idea."

"And what is Bennett doing about it?"

"He told me he can't be seen with me at the moment."

"That damn dog. I never would've taken him to be a coward. And I was liking him too." She runs her tongue over her teeth while shaking her head.

"I think he's as overwhelmed as I am. Mind you, I let him have it."

"Good! So you should."

"He offered to send someone to pick us up and take us somewhere to keep us safe."

May's mouth falls open. "That's fucked." May surprises me further with her choice of colorful words.

"It is, and he knows it is. I think he had a change of heart, or maybe he had a moment to deal with it because before you called me, he'd been trying to contact me, but..." I sigh. "What's the use, right? It's not like we can be together. Truthfully, I'd broken it off with him anyway, because I was terrified something like this would happen."

"It's a scary thing to have to go through."

"No, not for me. If I was on my own." I pointedly stare down the hallway. "I would've stayed and dealt with it. But I knew if the press got a whiff of this, his time in the Oval Office would've been over. And I definitely didn't want Emily to have to deal with the slurs, judgements, and assumptions of people. I didn't want her touched by this...but now she is."

"You broke it off for them?"

"Of course. Besides, it's not like I'm first lady material."

May lifts the corner of her mouth into a snarl. "Because you're an escort?"

"Because I'm a *twenty-five-year-old* escort, with a *ten-year-old* daughter. Do you honestly believe Bennett could be reelected if the public knew that about me? There's no way. Besides, my occupation is already out, and look at the uproar. The headline was 'The President and His Whore.'" I shake my head as I look down at the countertop.

"You have no faith in people. You'd be surprised how people would be if they got to know you."

"Seriously? Bennett has work to do, policies and changes he needs to implement. He won't be able to do any of that if he's not in the White House. Besides, you and I both know, he'll be forgiven for his indiscretions because he's a man, while I'll be persecuted until the day I die. I'm the woman. I must have seduced him, I'm the one who's responsible—that's what the public will think. My only regret is that I didn't end it earlier while I could protect Emily. But my stupid heart started falling for him." I exhale loudly. "Stupid me, right?"

"Was he falling for you?"

"I guess I'll never know. You'd have to ask him."

"Would you take him back?"

"How can this work, May? There's three-hundred and thirty-three million people standing in our way. Everyone will have an opinion."

"Opinions are like assholes; everyone has one. You know this. Besides, you don't strike me as the type of girl who cares what others think of her."

"It's not just me I have to worry about."

"Reece, that ship has sailed. That little girl in there knows what you do, and how you met Bennett."

I can feel my anger levels rising, because I don't want to talk about this anymore. Not at this stage, anyway. Besides, it's unfair for me to lash out at May for the choices I've made. "Thank you so much for allowing us to stay here," I say, steering the conversation away from what I don't want to talk about.

"Aha, I see. You're running from your feelings."

I finish preparing everything in silence, hating the fact May is so astute and observant. Even without turning, I can guarantee she'd be sitting on the stool behind me with a massive smirk. I turn around, and sure enough, May's sitting proudly with a grin on her face. "Whatever," I snap as I turn my back on May to start the cooking process of this damned frittata.

"If he wasn't the president, would you be attracted to him?"

"Would I ever," I mumble as a smile stretches my lips. "Yeah, absolutely I'd be interested in him."

"Then, what's the problem. He's not going to be president forever."

I look over my shoulder to May. "Yeah, but he's the president right now, and, if I'm on the scene, he can kiss reelection goodbye."

"I think you're being hard on yourself, Reece. Yes, this is going to explode, especially because people are hell-bent on leaving their attitudes shoved firmly up their asses, but I think eventually, people will be more than okay with you."

I burst into laughter at May's blunt ways. "Yeah, well. Let's agree to disagree. I'm a twenty-five-year-old escort with a kid who's in double digits. The public are going to want to know why."

"Hey!" May and I both look toward the front door. Hope waltzes in and does a double take when she sees me. "I was going to ask whose car that is, but now I know. The chick diddling the president," she says without a care in the world. "What are you doing here?" Hope walks over and gives May a kiss on the cheek before greeting me the same way.

"Um. Well."

"If you know, you know, right?" She winks at me. "Hey, tell me. What's he like in the sack? Does he have moves, or is he a dud?"

"Hope!" May scolds her.

"Oh come on, it's not like you haven't asked the same question."

"I actually haven't."

"What?" Hope stares at May with a gaping mouth. "How is that possible?"

"I haven't had the opportunity yet. I was working up to it. Then you waltz in, and start asking. What are you doing here anyway? Don't you have a house to build, or a damned TV program to film?"

I instantly freeze. "Shit," I whisper. "They can't know I'm here," I say to Hope. "Please."

"Hey, I'm not gonna say anything to anyone." Hope steps backward as she raises her hands in surrender.

With trembling hands and a quickened pulse I finish with the frittata. "I'm sorry, I shouldn't have been so irrational."

"Irrational?" Hope's voice is elevated. "Irrational? It's justified in this instance. You don't know us well enough to know if we're keepers of secrets, or if we'll hire a plane and skywrite it."

I sprinkle cheese on top of the frittata and place it in the broiler to finish cooking. "Well...you didn't answer Hope's question," May says after a moment of awkward silence.

"I haven't?" I keep an eye on breakfast to make sure it doesn't burn.

"Can our president move his hips, or not?" I turn to look at May and Hope, who are both eagerly waiting for my reply. "Can he?"

I shake my head as I laugh. "I can neither confirm or deny if the president of the United States is a generous," I pause and tap my finger to my lip as I think of the words to describe him. "Determined, explosive and incredibly mind-blowing lover. Nope, I cannot confirm or deny." I squat and notice the cheese bubbling under the broiler. I turn it off and with a tea towel, remove breakfast and set it on top of the range.

Turning, I see Hope leaning against the island counter, while May's staring at me with an arched brow. "Is he big?" Hope asks. "Like big?" She tries to indicate in size and waits for me to respond.

"Sorry, I signed an NDA."

"That means shit now that the entire planet knows he forked you good and proper." May slaps Hope. "What was that for?"

"Forked her?"

"Yeah, like stick a fork in me, I'm done. Tell me he's good? Please, tell me he's at least ten inches."

"Ten inches?" May shakes her head at Hope. "If he was ten inches, that poor girl would be split in two. Anyway, he'd be a porn star, not the president if he was ten inches." May huffs and rolls her eyes. "He's probably five inches."

Both May and Hope stare at me, waiting for any tendril of confirmation. I point to myself. "Signed an NDA."

"Oh, that's bullshit," Hope and May both echo. "I tell ya, that's bullshit." May lifts her hand and points at me.

"He's probably two inches hard," Hope adds and snorts.

"You two aren't going to give up until I tell you, are you?" I look around the kitchen. "Plates?"

"I'll set the table." Hope walks around the counter and opens the cupboards like she lives here. "The kid is here somewhere too, right?"

"She's reading."

"A book nerd? Yeah, I'm digging that." Hope takes out four of everything. I guess she's joining us for breakfast.

"So, tell me, I won't say anything to Hope," May whispers when Hope leaves the kitchen.

"I heard that." Hope quickly returns and stands with May. Both are staring at me.

"I'll say this about Bennett, he's above average."

Hope's eyes light up and she turns to May and holds her hand up, which May responds with a high five. They're like little kids. "Yes, I've always thought he was hot and secretly I hoped he'd be stellar between the sheets."

"And in the shower, and over a table," I murmur though I know they're both listening.

"I wanna be you," Hope says as she stares at me like she's seeing her first rainbow.

"You can take my place right now if you want."

"Oh no. I'll wait until all this bullshit dies down, then I'll have a turn with the president."

"What about River?" May asks. "I don't think your husband would be too happy with that."

"Pffft." Hope flicks her hand dismissively. "He knows I eye-fuck anything that's hot."

"Emily? Breakfast," I call down the hallway.

"I'll get her," Hope says as she's already heading toward the guest room.

"Follow me to the dining room." May stands and slowly shuffles with her cane. I place the hot frypan down on a trivet and wait to be told where I should sit. Emily and Hope appear, and they're happily talking about something.

"Are we having juice?" Hope asks everyone. "Do we have juice, old lady."

"Call me old lady again, and you're no longer welcome here." May pointedly looks at Hope.

"You're getting a bit touchy, aren't you? Haven't been getting any lately?"

I purse my lips together as tightly as I can to stop me from laughing. Emily scrunches her forehead and stares at Hope. "What do you mean?" she innocently asks.

May smirks and looks to Hope. "Yeah, Hope, what do you mean?"

It's at this point a lovely shade of red slowly drifts from Hope's neck all the way to her face. She clears her throat and widens her eyes. "I'll just get the juice." She lowers her head and disappears into the kitchen.

"Mom, can I stay and read today?"

I look to May for guidance, after all this is May's home. She gives me a discreet nod. "You can, but, if May asks you to leave, come straight back to the retreat."

"Okay." Emily smiles like her entire world is complete.

"Juice." Hope places a pitcher on the table, followed by a stack of glasses. "No iced tea?"

"No iced tea," May confirms.

We all sit and have breakfast, but I notice Emily shoveling it in like it's her last meal. "May I be excused, please?" She looks to me with hope once she's finished. I've barely even touched mine.

"Go for it."

"Thanks for breakfast," she calls as she rushes back to the room to read.

"Are you sure she's okay to stay here?"

"I'll probably forget she's in there."

"She's a quiet one, that's for sure." I pick at the food on my plate, worried and concerned about our future.

Hope reaches over and places her hand over mine. "It'll be okay. All of this is hard right now, but it'll all work out."

I look up and feel my eyes sting and my throat close. "I'm trying to be strong for Emily, but inside, I feel like I'm two breaths away from drowning." I lean my elbow on the table and bring my hand up to shield my face. "I don't know. It's overwhelming, and frustrating, and now I need to think about where Emily is going to go to school."

"School is the least of your problems. Seriously, this is going to blow over," Hope says as she rubs her hand up and down my back to comfort me.

"I'll forever be known as the President's Prostitute."

"This shit, right now, will all pass. Besides, look at it this way." May draws an evil smile. "You'll go down in history for going down on the president."

With my head still lowered and concealed by my hand, she's managed to make me smile. "I can't believe you said that." Hope scolds her.

"Pffft," May tsks.

I look up at them with tears in my eyes from being overwhelmed and grateful to both May and Hope for their support. "Thank you," I whisper as the tears finally fall.

"Eeeek, crying. I'm not good with crying." Hope awkwardly pats me on the back. "Here, here," she says as she angles away from me. "I'm sorry, I'm not the emotional one."

It's in that moment I burst into laughter at Hope's terror-filled features. My tears are falling for a plethora of reasons, but May and Hope make me feel like I shouldn't allow this to completely defeat me.

"The poor girl is terrified of you, Hope. Don't you have something to fix?"

"Ah, yes." Hope lifts her hand and points upward. "You asked me to change the showerhead in the retreat, and then I saw food, so...you know? Food." She stands and lifts her plate. "Are you okay if I go in to replace the showerhead?" she asks as she glimpses at me.

"Sure."

"I'll be back soon."

Hope walks out, leaving May and me alone. "You know you're welcome to stay here for as long as you like."

"Thank you, but I will eventually have to go back and face the media and everyone else."

"People will want to know your side of the story. Have you even had a chance to catch your breath and think about what you're going to say?"

"Not even for a moment." I pick at the rest of my breakfast.

"I'll say this, I have a lovely bathtub you can use, and a few good bottles of wine too. Emily and I will be fine together."

May has the largest and kindest heart. She's totally accepted me without any judgement. "I'm truly grateful to you, May."

"Good." She casts an eye over the table. "You can clean up then."

Standing, I begin to clear the table and hear the front door open again. "It's just me," Hope calls. She finds May and me still in the dining room. "I changed the showerhead, but the whole bathroom needs some work. Let me know when it's okay for me to get a crew out here to tear it out, so we can put it back together again."

"Um." My eyes widen in fear while my heart beats so quickly it feels like it's rising to the back of my throat.

"Don't worry, I'll make sure the crew doesn't even know you're here. So either you can hang out at my and River's house for a couple of days, or May can move you in here for the duration. Either way, no one is going to know you're here."

I instantly exhale a relieved breath. "Thank you."

"I got you." Hope smiles. "Right, I'm out of here. I'm looking at two houses this morning over in Mulberry Point. And, I need to get out to the fire station because one of the brothers wants me to do something on his house."

"It wouldn't be Dean. His and Joanne's house is new."

"And I built it, so I know there's nothing wrong with it. Nah, it's Alec. He and Serena are looking at extending their house so I have to talk to him about it."

"Those three brothers are good kids." May nods, giving her approval of three guys I've never heard of.

"Right, I'm out of here." Hope walks toward the bedroom, knocks once, then says, "See ya, kid."

"Bye!" Emily calls happily.

Hope walks back into the dining room and gives May a kiss on the cheek. "Let me know." She pointedly looks to me. "Whatever you're comfortable with."

"Thank you." Hope leaves, and I quickly clear the table. I fumble around the kitchen, trying to find a container to put the leftover breakfast in, and I rinse everything before stacking it in the dishwasher. Once done, I head back to the dining room, only to find May sitting on the sofa, nodding asleep. "May?"

"Yes." She opens her eyes and looks to me.

"Thank you for breakfast, I'll get Emily so we can let you have a nap."

"Leave her, she'll be fine. Why don't you go have a nap too?"

I lower my chin and stare at the floor for a moment. I'm desperately tired, and really do need a few hours. "Are you sure?"

"Of course."

"Thank you." I walk down the hallway and find Emily. She's on her back on the bed, holding the book up as she devours it. "I'm going back to the retreat for a nap, but May said you can stay and read. If you need anything, and May is sleeping, come down and get me, okay?"

"Sure, Mom." As quickly as she gave me her attention, I've already lost it to Harry Potter. I walk past May, who smiles although her eyes are struggling to stay open. "You can send her down if anything happens."

"We'll be fine." She flicks her hand at me.

I walk out of May's and head down to the retreat. It's peculiar, because other than Tash I've never had anyone be so caring about Emily or me. My own mother threw me out because I was a threat to her with her scum boyfriends.

I lie on the bed and look up at the ceiling.

My stomach churns with worry and my heart is beating fast.

I wonder how Bennett is coping. Is he hurting anywhere near as much as I am?

Chapter Twenty

Bennett

F our fucking days and I have no idea where she is. I'm going out of my fucking mind while I have to sit on my fucking hands, waiting for Brice to find Reece and Emily.

"Mr. President," Liam says as he walks into the Oval Office.

"What?" I snap in irritation.

Liam walks over and closes both doors the office and returns to lean against the armchair. This is his way of framing us as best friends, instead of boss and employee. "What's going on?"

I take my glasses off and toss them on the desk. "I find myself in unfamiliar territory." I rub at the tension across my brows. "I'm angry at myself for the way I treated her."

"The way you treated her?" Liam pushes.

"I treated Reece like she meant nothing when I should've protected her. And now she's gone, and I don't know where she is."

"Bennett, I have no idea what to say to you. If you think this is worth salvaging, then you need to address the American public." I look up to him. "Alison is getting hammered in the briefing room with the press corps demanding to know what's happening. You're going to have to address the public."

"What happened to the asshole who was asking for ten thousand?"

"Turns out he doesn't know anything. He was just looking for a quick payday."

Jamie enters my office and nods to Liam. "Mr. President, Brice is here."

"Good, show him in." Finally, he might have something for me. "Brice." I stand and hold my hand out to him to shake.

"Mr. President."

"What have you got?"

"My team has found her. As you know, Reece and Tash swapped cars, and Tash kept hold of Reece's phone. However, we've been tracking Tash's phone, and found she's been texting and calling a number that's only recently been activated. We've got it narrowed down to a small town called Hope River."

"Where?"

"Hope River, sir. We don't know exactly where in Hope River, but Frank is on his way there now. It's roughly a six-hour drive from here, possibly longer."

"ETA?"

"He's on route, should be there by three-ish."

Even though I don't know exactly where she is, I have the general location. I breathe a sigh of relief. "Thank you."

Brice acknowledges my gratitude and leaves my office. "Secret Service could've found her faster," Liam says.

"I can't use the public's money to find and protect her. Bad enough I had Mark start the process to find her; I know I need to answer for that, and I will."

"What about the pressure Alison is getting from the press corps? You're going to have to deal with that."

"I need to speak with Reece first."

"It's best if you get out there and tell the people something. Because right now, they're listening to anyone who's got an opinion. They need leadership, and…"

I hold my hand up to Liam. "I've screwed this whole thing up, Liam. I need to speak with Reece first before I address the nation. I just need time."

"But." Tipping my chin downward, I silence Liam with a tight jaw and arched brow. "Yes, sir." He nods once and pulls his shoulders back. "I'm meeting with the vice president in a few moments." He diplomatically backs out of my office.

I stare at the computer screen, then look around my office. My gaze lands on a photo of Kathryn and I'm instantly filled with remorse and sorrow. I pinch the bridge of my nose as I close my eyes. My mind is consumed as I cycle through every decision I made when it came to Reece. Standing, I pace back and forth in my office, unable to clear the disastrous whirlwind spinning out of control in my mind.

The door opens, and Jamie walks in holding a stack of papers. "Clear my schedule for today."

His blank stare is quickly replaced with his brows being drawn together. "Yes, sir." He leaves my office without asking me to do anything with the papers.

Walking over to my desk, I quickly pack it. "Mark," I call no louder than my normal tone. He enters the room and waits. "I'm going to the cemetery."

"Yes, sir." Mark is already communicating the orders to his team as he exits my office.

Once I'm packed, I head over to Liam's office where his personal assistant begins to stand as I walk into the room. I gesture for her to stay seated. "Is he in?"

"Yes, sir."

I knock once on the door and open it to find Liam on the phone. He holds a finger up to me and quickly finishes up the call. "Everything okay?"

I shove my hands in my pockets and click my tongue. "I'm heading up to the residence, then I'm going out to the cemetery. I won't be in the office for the rest of the day."

Liam's forehead crinkles. "Are you okay?"

I pace back and forth for a solid minute before I reply, "Yeah, I think so."

"Good, take whatever time you need." Liam smirks, lightening the mood for a brief moment. "As long as you're back in the office in the morning."

I stall in my pacing and turn to look at Liam. "Thank you...for everything."

There's an understanding that passes over Liam. He stands and pulls his shoulders back. "I serve at the pleasure of the president." Liam is a really good person who always has my back. I know, out of this crazy life I've chosen, he'll always do what's right for me.

Leaving his office, I head up to the residence until Mark and his team are ready for me.

⸱⸱ ———————— ✦ ———————— ⸱⸱

The Secret Service agents have fanned out, giving me space to speak with Kathryn. "Hey, baby," I say as I lay her favorite flowers, irises, on her grave. I clean away the few dead leaves laying on top of her headstone. "I miss you." I step back and kneel. "I'm stuck." I take a breath and look around noticing other than the Secret Service, I'm completely alone in the cemetery. "I think I'm falling for Reece." A massive rock-like lump forms in the base of my throat. "A part of me feels like I'm cheating on you, although I know I'm not."

There's a long hesitation as if I'm waiting for her to reply. What would Kathryn say to me if she were alive?

"I'm really struggling with this. Reece is nothing like you, not at all." I small smile pulls at the corners of my mouth. "Well, she's a little like you. She's feisty, that's for sure, and we both know you kept me in line." I snicker as I look down at the grass and sigh, my smile quickly disappearing. "I think you would've liked her. Not that I'd stray, that's not what I mean, so stop giving me judgmental stares." I take in a deep breath and hold it for a few seconds, before finally exhaling. "What do I do? Reece is an escort, and I was paying her for her time and her body. But, it's so much more than that now. I really like her and Emily. Oh, Emily is her daughter, she's a good kid and Reece has been a phenomenal mom in bringing her up. Which, by the way, is the reason she's an escort. Reece has had an awful start to life with no privileges at all, but she's never expected any, either. She's amazing and she's self-sufficient. She doesn't *need* me but damn it, I want her to."

I look around and notice the Secret Service are in a scattered pattern and all have their backs to me. "How would you feel if I started seeing her more permanently?" I shake my head at my stupidity. "I know," I say. "You'd want me to move on, just like I'd want the same thing for you, if the roles were reversed." I'm already feeling relieved by being here. I scrub at the stubble on my chin and stare at her grave. "This is one hell of a lonely job, Kathryn. I know, I know," I say as I hold my hands up in surrender. "It's what we signed up for, but I honestly thought I'd have you with me, by my side. It's exhausting being so isolated. Yes, I know, there are people around me all the time but it's not the same. I don't have you to come home to."

I roll my head back and look up toward the sky, letting out another long breath. There's a heaviness in my chest as I consider all my options. "I guess the question I need to ask myself is how I'd feel if I lost Reece forever, right?" I run my hand through my hair as I try to make sense of this craziness. "How would you feel, Kathryn?"

Obviously, my question is met with silence.

"I like her, and not because I'm lonely, but because she pushes back and isn't fazed by my being the president." My thoughts freeze for a moment as I find myself in a place, I never thought I'd be in. Speaking with my dead wife about me potentially dating an escort. Yep. Sounds insane, even to me. "What do I do, Kathryn? Would you be okay with me dating her?" I look down at the ground. "I feel like an idiot, but I'm struggling. God, I love you so much. Why did this happen?" I feel my eyes welling with tears, but I control myself. "This is so much harder than I thought it was going to be. If you were alive, we wouldn't be in this situation." I run my hand through my hair. "I'm sorry, I shouldn't have said that. But do you believe it's possible for me to..." I shake my head. "I haven't been sleeping, and I've been snapping at everyone. She's disappeared off the face of the earth. Well, yes, I know that's an overreaction and Brice has found out where she and Emily are, but she's..." A part of me is angry at Reece because she's not giving me the opportunity to apologize. "I deserve her silence. I've been a jerk. I told her I couldn't be seen with her when all this hit the media."

I know what Kathryn would be saying if she were alive, she'd be scolding me because of my behavior. "Was I a good husband?" My mouth dries. "Was I?" I ask in a quieter voice. "Reece has been through so much and I don't want to promise her anything if I was a lousy husband." I purse my lips together, wishing Kathryn was here. "If only I believed in signs from the other side, maybe you'd send me a butterfly, or have a blue feather drop at my feet to tell me you're okay and you approve of Reece." I snort to myself at the ridiculousness of the entire thing. "But we both know I don't believe in all that voodoo crap." I wet my lips and click my tongue. "You were my heartbeat, Kathryn. My reason *why*. Why I'd wake every morning, why I wanted to be a better man, why I did everything I did. I'd climb the highest mountain to see you, I'd swim in shark-infested waters to get to you, I'd do anything for you." I choke back the crack in my voice. "I hate myself for feeling this way about Reece, but I do." I look down at her grave. "You've always been my reason, but I have another one now."

Fuck, damn tears. My heart is rapidly beating. "Until we meet again, my love." I kiss the tips of my fingers and place the kiss on the tombstone. I take a moment to compose myself before I turn to head toward the car.

Mark is by my side and walks quietly with me.

He opens the door and waits until I'm in before sliding into the front. The convoy of vehicles proceeds out of the cemetery and back to the White House.

I need to take the rest of the day and get my head right, because the way I am at the moment, I'm no good to anyone.

Especially to the American people.

Chapter Twenty-one

Reece

"How are things back home?" I ask Tash.

"Crazy is an understatement. So many people are coming into the bookstore to ask about you. They're camped out the front of my house, even the news has trucks following me."

My heart sinks for Tash. "I'm sorry for getting you involved in this." I stand and walk to the slider, checking to see where Emily is. "This is a mess."

"Ah, yeah it is. But you don't have to worry about me, I'm fine. The bookstore hasn't ever been this busy before." Tash chuckles. "Good for business. At this rate, I'll be able to pay you back what you lent me to buy it."

"You know I'm not interested in your money."

"It's only fair," she pauses for a moment. "How's Emily handling this?"

"Well, I can't find her," I say with ease.

"What do you mean you can't find her? Where is she?" Panic sets in for Tash.

"She's probably holed up at May's reading. I'm not worried. I know she's looked after there."

"What's small-town living like? Have you met all five residents yet?"

"Smart-ass." I roll my eyes but can't hide the smile. "Emily and I have been hanging out here on the farm. We haven't gone anywhere. May's been so hospitable. The fridge and cupboards have been full of food, she hasn't asked for a single cent, and she allows Emily to hang out in her guest room where her library is."

"Hey, don't you dare!"

"Don't I dare what?" I ask, confused.

"Don't even think about moving there. I'll kick your butt if you decide to stay there."

"Truth be told, Tash, it's nice here, but it's not my home. And, I know I'm going to have to come back at some point and face the media. Although it makes me sick to my stomach thinking about what Emily is going to go through. If it were just me, I would never have left, but I have to think about what's best for Emily."

"Yeah, I know. Hey, listen, there's something I need to tell you."

My gut churns as I rub at the spot between my brows. I feel sick. "What is it?" my voice flattens as I brace for the worst.

"I spoke with Bennett."

I had a feeling she was going to say those exact words. "When?"

"It was sometime last week, just after you left for Hope River."

"I don't want to sound like a schoolgirl, but what was said?"

"I called him a jackass and told him he hurt you. He asked me if you and Emily are safe, and I said you were. But I promise you, I didn't tell him where you are, and I hung up on him too."

A small snicker vibrates through my chest. "A little while ago he was Mr. President, now he's Bennett to us."

"To you maybe, to me he's Jackass-in-Chief. Yep, that's his new name."

"I love you, Tash. But he still deserves to be addressed as—"

"Jackass," Tash cuts me off. "Until there's an apology, that's my new name for him."

"He'll apologize to the American public. His advisors will be pushing him to do that. I'm surprised he hasn't addressed it yet."

"He needs to apologize to you, Reece."

"I'm not expecting one from him, because let's be real here, Tash. He's a politician."

"He's also a man in the wrong."

I take a long and deep breath. "This whole thing has been wrong from the get-go. I knew I shouldn't have...you know."

"Have you fallen for him?" I slowly lift my shoulders. "Reece?"

"Stupid, right?" my voice is barely above a whisper. I close my eyes and shake my head. "Anyway, I have to go."

"No," she says. "No, it's not stupid. Everyone deserves a chance at love, and although he's a jackass, he deserves it too. You *especially* should be loved."

I wipe at the tears spilling from my eyes. "Maybe one day. But until then, I'll keep waiting."

"Reece," she whispers in a small breathy voice. I can feel her empathy for me from here.

"I have to go. Love you, Tash."

"Love you, too."

I hang up quickly, because I hate feeling so vulnerable. I'm not that girl, I can look after myself. I take a moment to compose myself before I go in search of my daughter. I'm a strong, independent woman, and I can't let this dark period I'm experiencing overtake my life.

Walking out, I call for Emily, but I'm met with silence. I make my way to the vegetable garden in case she's helping May, but I'm met with the chickens scratching around.

I walk up to May's and knock on the door. "Is that you, Reece?"

"Yeah, is Emily in there with you?" I holler from the door.

"Seriously, you're going to make me get up to let you in? You can open the damn door," May snaps at me. She's one forceful lady, that's for sure. I walk into her house and find her sitting at the kitchen counter, nursing a cup of coffee. She gestures toward the coffee machine. "Help yourself. I was about to go watch some TV."

I help her down from the stool before pouring myself a coffee. "Is Emily here?"

May nods as she shuffles toward the living room. "That girl is a ferocious reader."

"Yes, she is. Do you mind if I…" I place my mug on the dining table and point toward the hallway.

"Stop asking. Just go." She waves her hand at me, shooing me away.

"Thank you." I walk down the hallway and find Emily sitting on the floor, her back up against the bed, completely immersed in a book. "Hey."

"Hey, Mom." She looks up only long enough to acknowledge me before returning her attention to her book.

"New book?"

"Yeah, *Little Women*. Oh, my God! This is so good."

"I take it that you're enjoying it?"

She peers up from behind the book. "Loving it."

"Be careful with that book; it looks really old." I notice the deep green cover has worn edges. "Here, let me have a look at something." I hold my hand out for the book.

"Hang on." Emily takes the bookmark and places it at the spot she's up to before handing the book to me.

I open and flip the first few pages. "Shit."

"What is it?"

"I think this is a first edition." I take the book out to May. "May, is this a first edition?" I hold up the copy of *Little Women* Emily's been reading.

"Yeah," May casually replies.

"Oh my God! Do you know what this can be sold for?" Emily follows me out to the living room where May is sitting on the sofa, flicking through the channels on her TV.

"I have no idea, nor do I care." I stare at her, surprised by her lack of enthusiasm. "I'm not selling it, so I'm not interested in how much I could sell it for."

"Emily, you can't read this. It's worth too much."

"Pish posh! It's a book. it's meant to be read and enjoyed. So yes, you can read it, Emily. Besides, that story is groundbreaking and quite advanced for its time. You keep reading, darling girl."

"But, May, this is part of history."

"Which means it *should* be read by those who will go on to create future history. You have no idea what that book can do to a young mind. It might be the book that changes her world, so, let her read it. Because then you can say that book is worth so much more than money."

I slowly turn to Emily and hand her the book. "Thanks, Mom. Thanks, May. I'll be careful with it." Emily takes the book, opens it and continues reading as she heads back to the bedroom.

I pick my coffee up and go to sit with May. "You're an amazing woman, May. I wish we were..."

"I just miss my baby girl," the voice instantly stops me from speaking. A chill envelops me as I turn toward the TV.

I lift my hand and place it over my mouth as I stare at the woman on the screen. "What?" I whisper and carefully place my cup on the floor. The woman looks like a ghost. Her cheeks are sunken, she's missing teeth, and she's lucky to be pushing a hundred pounds.

"I miss her so much." She blinks several times and places her hand to her chest. "I don't know where she is. I wish she'd come home." The woman is not the same person I remember.

"Who is that vile woman?"

"She's my mother," I say in a small voice.

"*She's* your mother?" I nod slowly as I try to pay attention to the TV.

"Although I miss her, it's no wonder she ended up being a whore. But I still love her," Mom says. I scrunch my brows as I stare at her. I feel sick to my stomach.

"What do you mean by your statement that 'it's no wonder'?" the male interviewer asks.

Mom's sitting in a chair, dressed in what I can only describe as clothes that are way too young for her, with her sagging cleavage hanging out for everyone to see. My God, what happened to her? "When she was young, she'd always flirt with my boyfriends. She'd prance around in tiny shorts and skin-tight tank tops. She'd move her hips and bite her lip and seductively stare at them."

"I never did that," I whisper toward the TV.

"How old was she when she began to seduce your partners?"

"It started when she was about thirteen, maybe fourteen."

"I was a fucking child you refused to protect!" I yell at the TV.

"That's quite young to accuse her of attempting to seduce your partner," the interviewer says.

For a brief moment, I'm relieved he's made that statement.

"She was a deeply troubled child," Mom responds.

"I see," he says as he looks down at his paperwork.

Oh, God. I drop my head in the palms of my hands as my throat tightens with worry.

"I tried to help her, but she was always so much hard work. Reece would refuse to go to school, and when I'd take her there to make sure she went, she'd run away. She often made up lies about me and everything."

"This is getting worse by the moment." I look to May and burst into tears. "The things she's saying are all lies. Please, you have to believe me," I plead.

"You don't have to convince me, Reece. I completely believe you. Look at her. It's obvious she's drug-dependent, and she's probably being paid a few thousand dollars to give this interview. Let's face it, we both know what she's going to do with the money too."

"She's so disturbed, and full of lies. If Reece's mouth is moving and words are coming out, they're lies. But..." Mom stops and dabs at the corners of her eyes. "I miss her so much."

"If you could speak with Reece right now, what would you say?"

Mom turns to look into the camera and with a quivering chin and fake tears she says, "I miss you so much, baby. You can always come home. We can be a family again." She sucks in a breath and wipes at her eyes. "I forgive you for being a horrible child; I just need to make sure you're okay. I'm still your momma."

"She was never my mother," I whisper as I wipe at my own *real* tears. "How could she do this?"

"Do you know you're a grandmother?" the interviewer asks.

"I am?" Mom's eyes sparkle. "I had no idea. Do I have a grandson?" she asks with hope.

"No, a granddaughter."

Mom sinks in her seat and scowls. "She's probably like Reece. Good. I hope her kid treats her like Reece treated me." She arches a brow and sits back in the seat, crossing her arms in front of her nearly exposed chest.

"I'm a little confused here. First you say you miss her, then you're saying you hope her child treats her like she did you. Are you under the influence of any drugs?"

Mom's eyes widen as she sits straighter in the chair. "I'm a loving mother whose heart is breaking because that bitch ran away without even thinking about what it would do to me."

"Well, this interview is taking a turn for the worse for your mother," May points out.

I lift both my hands and rub at the pressure just above my eyebrows. "She's making a fool out of herself. I feel so sorry for her. She sounds terrible, and she looks even worse."

"Does Reece know how to get in contact with you? Has she ever reached out to you in the past?" The interviewer attempts to bring it back to our fractured relationship. Mom's staring downward, ignoring the question. "Julie?" he encourages.

"Yeah?" She lifts her chin and looks to him. "Sorry, what was the question?" He repeats it and Mom morphs back into her manipulative self.

"I had to move, so I don't live where I used to. I don't have a permanent home." She plays with her fingertips. "If my daughter ever loved me, you'd think she'd do everything in her power to help me. She's never sent me any money, or called or texted. Nothing. She just ran away and never came back. I have to be honest. I didn't even think she was still alive. I thought she died."

"What a despicable excuse for a woman," May groans.

"Did you search for her?" the interviewer asks. Mom touches her throat and averts her eyes for a split second. "Did you search for her?" he repeats.

"Well, of course."

"Did you go to the police?"

Mom's jaw tightens as she blinks rapidly, probably trying to formulate an answer. "Obviously," she finally replies.

"I can guarantee she didn't," May says.

"Considering she dragged me out of the house by my hair."

"She did what?" May shrieks as she slowly turns to look at me.

"Yeah, she wasn't a very nurturing mother."

"You poor child," May says.

"Please, I don't want sympathy. Mind you, I feel sorry for her." I pointedly glance to the TV. "She looks terrible, and she's spouting lies."

"She's actually doing you a favor."

I bark out a humorless laugh. "Really? I think it's making me look worse than I am."

"Think about this, Reece. Anyone with half a brain cell can see she's drug addicted. She's also proving that she's never cared about you. It shows anyone who's invested in this story how you were forced to survive. And really, consider that, because so many people are battling their own demons. You did what you had to do. Truthfully, this interview probably won't hurt you at all. You may even win some hearts with it."

"I see a woman successfully humiliating me."

"That's because she's talking about you."

I stand and begin to pace in the living room. "This is never going to go away, is it?"

May smiles sympathetically. "You're going to have to face this eventually, because there won't be a corner of the world where you can hide. Besides, do you really want to?"

"All I want is for everyone to forget my name, and leave Emily and me alone."

May shakes her head. "I'm afraid that ship has sailed, my dear Reece. Bennett Adams is a widower, young, very easy on the eyes, and a damn good president. He's a hot topic for so many reasons."

I walk over and kneel in front of May. "Do you think this'll hurt his chances of being reelected?"

May tenderly cups my cheek and gently runs her thumb across my skin. She drops it and sighs. "All I know is you're a good person, and that buffoon needs to get his priorities straight and come after you."

I grasp her hand in both of mine and softly squeeze. "Well, I don't know. It's not like we can be together."

"Why? Because you're an escort?" I nod slowly. "That's a load of bullshit if I ever heard any. If you love each other, this whole presidency thing is merely a temporary obstacle."

"That everyone has an opinion on."

May pushes up and reaches for her cane. "Pffft." She waves her cane at me. "I never would've taken you as someone so concerned by anyone's judgement."

"I'm not," I say in a small voice. "But I have to remember, it's not only about me." I look down the hallway, gesturing toward Emily. "I don't know what to do." I feel the start of a tension headache creeping up. "Would it be okay with you if I head back down to the retreat and crawl into bed...*forever*?" I whisper the last part.

"Emily can stay here for as long as you like. She can sleep here through the night, though I do believe she'll be awake reading to all hours."

"Probably." I lean down and give May a small kiss on the cheek. "Thank you."

She flicks her hand at me. "Go, and don't worry about Emily. She's in good hands. I'm sure Hope will pop around, she'll feed her sugar and bourbon."

"Bourbon?" I ask. May smirks and nods. "As long as it's top-shelf, and not that cheap nasty stuff."

"Only the best for us," May calls and adds a chuckle.

I walk down to the room to find Emily completely engrossed in *Little Women*. "Emily, I'm not feeling well, so I'm going to go back and take a nap. Are you okay to stay here with May?"

Emily jumps to her feet and carefully places the book on the bed. "Are you okay, Mommy? Do you want me to look after you?"

I wrap her in a warm hug and kiss the top of her head. "I've got a headache coming on, that's all. I'm going to have a shower and try to sleep it off."

Emily tightens her arms around me. "I'll stay here."

"If you need anything, either ask May, or come down."

"Okay." She breaks the hug first and turns back to the bed. Eagerly, Emily picks the book up and resumes her reading.

I walk out to find May has thankfully switched off that awful interview with my mother. "Emily's engrossed in *Little Women*."

"She's perfectly safe here," May says, easing my worry.

"Thank you." I leave May's and head back to the retreat.

I'm not sure I can handle too much more of this.

Who am I kidding? I have no choice *but* to handle whatever is thrown at me.

Chapter Twenty-two

Bennett

"Want me to beg?" Reece whispers.

"I want you to beg for my cock in your mouth." She leans in close, pushing her body against mine. I slide my hand between her legs feeling how wet she is. "You're such a greedy girl." Her panties are soaking wet from her hungry pussy. I slip my fingers under her panties and am rewarded when she grinds her hips against my hand. "You need to beg."

She licks my earlobe, then sucks it into her mouth. "May I suck your cock, Mr. President?"

My cock hardens as I finger fuck Reece's warm pussy. "I want you to cry out with my cock jammed down your throat."

Reece moans as her hips speed to a faster tempo. "I want to choke on your cock. Make me cry." She pulls back, drops to her knees and unzips my suit pants. Taking my cock out, she kisses the head before wrapping her mouth around my hard dick. She reaches for my hand and places it on her head. I push my fingers along her scalp and fist her hair, pulling her toward me. "Mmmm," she moans as her eyes roll closed and she sucks me with a ferocious need.

"There's my girl." I reach down and stroke her cheek while simultaneously using her mouth for my pleasure. My hips take over, pumping harder and harder into her mouth. Reece is choking and gagging, saliva dripping out of her mouth. My heart rate increases, my pulse quickens, and my balls draw up and tense.

"More," she shamelessly begs around my cock.

Opening my eyes, I'm covered in sweat. "What the fuck?" Sitting up in bed, I scrub my hand over my face and feel the effects of my hard-on. "Jesus," I grumble as I turn on the night-light and search for Reece, hoping that dream was real. Not because I want to fuck her face—which I do—but because I want her here with me. My heart is thumping against my chest as moments of my dream flash before me. Lying back, I close my eyes, push the covers back and snake my hand down to my dick. I grip my erect cock, desperate for release. Although a poor substitution to Reece's mouth, I grip and pull at my cock. She looks up at me and smirks as I keep driving my cock into her mouth. Reece is perfect on her knees. My body trembles as I groan my release, white ribbons of cum spurt onto my stomach. "Jesus," I mumble.

Saddened by the fact that Reece isn't with me, I blankly stare at the mess I've made. I hope Brice finds her soon, because I miss her so damn much.

***

The moment the elevator door opens, I'm accosted by Liam. "Morning, Mr. President," he says as we walk together toward the Oval Office.

"Morning, Liam. Why are you waiting for me?"

"There's an interview."

"With?"

"Reece's mother."

I stop walking and turn to look at Liam. "Press?" I ask, hoping he's not going to name one of the press corp.

"Small time TV tabloid."

I turn away from Liam and take a few slow steps to the garden adjacent to my office. I stare down at my feet before looking up toward the sky. "How bad was it?" I'm already dreading the answer.

"Actually, I think the interviewer did Reece a favor. The mother came off looking like she's trash, and has come out from under a rock for her fifteen minutes of fame."

Lowering my head, I do a double take at something that catches my attention. Only a few feet from me, a blue feather is poking out from under the hedge. "What the..." I bend and pick it up. "You've got to be kidding me." I turn to Liam and hold the feather up. "A blue feather."

"Uh, yes, it's a feather," Liam confirms in a baffled tone as he stares at me with wide eyes.

"Don't you..." I rapidly change my mind, choosing not to tell him about the conversation I had at Kathryn's grave yesterday. I shake my head, dislodging the thought as I tuck the feather into my suit coat's breast pocket before returning to the office.

"I think it might be a good idea to address the nation. Reece's mother seemed unhinged, and affected by some substance, and this might be a good lead-in to you giving a press conference."

"Until I speak with Reece, I won't be making a statement." I open my briefcase and remove my laptop.

"Mr. President, you need to address this soon. The interview with her mother..."

I slam my briefcase shut and stare up at Liam. "That woman is vulgar, and whatever she said would've been horrible lies."

"You can win the public with a strong statement," Liam pressures.

"I'm not giving a damn statement until I speak with Reece," I repeat.

"Mr. President—"

"Enough," I bellow, frustrated with Liam trying to push me on this.

Liam straightens and pulls his shoulders back. He visibly swallows and lifts his chin. "I'm sorry." He lowers his eyes, takes a deep breath, and heads out of the office in silence.

The other door opens, and Jamie enters my office. "Morning, Mr. President." He stands beside my desk. "You have four meetings this morning." Jamie continues to tell me all the appointments set for today as I set up my laptop.

"Thank you." I sit and search for my glasses. I pat my breast pocket, then my suit pant pockets. "Have you seen my glasses?"

Jamie looks around and opens my now-closed briefcase. He reaches into it and produces the case for my reading glasses. "Sir."

"Ugh, thank you." Jamie quietly exits my office and returns with my coffee, placing it beside me. For a brief moment, I'm left alone, but curiosity overtakes me and I search for the interview Reece's mother gave. I find it easily because it's heading every social media site. I click on it and look at the woman on the screen.

Julie, Reece's mother, speaks with no love or concern for her daughter. She's fidgeting in her seat and can barely string a sentence together. She's condescending toward Reece, and manipulative toward the interviewer. Julie's answers are filled with spite and hatred.

Esther opens the door, startling me. I quickly close the laptop. "You don't have to hide your porn from me, Mr. President. I've been around for a long time," she jokes and adds a snicker.

"And here I thought you were all innocence."

She places a stack of papers on my desk, lifts my pen and holds it out for me to take. "Oh, I may have been around the block once or twice." She snorts as she steps back and waits for me to sign the papers. Without missing a beat, the moment the papers are signed, Esther swoops in and takes them off my desk. "Alison is waiting for you."

"Send her in."

"He'll see you now," Esther says to Alison.

"Morning, Alison, how are you today?"

"Very well, Mr. President. The daily press briefing will be starting in approximately fifteen minutes." Alison purses her lips together and glances down at my desk before lifting her eyes to me. "How do you want me to approach the interview with Miss Maxwell's mother?"

It's obvious by Alison's reservation that this isn't a conversation she wants to revisit. But it's also clear, this isn't going to go away without me addressing it in some way. "Tell them I'll be making a statement within the next forty-eight hours." That should ease the pressure on her and quiet the press down for at least two days.

"Thank you, Mr. President."

Alison rapidly exits my office, and no sooner does she close the door, than it opens again. "Brice, sir," Jamie announces. I lift my hand and gesture to send him in. "You can go in." Jamie swings the door open and closes it once Brice has entered.

"Brice." I stand and offer my hand to shake.

"Mr. President." He extends his for a firm handshake.

"What have you got for me?"

"Well, Frank has reached Hope River. However, that's a tight-knit community that either doesn't know Reece and Emily are in town, or they're not talking."

I lean back on my desk and fold my arms in front of my chest. "What happens now?"

"Frank is good at his job, if they're there, which we absolutely believe they are, he'll find them. The town has a matriarch. Her name is May, and no one comes in or leaves that town without her knowledge."

"Is he going to see her?"

"He's waiting for approval to go." Brice lifts his brows, silently asking me for my permission.

"How positive are you she's in Hope River?"

"Her friend Tash is receiving calls and the closest cell tower is pinging in Hope River. I'm ninety-five percent sure they're there."

I push off my desk and pace back and forth as I think about this. I turn toward Brice and hold my hand out. "I'll call you."

He reaches for my hand and slowly nods. "Yes, sir. I'll have Frank pay attention, but not interfere until you give the go-ahead."

"Thank you."

Brice exits my office, and I head over to pour myself a scotch. The day has only started and already it feels long and exhausting. The door opens again, this time Liam enters my office. "You're doing a press conference?"

"Within the next forty-eight hours." I throw the scotch back and seriously consider pouring another.

"I'll have Elizabeth and Gavin start on a speech."

"I want to speak to them first."

Liam clears his throat and nods. "I'll have them come here."

"Thank you, Liam."

"May I speak frankly?"

My brows rise as I stare at Liam. "Do you really have to ask?"

"I think this is a good step forward, but let the speech writers do what they do best."

I purse my lips together as my jaw flexes. "I have nothing to apologize for." I pointedly look at him.

"I'll relay that information to them."

"I'm not sorry," I repeat in clearer more concise wording. "I won't say I'm sorry."

"I'll make that perfectly clear to Elizabeth and Gavin."

"Thank you."

He walks over to me and claps a hand to my shoulder. "I think you're doing the right thing, Bennett. Has Brice found her?"

"They know the area where she is." I intake a sharp breath. "I'm relieved she and Emily are both safe."

"You know that for sure?"

"They're in a small town and no one is talking, so yeah, I think they're both being protected and are safe there. Which leaves me in a difficult position."

"Why?"

"I want them safe, and I don't want to draw the media or the paparazzi to them." I shake my head as I walk over and sit at my desk. "I don't know what to do." I look up at Liam. "What would you do?"

"Pffft." He steps back and holds his hands up in surrender. "No use in asking me about affairs of the heart. I don't have one."

"Cold-blooded bastard," I tease.

"Don't you know it." He smirks and heads toward the door. "I'll speak with Elizabeth and Gavin about the speech." Liam quickly disappears back to his office, leaving me to do my work.

I slide my glasses on and stare at my open laptop. Jamie enters with a fresh cup of coffee, taking away the untouched one on my desk. "One of these days, sir, you'll drink the first coffee and surprise us all," he says in a lighter tone.

"Today my day started with a scotch, Jamie."

"Whoa. Sometimes we need the golden liquid to help us through."

"You drink?" I ask surprised.

"Me? No, sir. I'm not a fan of alcohol. Saw the nasty effects of when water is replaced by alcohol, and a person becomes dependent on it." I look up at him and sit back in my seat. Sliding my glasses down my nose, I stare at Jamie. "I disclosed this when I came for my interview, sir," his voice is shaky with panic.

"I'm not saying it wasn't disclosed, but I personally didn't know this."

He looks at the full cup of cold coffee in his hands. "It's not something I actively tell people. 'Hey, my mother was a nasty drunk who used to beat us.'" Jamie deflects the seriousness by spinning it with sarcasm. I've never seen Jamie so vulnerable.

"How's your mother now?"

"She's dead. Her liver couldn't cope with the amount of alcohol she put through it."

"I'm sorry, Jamie. That must've been difficult for you to go through."

"Not as much as my younger sister. She didn't cope well."

I gesture toward the chair opposite. Jamie's hands are shaking, the coffee spilling over the side. "Are you okay?"

"I've never really talked about this before, sir."

"You haven't had professional help for it?"

He slowly shakes his head and averts his eyes, looking down at his lap. "My sister has been getting help. She needs it more than I do."

I think this is an issue about money and health care. "Do you want to talk about it with anyone?"

"I thought that's what we're doing here, sir," he innocently replies.

"I'm not a professional, Jamie."

He reaches for the cup and clears his throat. "I'm so sorry, I shouldn't have said anything."

"Jamie, do you want to speak with someone?"

He stills his hands and stares at the coffee. "Eventually, once my sister is sorted, but for now, it's all about her."

"I'd like to get you help."

"Sir, you don't need to do that. You're way too busy running this country."

"Let me help you. We can make it discreet, and no one needs to know."

Jamie's eyes redden as he continues to stare at the cup. "Sir, I passed the psychological testing for my job."

He's misinterpreting my worry for him. "Jamie, I have no doubt you passed everything, but my concern is for you, for your mental health. Tell me about your father."

"He passed away years ago. It's just me and my sister, sir. But I disclosed all of this."

How did I never know this about my staff, especially someone who's as close to me as my personal assistant? "If you allow me to, I'd like to help."

It's clear by his rapid breathing and gulping that Jamie has never had anyone offer him help. "I'd appreciate that so much. Thank you."

I don't drag this out any longer. It's clear he's feeling uncomfortable and doesn't want to talk about it. "I'll arrange it."

"If it's too much, sir—"

"It's not," I cut him off. I pick my glasses up and look at the screen, essentially ending this.

"Thank you." He stands and with shaky hands, takes the first cup and leaves my office.

I chose to run for president so I can make a difference. Instead, I've been oblivious to the hurt those who work directly with me are going through. "I'm an asshole," I whisper to myself.

Completely unrelated, a thought pops into my mind. I take my cell out of my pocket, the feather I picked up gets caught with it. A sense of relief cascades over me. I lay the feather on my desk next to my laptop and stare at it. *Unbelievable.*

I stare at my phone and shake my head. Yeah, I have to do this, or I'll never forgive myself for not trying. If I don't succeed, then it's not going to be because of my pride. I'm not too proud to beg Reece for forgiveness.

Picking up my phone, I scroll and find Brice's number. "Hello?"

"Brice, it's Bennett Adams."

"Yes, Mr. President," his tone is slow and confused.

"I know you only left a short while ago, but can you please provide me with May's number?" There's a slight hesitation from him. "Either you give it to me, or I get it elsewhere."

"I'm sorry, but I'm not comfortable in providing that information to you. She's an older lady and hearing from the president may startle her."

I should be angry, but I'm not. Brice is doing his job and not caving to any pressure from me. Besides, he has a point about her age too. "I understand. If you have her number, can you call her and tell her to expect a call from me. Give her the heads-up." I'll have Jamie source her number.

"I'll call May and speak with her. I'll also ask her permission to pass her number on to you."

"Thank you." Ridiculous red tape. I'm the fucking president of the United States, I have fucking privilege. But I also know this has nothing to do with my office. It's personal.

The conversation lasts no longer than a few more seconds before the call is terminated.

I can see how some of my predecessors ran into trouble maintaining the line between the power of the office and using it to take care of personal problems. At times, the job is so all-consuming that it's hard to determine just where the line is. If the people around you are afraid to call you out when the line is breached, it's easy to get into trouble. I'm lucky I have Liam.

For now, I need to focus on work, and not on Reece Maxwell.

Chapter Twenty-three

Reece

My mother's interview yesterday has sent me into a tailspin. I've barely been able to get out of bed, let alone be a functioning mom to Emily. I stare out the window in the bedroom, having no energy to do anything but to lie in bed.

"Mom, do you want to help me in the garden?" Emily asks as she sits on the bed and stares at me.

"I'm not feeling my best again today, Emily. Do you mind if we do it tomorrow?"

Her features soften and her shoulders sink. "Yeah, that's okay," her voice can't hide the disappointment.

"I'm sorry, baby." I reach for Emily to drag her down onto the bed and hug her. "There's a lot of stuff going on in my head, and I'm kinda struggling a bit. Do you understand?"

"Has this got something to do with Bennett being the president and you being an escort? That shouldn't really matter, should it, Mom?"

"Some other things have happened too."

"Like what?"

I know Emily is only ten, but the fact is, she's in the middle if this too. "Um, yesterday, my mother gave an interview to a TV station about me."

Emily rapidly turns to look at me. "I have a grandma?" Her eyes widen and sparkle with anticipation.

My throat constricts as tears prickle my eyes. All I've been doing since yesterday is feeling sorry for myself and crying. "You do. But I haven't spoken to her since before you were born."

I fear Emily's going to ask *the* question. "Why?"

I can't hide the truth from her forever, not now considering the entire world knows our names. "Um." I close my eyes, dreading this conversation. "Okay, sit up." Emily sits on the edge of the bed. I push up and sit cross-legged on the bed. "Okay. Um." She mimics my posture and sits opposite me. Her big brown eyes are curiously staring and waiting for my explanation. I can barely look at Emily because this is the one time in my life, I'm so embarrassed about how we've ended up here. I don't want her to know how she was conceived, but at the same time I'm going to have to be transparent and honest.

"It's okay, Mommy." She reaches across and places her little hands over mine. "If you don't want..."

"No, I have to tell you." I look up at her and smile softly. "Um, so my mother is not a very nice person."

"What do you mean?"

I have no idea where to start. "My mom had boyfriends who'd come over and stay." Emily's brows draw in together. "I don't know who my dad is."

"Did he leave, like mine did?"

I close my eyes and lift my hand to run through my hair. My heart is racing as I struggle with having to be so honest with Emily at such a young age. "We'll get to him in a little bit, okay?" Emily's lips pull up into a tight smile as she nods. "Mom would like to drink quite a lot, and so did her boyfriends. When I was nearly thirteen her then-boyfriend stumbled into my room one night, and laid in my bed."

"Aha," Emily acknowledges but doesn't fully understand what I'm saying.

"The first time he did it, he had no idea he'd come into my room. He was so sorry, and apologized so much."

"That's good," Emily innocently replies.

"It was, but it didn't stop there. He started drinking less and less, and my mom would drink so much she'd pass out. He then started doing things to me." Emily's forehead crinkles with concern. "Bad things he shouldn't have done."

"Did he force himself on you?" I look down at my legs. I reach for the pillow and hug it toward my body before slowly nodding. "What happened?" she asks in a small voice.

I won't give her the specifics; she doesn't need to know. "Eventually mom found out, and threw me out of the house."

"But, you didn't do anything wrong...did you?" I shake my head, still unable to look at her. "Why did she throw *you* out?"

"Because she's nasty and thought I was trying to steal her boyfriend."

"That's disgusting." There's a long pause. "Where did you go to live?"

"I didn't live anywhere, Emily." I look up to see Emily turn her head to the side, and bite on her lower lip. "I'd hide through the day, and at nighttime I'd sneak back and sleep under the house."

"Oh my God," Emily sighs as she lifts her hand to cover her mouth. "Did it get better after that?"

I shake my head. "It only got worse. She found out the boyfriend was cheating on her with someone, so she got rid of him and basically said I could come back home."

"Wait, she caught him with someone else and she got rid of him, but when she found him with you, she was on his side?"

"Basically."

"What happened next?"

I give her the rundown of her next boyfriend, reducing Emily to tears. "I won't say anything more, baby." I drag her over toward me and wrap my arms around her tiny, quaking shoulders. "I'm sorry. I shouldn't have told you."

"I'm crying because I feel so bad for you, Mommy. She's a horrible person, and you shouldn't have gone through that."

I kiss the top of her head, contemplating not telling her how I was forced to sell my body, or even how I became pregnant with her. "I never wanted you to know about any of this."

"You don't have to tell me anymore."

But if I don't, her mind won't be at ease, and she might try to find the answers elsewhere. I'd rather she finds out the truth from me, than a twisted lie from someone else. "You need to know." I swallow back the hurt in my throat, then tell her everything. By the time I'm finished, Emily has tears streaking her pink cheeks.

"I'm sorry, Mommy. I'm sorry all those horrible things have happened to you. No one deserves that." My biggest worry is Emily now knows how she was conceived. As she's hugging me, she asks, "I'm sorry that man did that to you when you had no one. I'm sorry you became pregnant with me."

I pull back and clasp her cheeks in my hand and give her a warm smile. "Hey, you're the best thing that's ever happened to me, Emily. The. Best. Thing. You give me a reason to breathe every single day. I love you and have loved you from the moment I felt you kick for the first time. My heart beats for you, my sweet girl."

Emily lowers her gaze and bursts into tears. "I love you too, Mommy." She throws herself onto me, crying as she hugs me with all her might. "Thank you for being my mommy."

"Thank you for being my favorite person in the entire world."

She pulls back and manages a feeble smile. Emily's still staring down between us. "Um, Mommy, can I tell you something and you won't be mad?"

If she tells me someone has done to her what happened to me, I'll hunt them down and tear them limb from limb. My self-pity is being replaced by pure, undiluted fury. "You can tell me anything." I'm preparing myself for what I'm about to hear. I'll fucking end him, destroy his life before burying him in the ground. Whoever this fucker is, he's about to meet the wrath of a mother who's prepared to die for her child. "I told someone about Bennett," she whispers as she plays with the tips of her fingers.

I wasn't prepared for that. "What do you mean?"

"I told someone at school about him. We were sitting in the cafeteria having lunch, and someone said how Bennett Adams is a dick." She looks up at me and raises her hands. "That's their word, not mine."

"It's okay," I say as I find myself strangely calm. "Keep going."

"She was saying he's the worst president ever, and I said he's really nice."

Fuck. "What happened after that?"

"She asked me how I know, and I said he's been to our house and that you and him are friends. She said I was lying, and I said I wasn't. But then after lunch, she started asking me questions about him and you."

I try to hide my feelings from Emily. It's not her fault, she's just a kid who said she's met Bennett. "What's that girl's name?" Emily tells me and I instantly recognize the surname. Her mother is the anchor at a local TV station, and her father is the weatherman at one of the bigger stations.

"It's because of me, right?" Her chin quivers. "If I didn't say anything, then we wouldn't be here, would we?"

I lace my fingers through Emily's hair and kiss her forehead. "Nope. What's happened has nothing to do with you." If Emily thinks she's responsible for this, it could drown her in guilt. I refuse to allow her to think this happened because of her. "This is all me and Bennett, we're the people responsible, not you. You've done nothing wrong at all."

"But you told me not to say anything to anyone."

I shake my head, trying to form a logical and believable sentence for Emily. "The girl you told doesn't have the power or the influence to hurt us."

"But..." Emily's trying to claim responsibility. Although, it probably *is* because she told that girl at school that this has happened. But I'm taking that information to the grave with me. If I confirmed to Emily this happened because of her, her self-hatred would be just too much for a kid.

"There are no 'buts' to this, Emily. You're not responsible." I look her dead in the eye and smile warmly.

"Are you sure?"

"Without even the smallest shadow of doubt. You didn't do this. It's all on Bennett and me."

"But—"

"No!" I stop Emily before she ends up in her own head. "No, you didn't do a single thing to contribute to this mess. Not one. Do you hear me?"

Her shoulders slump forward, and Emily slightly nods. It's clear, she's not completely convinced, but over time I'll persuade her.

A short while passes with us entwined before there's a knock at the glass sider. "I'll see who it is," Emily says as she hesitantly stands. She walks out of the bedroom and calls out, "It's May."

"Open the door for her."

"Hey, I thought you were supposed to be helping me in the garden."

"Mom and I were talking."

"Ah, were you? You look like you've been crying. Where is your mom?"

"I'm in the bedroom," I call. "Give me a second." I stand and quickly throw my hair up in a loose bun on top of my head. I walk out to find May sitting at the sofa. "Sorry, I was monopolizing Emily."

May casts an eye over my disheveled appearance and turns toward Emily. "Emily, can you go collect the eggs for me? There's a basket up on the verandah."

"Sure." Emily turns to me and waits for my approval.

I think she's checking to make sure I'm okay. I smile and nod. Emily leaves and May taps her fingers on top of the cane she has in front of her. "You look like shit."

May does anything but mince her words. "I *feel* like shit," I reply earnestly. "The interview yesterday really screwed with my head. And..." I look out the door to make sure Emily isn't within earshot. "I know how this leaked out to the media. Emily was defending Bennett to one of the girls at school, and this girl's parents are both in media."

"Shit."

"Yeah, and she's feeling responsible. I'm trying to convince her it's not her fault, but she's internalizing it and blaming herself."

"Poor child. Well, it's not her fault."

"Of course, it isn't." I walk over to the sink and pour water from the faucet. "Drink?" I offer May.

"Actually, I'm here because I've made lunch and it needs to be eaten."

"I'm not really..."

"Hogwash." She flicks her hand dismissively. "Everyone needs to eat, so don't give me any lip about not being hungry."

"But, I'm not." May lifts her brows as her lips purse into a tight, thin line. I raise my hands in defeat. "Fine."

May lifts her chin and stands. "Good, I'll see you soon." She shuffles toward the door before stopping and turning toward me. "Have a shower, and make yourself presentable. You're a damn goddess, so own it." Without waiting for a reply, May leaves.

That woman is a rock star and an advocate for women everywhere. She's simply amazing. It truly hurts my heart that I never had a May in my life growing up. But, she's here now, and that's all that matters.

May's front door opens, and we hear someone waltz in. "It's me," I recognize Hope's voice. She walks further into the dining room and stops. Placing her hands on her hips, she lifts her brows and scoffs. "Seriously, there's food and I wasn't invited?"

"You know where everything is. Get a plate, sit down, and stop your whining," May counters.

"Ugh. Fine." Hope looks around and crinkles her forehead. "Where's the kid?"

"Where do you think?" I reply.

"Reading? Good." She places an old book on the table and heads back into the kitchen. Hope quickly returns with a plate and flatware. "I found this book in an attic of an old house we bought. Actually, I found a box of old books. Some were water damaged, some weren't suitable, but among those I found this." Hope sits opposite to me and fills her plate with the salad, potatoes, and meatloaf May has made. "Best potatoes ever." Hope shovels a heap into her mouth. She quickly chews, swallows and taps the book. "Kid!"

Emily emerges and sees Hope. She walks around the table and hugs her. "Hi, Hope."

"I'm rebuilding a house, and I found a box of books. But, this one here is for you. I saw it, and was totally vibing on it for you." Hope hands her the hardcover green book.

Emily opens it, and her eyes widen as a slow smile stretches her lips. "*Anne of Green Gables*? I've always wanted to read this, but never had a chance."

"Well, there you go, kid. You can read it now."

"Can I have a look at that?" I ask. Emily hands it to me, and I open and read it in my head. First edition, Fifth Impression, October 1908. "Wow," I whisper as I hand it back to Emily.

"What is it?" Emily asks.

"First *Little Women*, and now *Anne of Green Gabl*es." I look to Emily. "We're moving here with all these rare books. Maybe we'll find a rare copy of the *Old Testament* somewhere too!"

"You have no idea of the stuff I find when we're renovating a house. Honestly, books are one of the most common things. Sex toys too."

"Sex toys?" Emily asks innocently.

Hope's cheeks flush when she realizes what she's said. "Uh." Hope gulps and looks to me. I hold both my hands up to concede and shake my head. "One day your mom will explain that to you."

Emily shrugs as she cuddles the book. "Are you sure you've eaten enough?" I ask, trying to guide the conversation away from sex toys.

"Yeah. Can I go read?"

"Sure can."

Emily gives Hope a kiss on the cheek. "Thank you for my book. I love it." She heads back to the mini library in May's house.

"I really like that one." Hope shifts her eyes toward the hallway before jamming even more food into her mouth.

"Thank you. You didn't have to give her that book. It's probably worth at least a couple of thousand dollars."

"Kid! Give it back," Hope jokingly calls. "How do you know so much about books?"

"I really don't. But, my best friend, Tash, she wanted to get out of corporate life and wanted to own a bookstore, so I bought her one. She called it Books, Books and Coffee."

"Did you?" Hope asks. "I guess she sells books, books and coffee there." Hope smiles warmly.

"She did a lot for Emily and me when we moved to Washington. She took us in, and let us live with her. She literally saved us. Emily and I were living in my car, and I had no one to look after her when I worked, so I'd take her with me."

"Ewww." Hope screws her nose. "I mean, I don't care what you do, but taking the kid?"

"Stop being so judgmental," May snaps. "You have no idea what Reece has had to do."

"If you two are done, maybe I can elaborate." I stare at both Hope and May. "When I moved to Washington, I was working in a cafe and living in my car with Emily."

"Oh my God." Hope places her hand to her chest. "Sorry, Reece, my mind automatically responded, and obviously my mouth did too. I'm sorry."

"Yeah, so you should be," May says.

"Anyway, back to what I was saying, Tash let us live with her and she looked after Emily because she was working from home."

Hope chews on more food. "I'm sorry," she apologizes again.

"Both of you have been nothing but kind to Emily and me, so it's okay. I can tell you, other than Tash, I've never had anyone I can ask for help."

"I saw the interview your mother gave."

"Ugh," I groan.

"That woman doesn't deserve the title of 'mother.' Any asshole can have a child, but it takes selflessness to actually raise one." May turns to look at me. "Like you. You've done everything in your power to give that little girl her best chance in life." She points down the hallway. "No one should judge you for that, but let's be realistic, everyone has an opinion."

"Now I feel like a jerk," Hope says.

"Don't. How were you supposed to know?" I reach across the table and clasp Hope's hand, gently squeezing. "You've both been so good to us. I've already forgotten about it."

"You know what we need?"

"Dear Lord," May mumbles.

"Be quiet, old lady," Hope teases, making May shoot her an unimpressed glare with high brows and pursed lips. "We need to get drunk."

"It's barely one in the afternoon. Isn't it too early to drink?"

"Not now, but one night. Maybe Saturday? I'll get the girls together, and we'll come here with lots of alcohol. May can supervise."

I'm instantly terrified. "Um."

"No, that's not going to happen, Hope." Thankfully, May puts a stop to Hope's craziness. "Until everything is settled down, Reece can't do anything that'll make her look bad in the public eye."

"Who's going to tell them? I won't, you won't, Tabitha and Elle damn well won't."

I know who Tabitha is, but who's Elle? "Not a good idea," May insists.

"As much as I'd love a girls' night, I couldn't do it without Tash. So, when all this is forgotten, Tash and I will be down for some hard-core drinking and partying. If that's okay with May."

"My house is a safe place."

"Yay! So, it's a date. Sometime in the near future, we're drinking." Hope moves and takes her phone out of her cargo pants. She holds it up to her ear. "Yeah?" Oh, she got a call, I didn't even hear it ring. "Yeah." She picks up a piece of potato and pops it into her mouth. "What, how can that be? We just looked at it yesterday morning." She sighs and shakes her head. "Alright, I'll be there soon." Her shake changes to a nod. "That's what I said," Hope adds sarcastically. "Yeah, yeah. See ya, bro."

"Was that Charlie?" May asks.

"Yeah, I have to go. There's a problem with one of the houses." Hope stands and takes her plate into the kitchen. She returns and gives May a kiss on the cheek. "I love what I do, and I'm damn good at it, but my God, sometimes I wonder if it's worth flipping old houses."

"Can't really flip a brand new one, can you?" May snaps back.

"Well…" Hope fidgets and smirks. "I guess not. You know what? You're a cranky old biddy today."

May flicks her hand to playfully smack Hope. "Ha ha, you missed." She kisses May on the cheek once more. "Bye, kid!" she yells to Emily.

"See ya!" Emily calls from down the hallway. "Thank you for my book."

Hope smiles proudly. "I'll see you the next time I come out, Reece."

"Thank you for the book."

"You're welcome. Right, I'm out of here." She walks out of May's, leaving us alone.

"Hope was lost when she came to Hope River. She's really grown into an amazing young woman." May's loving smile beams. "She'll help anyone who needs help, and without expectation of anything in return. She's damn smart too and so incredibly talented. I'm so proud of her." I can see the love exuding from May's pores.

I stand and clear the table. When I'm done, I find May sitting on the sofa and I sit beside her. "Thank you so much for lunch, I feel better now."

May places her hand on my arm. "You need to get out of your head, because once you do, you'll see everything clearer."

I stare down at my flip-flops and nod slowly. "I might head back to the retreat and give Tash a call. I'm missing her."

"Emily is more than welcome to stay here."

"Please, don't say anything to her about..."

She gently pats my hand. "Don't worry about anything. If she broaches the subject with me, I'll make sure to listen and I'll reiterate that she's not at fault."

"Thank you." I stand and head toward the retreat after I inform Emily where I'm going.

One day, I hope I can build a family and be as kind as May's been to me.

Who knows, maybe one day in the future, that's exactly what'll happen. The moment I'm back in the retreat, I slide into bed and lift the covers over my head. Who am I kidding? Everyone knows who I am now. Is it possible to have a happy and healthy relationship with anyone?

Time will tell, I guess.

Chapter Twenty-four

Bennett

My eyes open and I let out a long sigh. Turning in the bed, my heart sinks when the realization that I'm alone again hits. These are the moments of quiet I know I screwed up by letting Reece go. I heartlessly broke the bond we were growing.

I allow myself a few minutes to mourn the love I once had with Kathryn, and the one I completely fucked up with Reece.

It's already been a long day, even though my eyes have only been open for minutes. I let out a long sigh before pushing up out of the bed and heading to the bathroom. Once out, I walk into my study and turn the TV on before I head out to grab a coffee. I open the door to find Mark standing opposite. "Morning, Mark."

"Sir. Sleep well?"

"Meh." I lift my hand and slightly wobble it. "You?"

"Like a damn baby." He smirks.

A little too much information for me, but I guess, Mark knows exactly when I'm intimate with Reece. The kitchen is cold and lifeless when I walk in. I spark the coffee machine awake and wait for it to come up to temperature before making myself a cup of joe. With my coffee in hand, I head back to my bedroom and study to process the morning before leaving for the office downstairs.

With the TV on in the background, I scroll through my tablet attempting to block out any media my name may be attached to. "What can you tell me about the character of Reece Maxwell?" Reece's name instantly stops me from scrolling through the Internet. I look up to see a woman on the screen. She's not that old, but she looks like she's seen a hard life.

The woman smiles and looks down at her hands. "Her character?" She lifts her eyes to look at the male interviewer.

"Yes, her character? Actually, let's back up a bit. How long have you known her?"

"We lost contact once she and her daughter moved to Washington." A tight humorless smile tugs at the corners of her mouth. "I always hoped they were doing well." Her brows pull in together as she flashes a genuine look of concern toward the interviewer.

"When she was here, what type of person was she?"

"What do you mean?" she asks for clarification.

"Was she aggressive, or dishonest, narcissistic, judgmental, predatory?"

The woman softly shakes her head. "Sounds like you've already made up your mind about her," she snaps. "You have to remember; she was a child with a child when I knew her. So, for you to sit there and ask me if she was aggressive, narcissistic and predatory tells me more about your judgements, simply because she's an escort." Oh, my God. She's serving it up to him. I bet he wasn't expecting that response from this woman.

He clears his throat, obviously uncomfortable with how she called him on his bullshit question. "How did you meet Reece?" he pulls his tone back, softening his approach.

"She was a kid in a bad situation, and although I've seen it many times, I wanted to help her. So, I started talking with her, and checking in on her."

"What did she tell you about why she was..." The interview pauses and rolls his eyes as if he's thinking about what to ask. "...soliciting?"

"Not much, and I didn't ask either. But, there were moments when I'd ask about family and her eyes would well up with tears. She'd lower her head and say family isn't something she'd ever had."

"What kind of relationship did you and Reece have?"

The woman looks over to the left and tilts her head in the same direction. "I tried to protect her. The streets aren't a place for a kid, but she survived, if that's what you can call it."

"How did you try to protect her?"

"I'd be there when she needed someone to be, and if she was running short of a few dollars, I'd give her some. But she really tried to be smart about a lot of things. She'd health-check her clients, and made sure she was safe."

"Tell me, Peggy, how did Reece end up pregnant at such a young age? Was she trying to trap a client?" Reece told me about Peggy and how kind she was toward her and Emily.

Peggy's left brow slowly rises, her lip curls and she clicks her tongue. "Take a step back and think about that question. You're asking me if a child was attempting to trap someone by getting pregnant by them. *A child.* You're putting a lot of emphasis on shaming the victim. That's not the interview I signed up for."

Yes. You go, Peggy. "I'm asking the questions the American public deserves to know an answer to," he snips with contempt.

"No. You're looking for me to say something perverse, to blame a child who was forced into selling her body," Peggy replies, keeping her cool.

I'm buying Peggy anything she wants, because she's not cracking under the pressure of this live interview.

The interviewer shifts in his seat, clearly feeling the pressure. "You said she was safe while she was working, so, can you explain how she ended up pregnant at such a tender age?"

Peggy opens her mouth, then closes it again. "She..." she stops talking and nervously adjusts the collar of her blouse. "That's not my story to tell, so I'm not going to. But I will say, the circumstances of her pregnancy are what we fear most."

"She was..."

Peggy holds her hand up and shakes her head. "I'm not going into that anymore."

The interviewer rustles some papers, reads them, then lifts his head to look at Peggy once again. "How did you lose contact with her and her child?"

A small candid smile pulls at her lips. "Reece didn't deserve to be on the streets, she was smart and had good instincts about people. She had a lot of street-smarts too, which helped her keep her head above water. I saw an advertisement for models and actresses, so I passed it onto Reece. Reece is naturally beautiful; she always has been. So, I thought this might have been the opportunity she deserved. Because no child should have to live the way she was living." Peggy swallows and looks down at her interlocked hands. "Obviously, that didn't work out for her and she still did what she had to in order to survive."

"Are you talking about prostitution?" he asks with a snide tone.

"I'm sorry, I believe she's an escort, not a prostitute. The difference is—"

"She still has sex for money," he abruptly cuts her off.

Peggy rolls her eyes and shakes her head. "It's not that simple."

"Well, yes, it is."

She shakes her head again. Peggy runs her tongue over her teeth and takes a visibly deep breath. "Would you let your child starve?"

"That has nothing to do with this."

"It has everything to do with it. Any parent who loves their child would walk through the gates of hell for them. You have no idea what Reece has had to go through, and clearly neither have I, considering we haven't spoken in years. But, instead of persecuting her, why don't you think about what she had to go through? She probably turned to being an escort because she loves her daughter so much that she'd rather sell her own body than see her daughter go without food, shelter and safety." Peggy pulls her shoulders back. "Wouldn't you do the same thing for your child? Because

I know I would if I had a child. I'd step in front of a bullet for them," she replies calmly.

"You seem quite hostile toward my questions."

"I'm disappointed that in today's day and age, you're questioning the difficult decisions a person has had to make for her child. We live in the United States of America, where no child should ever be put in that position, yet the narrative you keep circling back to is how Reece is paid for sex. Why aren't you asking about the people who procure these services? If there was no demand, there would be no supply."

"Wow," I whisper. "You should be working for me." I stare at the screen, completely impressed by Peggy.

"Why did you agree to do this interview?" he asks in a calmer tone.

"I needed to reach out and clear up all the deceptive speculations about Reece. It certainly isn't the money, because I declined any payment." My own brows rise with surprise.

"Thank you for your time, Peggy."

She smiles. "You're welcome."

I pick the remote up and turn off the TV. I suspect that interview wasn't supposed to go that way, but Peggy owned it. There's a knock on my bedroom door, and I call out for them enter. "In here," I call when I hear the door open.

Liam strolls in, picks up the remote and aims it at the TV. "There's an interview."

"It's done, I watched it. I may have missed the first few moments, but I caught the rest of it." Liam's jaw jumps and he shakes his head. "Are you worried about it? Because I'm not. And I'd be lying if I didn't say I want Peggy on my team."

"To do what?" Liam asks incredulous. "She's not qualified to do anything for you."

I stand and head back out to the kitchen to rummage around in the fridge. "I never took you to be such a damned snob."

Liam sighs. "You need to get on top of this now. We can't keep hearing from all these prostitutes about what a great person Reece is. First her mother, then Peggy." He groans and rolls his eyes.

"You already know I'm giving my speech today, but what's the problem with Peggy saying what she did? You know what she did? She showed the American public a serious flaw in our society. Point out what she said that wasn't true."

"Some of these things we can't fix, and we need to leave it to the next guy."

I slowly turn to look at him. "The next guy?" *Here we go again.*

Liam takes a frustrated step back and runs his hand through his hair. "You know what I mean, Bennett."

"I do, but we didn't sign up to leave problems to the next guy. We don't know what the next guy's agenda will be, and we need to do what's best for our country while we have the chance."

"There are things we can't deal with. This presidency is hanging on by a thread, if you don't go out there and renounce Reece, you can kiss a reelection goodbye."

I lean my hands on the kitchen counter and stare at Liam. "You want me to say there's *not* a problem in children selling their bodies to survive? Or do you want me to say prostitution is the cause, and not the cure?"

"No!" Liam lowers his chin and closes his eyes. "This is a fucking mess."

"Yeah, it is. But it's my mess."

"You don't get it, Bennett, it's all of our messes. If you're out, we're all out, and everything we've sacrificed has been for no reason."

"You're worried about your job?"

Liam lifts his gaze to look at me. "We all are," he admits. "We have so much left to do for our country, but we won't be able to if you lose the election. Right now, the polls aren't looking favorable, regardless of the good you've already done."

I reach for the milk I've taken out of the fridge, but slow before leaving it and looking to Liam. "You ran a poll?" I arch a brow and click my tongue to the roof of my mouth.

"Discreetly. Look, we have to know where we stand, and right now it's not looking good at all."

"When did you run the poll?"

"The day after her mother's spectacular TV performance."

"What did the poll say?"

"That you can't be trusted, and people wouldn't vote for you again."

This changes so many things. "Right." I lean back against the sink, crossing my arms in front of my chest. "Have Elizabeth and Gavin finished with the speech?"

"They're polishing it." Liam steps forward and sighs. "I'm sorry, Bennett, but there's no other way. You know what you have to do. You need to lead the country."

A massive hole tears through my chest. I simply give Liam one small nod before abandoning my breakfast and walking out of the kitchen. Liam heads toward the elevator, leaving me the time I need to wrap my head around this.

If I don't do this, my entire staff will be out of a job, and I have no idea if I get to keep the girl, because we're apart.

If I do this, I lose any opportunity I may have had with Reece.

In all my life, I've never feared both options as much as I am right now.

I sit back in my chair and stare at the open laptop. Reaching for my glasses, I hesitate before grabbing them off the desk. Jamie walks in with my coffee in hand. He places it on my desk and quietly leaves. Not even ten seconds from walking out, he opens the door again. "Elizabeth?"

"Send her in."

Jamie stands to the side, and Elizabeth walks in, holding several pages out to me. "Mr. President, your speech." She proudly hands me the papers.

"Thank you." I stand and walk around the desk and glance over the papers. "My eyes," I jokingly say as I turn for my glasses. Leaning against my desk, I skim through the pages.

"The speech will be uploaded to the teleprompter and will be emailed directly to the press once you've finished."

Standard procedure. "Okay." I look up over my glasses to Elizabeth. "We have..." I look at my watch, then back to Elizabeth. "Eighteen minutes before Alison starts the daily press briefing."

"Yes, sir."

"Thank you." Elizabeth leaves, giving me time to go over the speech more in depth.

I walk around to sit and see an email has come through, with the phone number of May from Hope River. Placing the speech down, I pull my phone out of my pocket and dial the number.

She answers virtually immediately. "Hello?"

"Is this May?"

"Who's this?"

"My name is Bennett Adams, ma'am."

She huffs into the phone. "How can I help you, Mr. President?" her voice carries no enthusiasm.

"I'm looking for someone and I've been informed you may know where they are."

"They?"

"Yes, Reece Maxwell and her daughter, Emily. They're in Hope River, and I'm trying to find them."

"Why?"

I lift my brows and smirk. "Because I need to speak with Reece," I admit openly.

"About?" Yeah, she knows where they are.

"Personal matters, ma'am."

"Personal matters? I do believe your and Miss Maxwell's personal matters are quite public."

Closing my eyes, I scrub my hand across my forehead. "Yes, they are. I need to speak to Reece. Would you be able to assist me with her location?"

"I'm sorry, sir, but even if I did know where she was, it would be a betrayal if I gave you that information."

"I just..." I swallow the lump in my throat. I shouldn't have made this call, it feels fruitless. "I need to tell her I'm sorry, and I shouldn't have abandoned her when I did. I'm..." This is harder than I thought it was going to be. "I'm..." I open my eyes and sit forward in my chair. "I let her go when I should've protected her. I let my job get in the way of how I feel, and now she's gone."

"Perhaps she's gone for a reason."

"She can't be." I take a breath while shaking my head. "This can't be the end of us. I can't let it end like this." Placing my hand to my heart, I struggle with the words I'm trying to convey. "If you do know where she is, ma'am, could you tell her that..." I pause as I stare at the laptop, trying to form some kind of coherent sentence. "Tell her..." Why can't I express how I'm feeling?

"Perhaps I might be able to reach her."

Suddenly, excitement bubbles through me. "Ma'am, I'll leave you my direct number in case she's lost it." By "lost" I mean, Reece has deleted it because she wants nothing to do with me any longer. "All I want to do is apologize to her."

"You can give me the number," May says seriously. "I may prank it a few times."

She brings a smile to my face. "It's a federal offence to prank people, especially the president," I quip.

I hear a small chuckle. "I'm going to be honest with you, Mr. President. I like you, and I think you have the potential to do good things for this country, but I'm also going to say if, when things get tough you drop the ball, what confidence should I have to vote for you again?"

It's my turn to laugh. "Ma'am, with all due respect, I doubt I'll have that chance again. I don't think there's anything I can do to win the public. And, I think I've come to terms with that, but what hurts me more is that I've lost Reece too." I lift one shoulder as I shake my head. "Thank you for your time today, and I'm sure if you know where Reece and her daughter are, you'll tell them I called. Can I ask just one more question?"

"You're on a roll, son, so why not?"

"Are they okay?"

There's a pause. "You should've led with that. But, yes, Reece and Emily are quite fine and healthy."

May absolutely knows where they are. "Thank you. If you do see her, please let her know I'm about to give a press conference about our...*relationship*."

Again, there's another long break before she says, "If I happen to cross paths with her, I'll let her know. Have a good day, Mr. President." She hangs up, leaving me to stew over my intense feelings for Reece. Jamie opens the door and returns with my second coffee, taking the first, untouched one to dispose of.

Liam waltzes in as Jamie is walking out and looks at the speech on my desk. "It's a good speech," he says.

"Yes, it is."

"Are you ready?"

I clear my throat and remove my glasses. "I am." I stand and shrug into my jacket, quickly making sure my tie is straight. There's a little nervous tingling in my fingertips as I tuck the speech into my pocket. My mouth is dry and my stomach twists with anticipation.

We walk through the corridors, my security detail following closely behind. As we approach the briefing room, Liam claps a hand to my back. There's a strong sense of comfort knowing he has my back.

Alisha opens the door to the briefing room and steps aside.

Alison walks toward me. "Copy of the speech on the podium, Mr. President," she whispers before standing against the wall with Liam, Alisha, Elizabeth and Gavin.

"Good morning," I start as I glance down at the speech waiting for me on the podium. I swallow the clump of dryness in my throat and look out to the eager press, waiting on every word I'm about to say so they can fling their questions at me.

With a thumping heart, I turn the paper over, completely disregarding the phenomenal speech they've written. There's a look of confusion on the reporters faces. "*Bennett Adams can't be trusted.*" I look around the room and lower my chin for a second. "Those are the words splashed everywhere along with *The President and His Whore.*" I despise that headline; it makes me sick to my stomach. Not one reporter has written a single thing, they're all waiting for me to speak. "Yes, I hired Reece Maxwell for her services." There's a collective gasp in the room. "I found the perfect woman for me. She challenged me at every turn, she supported and loved me unconditionally." I try to retain eye contact, but I'm struggling to do that. "That perfect woman..." I lift my hand to place on my chest. "...gave me her heart. I'd walk into a room with a thousand people and only see her. When I'd take her in my arms, she'd wrap hers around my waist and lean her head on my chest trying to snuggle close to me." I can't bring myself to look at anyone, instead I keep my eyes focused on the lip of the podium. "We could talk for hours about everything and nothing." I smile at my vivid memories. "It would drive me crazy when she'd brush her hair off her shoulder, because I'd get a small waft of the coconut in her shampoo, and she knew how much I loved coconuts." I rub my lips together remembering our intimate moments. "Shortly after five in the afternoon, eight days after inauguration, my beloved wife, Kathryn, was pronounced *dead*," my voice cracks as I attempt to hold in the emotions. It feels like hours pass as I compose myself. "There was a hole in my chest when Kathryn passed away that I thought could never be filled again." I take a deep breath and lower my eyes for a second.

"I never wanted to feel that pain again. I'd rather be alone than have to endure that horrible hurt and suffering. I didn't think I'd be able to fix my heart if it broke another time. So, I opted to protect myself by paying for the company of Reece Maxwell. She was supposed to be uncomplicated, and it was going to guard me against ever being in a position where I could have my heart destroyed.

"Something extraordinary happened when I was with her. My heart began to beat again." I smirk at my corny—though genuine—words. "Reece Maxwell has done nothing wrong. She has survived an astonishingly terrible childhood. She was forced to live a life no *child* should ever have to. But, instead of becoming another devastating statistic, she chose to not be a burden on society and did what she had to for herself and for her daughter. I have no remorse for paying Miss Maxwell for her company. In fact, the only regret I have is not fighting for her when the news broke."

I lift my hands to grip the edge of the podium as I stare out to all the press. "I was elected to serve the American public and I took an oath to faithfully execute the Office of the President. The last ten or so days, I've been nowhere near my best, and for that I apologize."

A lump of emotion gathers in my throat. "I've loved two women in my life. The first was torn away from me just as our lives were beginning. The second has been told she doesn't deserve to be loved because she's an escort." I swallow back the saliva pooling in my mouth. "Reece may be an escort, but she's also an amazing and loving mother." I feel a small smile tugging at my lips. "I have been absolutely honored to have met Reece's daughter, Emily, and what I witnessed was an amazingly well-adjusted, funny, bright little girl who's adored by her mother and now, by me too," I pause to wet my lips and take a breath.

"I can't apologize for loving Reece, nor will I." I drop my hands and take a small step back. "Thank you, everyone. Enjoy the rest of your day." I walk off the stage, not giving anyone a chance to ask questions, although the room has erupted, with every reporter on their feet shouting at me.

"I seem to have read a different speech from Elizabeth and Gavin," Liam says tartly as we walk through the corridors back to my office.

"Their speech was phenomenal," I say as I look over to him. "But the public deserved the truth, and not an overcomplicated political speech."

Liam closes my office door behind him and sighs. "This speech will either make, or break your presidency."

"What do you think?"

"Of the speech, or the presidency?"

"Whatever you have an opinion about." I sit on the sofa and invite Liam to join me.

"This is the first time you've ever made a speech where the public doesn't need to Google the meaning of words."

"It was simple."

"It was heartfelt," he corrects. "And I think that's given you a chance at reelection, because the public could relate to you, even if it's only for those minutes. They saw a man who's hurting because he's lost the only two women he's loved."

A small smile tugs at the corners of my lips. "I sounded like a marshmallow, but I don't regret it."

"You were vulnerable, and there's nothing wrong with that." Liam stands and claps his hands together. "Next time Elizabeth gives you a speech and you ignore it, I'll fucking wrestle you off the podium."

I snicker as I shake my head. "Get out, and go do some work." I flick my hand dismissively, though still smiling. I stay seated as Liam exits the office.

Staring out of the glass doors toward the garden, I can't help but miss both Kathryn and Reece. My cell vibrating in my suit jacket pocket startles me out of my cumbersome mindset. "Yes," I answer.

"Mr. President, it's May from Hope River."

"Hello, ma'am, how can I help you?"

"You've got a helicopter at your disposal, don't you?"

"Well, technically if it's…"

"It's a yes or no question, Mr. President."

Sassy old lady. "Marine One, yes, I do."

"Did you mean it in your speech when you said you loved her?"

I scrub my hand over my eyes, rubbing at the pressure mounting at the start of my brows. "I should try and save my career by saying no, but that would be a lie."

"Why do you love her?"

I'm being dragged over the coals by an old woman I've never met and with whom I've only had one brief conversation. But, if I don't have *this* conversation, then I run the risk of losing Reece and Emily forever. And I don't want that. "The only explanation I have to offer is because she's amazing." May doesn't respond, and I have to check my phone to make sure it's still connected. "Ma'am?" She must be thinking about her next step.

"I'll send you my address. You can have the helicopter land on my property. If I were you, I wouldn't leave it too long."

I jump off the sofa and head straight to speak with Mark. "Thank you."

"You're welcome. Don't scare my chickens."

"No, ma'am, I won't." I hang up and by the time I reach the door, she's texted me her address.

I'm going to Hope River. *Now.*

Chapter Twenty-five

Reece

Clutching at my chest, I watch as Bennett walks out of the room. The reporters are going crazy, hurling a barrage of questions about us to him. "Huh," May grumbles.

"I know," I say.

"He even mentioned me," Emily says.

"How could he not? You're the most wonderful little girl in the entire world." I drape my arm over her shoulders and bring her closer for a hug.

"It's clear he disregarded his speech writers' speech, because he didn't use impossible words even I don't understand." May turns her head toward me and glances at Emily. "He seems like a good man."

"He is," Emily chirps as she snuggles into me.

I stare down at the floor as my breath catches in my chest. "I don't know what to do."

"Emily, don't you have a book to read?" May asks.

"Can I go?" Emily looks to me for approval. I try to give her a smile as I nod. "Thanks, Mom." She gives me a small kiss on the cheek before taking off toward May's guest room.

My mind is racing as a flustered feeling overtakes me. "I don't know, May." Wringing my hands together, I look over to her. "What do I do?"

May slowly shrugs. "I'm not the best person to talk to about this. Why don't you call your friend Tash?"

It takes me a moment to wrap my head around this. Standing, I walk back into the kitchen and retrieve my phone from the kitchen counter. Tash has tried calling me over ten times. I hit dial and bring the phone to my ear. "You saw it?"

"The entire country saw it," Tash lovingly responds. "You have to call him."

"Am I setting myself up for disaster? It's not fair to lead me on. And what about Emily?" I lean against the island counter and absentmindedly pick at the quick around my nail. "This is all happening in a blur, Tash."

"Are you worried he'll hurt you? Or are you worried he's the first man who's ready to fight for you and Emily?"

"What if we..."

"You're talking out of your ass, Reece." She takes a breath. "Look, I'm sorry, but you have to stop fighting this."

"He betrayed me, Tash."

"Yeah, he did. And he not only made an apology, he did it in front of the whole country."

Blowing out my cheeks I keep looking down at the floor. "I'm terrified. I've been on my own since the day my mom threw me out of the house. I never thought I'd ever let someone in, not someone like him."

"I think you have a fear of abandonment."

"Of course, I do. It's easier to stay on my own than get into this relationship and eventually find out he doesn't want me anymore. Not only a relationship though, but a *public* one that'll be scrutinized by everyone."

"I never took you to be so soft."

"Soft? I'm not soft, I'm fucking scared."

"Good. You should be. Since when has that stopped you?"

I shake my head as a brow arches. "What do I do, Tash? Do I pretend I never saw this or do I call him?"

"I'm going to support you regardless of the outcome. You know that, right?"

"I know you'll support me, but, what do I do?"

"I can't make that decision for you. You have to do what's best for you and Emily. But can I say, that didn't sound like a speech written by anyone else. I think he spoke from the heart, not from a political point of view."

"He had the speech and he turned it over, he didn't use whatever speech his team gave him. I feel like I'm a bad person if I say I want this."

"What? You're cray-cray if you think you don't deserve to be happy. If anyone should be loved and happy, it should be you, Reece."

"Fuck..." I close my eyes to hold the tears back. "Do I though, do I deserve him?"

"Girl, I will get in my—*your*—car, and drive to where you are and slap the shit out of you! He's damned lucky to have you, just like you're damned lucky to have him." Tash intakes a sharp breath. "Do you love him?"

"I don't know," I answer honestly. "I never thought I'd have the opportunity to love anyone, so, I don't know. Maybe I do love him, but I can tell you right now, it hurt like hell when he said he couldn't be seen with me. It shredded my soul into so many pieces that I never thought I'd feel whole again. I miss him like crazy too, but I've been strong and burying those feelings."

"Sounds like love to me."

Tash's confirmation sends a tingle through me. "I'm scared," I whisper into the phone. "Something I never thought I'd ever have available to me is here. Bennett is..."

"He's being brave, and so should you."

"I should be brave," I affirm. "But I'm not sure I can be."

"Reece, that's all you've ever been. Let him in. See where this goes."

I take in several deep breaths as I nod. "I love you," I whisper.

"I know. It's because I'm the best friend anyone could ever have."

She brings a smile to my lips. "You are."

"As much as I want to talk to you, I have work to do. Look, I think you should at the very least talk to Bennett and hear him out. I mean, that was a pretty kick-ass grovel. And in front of the nation, too."

"Yeah, I guess. Alright, I guess, I'll be seeing you soon." I feel like a blubbering fool.

"Love you."

"Love you." I hang up and leave my phone on the kitchen counter. Heading back into the family room, I find May flicking through the channels. "Tash said I need to be brave."

"I heard all of your side of the conversation because I was eavesdropping. Yeah, you do need to be brave, and yes, you do deserve love, and you love him too." She turns the TV off and crosses her arms in front of her chest. "Look at your daughter. How fast have the last ten years gone?"

"In a blink of an eye," I honestly admit.

"She's going to be a young adult before you know it, going off to college and starting her own life. Don't let this chance slip out of your fingers, Reece, because for all you know he may be the love of your life." May's eyes soften as she lowers her chin and stares off to the side. "We have one chance at this thing called life, don't let fear stand in the way of reaching out for what you really want," May's tone is soft, as if she's speaking from personal experience.

I've never asked her about her life, perhaps one day soon I should. "What if..."

She snaps her gaze back to me, the almost whimsical look she had has now been replaced by cold, hard eyes. "You deserve the chance to find out if it *does* work." She huffs slightly and shuffles closer to the edge of her seat. She stands with a little difficulty and reaches for her cane. "Damn bladder. It's an asshole when you get older." She looks around her chair.

"What are you searching for?"

"My phone."

"I wouldn't take you for a person who has their phone in the bathroom."

She sees it caught between the chair cushion and the chair and lifts it out. "First of all, I've been trying to beat this hard level on Candy Crush, and second of all if you have to know, I ate a lot of prunes last night."

"Too much information, May." I wave my hand at her as I shake my head trying to dislodge that mental picture.

"Let me tell you, prunes will be your best friend when you're my age." She scuttles toward the bathroom.

I sit back on the sofa and close my eyes. I wasn't expecting Bennett to be so raw in his words. His speech wasn't a political agenda; it wasn't to win votes. It came from the heart.

Bennett looked so tired at the podium that all I wanted to do was be there with him, to wrap my arms around him and tell him everything would be okay. My stomach flutters just thinking about him; my heart hammers with desire.

I should have courage and reach out to him. "Be brave," I whisper to myself.

The bathroom door opens and May returns. There's a mischievous smirk on her face. "Enough now," she says as she stops in front of me.

"What?"

"I doubt you've run a brush through your hair in a couple of days. One of my chickens could lay an egg in that rat's nest you have going on and you'd never know it. And when was the last time you brushed your teeth? Get up and go take a shower." She points toward the retreat.

"What?"

"Enough, Reece. You've been moping around, barely changing out of your pajamas, feeling sorry for yourself. You've done life on your own; now it's time to let that man in. You've dragged yourself out of a bad situation and made a life for you and that little girl in there. Now it's time to let someone else care for you. He's a good man, and you're a damn good woman. You deserve this. Now, get your ass up, clean yourself up and be the woman you've always been. Strong, powerful, and damn sexy."

I burst into tears at May's tough love, but this is what I need. I jump to my feet and throw my arms around her. "You're right, May. I *do* deserve to be happy."

"I'm seldom wrong," she sassily replies. "Leave Emily here, and go have a shower. It's time you claim back your life."

She's right, it's time I start feeling more like me than the murky haze I've been in recently. "Thank you." I head past the kitchen and down to the retreat to have a shower and get ready so I can tackle this head-on. It's the least I can do for myself.

No one is going to save me, it's up to me to save myself.

⸰⸰———————✦———————⸰⸰

Once I'm showered, changed, and my hair is back in a ponytail, I feel like a massive burden has disappeared. I head back up to May's so I can talk with Emily.

"I'm back," I call as I walk into the house.

"Mom!" Emily runs to me, smiling, and hugs me. "You look so much better."

I catch May smirking from behind Emily. "I feel it." I smile at May and mouth "thank you." Then say, "I'm thinking tomorrow we head back home. What do you think?"

Emily looks over her shoulder to May, then back to me. Something passes between them, but I can't quite put my finger on it. "Sure, Mommy."

"What are you two up to?"

"Us? Nothing, why?" May asks. "I'm too old to be up to anything. Besides, haven't you seen me moving? It's not like I rushed out and quickly made arrangements for a party while you were in the shower." Emily giggles and covers her mouth.

I narrow my eyes as I stare between them. May is glaring at me, daring me to challenge her further. Emily can't even meet my stare. "You two are up to something."

"I'm too old."

"And I'm too young," Emily says immediately after May.

"You're too uptight," May snickers. "Loosen up a bit."

Coming from the left, I can hear a heavy, mechanical whooshing sound approaching. The closer it gets, the louder it is. "What's that?" I walk over to the massive window in the family room and look out.

"He's here!" Emily squeals with happiness as she takes off out of the house.

"Who's here?" I turn to find May with a cocked brow, smiling widely at me. Realization quickly dawns on me, and I look out the window again. "Is that Bennett?" I ask as my voice tightens.

"What if it is?"

I straighten my shoulders and run my hand over my hair. "How?"

"Does that really matter? That boy is coming here for you, are you really going to worry about the how?" The left side of her upper lip tugs upward. "Is that what's important here?"

I tidy and flatten my t-shirt and jeans, then clear my throat. I look out the window and see an army green helicopter begin its decent in the large open area. I turn to May and smile. "Thank you."

"I didn't do a single thing. I think you best get your butt out there." We both look out the window to watch the helicopter land. The top part of the helicopter is white, and the American flag is proudly painted on it along with the words United States of America.

"Are you going to go out and meet Bennett?"

"Sure am, but you go ahead, I'll get there."

I give May a hug before running out to greet my man. Emily and I stand at a safe distance and watch as the door opens and Mark jumps out of the helicopter first. A slew of his Secret Service guys all follow and yell some instructions to Bennett.

Emily and I are standing back, waiting for him. The moment he's out of the helicopter, Emily breaks out of my arms and runs up to him, throwing her arms around him. Bennett gives her a hug and says something. I can see the massive smile on her face as she nods, looks up at him, and responds to whatever he's said.

Bennett lifts his gaze to look at me and smiles. He straightens and offers his hand to Emily, who happily takes it and walks alongside of him.

"If he didn't mean what he said, he wouldn't be here," May says as she stands beside me.

"Any idea how he found me?"

May cheekily shrugs. "I have no idea, maybe he's psychic."

Bennett hasn't torn his eyes off of me as he gets closer to me. My breath catches as I watch his tall, suited frame walk toward me. He's truly a sexy, well-dressed man. *Damn.*

The moment he's in front of me, his steely gaze locks in on me. He winks at me and turns to May. "You must be the infamous May. It's a pleasure to meet you, ma'am." He holds his hand out for her to take.

May carefully casts a suspicious eye over him. She looks around her farm, then returns her attention to Bennett. "You didn't scare my chickens."

"No, ma'am. I'm far too scared of you to frighten your chickens."

May looks between us and offers him a nod. "You did good," she says to Bennett. "Emily, can you help me inside please?"

"Sure." Emily and May walk toward the house, leaving Bennett and me alone. Well, as alone as we can be with his team of Secret Service agents scattered around me.

"I watched your press conference."

Bennett steps closer to me. "I meant every single word, Reece. I've only loved two women in my life, and I'm totally crazy for you." He lifts his hands and gently cups my face. "I was a complete ass who panicked when it all got too real, but I'm also a man who can admit to his mistakes. I want you in my arms, and in my bed for the rest of my life."

My heart is beating rapidly as my pulse quickens and my palms sweat. God, I want to kiss him, but he has to work for it. I take a step backward and shake my head. "I don't know, Bennett. Why should you get my vote and not the other guy?"

He tilts his head slightly to the side and shoves his hands in his perfectly snug suit pants. Bennett begins to pace back and forth, a small smirk present. "I hear the other guy isn't so nice."

"You gotta do better than that. What will you offer me? What's the plan if I select you rather than the other guy?"

"Hmmm." He stops walking and taps his fingertip to his bottom lip. *Damn, his mouth is delicious.* "First of all, I'll be able to offer you stability and security."

"Meh." I shrug dramatically. "I can provide for myself. I don't need a man to do that. If that's all you have...well..."

He turns to look at me with wide eyes. "Now, hang on a moment, woman." *Woman? Really?* "You may not need me, but I need you."

I want to run into his arms, but he still needs to work for it. "That's a start, I guess." I feign disinterest by looking down at my nails. "What else have you got to offer?"

"Nothing more than my love." I lift my chin to look at him. "All I can tell you is that we're going to be thrust into the eye of every camera in the world. They're going to scrutinize everything about you, and me, and us," his voice darkens; it's not as carefree as it was a moment ago. "They're going to say horrible things about you and me. We'll forever be in the public eye, and we're going to have every religious organization come at us for an array of reasons. But I want you to know this..." He moves to take me in his arms. "I won't live another moment without you in my life."

"Bennett..."

"I made a decision on the way out here."

"What is it?" I lift my head to look up into his dark, seductive eyes.

"I'm resigning. I don't want this if I can't have you in my life."

There's a heaviness in my stomach, weighing me down. "You can't do that, Bennett."

"The only way I stay in office is if you're with me. I can't do my job effectively if I don't have you standing by my side."

I lower my chin to look down. "What are you asking me?"

"I'm asking you to move in with me. To love me like I love you. To be with me; and in time I'll be asking you another question, one that's more permanent."

"You're willing to walk away from the presidency to be with me?"

"In a heartbeat," he says instantly.

There's a moment of tension that passes between us. "Bennett Adams, you were a jerk in the way you treated me. But, I'm willing to let you make it up to me."

"You'll move in with me?" he asks, his voice full of hope. He clutches my hands tighter in his.

"On one condition."

"Anything."

"You need to ask Emily if she wants this too."

Bennett's eyes widen as an unrestrained smile fills his handsome face. "Deal. But first." He pulls me closer, smashing our bodies together. His strong lips are instantly on mine. "I love you," he murmurs against my mouth.

My body feels like it's floating as we stay connected for what feels like hours. "I love you," I whisper against his mouth.

Bennett Adams is the president of the United States, and he's mine. *All mine.*

Who would've thought a girl from shithole nowhere who was tossed out like trash at the age of fourteen by the one person who was supposed to protect her, who had a baby at fifteen and became a prostitute to survive would be standing in a field kissing the president of the United States?

Not me.

And I'm never letting him go.

Epilogue

Bennett

Opening my eyes, I roll over and smile when I see my beautiful girl in bed with me. The one thing I love to do, is wake her with my tongue buried deep inside her. I push the covers back and find her gloriously naked body waiting for me.

I lightly kiss down her body, being careful not to wake her yet. Mindfully, I move her right leg over my shoulder and skim my nose across her delicious pussy. God, I love the sweet smell of her cunt when she's excited. I hold her lips open and carefully lick her slit. "Hmmm." Reece wiggles once, unknowingly grinding herself against my face. There's no better way to start the morning than having my girl's pussy in my mouth. No. Better. Way.

I lick her slowly, waiting for her to react in her sleep. With every stroke of my tongue, Reece groans and breathes heavily. I nip and flick at her tender hood, dragging my teeth across her sensitive skin. Reece hooks her other leg over my shoulder, giving me total access to her intoxicating body. She isn't awake though, and I love how she's riding my face in her sleep.

I grip her ass, and drag her closer to me, making sure my face is completely immersed in my girl's pussy. If I die right now, I'll die the perfect death. My tongue flicks as it swirls around causing her to moan. Reece reaches down and pushes her fingers across my scalp. She grips my hair and tugs me closer as her hips take over and grind against me. My tongue plunges deeper inside her as my own desire is hurtling through me. "That's it," she breathlessly moans. "Keep doing that."

I'm about to lose my load, and I don't want it wasted. I want it inside of her. I pull back, grab her hips and yank her down as I kneel on the bed and impale her on my hard cock. Leaning over her, I fuck and kiss her at the same time. "Taste your pussy on my mouth," I mumble against her mouth.

She licks my mouth, devouring her own taste. "I'm nearly as delicious as you are."

"I was thirsty, I needed a drink." I pull back and easily flip her on her stomach. Opening her cheek, I smack my hard cock on her ass, causing Reece to grind backward. "You're so fucking greedy." I spank her ass hard, and it leaves a beautiful shade of red.

She looks over her shoulder and smiles. "You're insatiable." She wiggles her butt at me. While keeping my eyes on her, I spank her again causing her to bite on her lower lip and moan.

Her lips are glistening, desperate for attention. "I can't ignore this." I sink two fingers into Reece's greedy pussy before removing them and impaling her with my cock again. My fingers flex around her hips as I watch where my cock is disappearing into her perfect pussy. I'm fighting the urge to close my eyes and just feel how amazing she is around the end of my cock. "Jesus," I groan, a low rumble of desire bubbling inside my chest. I thrust into her, over and over again, attempting to control myself before gifting her with my cum.

Reece arches her back as her hands fist the bed sheets. "Oh, God," she whimpers while writhing under me. "More, more, keep going."

I tense as my hips take on a rhythm of their own, desperate for my own release. "Fucking you is pure heaven." My body tenses, my balls draw up and I quickly collapse onto her back as I snake my hand to her front so I can rub her clit.

"I love being your whore," she groans as her breath speeds up.

Smirking, I bite on her lobe and keep thrusting into her. "Be my whore between the sheets, and my first lady out of them." I bring her to the edge and tip her over.

Reece's body trembles against mine. "What?" she asks as she quivers beneath me.

"I want you to marry me."

With her lips pursed, she blinks rapidly. A mass of emotions pass through her. "Your cock is inside of me, and you're asking me to marry you?"

"What better time?"

She lowers her head and leans her forehead against the mattress. "You're impossible."

"That's not a no."

"How about you ask me when your dick isn't still inside me."

I move my hips back, removing my cock. "Marry me."

"That's not even a question." She maneuvers her body around so she's on her back. Her legs on either side of my body. I rub my hands up and down her legs. "You can't ask me something like that, Bennett."

I arch a brow. "It's Mr. President," I say as I lay across her body.

"Oh, and I serve at the pleasure of the president." Reece kisses across my chin.

"Damn right you do. Which also includes marrying me."

She scratches her nails slowly up and down my back as I move my head to nuzzle into her neck. "Why should you get my vote?" Reece teases.

"Because I want to be the only man you ever fuck again."

"Meh," she says with disinterest. "I have toys for that." Reaching across she feels around for the bedside table and removes her vibrator. "This one doesn't talk back."

I rip the vibrator out of her hands and throw it across the room. "That piece of plastic is no substitute for me."

Reece chuckles. "That's okay, I have more." She reaches again, but this time, I link our fingers together and bring her hand back so she doesn't delve into the treasure chest we both enjoy.

"I want you to be my wife." I stare into her intense brown eyes and lower my head to kiss her perky lips. "Then I want your mouth wrapped around my cock. I need these to be fucked, red and raw."

"You're a dirty bastard." She angles her head up to kiss me.

Reece isn't giving me an answer though. "Marry me?" I ask for a third time.

"You still haven't told me why I should give you my vote? The other guy might have more to offer me." The small, cute smirk tells me she's playing me.

I really haven't thought about a negotiation strategy. "I can only offer you one thing. I fucking love and adore you."

"In that case..." She wiggles down the bed and wraps her mouth around my hardening cock.

Fuck, I hope that's a yes because I'm sure as hell going to use her mouth for my own pleasure.

Reece

My stomach churns as I walk down to Emily's room. Opening the door, she's lounging on the bed, reading. "Hey, you need to start getting ready so we can go."

"One more chapter, Mom," she pleads. *Infamous last words.*

I sit on the edge of the bed and tap her leg. "Can you put the book down please?"

Emily searches for her bookmark and puts in place before closing her book. "What is it?"

"Um." I swallow my nerves and try to keep control. "Bennett asked me to marry him this morning."

Emily's eyes widen as she jumps up and throws her arms around me. "Yay!"

"I haven't said yes."

"What? Why? Don't you love him?" Emily unwraps her arms from around my neck and sits back on the bed.

"Of course, I do, but this involves you too. So, I wanted to talk to you about it before I give him my answer."

"Oh." She slowly nods. "Bennett is the only dad I know." She shrugs and looks off to the side. "If you marry him, do you think it would be okay if I called him Dad? Do you think he'd mind? I love him."

Tears well in my eyes. "I think he'd love that."

"I wanted to ask but I didn't know if I should. But, Mom, if you want to marry him, I think you should."

"Nothing will change if I do."

Emily searches around the room before she gently shakes her head. "Everything will change, Mom, because we'll be a family."

I drag her over to me and envelop her in a hug. "You're an amazing kid. You know that, right?"

"I have a great mom. Is Tash coming today too?"

"She is, and I think she'll be here soon. Can you please get dressed? We need to leave in less than an hour."

She picks her book up again and leans against her pillow. "Sure thing, Mom."

I shake my head as I leave her room and head back to the master suite so I can get ready for today.

Emily is standing in front of me, and Tash is at my side, both clapping. I watch as Bennett strides toward the chief justice of the Supreme Court. I can't tear my eyes off him as he reaches the chief justice, and the immense crowd below screams in happiness. It's no wonder they're yelling. He's a damn good president, and a sexy one too. Dressed in a beautifully fitted coat, and dark blue scarf, I know beneath that coat is an impeccable three-piece suit that fits his body like a damn glove. He is a fine specimen of a man.

"Wow," Tash whispers. "This is nothing like seeing it on TV."

"I know. It's crazy, isn't it? Wanna hear something awesome?"

"What?"

"The Bible being used is Kathryn's."

"Aww, that is so sweet. It's like she's here with him."

"I know, it's heartwarming, isn't it?"

A hush falls over everyone, it's all about to happen. "Are you prepared to take the oath, Mr. President?" the chief justice asks.

There's a slight hesitation from Bennett. He turns to glance at me and smiles. I'm so damn proud of him. "Not yet," he says.

"What the fuck?" Tash murmurs. "What's he doing?" She looks to me and I slowly lift my shoulders.

"I don't know."

"I can't do this without my family." Bennett strides back to where Emily and I are, and he gives me a kiss. "You're both my family." He looks between Emily and me.

"We are?" Emily asks, tears prickling her eyes. "You want us to be your family?"

"Only if you call me Dad," he says as he lightly touches her cheek.

Emily bursts into tears and throws her arms around him. "I've never had a dad before," she says through the tears.

My eyes are leaking, and I can't wipe the smile off my face. "Yes," I say to him, finally giving him the answer he's been pestering me for since this morning.

"Yes, what?" Bennett asks. I tilt my head to the side and widen my eyes. "You'll marry me?" I nod. Bennett gives Emily a kiss on top of her head, then swoops me up and spins me around. "I adore you."

Placing me to my feet, he kisses my forehead before linking our fingers together. "Let's get you sworn in, Mr. President."

"Best day of my life."

As a family we, walk toward the chief justice. "Ma'am," he greets me with a smile.

Emily and I stand beside Bennett. His shoulders are back, his chin is up, and his smile is so wide I think everyone here can see it. "Are you prepared to take the oath, Mr. President?" he repeats.

"I am." They both raise their right hands, while I hold Kathryn's Bible out for Bennett to place his left hand on it.

"I, Bennett Adams do solemnly swear," the chief justice starts.

"I, Bennett Adams do solemnly swear..."

I'm so proud and in love as I watch my man, the president of the United States.

Also By

Margaret McHeyzer

Hope River

Hope's River
Our Chance
Healing Hearts
A Hope River Christmas

Morgan Brothers

Dean
Alec
Rhett

Men of New York

Intrigue
Indulge
Entice

Perfectly Thin
Echoes of You
A Bump in the Road

Luna Caged
Luna Freed
Addiction
Drowning
The Gift
The Curse
Dying Wish
Mistrust
Ugly
Chef Pierre
Smoke and Mirrors
Grit
Yes, Master
A Life Less Broken
My Life for Yours

Printed in Great Britain
by Amazon

87300059R00174